Frontier Stories by Bret Harte

Francis Bret Harte was born on August 25, 1836 in Albany New York.

As a young boy Harte developed an early love of books and reading. He first published at the tender age of 11; a satirical poem titled "Autumn Musings." Expecting praise he encountered anything but and was later to write "Such a shock was their ridicule to me that I wonder that I ever wrote another line of verse."

By age 13 his formal education was at an end and four years later, in 1853, the family moved to California. Here the young man worked in a variety of capacities; miner, teacher, messenger, and journalist.

But it was also here on the West coast that he found the stories and inspiration for the works that would endure his fame across the literary world. He championed the early writings of Mark Twain. He was instrumental in propelling the short story genre forward and brought tales of the Old West and the Gold Rush to a greater audience. At the height of his fame we would entertain staggering monetary offers to write for monthly magazines.

His talents extended to poetry, plays, lectures, book reviews, editorials, and magazine sketches. As he moved location initially further east to New York and then through Consular appointments to Europe and finally to settle in England his audience diminished but he continued to experiment, to write and to publish.

Bret Harte died of throat cancer on May 5th 1902 and is buried in St Peter's Church in Frimley, Surrey, England.

Index Of Stories

FLIP: A CALIFORNIA ROMANCE

CHAPTER I.

Just where the red track of the Los Gatos road streams on and upward like the sinuous trail of a fiery rocket until it is extinguished in the blue shadows of the Coast Range, there is an embayed terrace near the summit, hedged by dwarf firs. At every bend of the heat-laden road the eye rested upon it wistfully; all along the flank of the mountain, which seemed to pant and quiver in the oven-like air, through rising dust, the slow creaking of dragging wheels, the monotonous cry of tired springs, and the muffled beat of plunging hoofs, it held out a promise of sheltered coolness and green silences beyond. Sunburned and anxious faces yearned toward it from the dizzy, swaying tops of stage-coaches, from lagging teams far below, from the blinding white canvas covers of "mountain schooners," and from scorching saddles that seemed to weigh down the scrambling, sweating animals beneath. But it would seem that the hope was vain, the promise illusive. When the terrace was reached it appeared not only to have caught and gathered all the heat of the valley below, but to have evolved a fire of its own from some hidden crater-like source unknown. Nevertheless, instead of prostrating and enervating man and beast, it was said to have induced the wildest exaltation. The heated air was filled and stifling with resinous exhalations. The delirious spices of balm, bay, spruce, juniper, yerba buena, wild syringa, and strange aromatic herbs as yet unclassified, distilled and evaporated in that mighty heat, and seemed to fire with a midsummer madness all who breathed their fumes. They stung, smarted, stimulated, intoxicated. It was said that the most jaded and foot-sore horses became furious and ungovernable under their influence; wearied teamsters and muleteers, who had exhausted their profanity in the ascent, drank fresh draughts of inspiration in this fiery air, extended their vocabulary, and created new and startling forms of objurgation. It is recorded that one bibulous stage-driver exhausted description and condensed its virtues in a single phrase: "Gin and ginger." This felicitous epithet, flung out in a generous comparison with his favorite drink, "rum and gum," clung to it ever after.

Such was the current comment on this vale of spices. Like most human criticism it was hasty and superficial. No one yet had been known to have penetrated deeply its mysterious recesses. It was still far below the summit and its wayside inn. It had escaped the intruding foot of hunter and prospector; and the inquisitive patrol of the county surveyor had only skirted its boundary. It remained for Mr. Lance Harriott to complete its exploration. His reasons for so doing were simple. He had made the journey thither underneath the stage-coach, and clinging to its axle. He had chosen this hazardous mode of conveyance at night, as the coach crept by his place of concealment in the wayside brush, to elude the sheriff of Monterey County and his posse, who were after him. He had not made himself known to his fellow-passengers, as they already knew him as a gambler, an outlaw, and a desperado; he deemed it unwise to present himself in his newer reputation of a man who had just slain a brother gambler in a quarrel, and for whom a reward was offered. He slipped from the axle as the stage-coach swirled past the brushing branches of fir, and for an instant lay unnoticed, a scarcely distinguishable mound of dust in the broken furrows of the road. Then, more like a beast than a man, he crept on his hands and knees into the steaming underbrush. Here he lay still until the clatter of harness and the sound of voices faded in the distance. Had he been followed, it would have been difficult to detect in that inert mass of rags any semblance to a known form or figure. A hideous, reddish mask of dust and clay obliterated his face; his hands were shapeless stumps exaggerated in his trailing sleeves. And when he rose, staggering like a drunken man, and plunged wildly into the recesses of the wood, a cloud of dust followed him, and pieces and patches of his frayed and rotten garments clung to the impeding branches. Twice he fell, but, maddened and upheld by the smarting spices and stimulating aroma of the air, he kept on his course.

Gradually the heat became less oppressive; once, when he stopped and leaned exhaustedly against a sapling, he fancied he saw the zephyr he could not yet feel in the glittering and trembling of leaves in the distance before him. Again the deep stillness was moved with a faint sighing rustle, and he knew he must be nearing the edge of the thicket. The spell of silence thus broken was followed by a fainter, more musical interruption, the glassy tinkle of water! A step further his foot trembled on the verge of a slight ravine, still closely canopied by the interlacing boughs overhead. A tiny stream that he could have dammed with his hand yet lingered in this parched red gash in the hillside and trickled into a deep, irregular, well-like cavity, that again overflowed and sent its slight surplus on. It had been the luxurious retreat of many a spotted trout; it was to be the bath of Lance Harriott. Without a moment's hesitation, without removing a single garment, he slipped cautiously into it, as if fearful of losing a single drop. His head disappeared from the level of the bank; the solitude was again unbroken. Only two objects remained upon the edge of the ravine, his revolver and tobacco pouch.

A few minutes elapsed. A fearless blue-jay alighted on the bank and made a prospecting peck at the tobacco pouch. It yielded in favor of a gopher, who endeavored to draw it toward his hole, but in turn gave way to a red squirrel, whose attention was divided, however, between the pouch and the revolver, which he regarded with mischievous fascination. Then there was a splash, a grunt, a sudden dispersion of animated nature, and the head of Mr. Lance Harriott appeared above the bank. It was a startling transformation. Not only that he had, by this wholesale process, washed himself and his light "drill" garments entirely clean, but that he had, apparently by the same operation, morally cleansed himself, and left every stain and ugly blot of his late misdeeds and reputation in his bath. His face, albeit scratched here and there, was rosy, round, shining with irrepressible good-humor and youthful levity. His large blue eyes were infantine in their innocent surprise and thoughtlessness. Dripping yet with water, and panting, he rested his elbows lazily on the bank, and became instantly absorbed with a boy's delight in the movements of the gopher, who, after the first alarm, returned cautiously to abduct the tobacco pouch. If any familiar had failed to detect Lance Harriott in this hideous masquerade of dust and grime and tatters, still less would any passing stranger have recognized in this blonde faun the possible outcast and murderer. And when with a swirl of his spattering sleeve he drove back the gopher in a shower of spray and leaped to the bank, he seemed to have accepted his felonious hiding-place as a mere picnicking bower.

A slight breeze was unmistakably permeating the wood from the west. Looking in that direction, Lance imagined that the shadow was less dark, and although the undergrowth was denser, he struck off carelessly toward it. As he went on, the wood became lighter and lighter; branches, and presently leaves, were painted against the vivid blue of the sky. He knew he must be near the summit, stopped, felt for his revolver, and then lightly put the few remaining branches aside.

The full glare of the noonday sun at first blinded him. When he could see more clearly, he found himself on the open western slope of the mountain, which in the Coast Range was seldom wooded. The spiced thicket stretched between him and the summit, and again between him and the stage road that plunges from the terrace, like forked lightning into the valley below. He could command all the approaches without being seen. Not that this seemed to occupy his thoughts or cause him any anxiety. His first act was to disencumber himself of his tattered coat; he then filled and lighted his pipe, and stretched himself full-length on the open hillside, as if to bleach in the fierce sun. While smoking he carelessly perused the fragment of a newspaper which had enveloped his tobacco, and being struck with some amusing paragraph, read it half aloud again to some imaginary auditor, emphasizing its humor with an hilarious slap upon his leg.

Possibly from the relaxation of fatigue and the bath, which had become a vapor one as he alternately rolled and dried himself in the baking grass, his eyes closed dreamily. He was awakened by the sound of voices. They were distant; they were vague; they approached no nearer. He rolled himself to the verge of the first precipitous grassy descent. There was another bank or plateau below him, and then a confused depth of olive shadows, pierced here and there by the spiked helmets of pines. There was no trace of habitation, yet the voices were those of some monotonous occupation, and Lance distinctly heard through them the click of crockery and the ring of some household utensil. It appeared to be the interjectional, half listless, half perfunctory, domestic dialogue of an old man and a girl, of which the words were unintelligible. Their voices indicated the solitude of the mountain, but without sadness; they were mysterious without being awe-inspiring. They might have uttered the dreariest commonplaces, but, in their vast isolation, they seemed musical and eloquent. Lance drew his first sigh, they had suggested dinner.

Careless as his nature was, he was too cautious to risk detection in broad daylight. He contented himself for the present with endeavoring to locate that particular part of the depths from which the voices seemed to rise. It was more difficult, however, to select some other way of penetrating it than by the stage road. "They're bound to have a fire or show a light when it's dark," he reasoned, and, satisfied with that reflection, lay down again. Presently he began to amuse himself by tossing some silver coins in the air. Then his attention was directed to a spur of the Coast Range which had been sharply silhouetted against the cloudless western sky. Something intensely white, something so small that it was scarcely larger than the silver coin in his hand, was appearing in a slight cleft of the range.

While he looked it gradually filled and obliterated the cleft. In another moment the whole serrated line of mountain had disappeared. The dense, dazzling white, encompassing host began to pour over and down every ravine and pass of the coast. Lance recognized the sea-fog, and knew that scarcely twenty miles away lay the ocean, and safety! The drooping sun was now caught and hidden in its soft embraces. A sudden chill breathed over the mountain. He shivered, rose, and plunged again for very warmth into the spice-laden thicket. The heated balsamic air began to affect him like a powerful sedative; his hunger was forgotten in the languor of fatigue: he slumbered. When he awoke it was dark. He groped his way through the thicket. A few stars were shining directly above him, but beyond and below, everything was lost in the soft, white, fleecy veil of fog. Whatever light or fire might have betokened human habitation was hidden. To push on blindly would be madness; he could only wait for morning. It suited the outcast's lazy philosophy. He crept back again to his bed in the hollow and slept. In that profound silence and shadow, shut out from human association and sympathy by the ghostly fog, what torturing visions conjured up by remorse and fear should have pursued him? What spirit passed before him, or slowly shaped itself out of the infinite blackness of the wood? None. As he slipped gently into that blackness he remembered with a slight regret, some biscuits that were dropped from the coach by a careless luncheon-consuming passenger. That pang over, he slept as sweetly, as profoundly, as divinely, as a child.

CHAPTER II.

He awoke with the aroma of the woods still steeping his senses. His first instinct was that of all young animals: he seized a few of the young, tender green leaves of the yerba buena vine that crept over his mossy pillow and ate them, being rewarded by a half berry-like flavor that seemed to soothe the cravings of his appetite. The languor of sleep being still upon him, he lazily watched the quivering of a sunbeam that was caught in the canopying boughs above. Then he dozed again. Hovering between sleeping and waking, he became conscious of a slight movement among the dead leaves on the bank beside the hollow in which he lay. The movement appeared to be intelligent, and directed toward his revolver, which glittered on the bank. Amused at this evident return of his larcenious friend of the previous day, he lay perfectly still. The movement and rustle continued, and it now seemed long and undulating. Lance's eyes suddenly became set; he was intensely, keenly awake. It was not a snake, but the hand of a human arm, half hidden in the moss, groping for the weapon. In that flash of perception he saw that it was small, bare, and deeply freckled. In an instant he grasped it firmly, and rose to his feet, dragging to his own level as he did so, the struggling figure of a young girl.

"Leave me go!" she said, more ashamed than frightened.

Lance looked at her. She was scarcely more than fifteen, slight and lithe, with a boyish flatness of breast and back. Her flushed face and bare throat were absolutely peppered with minute brown freckles, like grains of spent gunpowder. Her eyes, which were large and gray, presented the singular spectacle of being also freckled, at least they were shot through in pupil and cornea with tiny spots like powdered allspice. Her hair was even more remarkable in its tawny deer-skin color, full of lighter shades, and bleached to the faintest of blondes on the crown of her head, as if by the action of the sun. She had evidently outgrown her dress, which was made for a smaller child, and the too brief skirt disclosed a bare, freckled, and sandy desert of shapely limb, for which the darned stockings were equally too scant. Lance let his grasp slip from her thin wrist to her hand, and then with a good-humored gesture tossed it lightly back to her.

She did not retreat, but continued looking at him in a half-surly embarrassment.

"I ain't a bit frightened," she said; "I'm not going to run away, don't you fear."

"Glad to hear it," said Lance, with unmistakable satisfaction, "but why did you go for my revolver?"

She flushed again and was silent. Presently she began to kick the earth at the roots of the tree, and said, as if confidentially to her foot:

"I wanted to get hold of it before you did."

"You did? and why?"

"Oh, you know why."

Every tooth in Lance's head showed that he did, perfectly. But he was discreetly silent.

"I didn't know what you were hiding there for," she went on, still addressing the tree, "and," looking at him sideways under her white lashes, "I didn't see your face."

This subtle compliment was the first suggestion of her artful sex. It actually sent the blood into the careless rascal's face, and for a moment confused him. He coughed. "So you thought you'd freeze on to that six-shooter of mine until you saw my hand?"

She nodded. Then she picked up a broken hazel branch, fitted it into the small of her back, threw her tanned bare arms over the ends of it, and expanded her chest and her biceps at the same moment. This simple action was supposed to convey an impression at once of ease and muscular force.

"Perhaps you'd like to take it now," said Lance, handing her the pistol.

"I've seen six-shooters before now," said the girl, evading the proffered weapon and its suggestion. "Dad has one, and my brother had two derringers before he was half as big as me."

She stopped to observe in her companion the effect of this capacity of her family to bear arms. Lance only regarded her amusedly. Presently she again spoke abruptly:

"What made you eat that grass, just now?"

"Grass!" echoed Lance.

"Yes, there," pointing to the yerba buena.

Lance laughed. "I was hungry. Look!" he said, gayly tossing some silver into the air. "Do you think you could get me some breakfast for that, and have enough left to buy something for yourself?"

The girl eyed the money and the man with half-bashful curiosity.

"I reckon Dad might give ye suthing if he had a mind ter, though ez a rule he's down on tramps ever since they run off his chickens. Ye might try."

"But I want you to try. You can bring it to me here."

The girl retreated a step, dropped her eyes, and, with a smile that was a charming hesitation between bashfulness and impudence, said: "So you are hidin', are ye?"

"That's just it. Your head's level. I am," laughed Lance unconcernedly.

"Yur ain't one o' the McCarthy gang, are ye?"

Mr. Lance Harriott felt a momentary moral exaltation in declaring truthfully that he was not one of a notorious band of mountain freebooters known in the district under that name.

"Nor ye ain't one of them chicken lifters that raided Henderson's ranch? We don't go much on that kind o' cattle yer."

"No," said Lance, cheerfully.

"Nor ye ain't that chap ez beat his wife unto death at Santa Clara?"

Lance honestly scorned the imputation. Such conjugal ill treatment as he had indulged in had not been physical, and had been with other men's wives.

There was a moment's further hesitation on the part of the girl. Then she said shortly:

"Well, then, I reckon you kin come along with me."

"Where?" asked Lance.

"To the ranch," she replied simply.

"Then you won't bring me anything to eat here?"

"What for? You kin get it down there." Lance hesitated. "I tell you it's all right," she continued. "I'll make it all right with Dad."

"But suppose I reckon I'd rather stay here," persisted Lance, with a perfect consciousness, however, of affectation in his caution.

"Stay away then," said the girl coolly; "only as Dad perempted this yer woods" -

"Pre-empted," suggested Lance.

"Per-empted or pre-emp-ted, as you like," continued the girl scornfully, "ez he's got a holt on this yer woods, ye might ez well see him down thar ez here. For here he's like to come any minit. You can bet your life on that."

She must have read Lance's amusement in his eyes, for she again dropped her own with a frown of brusque embarrassment. "Come along, then; I'm your man," said Lance, gayly, extending his hand.

She would not accept it, eying it, however, furtively, like a horse about to shy. "Hand me your pistol first," she said.

He handed it to her with an assumption of gayety. She received it on her part with unfeigned seriousness, and threw it over her shoulder like a gun. This combined action of the child and heroine, it is quite unnecessary to say, afforded Lance undiluted joy.

"You go first," she said.

Lance stepped promptly out, with a broad grin. "Looks kinder as if I was a pris'ner, don't it?" he suggested.

"Go on, and don't fool," she replied.

The two fared onward through the wood. For one moment he entertained the facetious idea of appearing to rush frantically away, "just to see what the girl would do," but abandoned it. "It's an even thing if she wouldn't spot me the first pop," he reflected admiringly.

When they had reached the open hillside, Lance stopped inquiringly. "This way," she said, pointing toward the summit, and in quite an opposite direction to the valley where he had heard the voices, one of which he now recognized as hers. They skirted the thicket for a few moments, and then turned sharply into a trail which began to dip toward a ravine leading to the valley.

"Why do you have to go all the way round?" he asked.

"We don't," the girl replied with emphasis; "there's a shorter cut."

"Where?"

"That's telling," she answered shortly.

"What's your name?" asked Lance, after a steep scramble and a drop into the ravine.

"Flip."

"What?"

"Flip."

"I mean your first name, your front name."

"Flip."

"Flip! Oh, short for Felipa!"

"It ain't Flipper, it's Flip." And she relapsed into silence.

"You don't ask me mine?" suggested Lance.

She did not vouchsafe a reply.

"Then you don't want to know?"

"Maybe Dad will. You can lie to him."

This direct answer apparently sustained the agreeable homicide for some moments. He moved onward, silently exuding admiration.

"Only," added Flip, with a sudden caution, "you'd better agree with me."

The trail here turned again abruptly and reëntered the cañon. Lance looked up, and noticed they were almost directly beneath the bay thicket and the plateau that towered far above them. The trail here showed signs of clearing, and the way was marked by felled trees and stumps of pines.

"What does your father do here?" he finally asked. Flip remained silent, swinging the revolver. Lance repeated his question.

"Burns charcoal and makes diamonds," said Flip, looking at him from the corners of her eyes.

"Makes diamonds?" echoed Lance.

Flip nodded her head.

"Many of 'em?" he continued carelessly.

"Lots. But they're not big," she returned, with a sidelong glance.

"Oh, they're not big?" said Lance gravely.

They had by this time reached a small staked inclosure, whence the sudden fluttering and cackle of poultry welcomed the return of the evident mistress of this sylvan retreat. It was scarcely imposing. Further on, a cooking stove under a tree, a saddle and bridle, a few household implements scattered about, indicated the "ranch." Like most pioneer clearings, it was simply a disorganized raid upon nature that had left behind a desolate battlefield strewn with waste and decay. The fallen trees, the crushed thicket, the splintered limbs, the rudely torn-up soil, were made hideous by their grotesque juxtaposition with the wrecked fragments of civilization, in empty cans, broken bottles, battered hats, soleless boots, frayed stockings, cast-off rags, and the crowning absurdity of the twisted-wire skeleton of a hooped skirt hanging from a branch. The wildest defile, the densest thicket, the most virgin solitude, was less dreary and forlorn than this first footprint of man. The only redeeming feature of this prolonged bivouac was the cabin itself. Built of the half-cylindrical strips of pine bark, and thatched with the same material, it had a certain picturesque rusticity. But this was an accident of economy rather than taste, for which Flip apologized by saying that the bark of the pine was "no good" for charcoal.

"I reckon dad's in the woods," she added, pausing before the open door of the cabin. "Oh, Dad!" Her voice, clear and high, seemed to fill the whole long cañon, and echoed from the green plateau above. The monotonous strokes of an axe were suddenly intermitted, and somewhere from the depths of the close-set pines a voice answered "Flip." There was a pause of a few moments, with some muttering, stumbling, and crackling in the underbrush, and then the appearance of "Dad."

Had Lance first met him in the thicket, he would have been puzzled to assign his race to Mongolian, Indian, or Ethiopian origin. Perfunctory but incomplete washings of his hands and face, after charcoal burning, had gradually ground into his skin a grayish slate-pencil pallor, grotesquely relieved at the edges, where the washing had left off, with a border of a darker color. He looked like an overworked Christy minstrel with the briefest of intervals between his performances. There were black rims in the orbits of his eyes, as if he gazed feebly out of unglazed spectacles, which heightened his simian resemblance, already grotesquely exaggerated by what appeared to be repeated and spasmodic experiments in dyeing his gray hair. Without the slightest notice of Lance, he inflicted his protesting and querulous presence entirely on his daughter.

"Well! what's up now? Yer ye are calling me from work an hour before noon. Dog my skin, ef I ever get fairly limbered up afore it's 'Dad!' and 'Oh, Dad!'"

To Lance's intense satisfaction the girl received this harangue with an air of supreme indifference, and when "Dad" had relapsed into an unintelligible, and, as it seemed to Lance, a half-frightened muttering, she said coolly, -

"Ye'd better drop that axe and scoot round getten' this stranger some breakfast and some grub to take with him. He's one of them San Francisco sports out here trout-fishing in the branch. He's got adrift from his party, has lost his rod and fixins, and had to camp out last night in the Gin and Ginger Woods."

"That's just it; it's allers suthin like that," screamed the old man, dashing his fist on his leg in a feeble, impotent passion, but without looking at Lance. "Why in blazes don't he go up to that there blamed hotel on the summit? Why in thunder" - But here he caught his daughter's large, freckled eyes full in his own. He blinked feebly, his voice fell into a tone of whining entreaty. "Now, look yer, Flip, it's playing it rather low down on the old man, this yer running in o' tramps and desarted emigrants and cast-ashore sailors and forlorn widders and ravin' lunatics, on this yer ranch. I put it to you, Mister," he said abruptly, turning to Lance for the first time, but as if he had already taken an active part in the conversation, "I put it as a gentleman yourself, and a fair-minded sportin' man, if this is the square thing?"

Before Lance could reply, Flip had already begun. "That's just it! D'ye reckon, being a sportin' man and a A 1 feller, he's goin' to waltz down inter that hotel, rigged out ez he is? D'ye reckon he's goin' to let his partners get the laugh onter him? D'ye reckon he's goin' to show his head outer this yer ranch till he can do it square? Not much! Go 'long. Dad, you're talking silly!"

The old man weakened. He feebly trailed his axe between his legs to a stump and sat down, wiping his forehead with his sleeve, and imparting to it the appearance of a slate with a difficult sum partly rubbed out. He looked despairingly at Lance. "In course," he said, with a deep sigh, "you naturally ain't got any money. In course you left your pocketbook, containing fifty dollars, under a stone, and can't find it. In course," he continued, as he observed Lance put his hand to his pocket, "you've only got a blank check on Wells, Fargo & Co. for a hundred dollars, and you'd like me to give you the difference?"

Amused as Lance evidently was at this, his absolute admiration for Flip absorbed everything else. With his eyes fixed upon the girl, he briefly assured the old man that he would pay for everything he wanted. He did this with a manner quite different from the careless, easy attitude he had assumed toward Flip; at least the quickwitted girl noticed it, and wondered if he was angry. It was quite true that ever since his eye had fallen upon another of his own sex, its glance had been less frank and careless. Certain traits of possible impatience, which might develop into man-slaying, were coming to the fore. Yet a word or a gesture of Flip's was sufficient to change that manner, and when, with the fretful assistance of her father, she had prepared a somewhat sketchy and primitive repast, he questioned the old man about diamond-making. The eye of Dad kindled.

"I want ter know how ye knew I was making diamonds," he asked, with a certain bashful pettishness not unlike his daughter's.

"Heard it in 'Frisco," replied Lance, with glib mendacity, glancing at the girl.

"I reckon they're gettin' sort of skeert down there, them jewelers," chuckled Dad, "yet it's in nater that their figgers will have to come down. It's only a question of the price of charcoal. I suppose they didn't tell you how I made the discovery?"

Lance would have stopped the old man's narrative by saying that he knew the story, but he wished to see how far Flip lent herself to her father's delusion.

"Ye see, one night about two years ago I had a pit o' charcoal burning out there, and tho' it had been a-smouldering and a-smoking and a-blazing for nigh unto a month, somehow it didn't charcoal worth a cent. And yet, dog my skin, but the heat o' that er pit was suthin hidyus and frightful; ye couldn't stand within a hundred yards of it, and they could feel it on the stage road three miles over yon, t'other side the mountain. There was nights when me and Flip had to take our blankets up the ravine and camp out all night, and the back of this yer hut shriveled up like that bacon. It was about as nigh on to hell as any sample ye kin get here. Now, mebbe you think I built that air fire? Mebbe you'll allow the heat was just the nat'ral burning of that pit?"

"Certainly," said Lance, trying to see Flip's eyes, which were resolutely averted.

"Thet's whar you'd be lyin'! That yar heat kem out of the bowels of the yearth, kem up like out of a chimbley or a blast, and kep up that yar fire. And when she cools down a month after, and I got to strip her, there was a hole in the yearth, and a spring o' bilin', scaldin' water pourin' out of it ez big as your waist. And right in the middle of it was this yer." He rose with the instinct of a skillful raconteur, and whisked from under his bunk a chamois leather bag, which he emptied on the table before them. It contained a small fragment of native rock crystal, half-fused upon a petrified bit of pine. It was so glaringly truthful, so really what it purported to be, that the most unscientific woodman or pioneer would have understood it at a glance. Lance raised his mirthful eyes to Flip.

"It was cooled suddint, stunted by the water," said the girl, eagerly. She stopped, and as abruptly turned away her eyes and her reddened face.

"That's it, that's just it," continued the old man. "Thar's Flip, thar, knows it; she ain't no fool!" Lance did not speak, but turned a hard, unsympathizing look upon the old man, and rose almost roughly. The old man clutched his coat. "That's it, ye see. The carbon's just turning to di'mens. And stunted. And why? 'Cos the heat wasn't kep up long enough. Mebbe yer think I stopped thar? That ain't me. Thar's a pit out yar in the woods ez hez been burning six months; it hain't, in course, got the advantages o' the old one, for it's nat'ral heat. But I'm keeping that heat up. I've got a hole where I kin watch it every four hours. When the time comes, I'm thar! Don't you see? That's me! that's David Fairley, that's the old man, you bet!"

"That's so," said Lance, curtly. "And now, Mr. Fairley, if you'll hand me over a coat or jacket till I can get past these fogs on the Monterey road, I won't keep you from your diamond pit." He threw down a handful of silver on the table.

"Ther's a deerskin jacket yer," said the old man, "that one o' them vaqueros left for the price of a bottle of whiskey."

"I reckon it wouldn't suit the stranger," said Flip, dubiously producing a much-worn, slashed, and braided vaquero's jacket. But it did suit Lance, who found it warm, and also had suddenly found a certain satisfaction in opposing Flip. When he had put it on, and nodded coldly to the old man, and carelessly to Flip, he walked to the door.

"If you're going to take the Monterey road, I can show you a short cut to it," said Flip, with a certain kind of shy civility.

The paternal Fairley groaned. "That's it; let the chickens and the ranch go to thunder, as long as there's a stranger to trapse round with; go on!"

Lance would have made some savage reply, but Flip interrupted. "You know yourself, Dad, it's a blind trail, and as that 'ere constable that kem out here hunting French Pete, couldn't find it, and had to go round by the cañon, like ez not the stranger would lose his way, and have to come back!" This dangerous prospect silenced the old man, and Flip and Lance stepped into the road together. They walked on for some moments without speaking. Suddenly Lance turned upon his companion.

"You did n't swallow all that rot about the diamond, did you?" he asked, crossly.

Flip ran a little ahead, as if to avoid a reply.

"You don't mean to say that's the sort of hog wash the old man serves out to you regularly?" continued Lance, becoming more slangy in his ill temper.

"I don't know that it's any consarn o' yours what I think," replied Flip, hopping from boulder to boulder, as they crossed the bed of a dry watercourse.

"And I suppose you've piloted round and dry-nussed every tramp and dead-beat you've met since you came here," continued Lance, with unmistakable ill humor. "How many have you helped over this road?"

"It's a year since there was a Chinaman chased by some Irishmen from the Crossing into the brush about yer, and he was too afeered to come out, and nigh most starved to death in thar. I had to drag him out and start him on the mountain, for you couldn't get him back to the road. He was the last one but you."

"Do you reckon it's the right thing for a girl like you to run about with trash of this kind, and mix herself up with all sorts of roughs and bad company?" said Lance.

Flip stopped short. "Look! if you're goin' to talk like Dad, I'll go back."

The ridiculousness of such a resemblance struck him more keenly than a consciousness of his own ingratitude. He hastened to assure Flip that he was joking. When he had made his peace they fell into talk again, Lance becoming unselfish enough to inquire into one or two facts concerning her life which did not immediately affect him. Her mother had died on the plains when she was a baby, and her brother had run away from home at twelve. She fully expected to see him again, and thought he might sometime stray into their cañon. "That is why, then, you take so much stock in tramps," said Lance.

You expect to recognize him?"

"Well," replied Flip, gravely, "there is suthing in that, and there's suthing in this: some o' these chaps might run across brother and do him a good turn for the sake of me."

"Like me, for instance?" suggested Lance.

"Like you. You'd do him a good turn, wouldn't you?"

"You bet!" said Lance, with a sudden emotion that quite startled him; "only don't you go to throwing yourself round promiscuously." He was half conscious of an irritating sense of jealousy, as he asked if any of her protégés had ever returned.

"No," said Flip, "no one ever did. It shows," she added with sublime simplicity, "I had done 'em good, and they could get on alone. Don't it?"

"It does," responded Lance grimly. "Have you any other friends that come?"

"Only the Postmaster at the Crossing."

"The Postmaster?"

"Yes: he's reckonin' to marry me next year, if I'm big enough."

"And what do you reckon?" asked Lance earnestly.

Flip began a series of distortions with her shoulders, ran on ahead, picked up a few pebbles and threw them into the wood, glanced back at Lance with swimming mottled eyes, that seemed a piquant incarnation of everything suggestive and tantalizing, and said:

"That's telling."

They had by this time reached the spot where they were to separate. "Look," said Flip, pointing to a faint deflection of their path, which seemed, however, to lose itself in the underbrush a dozen yards away, "ther's your trail. It gets plainer and broader the further you get on, but you must use your eyes here, and get to know it well afore you get into the fog. Good-by."

"Good-by." Lance took her hand and drew her beside him. She was still redolent of the spices of the thicket, and to the young man's excited fancy seemed at that moment to personify the perfume and intoxication of her native woods. Half laughingly, half earnestly, he tried to kiss her: she struggled for some time strongly, but at the last moment yielded, with a slight return and the exchange of a subtle fire that thrilled him, and left him standing confused and astounded as she ran away. He watched her lithe, nymph-like figure disappear in the checkered shadows of the wood, and then he turned briskly down the half-hidden trail. His eyesight was keen, he made good progress, and was soon well on his way toward the distant ridge.

But Flip's return had not been as rapid. When she reached the wood she crept to its beetling verge, and looking across the cañon watched Lance's figure as it vanished and reappeared in the shadows and sinuosities of the ascent. When he reached the ridge the outlying fog crept across the summit, caught him in its embrace, and wrapped him from her gaze. Flip sighed, raised herself, put her alternate foot on a stump, and took a long pull at her too-brief stockings. When she had pulled down her skirt and endeavored once more to renew the intimacy that had existed in previous years between the edge of her petticoat and the top of her stockings, she sighed again, and went home.

CHAPTER III.

For six months the sea fogs monotonously came and went along the Monterey coast; for six months they beleaguered the Coast Range with afternoon sorties of white hosts that regularly swept over the mountain crest, and were as regularly beaten back again by the leveled lances of the morning sun. For six months that white veil which had once hidden Lance Harriott in its folds returned without him. For that amiable outlaw no longer needed disguise or hiding-place. The swift wave of pursuit that had dashed him on the summit had fallen back, and the next day was broken and scattered. Before the week had passed, a regular judicial inquiry relieved his crime of premeditation, and showed it to be a rude duel of two armed and equally desperate men. From a secure vantage in a sea-coast town Lance challenged a trial by his peers, and, as an already prejudged man escaping from his executioners, obtained a change of venue. Regular justice, seated by the calm Pacific, found the action of an interior, irregular jury rash and hasty. Lance was liberated on bail.

The Postmaster at Fisher's Crossing had just received the weekly mail and express from San Francisco, and was engaged in examining it. It consisted of five letters and two parcels. Of these, three of the letters and the two parcels were directed to Flip. It was not the first time during the last six months that this extraordinary event had occurred, and the curiosity of the Crossing was duly excited. As Flip had never called personally for the letters or parcels, but had sent one of her wild, irregular scouts or henchmen to bring them, and as she was seldom seen at the Crossing or on the stage road, that curiosity was never satisfied. The disappointment to the Postmaster, a man past the middle age, partook of a sentimental nature. He looked at the letters and parcels; he looked at his watch; it was yet early, he could return by noon. He again examined the addresses; they were in the same handwriting as the previous letters. His mind was made up, he would deliver them himself. The poetic, soulful side of his mission was delicately indicated by a pale blue necktie, a clean shirt, and a small package of ginger-nuts, of which Flip was extravagantly fond.

The common road to Fairley's Ranch was by the stage turnpike to a point below the Gin and Ginger Woods, where the prudent horseman usually left his beast and followed the intersecting trail afoot. It was here that the Postmaster suddenly observed on the edge of the wood the figure of an elegantly dressed woman; she was walking slowly, and apparently at her ease; one hand held her skirts lightly gathered between her gloved fingers, the other slowly swung a riding-whip. Was it a picnic of some people from Monterey or Santa Cruz? The spectacle was novel enough to justify his coming nearer. Suddenly she withdrew into the wood; he lost sight of her; she was gone. He remembered, however, that Flip was still to be seen, and as the steep trail was beginning to tax all his energies, he was fain to hurry forward. The sun was nearly vertical when he turned into the cañon, and saw the bark roof of the cabin beyond. At almost the same moment Flip appeared, flushed and panting, in the road before him.

"You've got something for me," she said, pointing to the parcel and letter. Completely taken by surprise, the Postmaster mechanically yielded them up, and as instantly regretted it. "They're paid for," continued Flip, observing his hesitation.

"That's so," stammered the official of the Crossing, seeing his last chance of knowing the contents of the parcel vanish; "but I thought ez it's a valooable package, maybe ye might want to examine it to see that it was all right afore ye receipted for it."

"I'll risk it," said Flip, coolly, "and if it ain't right I'll let ye know."

As the girl seemed inclined to retire with her property, the Postmaster was driven to other conversation. "We ain't had the pleasure of seeing you down at the Crossing for a month o' Sundays," he began, with airy yet pronounced gallantry. "Some folks let on you was keepin' company with some feller like Bijah Brown, and you were getting a little too set up for the Crossing." The individual here mentioned being the county butcher, and supposed to exhibit his hopeless affection for Flip by making a long and useless divergence from his weekly route to enter the cañon for "orders," Flip did not deem it necessary to reply. "Then I allowed how ez you might have company," he continued; "I reckon there's some city folks up at the summit. I saw a mighty smart, fash'n'ble gal cavorting round. Hed no end o' style and fancy fixin's. That's my kind, I tell you. I just weaken on that sort o' gal," he continued, in the firm belief that he had awakened Flip's jealousy, as he glanced at her well-worn homespun frock, and found her eyes suddenly fixed on his own.

"Strange I ain't got to see her yet," she replied coolly, shouldering her parcel, and quite ignoring any sense of obligation to him for his extra-official act.

"But you might get to see her at the edge of the Gin and Ginger Woods," he persisted feebly, in a last effort to detain her; "if you'll take a pasear there with me."

Flip's only response was to walk on toward the cabin, whence, with a vague complimentary suggestion of "drop-in' in to pass the time o' day" with her father, the Postmaster meekly followed.

The paternal Fairley, once convinced that his daughter's new companion required no pecuniary or material assistance from his hands, relaxed to the extent of entering into a querulous confidence with him, during which Flip took the opportunity of slipping away. As Fairley had that infelicitous tendency of most weak natures, to unconsciously exaggerate unimportant details in their talk, the Postmaster presently became convinced that the butcher was a constant and assiduous suitor of Flip's. The absurdity of his sending parcels and letters by post when he might bring them himself did not strike the official. On the contrary, he believed it to be a masterstroke of cunning. Fired by jealousy and Flip's indifference, he "deemed it his duty", using that facile form of cowardly offensiveness, to betray Flip.

Of which she was happily oblivious. Once away from the cabin, she plunged into the woods, with the parcel swung behind her like a knapsack. Leaving the trail, she presently struck off in a straight line through cover and underbrush with the unerring instinct of an animal, climbing hand over hand the steepest ascent, or fluttering like a bird from branch to branch down the deepest declivity. She soon reached that part of the trail where the susceptible Postmaster had seen the fascinating unknown. Assuring herself she was not followed, she crept through the thicket until she reached a little waterfall and basin that had served the fugitive Lance for a bath. The spot bore signs of later and more frequent occupancy, and when Flip carefully removed some bark and brushwood from a cavity in the rock and drew forth various folded garments, it was evident she used it as a sylvan dressing-room. Here she opened the parcel; it contained a small and delicate shawl of yellow China crèpe. Flip instantly threw it over her shoulders and stepped hurriedly toward the edge of the wood. Then she began to pass backward and forward before the trunk of a tree. At first nothing was visible on the tree, but a closer inspection showed a large pane of ordinary window glass stuck in the fork of the branches. It was placed at such a cunning angle against the darkness of the forest opening that it made a soft and mysterious mirror, not unlike a Claude Lorraine glass, wherein not only the passing figure of the young girl was seen, but the dazzling green and gold of the hillside, and the far-off silhouetted crests of the Coast Range.

But this was evidently only a prelude to a severer rehearsal. When she returned to the waterfall she unearthed from her stores a large piece of yellow soap and some yards of rough cotton "sheeting." These she deposited beside the basin and again crept to the edge of the wood to assure herself that she was alone. Satisfied that no intruding foot had invaded that virgin bower, she returned to her bath and began to undress. A slight wind followed her, and seemed to whisper to the circumjacent trees. It appeared to waken her sister naiads and nymphs, who, joining their leafy fingers, softly drew around her a gently moving band of trembling lights and shadows, of flecked sprays and inextricably mingled branches, and involved her in a chaste sylvan obscurity, veiled alike from pursuing god or stumbling shepherd. Within these hallowed precincts was the musical ripple of laughter and falling water, and at times the glimpse of a lithe brier-caught limb, or a ray of sunlight trembling over bright flanks, or the white austere outline of a childish bosom.

When she drew again the leafy curtain, and once more stepped out of the wood, she was completely transformed.

It was the figure that had appeared to the Postmaster; the slight, erect, graceful form of a young woman modishly attired. It was Flip, but Flip made taller by the lengthened skirt and clinging habiliments of fashion. Flip freckled, but, through the cunning of a relief of yellow color in her gown, her piquant brown-shot face and eyes brightened and intensified until she seemed like a spicy odor made visible. I cannot affirm that the judgment of Flip's mysterious modiste was infallible, or that the taste of Mr. Lance Harriott, her patron, was fastidious; enough that it was picturesque, and perhaps not more glaring and extravagant than the color in which Spring herself had once clothed the sere hillside where Flip was now seated. The phantom mirror in the tree fork caught and held her with the sky, the green leaves, the sunlight and all the graciousness of her surroundings, and the wind gently tossed her hair and the gay ribbons of her gypsy hat. Suddenly she started. Some remote sound in the trail below, inaudible to any ear less fine than hers, arrested her breathing. She rose swiftly and darted into cover.

Ten minutes passed. The sun was declining; the white fog was beginning to creep over the Coast Range. From the edge of the wood Cinderella appeared, disenchanted, and in her homespun garments. The clock had struck, the spell was past. As she disappeared down the trail even the magic mirror, moved by the wind, slipped from the tree-top to the ground, and became a piece of common glass.

CHAPTER IV.

The events of the day had produced a remarkable impression on the facial aspect of the charcoal-burning Fairley. Extraordinary processes of thought, indicated by repeated rubbing of his forehead, had produced a high light in the middle and a corresponding deepening of shadow at the sides, until it bore the appearance of a perfect sphere. It was this forehead that confronted Flip reproachfully as became a deceived comrade, menacingly as became an outraged parent in the presence of a third party and a Postmaster.

"Fine doin's this, yer receivin' clandecent bundles and letters, eh?" he began. Flip sent one swift, withering look of contempt at the Postmaster, who at once becoming invertebrate and groveling, mumbled that he must "get on" to the Crossing, and rose to go. But the old man, who had counted on his presence for moral support, and was clearly beginning to hate him for precipitating this scene with his daughter, whom he feared, violently protested.

"Sit down, can't ye? Don't you see you're a witness?" he screamed hysterically.

It was a fatal suggestion. "Witness," repeated Flip, scornfully.

"Yes, a witness! He gave ye letters and bundles."

"Weren't they directed to me?" asked Flip.

"Yes," said the Postmaster, hesitatingly; "in course, yes."

"Do you lay claim to them?" she said, turning to her father.

"No," responded the old man.

"Do you?" sharply, to the Postmaster.

"No," he replied.

"Then," said Flip, coolly, "if you're not claimin' 'em for yourself, and you hear father say they ain't his, I reckon the less you have to say about 'em the better."

"Thar's suthin' in that," said the old man, shamelessly abandoning the Postmaster.

"Then why don't she say who sent 'em, and what they are like," said the Postmaster, "if there's nothing in it?"

"Yes," echoed Dad. "Flip, why don't you?"

Without answering the direct question, Flip turned upon her father.

"Maybe you forget how you used to row and tear round here because tramps and such like came to the ranch for suthin', and I gave it to 'em? Maybe you'll quit tearin' round and letting yourself be made a fool of now by that man, just because one of those tramps gets up and sends us some presents back in turn?"

"'Twasn't me, Flip," said the old man, deprecatingly, but glaring at the astonished Postmaster. "'Twasn't my doin'. I allus said if you cast your bread on the waters it would come back to you by return mail. The fact is, the Gov'ment is getting too high-handed! Some o' these bloated officials had better climb down before next leckshen."

"Maybe," continued Flip to her father, without looking at her discomfited visitor, "ye'd better find out whether one of those officials comes up to this yer ranch to steal away a gal about my own size, or to get points about diamond-making. I reckon he don't travel round to find out who writes all the letters that go through the Post Office."

The Postmaster had seemingly miscalculated the old man's infirm temper, and the daughter's skillful use of it. He was unprepared for Flip's boldness and audacity, and when he saw that both barrels of the accusation had taken effect on the charcoal-burner, who was rising with epileptic rage, he fairly turned and fled. The old man would have followed him with objurgation beyond the door, but for the restraining hand of Flip.

Baffled and beaten, nevertheless Fate was not wholly unkind to the retreating suitor. Near the Gin and Ginger Woods he picked up a letter which had fallen from Flip's packet. He recognized the writing, and did not scruple to read it. It was not a love epistle, at least, not such a one as he would have written, it did not give the address nor the name of the correspondent; but he read the following with greedy eyes:

"Perhaps it's just as well that you don't rig yourself out for the benefit of those dead-beats at the Crossing, or any tramp that might hang round the ranch. Keep all your style for me when I come. I can't tell you when, it's mighty uncertain before the rainy season. But I'm coming soon. Don't go back on your promise about lettin' up on the tramps, and being a little more high-toned. And don't you give 'em so much. It's true I sent you hats twice. I clean forgot all about the first; but I wouldn't have given a ten-dollar hat to a nigger woman who had a sick baby because I had an extra hat. I'd have let that baby slide. I forgot to ask whether the skirt is worn separately; I must see that dressmaker sharp about it; but I think you'll want something on besides a jacket and skirt; at least, it looks like it up here. I don't think you could manage a piano down there without the old man knowing it, and raisin' the devil generally. I promised you I'd let up on him. Mind you keep all your promises to me. I'm glad you're gettin' on with the six-shooter; tin cans are good at fifteen yards, but try it on suthin' that moves! I forgot to say that I am on the track of your big brother. It's a three years' old track, and he was in Arizona. The friend who told me didn't expatiate much on what he did there, but I reckon they had a high old time. If he's above the earth I'll find him, you bet. The yerba buena and the southern wood came all right, they smelt like you. Say, Flip, do you remember the last, the very last, thing that happened when you said 'good-by' on the trail? Don't let me ever find out that you've let anybody else kiss" -

But here the virtuous indignation of the Postmaster found vent in an oath. He threw the letter away. He retained of it only two facts, Flip had a brother who was missing; she had a lover present in the flesh.

How much of the substance of this and previous letters Flip had confided to her father I cannot say. If she suppressed anything it was probably that which affected Lance's secret alone, and it was doubtful how much of that she herself knew. In her own affairs she was frank without being communicative, and never lost her shy obstinacy even with her father. Governing the old man as completely as she did, she appeared most embarrassed when she was most dominant; she had her own way without lifting her voice or her eyes; she seemed oppressed by mauvaise honte when she was most triumphant; she would end a discussion with a shy murmur addressed to herself, or a single gesture of self-consciousness.

The disclosure of her strange relations with an unknown man, and the exchange of presents and confidences, seemed to suddenly awake Fairley to a vague, uneasy sense of some unfulfilled duties as a parent. The first effect of this on his weak nature was a peevish antagonism to the cause of it. He had long, fretful monologues on the vanity of diamond-making, if accompanied with "pestering" by "interlopers;" on the wickedness of concealment and conspiracy, and their effects on charcoal-burning; on the nurturing of spies and "adders" in the family circle, and on the seditiousness of dark and mysterious councils in which a gray-haired father was left out. It was true that a word or look from Flip generally brought these monologues to an inglorious and abrupt termination, but they were none the less lugubrious as long as they lasted. In time they were succeeded by an affectation of contrite apology and self-depreciation. "Don't go out o' the way to ask the old man," he would say, referring to the quantity of bacon to be ordered; "it's nat'ral a young gal should have her own advisers." The state of the flour-barrel would also produce a like self-abasement. "Unless ye're already in correspondence about more flour, ye might take the opinion o' the first tramp ye meet ez to whether Santa Cruz Mills is a good brand, but don't ask the old man." If Flip was in conversation with the butcher, Fairley would obtrusively retire with the hope "he wasn't intrudin' on their secrets."

These phases of her father's weakness were not frequent enough to excite her alarm, but she could not help noticing they were accompanied with a seriousness unusual to him. He began to be tremulously watchful of her, returning often from work at an earlier hour, and lingering by the cabin in the morning. He brought absurd and useless presents for her, and presented them with a nervous anxiety, poorly concealed by an assumption of careless, paternal generosity. "Suthin' I picked up at the Crossin' for ye to-day," he would say, airily, and retire to watch the effect of a pair of shoes two sizes too large, or a fur cap in September. He would have hired a cheap parlor organ for her, but for the apparently unexpected revelation that she couldn't play. He had received the news of a clue to his long-lost son without emotion, but lately he seemed to look upon it as a foregone conclusion, and one that necessarily solved the question of companionship for Flip. "In course, when you've got your own flesh and blood with ye, ye can't go foolin' around with strangers." These autumnal blossoms of affection, I fear, came too late for any effect upon Flip, precociously matured by her father's indifference and selfishness. But she was good-humored, and, seeing him seriously concerned, gave him more of her time, even visited him in the sacred seclusion of the "diamond pit," and listened with far-off eyes to his fitful indictment of all things outside his grimy laboratory. Much of this patient indifference came with a capricious change in her own habits; she no longer indulged in the rehearsal of dress, she packed away her most treasured garments, and her leafy boudoir knew her no more. She sometimes walked on the hillside, and often followed the trail she had taken with Lance when she led him to the ranch. She once or twice extended her walk to the spot where she had parted from him, and as often came shyly away, her eyes downcast and her face warm with color. Perhaps because these experiences and some mysterious instinct of maturing womanhood had left a story in her eyes, which her two adorers, the Postmaster and the butcher, read with passion, she became famous without knowing it. Extravagant stories of her fascinations brought strangers into the valley. The effect upon her father may be imagined. Lance could not have desired a more effective guardian than he proved to be in this emergency. Those who had been told of this hidden pearl were surprised to find it so jealously protected.

CHAPTER V.

The long, parched summer had drawn to its dusty close. Much of it was already blown abroad and dissipated on trail and turnpike, or crackled in harsh, unelastic fibres on hillside and meadow. Some of it had disappeared in the palpable smoke by day and fiery crests by night of burning forests. The besieging fogs on the Coast Range daily thinned their hosts, and at last vanished. The wind changed from northwest to southwest. The salt breath of the sea was on the summit. And then one day the staring, unchanged sky was faintly touched with remote mysterious clouds, and grew tremulous in expression. The next morning dawned upon a newer face in the heavens, on changed woods, on altered outlines, on vanished crests, on forgotten distances. It was raining!

Four weeks of this change, with broken spaces of sunlight and intense blue aerial islands, and then a storm set in. All day the summit pines and redwoods rocked in the blast. At times the onset of the rain seemed to be held back by the fury of the gale, or was visibly seen in sharp waves on the hillside. Unknown and concealed watercourses suddenly overflowed the trails, pools became lakes and brooks rivers. Hidden from the storm, the sylvan silence of sheltered valleys was broken by the impetuous rush of waters; even the tiny streamlet that traversed Flip's retreat in the Gin and Ginger Woods became a cascade.

The storm drove Fairley from his couch early. The falling of a large tree across the trail, and the sudden overflow of a small stream beside it, hastened his steps.

But he was doomed to encounter what was to him a more disagreeable object, a human figure. By the bedraggled drapery that flapped and fluttered in the wind, by the long, unkempt hair that hid the face and eyes, and by the grotesquely misplaced bonnet, the old man recognized one of his old trespassers, an Indian squaw.

"Clear out 'er that! Come, make tracks, will ye?" the old man screamed; but here the wind stopped his voice, and drove him against a hazel-bush.

"Me heap sick," answered the squaw, shivering through her muddy shawl.

"I'll make ye a heap sicker if ye don't vamose the ranch," continued Fairley, advancing.

"Me wantee Wangee girl. Wangee girl give me heap grub," said the squaw, without moving.

"You bet your life," groaned the old man to himself. Nevertheless an idea struck him. "Ye ain't brought no presents, hev ye?" he asked cautiously. "Ye ain't got no pooty things for poor Wangee girl?" he continued insinuatingly.

"Me got heap cache nuts and berries," said the squaw.

"Oh, in course! in course! That's just it," screamed Fairley; "you've got 'em cached only two mile from yer, and you'll go and get 'em for a half dollar, cash down."

"Me bring Wangee girl to cache," replied the Indian, pointing to the wood. "Honest Injin."

Another bright idea struck Mr. Fairley; but it required some elaboration. Hurrying the squaw with him through the pelting rain, he reached the shelter of the corral. Vainly the shivering aborigine drew her tightly bandaged papoose closer to her square, flat breast, and looked longingly toward the cabin; the old man backed her against the palisade. Here he cautiously imparted his dark intentions to employ her to keep watch and ward over the ranch, and especially over its young mistress, "clear out all the tramps 'ceptin' yourself, and I'll keep ye in grub and rum." Many and deliberate repetitions of this offer in various forms at last seemed to affect the squaw; she nodded violently, and echoed the last word "rum." "Now," she added. The old man hesitated; she was in possession of his secret; he groaned, and, promising an immediate installment of liquor, led her to the cabin.

The door was so securely fastened against the impact of the storm that some moments elapsed before the bar was drawn, and the old man had become impatient and profane. When it was partly opened by Flip he hastily slipped in, dragging the squaw after him, and cast one single suspicious glance around the rude apartment which served as a sitting-room. Flip had apparently been writing. A small inkstand was still on the board table, but her paper had evidently been concealed before she allowed them to enter. The squaw instantly squatted before the adobe hearth, warmed her bundled baby, and left the ceremony of introduction to her companion. Flip regarded the two with calm preoccupation and indifference. The only thing that touched her interest was the old squaw's draggled skirt and limp neckerchief. They were Flip's own, long since abandoned and cast off in the Gin and Ginger Woods. "Secrets again," whined Fairley, still eying Flip furtively. "Secrets again, in course, in course, jiss so. Secrets that must be kep from the ole man. Dark doin's by one's own flesh and blood. Go on! go on! Don't mind me." Flip did not reply. She had even lost the interest in her old dress. Perhaps it had only touched some note in unison with her revery.

"Can't ye get the poor critter some whiskey?" he queried, fretfully. "Ye used to be peart enuff before." As Flip turned to the corner to lift the demijohn, Fairley took occasion to kick the squaw with his foot, and indicate by extravagant pantomime that the bargain was not to be alluded to before the girl. Flip poured out some whiskey in a tin cup, and, approaching the squaw, handed it to her. "It's like ez not," continued Fairley to his daughter, but looking at the squaw, "that she'll be huntin' the woods off and on, and kinder looking after the last pit near the Madroños; ye'll give her grub and licker ez she likes. Well, d'ye hear, Flip? Are ye moonin' agin with yer secrets? What's gone with ye?"

If the child were dreaming, it was a delicious dream. Her magnetic eyes were suffused by a strange light, as though the eye itself had blushed; her full pulse showed itself more in the rounding outline of her cheek than in any deepening of color; indeed, if there was any heightening of tint, it was in her freckles, which fairly glistened like tiny spangles. Her eyes were downcast, her shoulders slightly bent, but her voice was low and clear and thoughtful as ever.

"One o' the big pines above the Madroño pit has blown over into the run," she said. "It's choked up the water, and it's risin' fast. Like ez not it's pourin' over into the pit by this time."

The old man rose with a fretful cry. "And why in blazes didn't you say so first?" he screamed, catching up his axe and rushing to the door.

"Ye didn't give me a chance," said Flip, raising her eyes for the first time. With an impatient imprecation, Fairley darted by her and rushed into the wood. In an instant she had shut the door and bolted it. In the same instant the squaw arose, dashed the long hair not only from her eyes but from her head, tore away her shawl and blanket, and revealed the square shoulders of Lance Harriott! Flip remained leaning against the door; but the young man in rising dropped the bandaged papoose, which rolled from his lap into the fire. Flip, with a cry, sprang toward it; but Lance caught her by the waist with one arm, as with the other he dragged the bundle from the flames.

"Don't be alarmed," he said, gayly, "it's only" -

"What?" said Flip, trying to disengage herself.

"My coat and trousers."

Flip laughed, which encouraged Lance to another attempt to kiss her. She evaded it by diving her head into his waistcoat, and saying, "There's father."

"But he's gone to clear away that tree," suggested Lance.

One of Flip's significant silences followed.

"Oh, I see," he laughed. "That was a plan to get him away! Ah!" She had released herself.

"Why did you come like that?" she said, pointing to his wig and blanket.

"To see if you'd know me," he responded.

"No," said Flip, dropping her eyes. "It's to keep other people from knowing you. You're hidin' agin."

"I am," returned Lance; "but," he interrupted, "it's only the same old thing."

"But you wrote from Monterey that it was all over," she persisted.

"So it would have been," he said gloomily, "but for some dog down here who is hunting up an old scent. I'll spot him yet, and" - He stopped suddenly, with such utter abstraction of hatred in his fixed and glittering eyes that she almost feared him. She laid her hand quite unconsciously on his arm. He grasped it; his face changed.

"I couldn't wait any longer to see you, Flip, so I came here anyway," he went on. "I thought to hang round and get a chance to speak to you first, when I fell afoul of the old man. He didn't know me, and tumbled right in my little game. Why, do you believe he wants to hire me for my grub and liquor, to act as a sort of sentry over you and the ranch?" And here he related with great gusto the substance of his interview. "I reckon as he's that suspicious," he concluded, "I'd better play it out now as I've begun, only it's mighty hard I can't see you here before the fire in your fancy toggery, Flip, but must dodge in and out of the wet underbrush in these yer duds of yours that I picked up in the old place in the Gin and Ginger Woods."

"Then you came here just to see me?" asked Flip.

"I did."

"For only that?"

"Only that."

Flip dropped her eyes. Lance had got his other arm around her waist, but her resisting little hand was still potent.

"Listen," she said at last without looking up, but apparently talking to the intruding arm, "when Dad comes I'll get him to send you to watch the diamond pit. It isn't far; it's warm, and" -

"What?"

"I'll come, after a bit, and see you. Quit foolin' now. If you'd only have come here like yourself, like, like a white man."

"The old man," interrupted Lance, "would have just passed me on to the summit. I couldn't have played the lost fisherman on him at this time of year."

"Ye could have been stopped at the Crossing by high water, you silly," said the girl. "It was." This grammatical obscurity referred to the stage-coach.

"Yes, but I might have been tracked to this cabin. And look here, Flip," he said, suddenly straightening himself, and lifting the girl's face to a level with his own, "I don't want you to lie any more for me. It ain't right."

"All right. Ye needn't go to the pit, then, and I won't come."

"Flip!"

"And here's Dad coming. Quick!"

Lance chose to put his own interpretation on this last adjuration. The resisting little hand was now lying quite limp on his shoulder. He drew her brown, bright face near his own, felt her spiced breath on his lips, his cheeks, his hot eyelids, his swimming eyes, kissed her, hurriedly replaced his wig and blanket, and dropped beside the fire with the tremulous laugh of youth and innocent first passion. Flip had withdrawn to the window, and was looking out upon the rocking pines.

"He don't seem to be coming," said Lance, with a half-shy laugh.

"No," responded Flip demurely, pressing her hot oval cheek against the wet panes; "I reckon I was mistaken. You're sure," she added, looking resolutely another way, but still trembling like a magnetic needle toward Lance, as he moved slightly before the fire, "you're sure you'd like me to come to you?"

"Sure, Flip?"

"Hush!" said Flip, as this reassuring query of reproachful astonishment appeared about to be emphasized by a forward amatory dash of Lance's; "hush! he's coming this time, sure."

It was, indeed, Fairley, exceedingly wet, exceedingly bedraggled, exceedingly sponged out as to color, and exceedingly profane. It appeared that there was, indeed, a tree that had fallen in the "run," but that, far from diverting the overflow into the pit, it had established "back water," which had forced another outlet. All this might have been detected at once by any human intellect not distracted by correspondence with strangers, and enfeebled by habitually scorning the intellect of its own progenitor. This reckless selfishness had further only resulted in giving "rheumatics" to that progenitor, who now required the external administration of opodeldoc to his limbs, and the internal administration of whiskey. Having thus spoken, Mr. Fairley, with great promptitude and infantine simplicity, at once bared two legs of entirely different colors and mutely waited for his daughter to rub them. If Flip did this all unconsciously, and with the mechanical dexterity of previous habit, it was because she did not quite understand the savage eyes and impatient gestures of Lance in his encompassing wig and blanket, and because it helped her to voice her thought.

"Ye'll never be able to take yer watch at the diamond pit to-night, Dad," she said; "and I've been reck'nin' you might set the squaw there instead. I can show her what to do."

But to Flip's momentary discomfiture, her father promptly objected. "Mebbe I've got suthin' else for her to do. Mebbe I may have my secrets, too, eh?" he said, with dark significance, at the same time administering a significant nudge to Lance, which kept up the young man's exasperation. "No, she'll rest yer a bit just now. I'll set her to watchin' suthin' else, like as not, when I want her." Flip fell into one of her suggestive silences. Lance watched her earnestly, mollified by a single furtive glance from her significant eyes; the rain dashed against the windows, and occasionally spattered and hissed in the hearth of the broad chimney, and Mr. David Fairley, somewhat assuaged by the internal administration of whiskey, grew more loquacious. The genius of incongruity and inconsistency which generally ruled his conduct came out with freshened vigor under the gentle stimulation of spirit. "On an evening like this," he began, comfortably settling himself on the floor beside the chimney, "ye might rig yerself out in them new duds and fancy fixin's that that Sacramento shrimp sent ye, and let your own flesh and blood see ye. If that's too much to do for your old dad, ye might do it to please that digger squaw as a Christian act." Whether in the hidden depths of the old man's consciousness there was a feeling of paternal vanity in showing this wretched aborigine the value and importance of the treasure she was about to guard, I cannot say. Flip darted an interrogatory look at Lance, who nodded a quiet assent, and she flew into the inner room. She did not linger on the details of her toilet, but reappeared almost the next moment in her new finery, buttoning the neck of her gown as she entered the room, and chastely stopping at the window to characteristically pull up her stocking. The peculiarity of her situation increased her usual shyness; she played with the black and gold beads of a handsome necklace, Lance's last gift, as the merest child might; her unbuckled shoe gave the squaw a natural opportunity of showing her admiration and devotion by insisting upon buckling it, and gave Lance, under that disguise, an opportunity of covertly kissing the little foot and ankle in the shadow of the chimney; an event which provoked slight hysterical symptoms in Flip and caused her to sit suddenly down in spite of the remonstrances of her parent. "Ef you can't quit gigglin' and squirmin' like an Injin baby yourself, ye'd better get rid o' them duds," he ejaculated with peevish scorn.

Yet, under this perfunctory rebuke, his weak vanity could not be hidden, and he enjoyed the evident admiration of a creature, whom he believed to be half-witted and degraded, all the more keenly because it did not make him jealous. She could not take Flip from him. Rendered garrulous by liquor, he went to voice his contempt for those who might attempt it. Taking advantage of his daughter's absence to resume her homely garments, he whispered confidentially to Lance:

"Ye see these yer fine dresses, ye might think is presents. Pr'aps Flip lets on they are. Pr'aps she don't know any better. But they ain't presents. They're only samples o' dressmaking and jewelry that a vain, conceited shrimp of a feller up in Sacramento sends down here to get customers for. In course I'm to pay for 'em. In course he reckons I'm to do it. In course I calkilate to do it; but he needn't try to play 'em off as presents. He talks suthin' o' coming down here, sportin' hisself off on Flip as a fancy buck! Not ez long ez the old man's here, you bet!" Thoroughly carried away by his fancied wrongs, it was perhaps fortunate that he did not observe the flashing eyes of Lance behind his lank and lustreless wig; but seeing only the figure of Lance as he had conjured him, he went on: "That's why I want you to hang around her. Hang around her ontil my boy, him that's comin' home on a visit, gets here, and I reckon he'll clear out that yar Sacramento counter-jumper. Only let me get a sight o' him afore Flip does. Eh? D'ye hear? Dog my skin if I don't believe the damned Injin's drunk." It was fortunate that at that moment Flip reappeared and, dropping on the hearth between her father and the infuriated Lance, let her hand slip in his with a warning pressure. The light touch momentarily recalled him to himself and her, but not until the quick-witted girl had revealed to her, in one startled wave of consciousness, the full extent of Lance's infirmity of temper. With the instinct of awakened tenderness came a sense of responsibility, and a vague premonition of danger. The coy blossom of her heart was scarce unfolded before it was chilled by approaching shadows. Fearful of, she knew not what, she hesitated. Every moment of Lance's stay was imperiled by a single word that might spring from his suppressed white lips; beyond and above the suspicions his sudden withdrawal might awaken in her father's breast, she was dimly conscious of some mysterious terror without that awaited him. She listened to the furious onslaught of the wind upon the sycamores beside their cabin, and thought she heard it there; she listened to the sharp fusillade of rain upon roof and pane, and the turbulent roar and rush of leaping mountain torrents at their very feet, and fancied it was there. She suddenly sprang to the window, and, pressing her eyes to the pane, saw through the misty turmoil of tossing boughs and swaying branches the scintillating intermittent flames of torches moving on the trail above, and knew it was there!

In an instant she was collected and calm. "Dad," she said, in her ordinary indifferent tone, "there's torches movin; up toward the diamond pit. Likely it's tramps. I'll take the squaw and see." And before the old man could stagger to his feet she had dragged Lance with her into the road.

CHAPTER VI.

The wind charged down upon them, slamming the door at their backs, extinguishing the broad shaft of light that had momentarily shot out into the darkness, and swept them a dozen yards away. Gaining the lee of a madroño tree, Lance opened his blanketed arms, enfolded the girl, and felt her for one brief moment tremble and nestle in his bosom like some frightened animal. "Well," he said, gayly, "what next?" Flip recovered herself. "You're safe now anywhere outside the house. But did you expect them to-night?" Lance shrugged his shoulders. "Why not?" "Hush!" returned the girl; "they're coming this way."

The four flickering, scattered lights presently dropped into line. The trail had been found; they were coming nearer. Flip breathed quickly; the spiced aroma of her presence filled the blanket as he drew her tightly beside him. He had forgotten the storm that raged around them, the mysterious foe that was approaching, until Flip caught his sleeve with a slight laugh. "Why, it's Kennedy and Bijah!"

"Who's Kennedy and Bijah?" asked Lance, curtly.

"Kennedy's the Postmaster and Bijah's the Butcher."

"What do they want?" continued Lance.

"Me," said Flip, coyly.

"You?"

"Yes; let's run away."

Half leading, half dragging her friend, Flip made her way with unerring woodcraft down the ravine. The sound of voices and even the tumult of the storm became fainter, an acrid smell of burning green wood smarted Lance's lips and eyes; in the midst of the darkness beneath him gradually a faint, gigantic nimbus like a lurid eye glowed and sank, quivered and faded with the spent breath of the gale as it penetrated their retreat. "The pit," whispered Flip; "it's safe on the other side," she added, cautiously skirting the orbit of the great eye, and leading him to a sheltered nest of bark and sawdust. It was warm and odorous. Nevertheless, they both deemed it necessary to enwrap themselves in the single blanket. The eye beamed fitfully upon them, occasionally a wave of lambent tremulousness passed across it; its weirdness was an excuse for their drawing nearer each other in playful terror.

"Flip."

"Well?"

"What did the other two want? To see you, too?"

"Likely," said Flip, without the least trace of coquetry. "There's been a lot of strangers yer, off and on."

"Perhaps you'd like to go back and see them?"

"Do you want me to?"

Lance's reply was a kiss. Nevertheless he was vaguely uneasy. "Looks a little as if I were running away, don't it?" he suggested.

"No," said Flip; "they think you're only a squaw; it's me they're after." Lance smarted a little at this infelicitous speech. A strange and irritating sensation had been creeping over him, it was his first experience of shame and remorse. "I reckon I'll go back and see," he said, rising abruptly.

Flip was silent. She was thinking. Believing that the men were seeking her only, she knew that their intention would be directed from her companion when it was found out he was no longer with her, and she dreaded to meet them in his irritable presence.

"Go," she said; "tell Dad something's wrong in the diamond pit, and say I'm watching it for him here."

"And you?"

"I'll go there and wait for him. If he can't get rid of them, and they follow him there, I'll come back here and meet you. Anyhow, I'll manage to have Dad wait there a spell."

She took his hand and led him back by a different path to the trail. He was surprised to find that the cabin, its window glowing from the fire, was only a hundred yards away. "Go in the back way, by the shed. Don't go in the room, nor near the light, if you can. Don't talk inside, but call or beckon to Dad. Remember," she said, with a laugh, "you're keeping watch of me for him. Pull your hair down on your eyes, so." This operation, like most feminine embellishments of the masculine toilet, was attended by a kiss, and Flip, stepping back into the shadow, vanished in the storm.

Lance's first movements were inconsistent with his assumed sex. He picked up his draggled skirt and drew a bowie-knife from his boot. From his bosom he took a revolver, turning the chambers noiselessly as he felt the caps. He then crept toward the cabin softly and gained the shed. It was quite dark but for a pencil of light piercing a crack of the rude, ill-fitting door that opened on the sitting-room. A single voice not unfamiliar to him, raised in half-brutal triumph, greeted his ears. A name was mentioned, his own! His angry hand was on the latch. One moment more and he would have burst the door, but in that instant another name was uttered, a name that dropped his hand from the latch and the blood from his cheeks. He staggered backward, passed his hand swiftly across his forehead, recovered himself with a gesture of mingled rage and despair, and, sinking on his knees beside the door, pressed his hot temples against the crack.

"Do I know Lance Harriott?" said the voice. "Do I know the d-amned ruffian? Didn't I hunt him a year ago into the brush three miles from the Crossing? Didn't we lose sight of him the very day he turned up yer at this ranch, and got smuggled over into Monterey? Ain't it the same man as killed Arkansaw Bob, Bob Ridley, the name he went by in Sonora? And who was Bob Ridley, eh? Who? Why, you damned old fool, it was Bob Fairley, YOUR SON!"

The old man's voice rose querulous and indistinct.

"What are ye talkin' about?" interrupted the first speaker. I tell you I know. Look at these pictures. I found 'em on his body. Look at 'em. Pictures of you and your girl. Pr'aps you'll deny them. Pr'aps you'll tell me I lie when I tell you he told me he was your son; told me how he ran away from you; how you were livin' somewhere in the mountains makin' gold, or suthin' else, outer charcoal. He told me who he was as a secret. He never let on he told it to any one else. And when I found that the man who killed him, Lance Harriott, had been hidin' here, had been sendin' spies all around to find out all about your son, had been foolin' you, and tryin' to ruin your gal as he had killed your boy, I knew that he knew it too."

"LIAR!"

The door fell in with a crash. There was the sudden apparition of the demoniac face, still half hidden by the long trailing black locks of hair that curled like Medusa's around it. A cry of terror filled the room. Three of the men dashed from the door and fled precipitately. The man who had spoken sprang toward his rifle in the chimney corner. But the movement was his last; a blinding flash and shattering report interposed between him and his weapon. The impulse carried him forward headlong into the fire, that hissed and spluttered with his blood, and Lance Harriott, with his smoking pistol, strode past him to the door. Already far down the trail there were hurried voices, the crack and crackling of impending branches growing fainter and fainter in the distance. Lance turned back to the solitary living figure, the old man.

Yet he might have been dead too, he sat so rigid and motionless, his fixed eyes staring vacantly at the body on the hearth. Before him on the table lay the cheap photographs, one evidently of himself, taken in some remote epoch of complexion, one of a child which Lance recognized as Flip.

"Tell me," said Lance hoarsely, laying his quivering hand on the table, "was Bob Ridley your son?"

"My son," echoed the old man in a strange, far-off voice, without turning his eyes from the corpse, "my son-is-is-is there!" pointing to the dead man. "Hush! Didn't he tell you so? Didn't you hear him say it? Dead, dead, shot, shot!"

"Silence! are you crazy, man?" interposed Lance, tremblingly; "that is not Bob Ridley, but a dog, a coward, a liar, gone to his reckoning. Hear me! If your son was Bob Ridley, I swear to God I never knew it, now or, or then. Do you hear me? Tell me! Do you believe me? Speak! You shall speak!"

He laid his hand almost menacingly on the old man's shoulder. Fairley slowly raised his head. Lance fell back with a groan of horror. The weak lips were wreathed with a feeble imploring smile, but the eyes wherein the fretful, peevish, suspicious spirit had dwelt were blank and tenantless; the flickering intellect that had lit them was blown out and vanished.

Lance walked toward the door and remained motionless for a moment, gazing into the night. When he turned back again toward the fire his face was as colorless as the dead man's on the hearth; the fire of passion was gone from his beaten eyes; his step was hesitating and slow. He went up to the table.

"I say, old man," he said, with a strange smile and an odd, premature suggestion of the infinite weariness of death in his voice, "you wouldn't mind giving me this, would you?" and he took up the picture of Flip. The old man nodded repeatedly. "Thank you," said Lance. He went to the door, paused a moment, and returned. "Good-by, old man," he said, holding out his hand. Fairley took it with a childish smile. "He's dead," said the old man softly, holding Lance's hand, but pointing to the hearth. "Yes," said Lance, with the faintest of smiles on the palest of faces. "You feel sorry for any one that's dead, don't you?" Fairley nodded again. Lance looked at him with eyes as remote as his own, shook his head, and turned away. When he reached the door he laid his revolver carefully, and, indeed, somewhat ostentatiously, upon a chair. But when he stepped from the threshold he stopped a moment in the light of the open door to examine the lock of a small derringer which he drew from his pocket. He then shut the door carefully, and with the same slow, hesitating step, felt his way into the night.

He had but one idea in his mind, to find some lonely spot; some spot where the footsteps of man would never penetrate, some spot that would yield him rest, sleep, obliteration, forgetfulness, and, above all, where he would be forgotten. He had seen such places; surely there were many, where bones were picked up of dead men who had faded from the earth and had left no other record. If he could only keep his senses now he might find such a spot, but he must be careful, for her little feet went everywhere, and she must never see him again alive or dead. And in the midst of his thoughts, and the darkness, and the storm, he heard a voice at his side, "Lance, how long you have been!"

Left to himself, the old man again fell into a vacant contemplation of the dead body before him, until a stronger blast swept down like an avalanche upon the cabin, burst through the ill-fastened door and broken chimney, and, dashing the ashes and living embers over the floor, filled the room with blinding smoke and flame. Fairley rose with a feeble cry, and then, as if acted upon by some dominant memory, groped under the bed until he found his buckskin bag and his precious crystal, and fled precipitately from the room. Lifted by this second shock from his apathy, he returned to the fixed idea of his life, the discovery and creation of the diamond, and forgot all else. The feeble grasp that his shaken intellect kept of the events of the night relaxed, the disguised Lance, the story of his son, the murder, slipped into nothingness; there remained only the one idea, his nightly watch by the diamond pit. The instinct of long habit was stronger than the darkness or the onset of the storm, and he kept his tottering way over stream and fallen timber until he reached the spot. A sudden tremor seemed to shake the lambent flame that had lured him on. He thought he heard the sound of voices; there were signs of recent disturbance, footprints in the sawdust! With a cry of rage and suspicion, Fairley slipped into the pit and sprang toward the nearest opening. To his frenzied fancy it had been tampered with, his secret discovered, the fruit of his long labors stolen from him that very night. With superhuman strength he began to open the pit, scattering the half-charred logs right and left, and giving vent to the suffocating gases that rose from the now incandescent charcoal. At times the fury of the gale would drive it back and hold it against the sides of the pit, leaving the opening free; at times, following the blind instinct of habit, the demented man would fall upon his face and bury his nose and mouth in the wet bark and sawdust. At last, the paroxysm past, he sank back again into his old apathetic attitude of watching, the attitude he had so often kept beside his sylvan crucible. In this attitude and in silence he waited for the dawn.

It came with a hush in the storm; it came with blue openings in the broken up and tumbled heavens; it came with stars that glistened first, and then paled, and at last sank drowning in those deep cerulean lakes; it came with those cerulean lakes broadening into vaster seas, whose shores expanded at last into one illimitable ocean, cerulean no more, but flecked with crimson and opal dyes; it came with the lightly lifted misty curtain of the day, torn and rent on crag and pine-top, but always lifting, lifting. It came with the sparkle of emerald in the grasses, and the flash of diamonds in every spray, with a whisper in the awakening woods, and voices in the traveled roads and trails.

The sound of these voices stopped before the pit, and seemed to interrogate the old man. He came, and, putting his finger on his lips, made a sign of caution. When three or four men had descended he bade them follow him, saying, weakly and disjointedly, but persistently: "My boy, my son Robert, came home, came home at last, here with Flip, both of them, come and see!"

He had reached a little niche or nest in the hillside, and stopped, and suddenly drew aside a blanket. Beneath it, side by side, lay Flip and Lance, dead, with their cold hands clasped in each other's.

"Suffocated!" said two or three, turning with horror toward the broken up and still smouldering pit.

"Asleep!" said the old man. "Asleep! I've seen 'em lying that way when they were babies together. Don't tell me! Don't say I don't know my own flesh and blood! So! so! So, my pretty ones!" He stooped and kissed them. Then, drawing the blanket over them gently, he rose and said softly, "Good night!"

FOUND AT BLAZING STAR.

The rain had only ceased with the gray streaks of morning at Blazing Star, and the settlement awoke to a moral sense of cleanliness, and the finding of forgotten knives, tin cups, and smaller camp utensils, where the heavy showers had washed away the débris and dust heaps before the cabin-doors. Indeed, it was recorded in Blazing Star that a fortunate early riser had once picked up on the highway a solid chunk of gold quartz which the rain had freed from its incumbering soil, and washed into immediate and glittering popularity. Possibly this may have been the reason why early risers in that locality, during the rainy season, adopted a thoughtful habit of body, and seldom lifted their eyes to the rifted or india-ink washed skies above them.

"Cass" Beard had risen early that morning, but not with a view to discovery. A leak in his cabin roof, quite consistent with his careless, improvident habits, had roused him at 4 A.M., with a flooded "bunk" and wet blankets. The chips from his wood pile refused to kindle a fire to dry his bedclothes, and he had recourse to a more provident neighbor's to supply the deficiency. This was nearly opposite. Mr. Cassius crossed the highway, and stopped suddenly. Something glittered in the nearest red pool before him. Gold, surely! But, wonderful to relate, not an irregular, shapeless fragment of crude ore, fresh from Nature's crucible, but a bit of jeweler's handicraft in the form of a plain gold ring. Looking at it more attentively, he saw that it bore the inscription, "May to Cass."

Like most of his fellow gold-seekers, Cass was superstitious. "Cass!" His own name! He tried the ring. It fitted his little finger closely. It was evidently a woman's ring. He looked up and down the highway. No one was yet stirring. Little pools of water in the red road were beginning to glitter and grow rosy from the far-flushing east, but there was no trace of the owner of the shining waif. He knew that there was no woman in camp, and among his few comrades in the settlement he remembered to have seen none wearing an ornament like that. Again, the coincidence of the inscription to his rather peculiar nickname would have been a perennial source of playful comment in a camp that made no allowance for sentimental memories. He slipped the glittering little hoop into his pocket, and thoughtfully returned to his cabin.

Two hours later, when the long, straggling procession, which every morning wended its way to Blazing Star Gulch, the seat of mining operations in the settlement, began to move, Cass saw fit to interrogate his fellows.

"Ye didn't none on ye happen to drop anything round yer last night?" he asked, cautiously.

"I dropped a pocketbook containing government bonds and some other securities, with between fifty and sixty thousand dollars," responded Peter Drummond, carelessly; "but no matter, if any man will return a few autograph letters from foreign potentates that happened to be in it, of no value to anybody but the owner, he can keep the money. Thar's nothin' mean about me," he concluded, languidly.

This statement, bearing every evidence of the grossest mendacity, was lightly passed over, and the men walked on with the deepest gravity.

"But hev you?" Cass presently asked of another.

"I lost my pile to Jack Hamlin at draw-poker, over at Wingdam last night," returned the other, pensively, "but I don't calkilate to find it lying round loose."

Forced at last by this kind of irony into more detailed explanation, Cass confided to them his discovery, and produced his treasure. The result was a dozen vague surmises, only one of which seemed to be popular, and to suit the dyspeptic despondency of the party, a despondency born of hastily masticated fried pork and flapjacks. The ring was believed to have been dropped by some passing "road agent" laden with guilty spoil.

"Ef I was you," said Drummond gloomily, "I wouldn't flourish that yer ring around much afore folks. I've seen better men nor you strung up a tree by Vigilantés for having even less than that in their possession."

"And I wouldn't say much about bein' up so damned early this morning," added an even more pessimistic comrade; "it might look bad before a jury."

With this the men sadly dispersed, leaving the innocent Cass with the ring in his hand, and a general impression on his mind that he was already an object of suspicion to his comrades, an impression, it is hardly necessary to say, they fully intended should be left to rankle in his guileless bosom.

Notwithstanding Cass's first hopeful superstition, the ring did not seem to bring him nor the camp any luck. Daily the "clean up" brought the same scant rewards to their labors, and deepened the sardonic gravity of Blazing Star. But, if Cass found no material result from his treasure, it stimulated his lazy imagination, and, albeit a dangerous and seductive stimulant, at least lifted him out of the monotonous grooves of his half-careless, half-slovenly, but always self-contented camp life. Heeding the wise caution of his comrades, he took the habit of wearing the ring only at night. Wrapped in his blanket, he stealthily slipped the golden circlet over his little finger, and, as he averred, "slept all the better for it." Whether it ever evoked any warmer dream or vision during those calm, cold, virgin-like spring nights, when even the moon and the greater planets retreated into the icy blue, steel-like firmament, I cannot say. Enough that this superstition began to be colored a little by fancy, and his fatalism somewhat mitigated by hope. Dreams of this kind did not tend to promote his efficiency in the communistic labors of the camp, and brought him a self-isolation that, however gratifying at first, soon debarred him the benefits of that hard practical wisdom which underlaid the grumbling of his fellow-workers.

"I'm dog-goned," said one commentator, "ef I don't believe that Cass is looney over that yer ring he found. Wears it on a string under his shirt."

Meantime, the seasons did not wait the discovery of the secret. The red pools in Blazing Star highway were soon dried up in the fervent June sun and riotous night winds of those altitudes. The ephemeral grasses that had quickly supplanted these pools and the chocolate-colored mud, were as quickly parched and withered. The footprints of spring became vague and indefinite, and were finally lost in the impalpable dust of the summer highway.

In one of his long, aimless excursions, Cass had penetrated a thick undergrowth of buckeye and hazel, and found himself quite unexpectedly upon the high road to Red Chief's Crossing. Cass knew by the lurid cloud of dust that hid the distance, that the up coach had passed. He had already reached that stage of superstition when the most trivial occurrence seemed to point in some way to an elucidation of the mystery of his treasure. His eyes had mechanically fallen to the ground again, as if he half expected to find in some other waif a hint or corroboration of his imaginings. Thus abstracted, the figure of a young girl on horseback, in the road directly before the bushes he emerged from, appeared to have sprung directly from the ground.

"Oh, come here, please do; quick!"

Cass stared, and then moved hesitatingly toward her.

"I heard someone coming through the bushes, and I waited," she went on. "Come quick. It's something too awful for anything."

In spite of this appalling introduction, Cass could not but notice that the voice, although hurried and excited, was by no means agitated or frightened; that the eyes which looked into his sparkled with a certain kind of pleased curiosity.

"It was just here," she went on vivaciously, "just here that I went into the bush and cut a switch for my mare, and," - leading him along at a brisk trot by her side, - "just here, look, see! this is what I found."

It was scarcely thirty feet from the road. The only object that met Cass's eye was a man's stiff, tall hat, lying emptily and vacantly in the grass. It was new, shiny, and of modish shape. But it was so incongruous, so perkily smart, and yet so feeble and helpless lying there, so ghastly ludicrous in its very appropriateness and incapacity to adjust itself to the surrounding landscape, that it affected him with something more than a sense of its grotesqueness, and he could only stare at it blankly.

"But you're not looking the right way," the girl went on sharply; "look there!"

Cass followed the direction of her whip. At last, what might have seemed a coat thrown carelessly on the ground met his eye, but presently he became aware of a white, rigid, aimlessly-clinched hand protruding from the flaccid sleeve; mingled with it in some absurd way and half hidden by the grass, lay what might have been a pair of cast-off trousers but for two rigid boots that pointed in opposite angles to the sky. It was a dead man! So palpably dead that life seemed to have taken flight from his very clothes. So impotent, feeble, and degraded by them that the naked subject of a dissecting table would have been less insulting to humanity. The head had fallen back, and was partly hidden in a gopher burrow, but the white, upturned face and closed eyes had less of helpless death in them than those wretched enwrappings. Indeed, one limp hand that lay across the swollen abdomen lent itself to the grotesquely hideous suggestion of a gentleman sleeping off the excesses of a hearty dinner.

"Ain't he horrid?" continued the girl; "but what killed him?"

Struggling between a certain fascination at the girl's cold-blooded curiosity and horror of the murdered man, Cass hesitatingly lifted the helpless head. A bluish hole above the right temple, and a few brown paint-like spots on the forehead, shirt collar, and matted hair, proved the only record.

"Turn him over again," said the girl, impatiently, as Cass was about to relinquish his burden. "Maybe you'll find another wound."

But Cass was dimly remembering certain formalities that in older civilizations attend the discovery of dead bodies, and postponed a present inquest.

"Perhaps you'd better ride on, Miss, afore you get summoned as a witness. I'll give warning at Red Chief's Crossing, and send the coroner down here."

"Let me go with you," she said, earnestly; "it would be such fun. I don't mind being a witness. Or," she added, without heeding Cass's look of astonishment, "I'll wait here till you come back."

"But you see, Miss, it wouldn't seem right," began Cass.

"But I found him first," interrupted the girl, with a pout.

Staggered by this preemptive right, sacred to all miners, Cass stopped.

"Who is the coroner?" she asked.

"Joe Hornsby."

"The tall, lame man, who was half eaten by a grizzly?"

"Yes."

"Well, look now! I'll ride on and bring him back in half an hour. There!"

"But, Miss!"

"Oh, don't mind me. I never saw anything of this kind before, and I want to see it all."

"Do you know Hornsby?" asked Cass, unconsciously a trifle irritated.

"No, but I'll bring him." She wheeled her horse into the road.

In the presence of this living energy Cass quite forgot the helpless dead. "Have you been long in these parts, Miss?" he asked.

"About two weeks," she answered, shortly. "Good-by, just now. Look around for the pistol or anything else you can find, although I have been over the whole ground twice already."

A little puff of dust as the horse sprang into the road, a muffled shuffle, struggle, then the regular beat of hoofs, and she was gone.

After five minutes had passed, Cass regretted that he had not accompanied her: waiting in such a spot was an irksome task. Not that there was anything in the scene itself to awaken gloomy imaginings; the bright, truthful Californian sunshine scoffed at any illusion of creeping shadows or waving branches. Once, in the rising wind, the empty hat rolled over, but only in a ludicrous, drunken way. A search for any further sign or token had proved futile, and Cass grew impatient. He began to hate himself for having stayed; he would have fled but for shame. Nor was his good-humor restored when at the close of a weary half hour two galloping figures emerged from the dusty horizon, Hornsby and the young girl.

His vague annoyance increased as he fancied that both seemed to ignore him, the coroner barely acknowledging his presence with a nod. Assisted by the young girl, whose energy and enthusiasm evidently delighted him, Hornsby raised the body for a more careful examination. The dead man's pockets were carefully searched. A few coins, a silver pencil, knife, and tobacco-box were all they found. It gave no clew to his identity. Suddenly the young girl, who had, with unabashed curiosity, knelt beside the exploring official hands of the Red Chief, uttered a cry of gratification.

"Here's something! It dropped from the bosom of his shirt on the ground. Look!"

She was holding in the air, between her thumb and forefinger, a folded bit of well-worn newspaper. Her eyes sparkled.

"Shall I open it?" she asked.

"Yes."

"It's a little ring," she said; "looks like an engagement ring. Something is written on it. Look! 'May to Cass.'"

Cass darted forward. "It's mine," he stammered, "mine! I dropped it. It's nothing, nothing," he went on, after a pause, embarrassed and blushing, as the girl and her companion both stared at him, "a mere trifle. I'll take it."

But the coroner opposed his outstretched hand. "Not much," he said, significantly.

"But it's mine," continued Cass, indignation taking the place of shame at his discovered secret. "I found it six months ago in the road. I picked it up."

"With your name already written on it! How handy!" said the coroner, grimly.

"It's an old story," said Cass, blushing again under the half mischievous, half searching eyes of the girl. "All Blazing Star knows I found it."

"Then ye'll have no difficulty in provin' it," said Hornsby, coolly. "Just now, however, we've found it, and we propose to keep it for the inquest."

Cass shrugged his shoulders. Further altercation would have only heightened his ludicrous situation in the girl's eyes. He turned away, leaving his treasure in the coroner's hands.

The inquest, a day or two later, was prompt and final. No clew to the dead man's identity; no evidence sufficiently strong to prove murder or suicide; no trace of any kind, inculpating any party, known or unknown, were found. But much publicity and interest were given to the proceedings by the presence of the principal witness, a handsome girl. "To the pluck, persistency, and intellect of Miss Porter," said the "Red Chief Recorder," "Tuolumne County owes the recovery of the body."

No one who was present at the inquest failed to be charmed with the appearance and conduct of this beautiful young lady.

"Miss Porter has but lately arrived in this district, in which, it is hoped, she will become an honored resident, and continue to set an example to all lackadaisical and sentimental members of the so-called 'sterner sex.'" After this universally recognized allusion to Cass Beard, the "Recorder" returned to its record: "Some interest was excited by what appeared to be a clew to the mystery in the discovery of a small gold engagement ring on the body. Evidence was afterward offered to show it was the property of a Mr. Cass Beard of Blazing Star, who appeared upon the scene after the discovery of the corpse by Miss Porter. He alleged he had dropped it in lifting the unfortunate remains of the deceased. Much amusement was created in court by the sentimental confusion of the claimant, and a certain partisan spirit shown by his fellow-miners of Blazing Star. It appearing, however, by the admission of this sighing Strephon of the Foot Hills, that he had himself found this pledge of affection lying in the highway six months previous, the coroner wisely placed it in the safe-keeping of the county court until the appearance of the rightful owner."

Thus on the 13th of September, 186-, the treasure found at Blazing Star passed out of the hands of its finder.

Autumn brought an abrupt explanation of the mystery. Kanaka Joe had been arrested for horse-stealing, but had with noble candor confessed to the finer offense of manslaughter. That swift and sure justice which overtook the horse-stealer in these altitudes was stayed a moment and hesitated, for the victim was clearly the mysterious unknown. Curiosity got the better of an extempore judge and jury.

"It was a fair fight," said the accused, not without some human vanity, feeling that the camp hung upon his words, "and was settled by the man az was peartest and liveliest with his weapon. We had a sort of unpleasantness over at Lagrange the night afore, along of our both hevin' a monotony of four aces. We had a clinch and a stamp around, and when we was separated it was only a question of shootin' on sight. He left Lagrange at sun up the next morning, and I struck across a bit o' buckeye and underbrush and came upon him, accidental like, on the Red Chief Road. I drawed when I sighted him, and called out. He slipped from his mare and covered himself with her flanks, reaching for his holster, but she rared and backed down on him across the road and into the grass, where I got in another shot and fetched him."

"And you stole his mare?" suggested the Judge.

"I got away," said the gambler, simply.

Further questioning only elicited the fact that Joe did not know the name or condition of his victim. He was a stranger in Lagrange.

It was a breezy afternoon, with some turbulency in the camp, and much windy discussion over this unwonted delay of justice. The suggestion that Joe should be first hanged for horse stealing and then tried for murder was angrily discussed, but milder counsels were offered, that the fact of the killing should be admitted only as proof of the theft. A large party from Red Chief had come over to assist in judgment, among them the coroner.

Cass Beard had avoided these proceedings, which only recalled an unpleasant experience, and was wandering with pick, pan, and wallet far from the camp. These accoutrements, as I have before intimated, justified any form of aimless idleness under the equally aimless title of "prospecting." He had at the end of three hours' relaxation reached the highway to Red Chief, half hidden by blinding clouds of dust torn from the crumbling red road at every gust which swept down the mountain side. The spot had a familiar aspect to Cass, although some freshly-dug holes near the wayside, with scattered earth beside them, showed the presence of a recent prospector. He was struggling with his memory, when the dust was suddenly dispersed and he found himself again at the scene of the murder. He started: he had not put foot on the road since the inquest. There lacked only the helpless dead man and the contrasting figure of the alert young woman to restore the picture. The body was gone, it was true, but as he turned he beheld Miss Porter, at a few paces distant, sitting her horse as energetic and observant as on the first morning they had met. A superstitious thrill passed over him and awoke his old antagonism.

She nodded to him slightly. "I came here to refresh my memory," she said, "as Mr. Hornsby thought I might be asked to give my evidence again at Blazing Star."

Cass carelessly struck an aimless blow with his pick against the sod and did not reply.

"And you?" she queried.

"I stumbled upon the place just now while prospecting, or I shouldn't be here."

"Then it was you made these holes?"

"No," said Cass, with ill-concealed disgust. "Nobody but a stranger would go foolin' round such a spot."

He stopped, as the rude significance of his speech struck him, and added surlily, "I mean no one would dig here."

The girl laughed and showed a set of very white teeth in her square jaw. Cass averted his face.

"Do you mean to say that every miner doesn't know that it's lucky to dig wherever human blood has been spilt?"

Cass felt a return of his superstition, but he did not look up. "I never heard it before," he said, severely.

"And you call yourself a California miner?"

"I do."

It was impossible for Miss Porter to misunderstand his curt speech and unsocial manner. She stared at him and colored slightly. Lifting her reins lightly, she said: "You certainly do not seem like most of the miners I have met."

"Nor you like any girl from the East I ever met," he responded.

"What do you mean?" she asked, checking her horse.

"What I say," he answered, doggedly. Reasonable as this reply was, it immediately struck him that it was scarcely dignified or manly. But before he could explain himself Miss Porter was gone.

He met her again that very evening. The trial had been summarily suspended by the appearance of the Sheriff of Calaveras and his posse, who took Joe from that self-constituted tribunal of Blazing Star and set his face southward and toward authoritative although more cautious justice. But not before the evidence of the previous inquest had been read, and the incident of the ring again delivered to the public. It is said the prisoner burst into an incredulous laugh and asked to see this mysterious waif. It was handed to him. Standing in the very shadow of the gallows tree, which might have been one of the pines that sheltered the billiard room in which the Vigilance Committee held their conclave, the prisoner gave way to a burst of merriment, so genuine and honest that the judge and jury joined in automatic sympathy. When silence was restored an explanation was asked by the Judge. But there was no response from the prisoner except a subdued chuckle.

"Did this ring belong to you?" asked the Judge, severely, the jury and spectators craning their ears forward with an expectant smile already on their faces. But the prisoner's eyes only sparkled maliciously as he looked around the court.

"Tell us, Joe," said a sympathetic and laughter-loving juror, under his breath. "Let it out and we'll make it easy for you."

"Prisoner," said the Judge, with a return of official dignity, "remember that your life is in peril. Do you refuse?"

Joe lazily laid his arm on the back of his chair with (to quote the words of an animated observer) "the air of having a Christian hope and a sequence flush in his hand," and said: "Well, as I reckon I'm not up yer for stealin' a ring that another man lets on to have found, and as fur as I kin see, hez nothin' to do with the case, I do!" And as it was here that the Sheriff of Calaveras made a precipitate entry into the room, the mystery remained unsolved.

The effect of this freshly-important ridicule on the sensitive mind of Cass might have been foretold by Blazing Star had it ever taken that sensitiveness into consideration. He had lost the good-humor and easy pliability which had tempted him to frankness, and he had gradually become bitter and hard. He had at first affected amusement over his own vanished day dream, hiding his virgin disappointment in his own breast; but when he began to turn upon his feelings he turned upon his comrades also. Cass was for a while unpopular. There is no ingratitude so revolting to the human mind as that of the butt who refuses to be one any longer. The man who rejects that immunity which laughter generally casts upon him and demands to be seriously considered deserves no mercy.

It was under these hard conditions that Cass Beard, convicted of overt sentimentalism, aggravated by inconsistency, stepped into the Red Chief coach that evening. It was his habit usually to ride with the driver, but the presence of Hornsby and Miss Porter on the box seat changed his intention. Yet he had the satisfaction of seeing that neither had noticed him, and as there was no other passenger inside, he stretched himself on the cushion of the back seat and gave way to moody reflections. He quite determined to leave Blazing Star, to settle himself seriously to the task of money-getting, and to return to his comrades, some day, a sarcastic, cynical, successful man, and so overwhelm them with confusion. For poor Cass had not yet reached that superiority of knowing that success would depend upon his ability to forego his past. Indeed, part of his boyhood had been cast among these men, and he was not old enough to have learned that success was not to be gauged by their standard. The moon lit up the dark interior of the coach with a faint poetic light. The lazy swinging of the vehicle that was bearing him away, albeit only for a night and a day, the solitude, the glimpses from the window of great distances full of vague possibilities, made the abused ring potent as that of Gyges. He dreamed with his eyes open. From an Alnaschar vision he suddenly awoke. The coach had stopped. The voices of men, one in entreaty, one in expostulation, came from the box. Cass mechanically put his hand to his pistol pocket.

"Thank you, but I insist upon getting down."

It was Miss Porter's voice. This was followed by a rapid, half restrained interchange of words between Hornsby and the driver. Then the latter said gruffly:

"If the lady wants to ride inside, let her."

Miss Porter fluttered to the ground. She was followed by Hornsby. "Just a minit, Miss," he expostulated, half shamedly, half brusquely, "ye don't onderstand me. I only" -

But Miss Porter had jumped into the coach.

Hornsby placed his hand on the handle of the door. Miss Porter grasped it firmly from the inside. There was a slight struggle.

All of which was part of a dream to the boyish Cass. But he awoke from it a man! "Do you," he asked, in a voice he scarcely recognized himself, - "do you want this man inside?"

"No!"

Cass caught at Hornsby's wrist like a young tiger. But alas! what availed instinctive chivalry against main strength? He only succeeded in forcing the door open in spite of Miss Porter's superior strategy, and, I fear I must add, muscle also, and threw himself passionately at Hornsby's throat, where he hung on and calmly awaited dissolution. But he had, in the onset, driven Hornsby out into the road and the moonlight.

"Here! somebody take my lines." The voice was "Mountain Charley's," the driver. The figure that jumped from the box and separated the struggling men belonged to this singularly direct person.

"You're riding inside?" said Charley, interrogatively, to Cass. Before he could reply Miss Porter's voice came from the window:

"He is!"

Charley promptly bundled Cass into the coach.

"And you?" to Hornsby, "onless you're kalkilatin' to take a little 'pasear' you're booked outside. Get up."

It is probable that Charley assisted Mr. Hornsby as promptly to his seat, for the next moment the coach was rolling on.

Meanwhile Cass, by reason of his forced entry, had been deposited in Miss Porter's lap, whence, freeing himself, he had attempted to climb over the middle seat, but in the starting of the coach was again thrown heavily against her hat and shoulder; all of which was inconsistent with the attitude of dignified reserve he had intended to display. Miss Porter, meanwhile, recovered her good-humor.

"What a brute he was, ugh!" she said, re-tying the ribbons of her bonnet under her square chin, and smoothing out her linen duster.

Cass tried to look as if he had forgotten the whole affair. "Who? Oh, yes! I see!" he responded, absently.

"I suppose I ought to thank you," she went on with a smile, "but you know, really, I could have kept him out if you hadn't pulled his wrist from outside. I'll show you. Look! Put your hand on the handle there! Now, I'll hold the lock inside firmly. You see, you can't turn the catch!"

She indeed held the lock fast. It was a firm hand, yet soft, their fingers had touched over the handle, and looked white in the moonlight. He made no reply, but sank back again in his seat with a singular sensation in the fingers that had touched hers. He was in the shadow, and, without being seen, could abandon his reserve and glance at her face. It struck him that he had never really seen her before. She was not so tall as she had appeared to be. Her eyes were not large, but her pupils were black, moist, velvety, and so convex as to seem embossed on the white. She had an indistinctive nose, a rather colorless face, whiter at the angles of the mouth and nose through the relief of tiny freckles like grains of pepper. Her mouth was straight, dark, red, but moist as her eyes. She had drawn herself into the corner of the back seat, her wrist put through and hanging over the swinging strap, the easy lines of her plump figure swaying from side to side with the motion of the coach. Finally, forgetful of any presence in the dark corner opposite, she threw her head a little farther back, slipped a trifle lower, and placing two well-booted feet upon the middle seat, completed a charming and wholesome picture.

Five minutes elapsed. She was looking straight at the moon. Cass Beard felt his dignified reserve becoming very much like awkwardness. He ought to be coldly polite.

"I hope you're not flustered, Miss, by the, by the" - he began.

"I?" She straightened herself up in the seat, cast a curious glance into the dark corner, and then, letting herself down again, said: "Oh dear, no!"

Another five minutes elapsed. She had evidently forgotten him. She might, at least, have been civil. He took refuge again in his reserve. But it was now mixed with a certain pique.

Yet how much softer her face looked in the moonlight! Even her square jaw had lost that hard, matter-of-fact, practical indication which was so distasteful to him, and always had suggested a harsh criticism of his weakness. How moist her eyes were, actually shining in the light! How that light seemed to concentrate in the corners of the lashes, and then slipped, a flash, away! Was she? Yes, she was crying.

Cass melted. He moved. Miss Porter put her head out of the window and drew it back in a moment dry-eyed.

"One meets all sorts of folks traveling," said Cass, with what he wished to make appear a cheerful philosophy.

"I dare say. I don't know. I never before met anyone who was rude to me. I have traveled all over the country alone, and with all kinds of people ever since I was so high. I have always gone my own way, without hindrance or trouble. I always do. I don't see why I shouldn't. Perhaps other people mayn't like it. I do. I like excitement. I like to see all that there is to see. Because I'm a girl I don't see why I can't go out without a keeper, and why I cannot do what any man can do that isn't wrong; do you? Perhaps you do, perhaps you don't. Perhaps you like a girl to be always in the house dawdling or thumping a piano or reading novels. Perhaps you think I'm bold because I don't like it, and won't lie and say I do."

She spoke sharply and aggressively, and so evidently in answer to Cass's unspoken indictment against her, that he was not surprised when she became more direct.

"You know you were shocked when I went to fetch that Hornsby, the coroner, after we found the dead body."

"Hornsby wasn't shocked," said Cass, a little viciously.

"What do you mean?" she said, abruptly.

"You were good friends enough until" -

"Until he insulted me just now; is that it?"

"Until he thought," stammered Cass, "that because you were, you know, not so, so, so careful as other girls, he could be a little freer."

"And so, because I preferred to ride a mile with him to see something real that had happened, and tried to be useful instead of looking in shop-windows in Main Street or promenading before the hotel" -

"And being ornamental," interrupted Cass. But this feeble and un-Cass-like attempt at playful gallantry met with a sudden check.

Miss Porter drew herself together, and looked out of the window. "Do you wish me to walk the rest of the way home?"

"No," said Cass, hurriedly, with a crimson face and a sense of gratuitous rudeness.

"Then stop that kind of talk, right there!"

There was an awkward silence. "I wish I was a man," she said, half bitterly, half earnestly. Cass Beard was not old and cynical enough to observe that this devout aspiration is usually uttered by those who have least reason to deplore their own femininity; and, but for the rebuff he had just received, would have made the usual emphatic dissent of our sex, when the wish is uttered by warm red lips and tender voices, a dissent, it may be remarked, generally withheld, however, when the masculine spinster dwells on the perfection of woman. I dare say Miss Porter was sincere, for a moment later she continued, poutingly:

"And yet I used to go to fires in Sacramento when I was only ten years old. I saw the theatre burnt down. Nobody found fault with me then."

Something made Cass ask if her father and mother objected to her boyish tastes. The reply was characteristic if not satisfactory:

"Object? I'd like to see them do it!"

The direction of the road had changed. The fickle moon now abandoned Miss Porter and sought out Cass on the front seat. It caressed the young fellow's silky moustache and long eyelashes, and took some of the sunburn from his cheek.

"What's the matter with your neck?" said the girl, suddenly.

Cass looked down, blushing to find that the collar of his smart "duck" sailor shirt was torn open. But something more than his white, soft, girlish skin was exposed; the shirt front was dyed quite red with blood from a slight cut on the shoulder. He remembered to have felt a scratch while struggling with Hornsby.

The girl's soft eyes sparkled. "Let me," she said, vivaciously. "Do! I'm good at wounds. Come over here. No, stay there. I'll come over to you."

She did, bestriding the back of the middle seat and dropping at his side. The magnetic fingers again touched his; he felt her warm breath on his neck as she bent toward him.

"It's nothing," he said, hastily, more agitated by the treatment than the wound.

"Give me your flask," she responded, without heeding. A stinging sensation as she bathed the edges of the cut with the spirit brought him back to common sense again. "There," she said, skillfully extemporizing a bandage from her handkerchief and a compress from his cravat. "Now, button your coat over your chest, so, and don't take cold." She insisted upon buttoning it for him; greater even than the feminine delight in a man's strength is the ministration to his weakness. Yet, when this was finished, she drew a little away from him in some embarrassment, an embarrassment she wondered at, as his skin was finer, his touch gentler, his clothes cleaner, and, not to put too fine a point upon it, he exhaled an atmosphere much sweeter than belonged to most of the men her boyish habits had brought her in contact with, not excepting her own father. Later she even exempted her mother from the possession of this divine effluence. After a moment she asked, suddenly, "What are you going to do with Hornsby?"

Cass had not thought of him. His short-lived rage was past with the occasion that provoked it. Without any fear of his adversary, he would have been content quite willing to meet him no more. He only said, "That will depend upon him."

"Oh, you won't hear from him again," said she, confidently; "but you really ought to get up a little more muscle. You've no more than a girl." She stopped, a little confused.

"What shall I do with your handkerchief?" asked the uneasy Cass, anxious to change the subject.

"Oh, keep it, if you want to; only don't show it to everybody as you did that ring you found." Seeing signs of distress in his face, she added: "Of course that was all nonsense. If you had cared so much for the ring you couldn't have talked about it, or shown it; could you?"

It relieved him to think that this might be true; he certainly had not looked at it in that light before.

"But did you really find it?" she asked, with sudden gravity. "Really, now?"

"Yes."

"And there was no real May in the case?"

"Not that I know of," laughed Cass, secretly pleased.

But Miss Porter, after eying him critically for a moment, jumped up and climbed back again to her seat. "Perhaps you had better give me that handkerchief back."

Cass began to unbutton his coat.

"No! no! Do you want to take your death of cold?" she screamed. And Cass, to avoid this direful possibility, rebuttoned his coat again over the handkerchief and a peculiarly pleasing sensation.

Very little now was said until the rattling, bounding descent of the coach denoted the approach to Red Chief. The straggling main street disclosed itself, light by light. In the flash of glittering windows and the sound of eager voices Miss Porter descended, without waiting for Cass's proffered assistance, and anticipated Mountain Charley's descent from the box. A few undistinguishable words passed between them.

"You kin freeze to me, Miss," said Charley; and Miss Porter, turning her frank laugh and frankly opened palm to Cass, half returned the pressure of his hand and slipped away.

A few days after the stage-coach incident Mountain Charley drew up beside Cass on the Blazing Star turnpike, and handed him a small packet. "I was told to give ye that by Miss Porter. Hush, listen! It's that rather old dog-goned ring o' yours that's bin in all the papers. She's bamboozled that sap-headed county judge, Boompointer, into givin' it to her. Take my advice and sling it away for some other feller to pick up and get looney over. That's all!"

"Did she say anything?" asked Cass, anxiously, as he received his lost treasure somewhat coldly.

"Well, yes! I reckon. She asked me to stand betwixt Hornsby and you. So don't you tackle him, and I'll see he don't tackle you," and with a portentous wink Mountain Charley whipped up his horses and was gone.

Cass opened the packet. It contained nothing but the ring. Unmitigated by any word of greeting, remembrance, or even raillery, it seemed almost an insult. Had she intended to flaunt his folly in his face, or had she believed he still mourned for it and deemed its recovery a sufficient reward for his slight service? For an instant he felt tempted to follow Charley's advice, and cast this symbol of folly and contempt in the dust of the mountain road. And had she not made his humiliation complete by begging Charley's interference between him and his enemy? He would go home and send her back the handkerchief she had given him. But here the unromantic reflection that although he had washed it that very afternoon in the solitude of his own cabin, he could not possibly iron it, but must send it "rough dried," stayed his indignant feet.

Two or three days, a week, a fortnight even, of this hopeless resentment filled Cass's breast. Then the news of Kanaka Joe's acquittal in the state court momentarily revived the story of the ring, and revamped a few stale jokes in the camp. But the interest soon flagged; the fortunes of the little community of Blazing Star had been for some months failing; and with early snows in the mountain and wasted capital in fruitless schemes on the river, there was little room for the indulgence of that lazy and original humor which belonged to their lost youth and prosperity. Blazing Star truly, in the grim figure of their slang, was "played out." Not dug out, worked out, or washed out, but dissipated in a year of speculation and chance.

Against this tide of fortune Cass struggled manfully, and even evoked the slow praise of his companions. Better still, he won a certain praise for himself, in himself, in a consciousness of increased strength, health, power, and self-reliance. He began to turn his quick imagination and perception to some practical account, and made one or two discoveries which quite startled his more experienced, but more conservative companions. Nevertheless, Cass's discoveries and labors were not of a kind that produced immediate pecuniary realization, and Blazing Star, which consumed so many pounds of pork and flour daily, did not unfortunately produce the daily equivalent in gold. Blazing Star lost its credit. Blazing Star was hungry, dirty, and ragged. Blazing Star was beginning to set.

Participating in the general ill-luck of the camp, Cass was not without his own individual mischance. He had resolutely determined to forget Miss Porter and all that tended to recall the unlucky ring, but, cruelly enough, she was the only thing that refused to be forgotten, whose undulating figure reclined opposite to him in the weird moonlight of his ruined cabin, whose voice mingled with the song of the river by whose banks he toiled, and whose eyes and touch thrilled him in his dreams. Partly for this reason, and partly because his clothes were beginning to be patched and torn, he avoided Red Chief and any place where he would be likely to meet her. In spite of this precaution he had once seen her driving in a pony carriage, but so smartly and fashionably dressed that he drew back in the cover of a wayside willow that she might pass without recognition. He looked down upon his red-splashed clothes and grimy, soil-streaked hands, and for a moment half hated her. His comrades seldom spoke of her, instinctively fearing some temptation that might beset his Spartan resolutions, but he heard from time to time that she had been seen at balls and parties, apparently enjoying those very frivolities of her sex she affected to condemn. It was a Sabbath morning in early spring that he was returning from an ineffectual attempt to enlist a capitalist at the county town to redeem the fortunes of Blazing Star. He was pondering over the narrowness of that capitalist, who had evidently but illogically connected Cass's present appearance with the future of that struggling camp, when he became so footsore that he was obliged to accept a "lift" from a wayfaring teamster. As the slowly lumbering vehicle passed the new church on the outskirts of the town, the congregation were sallying forth. It was too late to jump down and run away, and Cass dared not ask his new-found friend to whip up his cattle. Conscious of his unshorn beard and ragged garments, he kept his eyes fixed upon the road. A voice that thrilled him called his name. It was Miss Porter, a resplendent vision of silk, laces, and Easter flowers, yet actually running, with something of her old dash and freedom, beside the wagon. As the astonished teamster drew up before this elegant apparition, she panted:

"Why did you make me run so far, and why didn't you look up?"

Cass, trying to hide the patches on his knees beneath a newspaper, stammered that he had not seen her.

"And you did not hold down your head purposely?"

"No," said Cass.

"Why have you not been to Red Chief? Why didn't you answer my message about the ring?" she asked, swiftly.

"You sent nothing but the ring," said Cass, coloring, as he glanced at the teamster.

"Why, that was a message, you born idiot."

Cass stared. The teamster smiled. Miss Porter gazed anxiously at the wagon. "I think I'd like a ride in there; it looks awfully good." She glanced mischievously around at the lingering and curious congregation. "May I?"

But Cass deprecated that proceeding strongly. It was dirty; he was not sure it was even wholesome; she would be so uncomfortable; he himself was only going a few rods farther, and in that time she might ruin her dress -

"Oh, yes," she said, a little bitterly, "certainly, my dress must be looked after. And, what else?"

"People might think it strange, and believe I had invited you," continued Cass, hesitatingly.

"When I had only invited myself? Thank you. Good-by."

She waved her hand and stepped back from the wagon. Cass would have given worlds to recall her, but he sat still, and the vehicle moved on in moody silence. At the first cross road he jumped down. "Thank you," he said to the teamster. "You're welcome," returned that gentleman, regarding him curiously, "but the next time a gal like that asks to ride in this yer wagon, I reckon I won't take the vote of any deadhead passenger. Adios, young fellow. Don't stay out late; ye might be ran off by some gal, and what would your mother say?" Of course the young man could only look unutterable things and walk away, but even in that dignified action he was conscious that its effect was somewhat mitigated by a large patch from a material originally used as a flour-sack, which had repaired his trousers, but still bore the ironical legend, "Best Superfine."

The summer brought warmth and promise and some blossom, if not absolute fruition to Blazing Star. The long days drew Nature into closer communion with the men, and hopefulness followed the discontent of their winter seclusion. It was easier, too, for Capital to be wooed and won into making a picnic in these mountain solitudes than when high water stayed the fords and drifting snow the Sierran trails. At the close of one of these Arcadian days Cass was smoking before the door of his lonely cabin when he was astounded by the onset of a dozen of his companions. Peter Drummond, far in the van, was waving a newspaper like a victorious banner. "All's right now, Cass, old man!" he panted as he stopped before Cass and shoved back his eager followers.

"What's all right?" asked Cass, dubiously.

"You! You kin rake down the pile now. You're hunky! You're on velvet. Listen!"

He opened the newspaper and read, with annoying deliberation, as follows:

"LOST. If the finder of a plain gold ring, bearing the engraved inscription, 'May to Cass,' alleged to have been picked up on the high road near Blazing Star on the 4th March, 186-, will apply to Bookham & Sons, bankers, 1007 Y. Street, Sacramento, he will be suitably rewarded either for the recovery of the ring, or for such facts as may identify it, or the locality where it was found."

Cass rose and frowned savagely on his comrades. "No! no!" cried a dozen voices assuringly. "It's all right! Honest Injun! True as gospel! No joke, Cass!"

"Here's the paper, Sacramento 'Union' of yesterday. Look for yourself," said Drummond, handing him the well-worn journal. "And you see," he added, "how darned lucky you are. It ain't necessary for you to produce the ring, so if that old biled owl of a Boompointer don't giv' it back to ye, it's all the same."

"And they say nobody but the finder need apply," interrupted another. "That shuts out Boompointer or Kanaka Joe for the matter o' that."

"It's clar that it means you, Cass, ez much ez if they'd given your name," added a third.

For Miss Porter's sake and his own Cass had never told them of the restoration of the ring, and it was evident that Mountain Charley had also kept silent. Cass could not speak now without violating a secret, and he was pleased that the ring itself no longer played an important part in the mystery. But what was that mystery, and why was the ring secondary to himself? Why was so much stress laid upon his finding it?

"You see," said Drummond, as if answering his unspoken thought, "that'ar gal, for it is a gal in course, hez read all about it in the papers, and hez sort o' took a shine to ye. It don't make a bit o' difference who in thunder Cass is or waz, for I reckon she's kicked him over by this time" -

"Sarved him right, too, for losing the girl's ring and then lying low and keeping dark about it," interrupted a sympathizer.

"And she's just weakened over the romantic, high-toned way you stuck to it," continued Drummond, forgetting the sarcasms he had previously hurled at this romance. Indeed the whole camp, by this time, had become convinced that it had fostered and developed a chivalrous devotion which was now on the point of pecuniary realization. It was generally accepted that "she" was the daughter of this banker, and also felt that in the circumstances the happy father could not do less than develop the resources of Blazing Star at once. Even if there were no relationship, what opportunity could be more fit for presenting to capital a locality that even produced engagement rings, and, as Jim Fauquier put it, "the men ez knew how to keep 'em." It was this sympathetic Virginian who took Cass aside with the following generous suggestion: "If you find that you and the old gal couldn't hitch hosses, owin' to your not likin' red hair or a game leg" (it may be here recorded that Blazing Star had, for no reason whatever, attributed these unprepossessing qualities to the mysterious advertiser), "you might let me in. You might say ez how I used to jest worship that ring with you, and allers wanted to borrow it on Sundays. If anything comes of it, why, we're pardners!"

A serious question was the outfitting of Cass for what now was felt to be a diplomatic representation of the community. His garments, it hardly need be said, were inappropriate to any wooing except that of the "maiden all forlorn," which the advertiser clearly was not. "He might," suggested Fauquier, "drop in jest as he is, kinder as if he'd got keerless of the world, being lovesick." But Cass objected strongly, and was borne out in his objection by his younger comrades. At last a pair of white duck trousers, a red shirt, a flowing black silk scarf, and a Panama hat were procured at Red Chief, on credit, after a judicious exhibition of the advertisement. A heavy wedding-ring, the property of Drummond (who was not married), was also lent as a graceful suggestion, and at the last moment Fauquier affixed to Cass's scarf an enormous specimen pin of gold and quartz. "It sorter indicates the auriferous wealth o' this yer region, and the old man (the senior member of Bookham & Sons) needn't know I won it at draw-poker in Frisco," said Fauqier. "Ef you 'pass' on the gal, you kin hand it back to me and I'll try it on."

Forty dollars for expenses was put into Cass's hands, and the entire community accompanied him to the cross roads where he was to meet the Sacramento coach, which eventually carried him away, followed by a benediction of waving hats and exploding revolvers.

That Cass did not participate in the extravagant hopes of his comrades, and that he rejected utterly their matrimonial speculations in his behalf, need not be said.

Outwardly, he kept his own counsel with good-humored assent. But there was something fascinating in the situation, and while he felt he had forever abandoned his romantic dream, he was not displeased to know that it might have proved a reality. Nor was it distasteful to him to think that Miss Porter would hear of it and regret her late inability to appreciate his sentiment. If he really were the object of some opulent maiden's passion, he would show Miss Porter how he could sacrifice the most brilliant prospects for her sake. Alone, on the top of the coach, he projected one of those satisfying conversations in which imaginative people delight, but which unfortunately never come quite up to rehearsal. "Dear Miss Porter," he would say, addressing the back of the driver, "if I could remain faithful to a dream of my youth, however illusive and unreal, can you believe that for the sake of lucre I could be false to the one real passion that alone supplanted it?" In the composition and delivery of this eloquent statement an hour was happily forgotten: the only drawback to its complete effect was that a misplacing of epithets in rapid repetition did not seem to make the slightest difference, and Cass found himself saying "Dear Miss Porter, if I could be false to a dream of my youth, etc., etc., can you believe I could be faithful to the one real passion, etc., etc.," with equal and perfect satisfaction. As Miss Porter was reputed to be well off, if the unknown were poor, that might be another drawback.

The banking house of Bookham & Sons did not present an illusive nor mysterious appearance. It was eminently practical and matter of fact; it was obtrusively open and glassy; nobody would have thought of leaving a secret there that would have been inevitably circulated over the counter. Cass felt an uncomfortable sense of incongruity in himself, in his story, in his treasure, to this temple of disenchanting realism. With the awkwardness of an embarrassed man he was holding prominently in his hand an envelope containing the ring and advertisement as a voucher for his intrusion, when the nearest clerk took the envelope from his hand, opened it, took out the ring, returned it, said briskly, "T' other shop, next door, young man," and turned to another customer.

Cass stepped to the door, saw that "T'other shop" was a pawnbroker's, and returned again with a flashing eye and heightened color. "It's an advertisement I have come to answer," he began again.

The clerk cast a glance at Cass's scarf and pin. "Place taken yesterday, no room for any more," he said, abruptly.

Cass grew quite white. But his old experience in Blazing Star repartee stood him in good stead. "If it's your place you mean," he said coolly, "I reckon you might put a dozen men in the hole you're rattlin' round in, but it's this advertisement I'm after. If Bookham isn't in, maybe you'll send me one of the grown-up sons." The production of the advertisement and some laughter from the bystanders had its effect. The pert young clerk retired, and returned to lead the way to the bank parlor. Cass's heart sank again as he was confronted by a dark, iron-gray man, in dress, features, speech, and action, uncompromisingly opposed to Cass, his ring and his romance. When the young man had told his story and produced his treasure he paused. The banker scarcely glanced at it, but said, impatiently:

"Well, your papers?"

"My papers?"

"Yes. Proof of your identity. You say your name is Cass Beard. Good! What have you got to prove it? How can I tell who you are?"

To a sensitive man there is no form of suspicion that is as bewildering and demoralizing at the moment as the question of his identity. Cass felt the insult in the doubt of his word, and the palpable sense of his present inability to prove it. The banker watched him keenly but not unkindly.

"Come," he said at length, "this is not my affair; if you can legally satisfy the lady for whom I am only agent, well and good. I believe you can; I only warn you that you must. And my present inquiry was to keep her from losing her time with impostors, a class I don't think you belong to. There's her card. Good day."

"MISS MORTIMER."

It was not the banker's daughter. The first illusion of Blazing Star was rudely dispelled. But the care taken by the capitalist to shield her from imposture indicated a person of wealth. Of her youth and beauty Cass no longer thought.

The address given was not distant. With a beating heart he rung the bell of a respectable-looking house, and was ushered into a private drawing-room. Instinctively he felt that the room was only temporarily inhabited; an air peculiar to the best lodgings, and when the door opened upon a tall lady in deep mourning, he was still more convinced of an incongruity between the occupant and her surroundings. With a smile that vacillated between a habit of familiarity and ease, and a recent restraint, she motioned him to a chair.

"Miss Mortimer" was still young, still handsome, still fashionably dressed, and still attractive. From her first greeting to the end of the interview Cass felt that she knew all about him. This relieved him from the onus of proving his identity, but seemed to put him vaguely at a disadvantage. It increased his sense of inexperience and youthfulness.

"I hope you will believe," she began, "that the few questions I have to ask you are to satisfy my own heart, and for no other purpose." She smiled sadly as she went on. "Had it been otherwise, I should have instituted a legal inquiry, and left this interview to some one cooler, calmer, and less interested than myself. But I think, I know I can trust you. Perhaps we women are weak and foolish to talk of an instinct, and when you know my story you may have reason to believe that but little dependence can be placed on that; but I am not wrong in saying, am I?" (with a sad smile) "that you are not above that weakness?" She paused, closed her lips tightly, and grasped her hands before her. "You say you found that ring in the road some three months before, the, the, you know what I mean, the body was discovered?"

"Yes."

"You thought it might have been dropped by someone in passing?"

"I thought so, yes, it belonged to no one in the camp."

"Before your cabin or on the highway?"

"Before my cabin."

"You are sure?" There was something so very sweet and sad in her smile that it oddly made Cass color.

"But my cabin is near the road," he suggested.

"I see! And there was nothing else; no paper nor envelope?"

"Nothing."

"And you kept it because of the odd resemblance one of the names bore to yours?"

"Yes."

"For no other reason?"

"None." Yet Cass felt he was blushing.

"You'll forgive my repeating a question you have already answered, but I am so anxious. There was some attempt to prove at the inquest that the ring had been found on the body of the unfortunate man. But you tell me it was not so?"

"I can swear it."

"Good God, the traitor!" She took a hurried step forward, turned to the window, and then came back to Cass with a voice broken with emotion. "I have told you I could trust you. That ring was mine!"

She stopped, and then went on hurriedly. "Years ago I gave it to a man who deceived and wronged me; a man whose life since then has been a shame and disgrace to all who knew him; a man who, once a gentleman, sank so low as to become the associate of thieves and ruffians; sank so low, that when he died, by violence, a traitor even to them, his own confederates shrunk from him, and left him to fill a nameless grave. That man's body you found!"

Cass started. "And his name was?"

"Part of your surname. Cass, Henry Cass."

"You see why Providence seems to have brought that ring to you," she went on. "But you ask me why, knowing this, I am so eager to know if the ring was found by you in the road, or if it were found on his body. Listen! It is part of my mortification that the story goes that this man once showed this ring, boasted of it, staked, and lost it at a gambling table to one of his vile comrades."

"Kanaka Joe," said Cass, overcome by a vivid recollection of Joe's merriment at the trial.

"The same. Don't you see," she said, hurriedly, "if the ring had been found on him I could believe that somewhere in his heart he still kept respect for the woman he had wronged. I am a woman, a foolish woman, I know, but you have crushed that hope forever."

"But why have you sent for me?" asked Cass, touched by her emotion.

"To know it for certain," she said, almost fiercely. "Can you not understand that a woman like me must know a thing once and forever? But you can help me. I did not send for you only to pour my wrongs in your ears. You must take me with you to this place, to the spot where you found the ring, to the spot where you found the body, to the spot where, where he lies. You must do it secretly, that none shall know me."

Cass hesitated. He was thinking of his companions and the collapse of their painted bubble. How could he keep the secret from them?

"If it is money, you need, let not that stop you. I have no right to your time without recompense. Do not misunderstand me. There has been a thousand dollars awaiting my order at Bookham's when the ring should be delivered. It shall be doubled if you help me in this last moment."

It was possible. He could convey her safely there, invent some story of a reward delayed for want of proofs, and afterward share that reward with his friends. He answered promptly, "I will take you there."

She took his hands in both of hers, raised them to her lips, and smiled. The shadow of grief and restraint seemed to have fallen from her face, and a half mischievous, half coquettish gleam in her dark eyes touched the susceptible Cass in so subtle a fashion that he regained the street in some confusion. He wondered what Miss Porter would have thought. But was he not returning to her, a fortunate man, with one thousand dollars in his pocket! Why should he remember he was handicapped by a pretty woman and a pathetic episode? It did not make the proximity less pleasant as he helped her into the coach that evening, nor did the recollection of another ride with another woman obtrude itself upon those consolations which he felt it his duty, from time to time, to offer. It was arranged that he should leave her at the "Red Chief" Hotel, while he continued on to Blazing Star, returning at noon to bring her with him when he could do it without exposing her to recognition. The gray dawn came soon enough, and the coach drew up at "Red Chief" while the lights in the bar-room and dining-room of the hotel were still struggling with the far flushing east. Cass alighted, placed Miss Mortimer in the hands of the landlady, and returned to the vehicle. It was still musty, close, and frowzy, with half awakened passengers. There was a vacated seat on the top, which Cass climbed up to, and abstractedly threw himself beside a figure muffled in shawls and rugs. There was a slight movement among the multitudinous enwrappings, and then the figure turned to him and said dryly, "Good morning!" It was Miss Porter!

"Have you been long here?" he stammered.

"All night."

He would have given worlds to leave her at that moment. He would have jumped from the starting coach to save himself any explanation of the embarrassment he was furiously conscious of showing, without, as he believed, any adequate cause. And yet, like all inexperienced, sensitive men, he dashed blindly into that explanation; worse, he even told his secret at once, then and there, and then sat abashed and conscience-stricken, with an added sense of its utter futility.

"And this," summed up the young girl, with a slight shrug of her pretty shoulders, "is your May?"

Cass would have recommenced his story.

"No, don't, pray! It isn't interesting, nor original. Do you believe it?"

"I do," said Cass, indignantly.

"How lucky! Then let me go to sleep."

Cass, still furious, but uneasy, did not again address her. When the coach stopped at Blazing Star she asked him, indifferently: "When does this sentimental pilgrimage begin?"

"I return for her at one o'clock," replied Cass, stiffly. He kept his word. He appeased his eager companions with a promise of future fortune, and exhibited the present and tangible reward. By a circuitous route known only to himself, he led Miss Mortimer to the road before the cabin. There was a pink flush of excitement on her somewhat faded cheek.

"And it was here?" she asked, eagerly.

"I found it here."

"And the body?"

"That was afterward. Over in that direction, beyond the clump of buckeyes, on the Red Chief turnpike."

"And anyone coming from the road we left just now and going to, to that place, would have to cross just here? Tell me," she said, with a strange laugh, laying her cold nervous hand on his, "wouldn't they?"

"They would."

"Let us go to that place."

Cass stepped out briskly to avoid observation and gain the woods beyond the highway. "You have crossed here before," she said. "There seems to be a trail."

"I may have made it: it's a short cut to the buckeyes."

"You never found anything else on the trail?"

"You remember, I told you before, the ring was all I found."

"Ah, true!" she smiled sweetly; "it was that which made it seem so odd to you. I forgot."

In half an hour they reached the buckeyes. During the walk she had taken rapid recognizance of everything in her path. When they crossed the road and Cass had pointed out the scene of the murder, she looked anxiously around. "You are sure we are not seen?"

"Quite."

"You will not think me foolish if I ask you to wait here while I go in there", she pointed to the ominous thicket near them, "alone?" She was quite white.

Cass's heart, which had grown somewhat cold since his interview with Miss Porter, melted at once.

"Go; I will stay here."

He waited five minutes. She did not return. What if the poor creature had determined upon suicide on the spot where her faithless lover had fallen? He was reassured in another moment by the rustle of skirts in the undergrowth.

"I was becoming quite alarmed," he said, aloud.

"You have reason to be," returned a hurried voice. He started. It was Miss Porter, who stepped swiftly out of the cover. "Look," she said, "look at that man down the road. He has been tracking you two ever since you left the cabin. Do you know who he is?"

"No!"

"Then listen. It is three-fingered Dick, one of the escaped road agents. I know him!"

"Let us go and warn her," said Cass, eagerly.

Miss Porter laid her hand upon his shoulder.

"I don't think she'll thank you," she said, dryly. "Perhaps you'd better see what she's doing, first."

Utterly bewildered, yet with a strong sense of the masterfulness of his companion, he followed her. She crept like a cat through the thicket. Suddenly she paused. "Look!" she whispered, viciously, "look at the tender vigils of your heart-broken May!"

Cass saw the woman who had left him a moment before on her knees on the grass, with long thin fingers digging like a ghoul in the earth. He had scarce time to notice her eager face and eyes, cast now and then back toward the spot where she had left him, before there was a crash in the bushes, and a man, the stranger of the road, leaped to her side. "Run," he said; "run for it now. You're watched!"

"Oh! that man, Beard!" she said, contemptuously.

"No, another in a wagon. Quick. Fool, you know the place now, you can come later; run!" And half-dragging, half-lifting her, he bore her through the bushes. Scarcely had they closed behind the pair when Miss Porter ran to the spot vacated by the woman. "Look!" she cried, triumphantly, "look!"

Cass looked, and sank on his knees beside her.

"It was worth a thousand dollars, wasn't it?" she repeated, maliciously, "wasn't it? But you ought to return it! Really you ought."

Cass could scarcely articulate. "But how did you know it?" he finally gasped.

"Oh, I suspected something; there was a woman, and you know you're such a fool!"

Cass rose, stiffly.

"Don't be a greater fool now, but go and bring my horse and wagon from the hill, and don't say anything to the driver."

"Then you did not come alone?"

"No; it would have been bold and improper."

"Please!"

"And to think it was the ring, after all, that pointed to this," she said.

"The ring that you returned to me."

"What did you say?"

"Nothing."

"Don't, please, the wagon is coming."

In the next morning's edition of the "Red Chief Chronicle" appeared the following startling intelligence:

EXTRAORDINARY DISCOVERY!

FINDING OF THE STOLEN TREASURE OF WELLS, FARGO & CO. OVER $300,000 RECOVERED.

Our readers will remember the notorious robbery of Wells, Fargo & Co.'s treasure from the Sacramento and Red Chief Pioneer Coach on the night of September 1. Although most of the gang were arrested, it is known that two escaped, who, it was presumed, cached the treasure, amounting to nearly $500,000 in gold, drafts, and jewelry, as no trace of the property was found. Yesterday our esteemed fellow citizen, Mr. Cass Beard, long and favorably known in this county, succeeded in exhuming the treasure in a copse of hazel near the Red Chief turnpike, adjacent to the spot where an unknown body was lately discovered. This body is now strongly suspected to be that of one Henry Cass, a disreputable character, who has since been ascertained to have been one of the road agents who escaped. The matter is now under legal investigation. The successful result of the search is due to a systematic plan evolved from the genius of Mr. Beard, who has devoted over a year to this labor. It was first suggested to him by the finding of a ring, now definitely identified as part of the treasure which was supposed to have been dropped from Wells, Fargo & Co.'s boxes by the robbers in their midnight flight through Blazing Star.

In the same journal appeared the no less important intelligence, which explains, while it completes this veracious chronicle:

"It is rumored that a marriage is shortly to take place between the hero of the late treasure discovery and a young lady of Red Chief, whose devoted aid and assistance to this important work is well known to this community."

IN THE CARQUINEZ WOODS.

CHAPTER I.

The sun was going down on the Carquinez Woods. The few shafts of sunlight that had pierced their pillared gloom were lost in unfathomable depths, or splintered their ineffectual lances on the enormous trunks of the redwoods. For a time the dull red of their vast columns, and the dull red of their cast-off bark which matted the echoless aisles, still seemed to hold a faint glow of the dying day. But even this soon passed. Light and color fled upwards. The dark, interlaced tree-tops, that had all day made an impenetrable shade, broke into fire here and there; their lost spires glittered, faded, and went utterly out. A weird twilight that did not come from an outer world, but seemed born of the wood itself, slowly filled and possessed the aisles. The straight, tall, colossal trunks rose dimly like columns of upward smoke. The few fallen trees stretched their huge length into obscurity, and seemed to lie on shadowy trestles. The strange breath that filled these mysterious vaults had neither coldness nor moisture; a dry, fragrant dust arose from the noiseless foot that trod their bark-strewn floor; the aisles might have been tombs, the fallen trees, enormous mummies; the silence, the solitude of the forgotten past.

And yet this silence was presently broken by a recurring sound like breathing, interrupted occasionally by inarticulate and stertorous gasps. It was not the quick, panting, listening breath of some stealthy feline or canine animal, but indicated a larger, slower, and more powerful organization, whose progress was less watchful and guarded, or as if a fragment of one of the fallen monsters had become animate. At times this life seemed to take visible form, but as vaguely, as misshapenly, as the phantom of a nightmare. Now it was a square object moving sideways, endways, with neither head nor tail and scarcely visible feet; then an arched bulk rolling against the trunks of the trees and recoiling again, or an upright cylindrical mass, but always oscillating and unsteady, and striking the trees on either hand. The frequent occurrence of the movement suggested the figures of some weird rhythmic dance to music heard by the shape alone. Suddenly it either became motionless or faded away.

There was the frightened neighing of a horse, the sudden jingling of spurs, a shout and outcry, and the swift apparition of three dancing torches in one of the dark aisles; but so intense was the obscurity that they shed no light on surrounding objects, and seemed to advance at their own volition without human guidance, until they disappeared suddenly behind the interposing bulk of one of the largest trees. Beyond its eighty feet of circumference the light could not reach, and the gloom remained inscrutable. But the voices and jingling spurs were heard distinctly.

"Blast the mare! She's shied off that cursed trail again."

"Ye ain't lost it agin, hev ye?" growled a second voice.

"That's jist what I hev. And these blasted pine-knots don't give light an inch beyond 'em. Damned if I don't think they make this cursed hole blacker."

There was a laugh, a woman's laugh, hysterical, bitter, sarcastic, exasperating. The second speaker, without heeding it, went on:

"What in thunder skeert the hosses? Did you see or hear anything?"

"Nothin'. The wood is like a graveyard."

The woman's voice again broke into a hoarse, contemptuous laugh. The man resumed angrily:

"If you know anything, why in hell don't you say so, instead of cackling like a damned squaw there? P'raps you reckon you ken find the trail too."

"Take this rope off my wrist," said the woman's voice, "untie my hands, let me down, and I'll find it." She spoke quickly and with a Spanish accent.

It was the men's turn to laugh. "And give you a show to snatch that six-shooter and blow a hole through me, as you did to the Sheriff of Calaveras, eh? Not if this court understands itself," said the first speaker dryly.

"Go to the devil, then," she said curtly.

"Not before a lady," responded the other. There was another laugh from the men, the spurs jingled again, the three torches reappeared from behind the tree, and then passed away in the darkness.

For a time silence and immutability possessed the woods; the great trunks loomed upwards, their fallen brothers stretched their slow length into obscurity. The sound of breathing again became audible; the shape reappeared in the aisle, and recommenced its mystic dance. Presently it was lost in the shadow of the largest tree, and to the sound of breathing succeeded a grating and scratching of bark. Suddenly, as if riven by lightning, a flash broke from the centre of the tree-trunk, lit up the woods, and a sharp report rang through it. After a pause the jingling of spurs and the dancing of torches were revived from the distance.

"Hallo?"

No answer.

"Who fired that shot?"

But there was no reply. A slight veil of smoke passed away to the right, there was the spice of gunpowder in the air, but nothing more.

The torches came forward again, but this time it could be seen they were held in the hands of two men and a woman. The woman's hands were tied at the wrist to the horse-hair reins of her mule, while a riata, passed around her waist and under the mule's girth, was held by one of the men, who were both armed with rifles and revolvers. Their frightened horses curveted, and it was with difficulty they could be made to advance.

"Ho! stranger, what are you shooting at?"

The woman laughed and shrugged her shoulders. "Look yonder at the roots of the tree. You're a damned smart man for a sheriff, ain't you?"

The man uttered an exclamation and spurred his horse forward, but the animal reared in terror. He then sprang to the ground and approached the tree. The shape lay there, a scarcely distinguishable bulk.

"A grizzly, by the living Jingo! Shot through the heart."

It was true. The strange shape lit up by the flaring torches seemed more vague, unearthly, and awkward in its dying throes, yet the small shut eyes, the feeble nose, the ponderous shoulders, and half-human foot armed with powerful claws were unmistakable. The men turned by a common impulse and peered into the remote recesses of the wood again.

"Hi, Mister! come and pick up your game. Hallo there!"

The challenge fell unheeded on the empty woods.

"And yet," said he whom the woman had called the sheriff, "he can't be far off. It was a close shot, and the bear hez dropped in his tracks. Why, wot's this sticking in his claws?"

The two men bent over the animal. "Why, it's sugar, brown sugar, look!" There was no mistake. The huge beast's fore paws and muzzle were streaked with the unromantic household provision, and heightened the absurd contrast of its incongruous members. The woman, apparently indifferent, had taken that opportunity to partly free one of her wrists.

"If we hadn't been cavorting round this yer spot for the last half hour, I'd swear there was a shanty not a hundred yards away," said the sheriff.

The other man, without replying, remounted his horse instantly.

"If there is, and it's inhabited by a gentleman that kin make centre shots like that in the dark, and don't care to explain how, I reckon I won't disturb him."

The sheriff was apparently of the same opinion, for he followed his companion's example, and once more led the way. The spurs tinkled, the torches danced, and the cavalcade slowly reëntered the gloom. In another moment it had disappeared.

The wood sank again into repose, this time disturbed by neither shape nor sound. What lower forms of life might have crept close to its roots were hidden in the ferns, or passed with deadened tread over the bark-strewn floor. Towards morning a coolness like dew fell from above, with here and there a dropping twig or nut, or the crepitant awakening and stretching-out of cramped and weary branches. Later a dull, lurid dawn, not unlike the last evening's sunset, filled the aisles. This faded again, and a clear gray light, in which every object stood out in sharp distinctness, took its place. Morning was waiting outside in all its brilliant, youthful coloring, but only entered as the matured and sobered day.

Seen in that stronger light, the monstrous tree near which the dead bear lay revealed its age in its denuded and scarred trunk, and showed in its base a deep cavity, a foot or two from the ground, partly hidden by hanging strips of bark which had fallen across it. Suddenly one of these strips was pushed aside, and a young man leaped lightly down.

But for the rifle he carried and some modern peculiarities of dress, he was of a grace so unusual and unconventional that he might have passed for a faun who was quitting his ancestral home. He stepped to the side of the bear with a light elastic movement that was as unlike customary progression as his face and figure were unlike the ordinary types of humanity. Even as he leaned upon his rifle, looking down at the prostrate animal, he unconsciously fell into an attitude that in any other mortal would have been a pose, but with him was the picturesque and unstudied relaxation of perfect symmetry.

"Hallo, Mister!"

He raised his head so carelessly and listlessly that he did not otherwise change his attitude. Stepping from behind the tree, the woman of the preceding night stood before him. Her hands were free except for a thong of the riata, which was still knotted around one wrist, the end of the thong having been torn or burnt away. Her eyes were bloodshot, and her hair hung over her shoulders in one long black braid.

"I reckoned all along it was you who shot the bear," she said; "at least some one hidin' yer," and she indicated the hollow tree with her hand. "It wasn't no chance shot." Observing that the young man, either from misconception or indifference, did not seem to comprehend her, she added, "We came by here, last night, a minute after you fired."

"Oh, that was you kicked up such a row, was it?" said the young man, with a shade of interest.

"I reckon," said the woman, nodding her head, "and them that was with me."

"And who are they?"

"Sheriff Dunn, of Yolo, and his deputy."

"And where are they now?"

"The deputy, in hell, I reckon. I don't know about the sheriff."

"I see," said the young man quietly; "and you?"

"I got away," she said savagely. But she was taken with a sudden nervous shiver, which she at once repressed by tightly dragging her shawl over her shoulders and elbows, and folding her arms defiantly.

"And you're going?"

"To follow the deputy, may be," she said gloomily. "But come, I say, ain't you going to treat? It's cursed cold here."

"Wait a moment." The young man was looking at her, with his arched brows slightly knit and a half smile of curiosity. "Ain't you Teresa?"

She was prepared for the question, but evidently was not certain whether she would reply defiantly or confidently. After an exhaustive scrutiny of his face she chose the latter, and said, "You can bet your life on it, Johnny."

"I don't bet, and my name isn't Johnny. Then you're the woman who stabbed Dick Curson over at Lagrange's?"

She became defiant again. "That's me, all the time. What are you going to do about it?"

"Nothing. And you used to dance at the Alhambra?"

She whisked the shawl from her shoulders, held it up like a scarf, and made one or two steps of the sembicuacua. There was not the least gayety, recklessness, or spontaneity in the action; it was simply mechanical bravado. It was so ineffective, even upon her own feelings, that her arms presently dropped to her side, and she coughed embarrassedly. "Where's that whiskey, pardner?" she asked.

The young man turned toward the tree he had just quitted, and without further words assisted her to mount to the cavity. It was an irregular-shaped vaulted chamber, pierced fifty feet above by a shaft or cylindrical opening in the decayed trunk, which was blackened by smoke as if it had served the purpose of a chimney. In one corner lay a bearskin and blanket; at the side were two alcoves or indentations, one of which was evidently used as a table, and the other as a cupboard. In another hollow, near the entrance, lay a few small sacks of flour, coffee, and sugar, the sticky contents of the latter still strewing the floor. From this storehouse the young man drew a wicker flask of whiskey, and handed it, with a tin cup of water, to the woman. She waved the cup aside, placed the flask to her lips, and drank the undiluted spirit. Yet even this was evidently bravado, for the water started to her eyes, and she could not restrain the paroxysm of coughing that followed.

"I reckon that's the kind that kills at forty rods," she said, with a hysterical laugh. "But I say, pardner, you look as if you were fixed here to stay," and she stared ostentatiously around the chamber. But she had already taken in its minutest details, even to observing that the hanging strips of bark could be disposed so as to completely hide the entrance.

"Well, yes," he replied; "it wouldn't be very easy to pull up the stakes and move the shanty further on."

Seeing that either from indifference or caution he had not accepted her meaning, she looked at him fixedly, and said, -

"What is your little game?"

"Eh?"

"What are you hiding for, here in this tree?"

"But I'm not hiding."

"Then why didn't you come out when they hailed you last night?"

"Because I didn't care to."

Teresa whistled incredulously. "All right, then if you're not hiding, I'm going to." As he did not reply, she went on: "If I can keep out of sight for a couple of weeks, this thing will blow over here, and I can get across into Yolo. I could get a fair show there, where the boys know me. Just now the trails are all watched, but no one would think of lookin' here."

"Then how did you come to think of it?" he asked carelessly.

"Because I knew that bear hadn't gone far for that sugar; because I knew he hadn't stole it from a cache, it was too fresh, and we'd have seen the torn-up earth; because we had passed no camp; and because I knew there was no shanty here. And, besides," she added in a low voice, "may be I was huntin' a hole myself to die in, and spotted it by instinct."

There was something in this suggestion of a hunted animal that, unlike anything she had previously said or suggested, was not exaggerated, and caused the young man to look at her again. She was standing under the chimney-like opening, and the light from above illuminated her head and shoulders. The pupils of her eyes had lost their feverish prominence, and were slightly suffused and softened as she gazed abstractedly before her. The only vestige of her previous excitement was in her left-hand fingers, which were incessantly twisting and turning a diamond ring upon her right hand, but without imparting the least animation to her rigid attitude. Suddenly, as if conscious of his scrutiny, she stepped aside out of the revealing light, and by a swift feminine instinct raised her hand to her head as if to adjust her straggling hair. It was only for a moment, however, for, as if aware of the weakness, she struggled to resume her aggressive pose.

"Well," she said. "Speak up. Am I goin' to stop here, or have I got to get up and get?"

"You can stay," said the young man quietly; "but as I've got my provisions and ammunition here, and haven't any other place to go to just now, I suppose we'll have to share it together."

She glanced at him under her eyelids, and a half-bitter, half-contemptuous smile passed across her face. "All right, old man," she said, holding out her hand, "it's a go. We'll start in housekeeping at once, if you like."

"I'll have to come here once or twice a day," he said, quite composedly, "to look after my things, and get something to eat; but I'll be away most of the time, and what with camping out under the trees every night I reckon my share won't incommode you."

She opened her black eyes upon him, at this original proposition. Then she looked down at her torn dress. "I suppose this style of thing ain't very fancy, is it?" she said, with a forced laugh.

"I think I know where to beg or borrow a change for you, if you can't get any," he replied simply.

She stared at him again. "Are you a family man?"

"No."

She was silent for a moment. "Well," she said, "you can tell your girl I'm not particular about its being in the latest fashion."

There was a slight flush on his forehead as he turned toward the little cupboard, but no tremor in his voice as he went on: "You'll find tea and coffee here, and, if you're bored, there's a book or two. You read, don't you, I mean English?"

She nodded, but cast a look of undisguised contempt upon the two worn, coverless novels he held out to her. "You haven't got last week's 'Sacramento Union,' have you? I hear they have my case all in; only them lying reporters made it out against me all the time."

"I don't see the papers," he replied curtly.

"They say there's a picture of me in the 'Police Gazette,' taken in the act," and she laughed.

He looked a little abstracted, and turned as if to go. "I think you'll do well to rest a while just now, and keep as close hid as possible until afternoon. The trail is a mile away at the nearest point, but someone might miss it and stray over here. You're quite safe if you're careful, and stand by the tree. You can build a fire here," he stepped under the chimney-like opening, "without its being noticed. Even the smoke is lost and cannot be seen so high."

The light from above was falling on his head and shoulders, as it had on hers. She looked at him intently.

"You travel a good deal on your figure, pardner, don't you?" she said, with a certain admiration that was quite sexless in its quality; "but I don't see how you pick up a living by it in the Carquinez Woods. So you're going, are you? You might be more sociable. Good-by."

"Good-by!" He leaped from the opening.

"I say, pardner!"

He turned a little impatiently. She had knelt down at the entrance, so as to be nearer his level, and was holding out her hand. But he did not notice it, and she quietly withdrew it.

"If anybody dropped in and asked for you, what name will they say?"

He smiled. "Don't wait to hear."

"But suppose I wanted to sing out for you, what will I call you?"

He hesitated. "Call me Lo."

"Lo, the poor Indian?" [The first word of Pope's familiar apostrophe is humorously used in the far West as a distinguishing title for the Indian.]

"Exactly."

It suddenly occurred to the woman, Teresa, that in the young man's height, supple, yet erect carriage, color, and singular gravity of demeanor there was a refined, aboriginal suggestion. He did not look like any Indian she had ever seen, but rather as a youthful chief might have looked. There was a further suggestion in his fringed buckskin shirt and moccasins; but before she could utter the half-sarcastic comment that rose to her lips he had glided noiselessly away, even as an Indian might have done.

She readjusted the slips of hanging bark with feminine ingenuity, dispersing them so as to completely hide the entrance. Yet this did not darken the chamber, which seemed to draw a purer and more vigorous light through the soaring shaft that pierced the room than that which came from the dim woodland aisles below. Nevertheless, she shivered, and drawing her shawl closely around her began to collect some half-burnt fragments of wood in the chimney to make a fire. But the preoccupation of her thoughts rendered this a tedious process, as she would from time to time stop in the middle of an action and fall into an attitude of rapt abstraction, with far-off eyes and rigid mouth. When she had at last succeeded in kindling a fire and raising a film of pale blue smoke, that seemed to fade and dissipate entirely before it reached the top of the chimney shaft, she crouched beside it, fixed her eyes on the darkest corner of the cavern, and became motionless.

What did she see through that shadow?

Nothing at first but a confused medley of figures and incidents of the preceding night; things to be put away and forgotten; things that would not have happened but for another thing, the thing before which everything faded! A ball-room; the sounds of music; the one man she had cared for insulting her with the flaunting ostentation of his unfaithfulness; herself despised, put aside, laughed at, or worse, jilted. And then the moment of delirium, when the light danced; the one wild act that lifted her, the despised one, above them all, made her the supreme figure, to be glanced at by frightened women, stared at by half-startled, half-admiring men! "Yes," she laughed; but struck by the sound of her own voice, moved twice round the cavern nervously, and then dropped again into her old position.

As they carried him away he had laughed at her, like a hound that he was; he who had praised her for her spirit, and incited her revenge against others; he who had taught her to strike when she was insulted; and it was only fit he should reap what he had sown. She was what he, what other men, had made her. And what was she now? What had she been once?

She tried to recall her childhood: the man and woman who might have been her father and mother; who fought and wrangled over her precocious little life; abused or caressed her as she sided with either; and then left her with a circus troupe, where she first tasted the power of her courage, her beauty, and her recklessness. She remembered those flashes of triumph that left a fever in her veins, a fever that when it failed must be stimulated by dissipation, by anything, by everything that would keep her name a wonder in men's mouths, an envious fear to women. She recalled her transfer to the strolling players; her cheap pleasures, and cheaper rivalries and hatred, but always Teresa! the daring Teresa! the reckless Teresa! audacious as a woman, invincible as a boy; dancing, flirting, fencing, shooting, swearing, drinking, smoking, fighting Teresa! "Oh, yes; she had been loved, perhaps, who knows? but always feared. Why should she change now? Ha, he should see."

She had lashed herself in a frenzy, as was her wont, with gestures, ejaculations, oaths, adjurations, and passionate apostrophes, but with this strange and unexpected result. Heretofore she had always been sustained and kept up by an audience of some kind or quality, if only perhaps a humble companion; there had always been some one she could fascinate or horrify, and she could read her power mirrored in their eyes. Even the half-abstracted indifference of her strange host had been something. But she was alone now. Her words fell on apathetic solitude; she was acting to viewless space. She rushed to the opening, dashed the hanging bark aside and leaped to the ground.

She ran forward wildly a few steps, and stopped.

"Hallo!" she cried. "Look, 'tis I, Teresa!"

The profound silence remained unbroken. Her shrillest tones were lost in an echoless space, even as the smoke of her fire had faded into pure ether. She stretched out her clenched fists as if to defy the pillared austerities of the vaults around her.

"Come and take me if you dare!"

The challenge was unheeded. If she had thrown herself violently against the nearest tree-trunk, she could not have been stricken more breathless than she was by the compact, embattled solitude that encompassed her. The hopelessness of impressing these cold and passive vaults with her selfish passion filled her with a vague fear. In her rage of the previous night she had not seen the wood in its profound immobility. Left alone with the majesty of those enormous columns, she trembled and turned faint. The silence of the hollow tree she had just quitted seemed to her less awful than the crushing presence of these mute and monstrous witnesses of her weakness. Like a wounded quail with lowered crest and trailing wing, she crept back to her hiding-place.

Even then the influence of the wood was still upon her. She picked up the novel she had contemptuously thrown aside only to let it fall again in utter weariness. For a moment her feminine curiosity was excited by the discovery of an old book, in whose blank leaves were pressed a variety of flowers and woodland grasses. As she could not conceive that these had been kept for any but a sentimental purpose, she was disappointed to find that underneath each was a sentence in an unknown tongue, that even to her untutored eye did not appear to be the language of passion. Finally she rearranged the couch of skins and blankets, and, imparting to it in three clever shakes an entirely different character, lay down to pursue her reveries. But nature asserted herself, and ere she knew it she was fast asleep.

So intense and prolonged had been her previous excitement that, the tension once relieved, she passed into a slumber of exhaustion so deep that she seemed scarce to breathe. High noon succeeded morning, the central shaft received a single ray of upper sunlight, the afternoon came and went, the shadows gathered below, the sunset fires began to eat their way through the groined roof, and she still slept. She slept even when the bark hangings of the chamber were put aside, and the young man reentered.

He laid down a bundle he was carrying, and softly approached the sleeper. For a moment he was startled from his indifference; she lay so still and motionless. But this was not all that struck him; the face before him was no longer the passionate, haggard visage that confronted him that morning; the feverish air, the burning color, the strained muscles of mouth and brow, and the staring eyes were gone; wiped away, perhaps, by the tears that still left their traces on cheek and dark eyelash. It was a face of a handsome woman of thirty, with even a suggestion of softness in the contour of the cheek and arching of her upper lip, no longer rigidly drawn down in anger, but relaxed by sleep on her white teeth.

With the lithe, soft tread that was habitual to him, the young man moved about, examining the condition of the little chamber and its stock of provisions and necessaries, and withdrew presently, to reappear as noiselessly with a tin bucket of water. This done he replenished the little pile of fuel with an armful of bark and pine cones, cast an approving glance about him, which included the sleeper, and silently departed.

It was night when she awoke. She was surrounded by a profound darkness, except where the shaft-like opening made a nebulous mist in the corner in her wooden cavern. Providentially she struggled back to consciousness slowly, so that the solitude and silence came upon her gradually, with a growing realization of the events of the past twenty-four hours, but without a shock. She was alone here, but safe still, and every hour added to her chances of ultimate escape. She remembered to have seen a candle among the articles on the shelf, and she began to grope her way toward the matches. Suddenly she stopped. What was that panting?

Was it her own breathing, quickened with a sudden nameless terror? or was there something outside? Her heart seemed to stop beating while she listened. Yes! it was a panting outside, a panting now increased, multiplied, redoubled, mixed with the sounds of rustling, tearing, craunching, and occasionally a quick, impatient snarl. She crept on her hands and knees to the opening and looked out. At first the ground seemed to be undulating between her and the opposite tree. But a second glance showed her the black and gray, bristling, tossing backs of tumbling beasts of prey, charging the carcass of the bear that lay at its roots, or contesting for the prize with gluttonous choked breath, sidelong snarls, arched spines, and recurved tails. One of the boldest had leaped upon a buttressing root of her tree within a foot of the opening.

The excitement, awe, and terror she had undergone culminated in one wild, maddened scream, that seemed to pierce even the cold depths of the forest, as she dropped on her face, with her hands clasped over her eyes in an agony of fear.

Her scream was answered, after a pause, by a sudden volley of firebrands and sparks into the midst of the panting, crowding pack; a few smothered howls and snaps, and a sudden dispersion of the concourse. In another moment the young man, with a blazing brand in either hand, leaped upon the body of the bear.

Teresa raised her head, uttered a hysterical cry, slid down the tree, flew wildly to his side, caught convulsively at his sleeve, and fell on her knees beside him.

"Save me! save me!" she gasped, in a voice broken by terror. "Save me from those hideous creatures. No, no!" she implored, as he endeavored to lift her to her feet. "No, let me stay here close beside you. So," clutching the fringe of his leather hunting-shirt, and dragging herself on her knees nearer him, "so don't leave me, for God's sake!"

"They are gone," he replied, gazing down curiously at her, as she wound the fringe around her hand to strengthen her hold; "they're only a lot of cowardly coyotes and wolves, that dare not attack anything that lives and can move."

The young woman responded with a nervous shudder. "Yes, that's it," she whispered, in a broken voice; "it's only the dead they want. Promise me, swear to me, if I'm caught, or hung, or shot, you won't let me be left here to be torn and, ah! my God! what's that?"

She had thrown her arms around his knees, completely pinioning him to her frantic breast. Something like a smile of disdain passed across his face as he answered, "It's nothing. They will not return. Get up!"

Even in her terror she saw the change in his face. "I know, I know!" she cried. "I'm frightened, but I cannot bear it any longer. Hear me! Listen! Listen, but don't move! I didn't mean to kill Curson, no! I swear to God, no! I didn't mean to kill the sheriff, and I didn't. I was only bragging, do you hear? I lied! I lied, don't move, I swear to God I lied. I've made myself out worse than I was. I have. Only don't leave me now, and if I die, and it's not far off, may be, get me away from here, and from them. Swear it!"

"All right," said the young man, with a scarcely concealed movement of irritation. "But get up now, and go back to the cabin."

"No; not there alone." Nevertheless, he quietly but firmly released himself.

"I will stay here," he replied. "I would have been nearer to you, but I thought it better for your safety that my camp-fire should be further off. But I can build it here, and that will keep the coyotes off."

"Let me stay with you, beside you," she said imploringly.

She looked so broken, crushed, and spiritless, so unlike the woman of the morning that, albeit with an ill grace, he tacitly consented, and turned away to bring his blankets. But in the next moment she was at his side, following him like a dog, silent and wistful, and even offering to carry his burden. When he had built the fire, for which she had collected the pine, cones and broken branches near them, he sat down, folded his arms, and leaned back against the tree in reserved and deliberate silence. Humble and submissive, she did not attempt to break in upon a reverie she could not help but feel had little kindliness to herself. As the fire snapped and sparkled, she pillowed her head upon a root, and lay still to watch it.

It rose and fell, and dying away at times to a mere lurid glow, and again, agitated by some breath scarcely perceptible to them, quickening into a roaring flame. When only the embers remained, a dead silence filled the wood. Then the first breath of morning moved the tangled canopy above, and a dozen tiny sprays and needles detached from the interlocked boughs winged their soft way noiselessly to the earth. A few fell upon the prostrate woman like a gentle benediction, and she slept. But even then, the young man, looking down, saw that the slender fingers were still aimlessly but rigidly twisted in the leather fringe of his hunting-shirt.

CHAPTER II.

It was a peculiarity of the Carquinez Wood that it stood apart and distinct in its gigantic individuality. Even where the integrity of its own singular species was not entirely preserved, it admitted no inferior trees. Nor was there any diminishing fringe on its outskirts; the sentinels that guarded the few gateways of the dim trails were as monstrous as the serried ranks drawn up in the heart of the forest. Consequently, the red highway that skirted the eastern angle was bare and shadeless, until it slipped a league off into a watered valley and refreshed itself under lesser sycamores and willows. It was here the newly-born city of Excelsior, still in its cradle, had, like an infant Hercules, strangled the serpentine North Fork of the American river, and turned its life-current into the ditches and flumes of the Excelsior miners.

Newest of the new houses that seemed to have accidentally formed its single, straggling street was the residence of the Rev. Winslow Wynn, not unfrequently known as "Father Wynn," pastor of the first Baptist church. The "pastorage," as it was cheerfully called, had the glaring distinction of being built of brick, and was, as had been wickedly pointed out by idle scoffers, the only "fireproof" structure in town. This sarcasm was not, however, supposed to be particularly distasteful to "Father Wynn," who enjoyed the reputation of being "hail fellow, well met" with the rough mining element, who called them by their Christian names, had been known to drink at the bar of the Polka Saloon while engaged in the conversion of a prominent citizen, and was popularly said to have no "gospel starch" about him. Certain conscious outcasts and transgressors were touched at this apparent unbending of the spiritual authority. The rigid tenets of Father Wynn's faith were lost in the supposed catholicity of his humanity. "A preacher that can jine a man when he's histin' liquor into him, without jawin' about it, ought to be allowed to wrestle with sinners and splash about in as much cold water as he likes," was the criticism of one of his converts. Nevertheless, it was true that Father Wynn was somewhat loud and intolerant in his tolerance. It was true that he was a little more rough, a little more frank, a little more hearty, a little more impulsive, than his disciples. It was true that often the proclamation of his extreme liberality and brotherly equality partook somewhat of an apology. It is true that a few who might have been most benefited by this kind of gospel regarded him with a singular disdain. It is true that his liberality was of an ornamental, insinuating quality, accompanied with but little sacrifice; his acceptance of a collection taken up in a gambling-saloon for the rebuilding of his church, destroyed by fire, gave him a popularity large enough, it must be confessed, to cover the sins of the gamblers themselves, but it was not proven that he had ever organized any form of relief. But it was true that local history somehow accepted him as an exponent of mining Christianity, without the least reference to the opinions of the Christian miners themselves.

The Rev. Mr. Wynn's liberal habits and opinions were not, however, shared by his only daughter, a motherless young lady of eighteen. Nellie Wynn was in the eye of Excelsior an unapproachable divinity, as inaccessible and cold as her father was impulsive and familiar. An atmosphere of chaste and proud virginity made itself felt even in the starched integrity of her spotless skirts, in her neatly-gloved finger-tips, in her clear amber eyes, in her imperious red lips, in her sensitive nostrils. Need it be said that the youth and middle age of Excelsior were madly, because apparently hopelessly, in love with her? For the rest, she had been expensively educated, was profoundly ignorant in two languages, with a trained misunderstanding of music and painting, and a natural and faultless taste in dress.

The Rev. Mr. Wynn was engaged in a characteristic hearty parting with one of his latest converts upon his own doorstep, with admirable al fresco effect. He had just clapped him on the shoulder. "Good-by, good-by, Charley, my boy, and keep in the right path; not up, or down, or round the gulch, you know, ha, ha! but straight across lots to the shining gate." He had raised his voice under the stimulus of a few admiring spectators, and backed his convert playfully against the wall. "You see! we're goin' in to win, you bet. Good-by! I'd ask you to step in and have a chat, but I've got my work to do, and so have you. The gospel mustn't keep us from that, must it, Charley? Ha, ha!"

The convert (who elsewhere was a profane expressman, and had become quite imbecile under Mr. Wynn's active heartiness and brotherly horse-play before spectators) managed, however, to feebly stammer with a blush something about "Miss Nellie."

"Ah, Nellie. She, too, is at her tasks, trimming her lamp, you know, the parable of the wise virgins," continued Father Wynn hastily, fearing that the convert might take the illustration literally. "There, there, good-by. Keep in the right path." And with a parting shove he dismissed Charley and entered his own house.

That "wise virgin," Nellie, had evidently finished with the lamp, and was now going out to meet the bridegroom, as she was fully dressed and gloved, and had a pink parasol in her hand, as her father entered the sitting-room.

His bluff heartiness seemed to fade away as he removed his soft, broad-brimmed hat and glanced across the too fresh-looking apartment. There was a smell of mortar still in the air, and a faint suggestion that at any moment green grass might appear between the interstices of the red-brick hearth. The room, yielding a little in the point of coldness, seemed to share Miss Nellie's fresh virginity, and, barring the pink parasol, set her off as in a vestal's cell.

"I supposed you wouldn't care to see Brace, the expressman, so I got rid of him at the door," said her father, drawing one of the new chairs towards him slowly, and sitting down carefully, as if it were a hitherto untried experiment.

Miss Nellie's face took a tint of interest. "Then he doesn't go with the coach to Indian Spring to-day?"

"No; why?"

"I thought of going over myself to get the Burnham girls to come to choir-meeting," replied Miss Nellie carelessly, "and he might have been company."

"He'd go now if he knew you were going," said her father; "but it's just as well he shouldn't be needlessly encouraged. I rather think that Sheriff Dunn is a little jealous of him. By the way, the sheriff is much better. I called to cheer him up to-day" (Mr. Wynn had in fact tumultuously accelerated the sick man's pulse), "and he talked of you, as usual. In fact, he said he had only two things to get well for. One was to catch and hang that woman Teresa, who shot him; the other, can't you guess the other?" he added archly, with a faint suggestion of his other manner.

Miss Nellie coldly could not.

The Rev. Mr. Wynn's archness vanished. "Don't be a fool," he said dryly. "He wants to marry you, and you know it."

"Most of the men here do," responded Miss Nellie, without the least trace of coquetry. "Is the wedding or the hanging to take place first, or together, so he can officiate at both?"

"His share in the Union Ditch is worth a hundred thousand dollars," continued her father; "and if he isn't nominated for district judge this fall, he's bound to go to the legislature, any way. I don't think a girl with your advantages and education can afford to throw away the chance of shining in Sacramento, San Francisco, or, in good time, perhaps even Washington."

Miss Nellie's eyes did not reflect entire disapproval of this suggestion, although she replied with something of her father's practical quality.

"Mr. Dunn is not out of his bed yet, and they say Teresa's got away to Arizona, so there isn't any particular hurry."

"Perhaps not; but see here, Nellie, I've some important news for you. You know your young friend of the Carquinez Woods, Dorman, the botanist, eh? Well, Brace knows all about him. And what do you think he is?"

Miss Nellie took upon herself a few extra degrees of cold, and didn't know.

"An Injin! Yes, an out-and-out Cherokee. You see he calls himself Dorman, Low Dorman. That's only French for 'Sleeping Water,' his Injin name, 'Low Dorman.'"

"You mean 'L'Eau Dormante,'" said Nellie.

"That's what I said. The chief called him 'Sleeping Water' when he was a boy, and one of them French Canadian trappers translated it into French when he brought him to California to school. But he's an Injin, sure. No wonder he prefers to live in the woods."

"Well?" said Nellie.

"Well," echoed her father impatiently, "he's an Injin, I tell you, and you can't of course have anything to do with him. He mustn't come here again."

"But you forget," said Nellie imperturbably, "that it was you who invited him here, and were so much exercised over him. You remember you introduced him to the Bishop and those Eastern clergymen as a magnificent specimen of a young Californian. You forget what an occasion you made of his coming to church on Sunday, and how you made him come in his buckskin shirt and walk down the street with you after service!"

"Yes, yes," said the Rev. Mr. Wynn hurriedly.

"And," continued Nellie carelessly, "how you made us sing out of the same book 'Children of our Father's Fold,' and how you preached at him until he actually got a color!"

"Yes," said her father; "but it wasn't known then he was an Injin, and they are frightfully unpopular with those Southwestern men among whom we labor. Indeed, I am quite convinced that when Brace said 'the only good Indian was a dead one' his expression, though extravagant, perhaps, really voiced the sentiments of the majority. It would be only kindness to the unfortunate creature to warn him from exposing himself to their rude but conscientious antagonism."

"Perhaps you'd better tell him, then, in your own popular way, which they all seem to understand so well," responded the daughter. Mr. Wynn cast a quick glance at her, but there was no trace of irony in her face, nothing but a half-bored indifference as she walked toward the window.

"I will go with you to the coach-office," said her father, who generally gave these simple paternal duties the pronounced character of a public Christian example.

"It's hardly worth while," replied Miss Nellie. "I've to stop at the Watsons', at the foot of the hill, and ask after the baby; so I shall go on to the Crossing and pick up the coach as it passes. Good-by."

Nevertheless, as soon as Nellie had departed, the Rev. Mr. Wynn proceeded to the coach-office, and publicly grasping the hand of Yuba Bill, the driver, commended his daughter to his care in the name of the universal brotherhood of man and the Christian fraternity. Carried away by his heartiness, he forgot his previous caution, and confided to the expressman Miss Nellie's regrets that she was not to have that gentleman's company. The result was that Miss Nellie found the coach with its passengers awaiting her with uplifted hats and wreathed smiles at the Crossing, and the box-seat (from which an unfortunate stranger, who had expensively paid for it, had been summarily ejected) at her service beside Yuba Bill, who had thrown away his cigar and donned a new pair of buckskin gloves to do her honor. But a more serious result to the young beauty was the effect of the Rev. Mr. Wynn's confidences upon the impulsive heart of Jack Brace, the expressman. It has been already intimated that it was his "day off." Unable to summarily reassume his usual functions beside the driver without some practical reason, and ashamed to go so palpably as a mere passenger, he was forced to let the coach proceed without him. Discomfited for the moment, he was not, however, beaten. He had lost the blissful journey by her side, which would have been his professional right, but she was going to Indian Spring! could he not anticipate her there? Might they not meet in the most accidental manner? And what might not come from that meeting away from the prying eyes of their own town? Mr. Brace did not hesitate, but saddling his fleet Buckskin, by the time the stagecoach had passed the Crossing in the high-road he had mounted the hill and was dashing along the "cut-off" in the same direction, a full mile in advance. Arriving at Indian Spring, he left his horse at a Mexican posada on the confines of the settlement, and from the piled débris of a tunnel excavation awaited the slow arrival of the coach. On mature reflection he could give no reason why he had not boldly awaited it at the express office, except a certain bashful consciousness of his own folly, and a belief that it might be glaringly apparent to the bystanders. When the coach arrived and he had overcome this consciousness, it was too late. Yuba Bill had discharged his passengers for Indian Spring and driven away. Miss Nellie was in the settlement, but where? As time passed he became more desperate and bolder. He walked recklessly up and down the main street, glancing in at the open doors of shops, and even in the windows of private dwellings. It might have seemed a poor compliment to Miss Nellie, but it was an evidence of his complete preoccupation, when the sight of a female face at a window, even though it was plain or perhaps painted, caused his heart to bound, or the glancing of a skirt in the distance quickened his feet and his pulses. Had Jack contented himself with remaining at Excelsior he might have vaguely regretted, but as soon become as vaguely accustomed to, Miss Nellie's absence. But it was not until his hitherto quiet and passive love took this first step of action that it fully declared itself. When he had made the tour of the town a dozen times unsuccessfully, he had perfectly made up his mind that marriage with Nellie or the speedy death of several people, including possibly himself, was the only alternative. He regretted he had not accompanied her; he regretted he had not demanded where she was going; he contemplated a course of future action that two hours ago would have filled him with bashful terror. There was clearly but one thing to do, to declare his passion the instant he met her, and return with her to Excelsior an accepted suitor, or not to return at all.

Suddenly he was vexatiously conscious of hearing his name lazily called, and looking up found that he was on the outskirts of the town, and interrogated by two horsemen.

"Got down to walk, and the coach got away from you, Jack, eh?"

A little ashamed of his preoccupation, Brace stammered something about "collections." He did not recognize the men, but his own face, name, and business were familiar to everybody for fifty miles along the stage-road.

"Well, you can settle a bet for us, I reckon. Bill Dacre thar bet me five dollars and the drinks that a young gal we met at the edge of the Carquinez Woods, dressed in a long brown duster and half muffled up in a hood, was the daughter of Father Wynn of Excelsior. I did not get a fair look at her, but it stands to reason that a high-toned young lady like Nellie Wynn don't go trap'sing along the wood like a Pike County tramp. I took the bet. May be you know if she's here or in Excelsior?"

Mr. Brace felt himself turning pale with eagerness and excitement. But the near prospect of seeing her presently gave him back his caution, and he answered truthfully that he had left her in Excelsior, and that in his two hours' sojourn in Indian Spring he had not once met her. "But," he added, with a Californian's reverence for the sanctity of a bet, "I reckon you'd better make it a standoff for twenty-four hours, and I'll find out and let you know." Which, it is only fair to say, he honestly intended to do.

With a hurried nod of parting, he continued in the direction of the Woods. When he had satisfied himself that the strangers had entered the settlement and would not follow him for further explanation, he quickened his pace. In half an hour he passed between two of the gigantic sentinels that guarded the entrance to a trail. Here he paused to collect his thoughts. The Woods were vast in extent, the trail dim and uncertain, at times apparently breaking off, or intersecting another trail as faint as itself. Believing that Miss Nellie had diverged from the highway only as a momentary excursion into the shade, and that she would not dare to penetrate its more sombre and unknown recesses, he kept within sight of the skirting plain. By degrees the sedate influence of the silent vaults seemed to depress him. The ardor of the chase began to flag. Under the calm of their dim roof the fever of his veins began to subside; his pace slackened; he reasoned more deliberately. It was by no means probable that the young woman in a brown duster was Nellie; it was not her habitual traveling dress; it was not like her to walk unattended in the road; there was nothing in her tastes and habits to take her into this gloomy forest, allowing that she had even entered it; and on this absolute question of her identity the two witnesses were divided. He stopped irresolutely, and cast a last, long, half-despairing look around him. Hitherto he had given that part of the wood nearest the plain his greatest attention. His glance now sought its darker recesses. Suddenly he became breathless. Was it a beam of sunlight that had pierced the groined roof above, and now rested against the trunk of one of the dimmer, more secluded giants? No, it was moving; even as he gazed it slipped away, glanced against another tree, passed across one of the vaulted aisles, and then was lost again. Brief as was the glimpse, he was not mistaken, it was the figure of a woman.

In another moment he was on her track, and soon had the satisfaction of seeing her reappear at a lesser distance. But the continual intervention of the massive trunks made the chase by no means an easy one, and as he could not keep her always in sight he was unable to follow or understand the one intelligent direction which she seemed to invariably keep. Nevertheless, he gained upon her breathlessly, and, thanks to the bark-strewn floor, noiselessly. He was near enough to distinguish and recognize the dress she wore, a pale yellow, that he had admired when he first saw her. It was Nellie, unmistakably; if it were she of the brown duster, she had discarded it, perhaps for greater freedom. He was near enough to call out now, but a sudden nervous timidity overcame him; his lips grew dry. What should he say to her? How account for his presence? "Miss Nellie, one moment!" he gasped. She darted forward and vanished.

At this moment he was not more than a dozen yards from her. He rushed to where she had been standing, but her disappearance was perfect and complete. He made a circuit of the group of trees within whose radius she had last appeared, but there was neither trace of her, nor suggestion of her mode of escape. He called aloud to her; the vacant Woods let his helpless voice die in their unresponsive depths. He gazed into the air and down at the bark-strewn carpet at his feet. Like most of his vocation, he was sparing of speech, and epigrammatic after his fashion. Comprehending in one swift but despairing flash of intelligence the existence of some fateful power beyond his own weak endeavor, he accepted its logical result with characteristic grimness, threw his hat upon the ground, put his hands in his pockets, and said -

"Well, I'm damned!"

CHAPTER III.

Out of compliment to Miss Nellie Wynn, Yuba Bill, on reaching Indian Spring, had made a slight détour to enable him to ostentatiously set down his fair passenger before the door of the Burnhams. When it had closed on the admiring eyes of the passengers and the coach had rattled away, Miss Nellie, without any undue haste or apparent change in her usual quiet demeanor, managed, however, to dispatch her business promptly, and, leaving an impression that she would call again before her return to Excelsior, parted from her friends, and slipped away through a side street, to the General Furnishing Store of Indian Spring. In passing this emporium, Miss Nellie's quick eye had discovered a cheap brown linen duster hanging in its window. To purchase it, and put it over her delicate cambric dress, albeit with a shivering sense that she looked like a badly-folded brown-paper parcel, did not take long. As she left the shop it was with mixed emotions of chagrin and security that she noticed that her passage through the settlement no longer turned the heads of its male inhabitants. She reached the outskirts of Indian Spring and the high-road at about the time Mr. Brace had begun his fruitless patrol of the main street. Far in the distance a faint olive-green table mountain seemed to rise abruptly from the plain. It was the Carquinez Woods. Gathering her spotless skirts beneath her extemporized brown domino, she set out briskly towards them.

But her progress was scarcely free or exhilarating. She was not accustomed to walking in a country where "buggy-riding" was considered the only genteel young, lady-like mode of progression, and its regular provision the expected courtesy of mankind. Always fastidiously booted, her low-quartered shoes were charming to the eye, but hardly adapted to the dust and inequalities of the high-road. It was true that she had thought of buying a coarser pair at Indian Spring, but once face to face with their uncompromising ugliness, she had faltered and fled. The sun was unmistakably hot, but her parasol was too well known and offered too violent a contrast to the duster for practical use. Once she stopped with an exclamation of annoyance, hesitated, and looked back. In half an hour she had twice lost her shoe and her temper; a pink flush took possession of her cheeks, and her eyes were bright with suppressed rage. Dust began to form grimy circles around their orbits; with cat-like shivers she even felt it pervade the roots of her blonde hair. Gradually her breath grew more rapid and hysterical, her smarting eyes became humid, and at last, encountering two observant horsemen in the road, she turned and fled, until, reaching the wood, she began to cry.

Nevertheless she waited for the two horsemen to pass, to satisfy herself that she was not followed; then pushed on vaguely, until she reached a fallen tree, where, with a gesture of disgust, she tore off her hapless duster and flung it on the ground. She then sat down sobbing, but after a moment dried her eyes hurriedly and started to her feet. A few paces distant, erect, noiseless, with outstretched hand, the young solitary of the Carquinez Woods advanced towards her. His hand had almost touched hers, when he stopped.

"What has happened?" he asked gravely.

"Nothing," she said, turning half away, and searching the ground with her eyes, as if she had lost something. "Only I must be going back now."

"You shall go back at once, if you wish it," he said, flushing slightly. "But you have been crying; why?"

Frank as Miss Nellie wished to be, she could not bring herself to say that her feet hurt her, and the dust and heat were ruining her complexion. It was therefore with a half-confident belief that her troubles were really of a moral quality that she answered, "Nothing, nothing, but, but it's wrong to come here."

"But you did not think it was wrong when you agreed to come, at our last meeting," said the young man, with that persistent logic which exasperates the inconsequent feminine mind. "It cannot be any more wrong to-day."

"But it was not so far off," murmured the young girl, without looking up.

"Oh, the distance makes it more improper, then," he said abstractedly; but after a moment's contemplation of her half-averted face, he asked gravely, "Has any one talked to you about me?"

Ten minutes before, Nellie had been burning to unburden herself of her father's warning, but now she felt she would not. "I wish you wouldn't call yourself Low," she said at last.

"But it's my name," he replied quietly.

"Nonsense! It's only a stupid translation of a stupid nickname. They might as well call you 'Water' at once."

"But you said you liked it."

"Well, so I do. But don't you see, I, oh dear! you don't understand."

Low did not reply, but turned his head with resigned gravity towards the deeper woods. Grasping the barrel of his rifle with his left hand, he threw his right arm across his left wrist and leaned slightly upon it with the habitual ease of a Western hunter, doubly picturesque in his own lithe, youthful symmetry. Miss Nellie looked at him from under her eyelids, and then half defiantly raised her head and her dark lashes. Gradually an almost magical change came over her features; her eyes grew larger and more and more yearning, until they seemed to draw and absorb in their liquid depths the figure of the young man before her; her cold face broke into an ecstasy of light and color; her humid lips parted in a bright, welcoming smile, until, with an irresistible impulse, she arose, and throwing back her head stretched towards him two hands full of vague and trembling passion.

In another moment he had seized them, kissed them, and, as he drew her closer to his embrace, felt them tighten around his neck. "But what name do you wish to call me?" he asked, looking down into her eyes.

Miss Nellie murmured something confidentially to the third button of his hunting-shirt. "But that," he replied, with a faint smile, "that wouldn't be any more practical, and you wouldn't want others to call me dar -" Her fingers loosened around his neck, she drew her head back, and a singular expression passed over her face, which to any calmer observer than a lover would have seemed, however, to indicate more curiosity than jealousy.

"Who else does call you so?" she added earnestly. "How many, for instance?"

Low's reply was addressed not to her ear, but her lips. She did not avoid it, but added, "And do you kiss them all like that?" Taking him by the shoulders, she held him a little way from her, and gazed at him from head to foot. Then drawing him again to her embrace, she said, "I don't care, at least no woman has kissed you like that." Happy, dazzled, and embarrassed, he was beginning to stammer the truthful protestation that rose to his lips, but she stopped him: "No, don't protest! say nothing! Let me love you, that is all. It is enough." He would have caught her in his arms again, but she drew back. "We are near the road," she said quietly. "Come! you promised to show me where you camped. Let us make the most of our holiday. In an hour I must leave the woods."

"But I shall accompany you, dearest."

"No, I must go as I came, alone."

"But Nellie" -

"I tell you no," she said, with an almost harsh practical decision, incompatible with her previous abandonment. "We might be seen together."

"Well, suppose we are; we must be seen together eventually," he remonstrated.

The young girl made an involuntary gesture of impatient negation, but checked herself. "Don't let us talk of that now. Come, while I am here under your own roof", she pointed to the high interlaced boughs above them, "you must be hospitable. Show me your home; tell me, isn't it a little gloomy sometimes?"

"It never has been; I never thought it would be until the moment you leave it to-day."

She pressed his hand briefly and in a half-perfunctory way, as if her vanity had accepted and dismissed the compliment. "Take me somewhere," she said inquisitively, "where you stay most; I do not seem to see you here," she added, looking around her with a slight shiver. "It is so big and so high. Have you no place where you eat and rest and sleep?"

"Except in the rainy season, I camp all over the place, at any spot where I may have been shooting or collecting."

"Collecting?" queried Nellie.

"Yes; with the herbarium, you know."

"Yes," said Nellie dubiously. "But you told me once, the first time we ever talked together," she added, looking in his eyes, "something about your keeping your things like a squirrel in a tree. Could we not go there? Is there not room for us to sit and talk without being browbeaten and looked down upon by these supercilious trees?"

"It's too far away," said Low truthfully, but with a somewhat pronounced emphasis, "much too far for you just now; and it lies on another trail that enters the wood beyond. But come, I will show you a spring known only to myself, the wood ducks, and the squirrels. I discovered it the first day I saw you, and gave it your name. But you shall christen it yourself. It will be all yours, and yours alone, for it is so hidden and secluded that I defy any feet but my own or whoso shall keep step with mine to find it. Shall that foot be yours, Nellie?"

Her face beamed with a bright assent. "It may be difficult to track it from here," he said, "but stand where you are a moment, and don't move, rustle, nor agitate the air in any way. The woods are still now." He turned at right angles with the trail, moved a few paces into the ferns and underbrush, and then stopped with his finger on his lips. For an instant both remained motionless; then, with his intent face bent forward and both arms extended, he began to sink slowly upon one knee and one side, inclining his body with a gentle, perfectly-graduated movement until his ear almost touched the ground. Nellie watched his graceful figure breathlessly, until, like a bow unbent, he stood suddenly erect again, and beckoned to her without changing the direction of his face.

"What is it?" she asked eagerly.

"All right; I have found it," he continued, moving forward without turning his head.

"But how? What did you kneel for?" He did not reply, but taking her hand in his continued to move slowly on through the underbrush, as if obeying some magnetic attraction. "How did you find it?" again asked the half-awed girl, her voice unconsciously falling to a whisper. Still silent, Low kept his rigid face and forward tread for twenty yards further; then he stopped and released the girl's half-impatient hand. "How did you find it?" she repeated sharply.

"With my ears and nose," replied Low gravely.

"With your nose?"

"Yes; I smelt it."

Still fresh with the memory of his picturesque attitude, the young man's reply seemed to involve something more irritating to her feelings than even that absurd anti-climax. She looked at him coldly and critically, and appeared to hesitate whether to proceed. "Is it far?" she asked.

"Not more than ten minutes now, as I shall go."

"And you won't have to smell your way again?"

"No; it is quite plain now," he answered seriously, the young girl's sarcasm slipping harmlessly from his Indian stolidity. "Don't you smell it yourself?"

But Miss Nellie's thin, cold nostrils refused to take that vulgar interest.

"Nor hear it? Listen!"

"You forget I suffer the misfortune of having been brought up under a roof," she replied coldly.

"That's true," repeated Low, in all seriousness; "it's not your fault. But do you know, I sometimes think I am peculiarly sensitive to water; I feel it miles away. At night, though I may not see it or even know where it is, I am conscious of it. It is company to me when I am alone, and I seem to hear it in my dreams. There is no music as sweet to me as its song. When you sang with me that day in church, I seemed to hear it ripple in your voice. It says to me more than the birds do, more than the rarest plants I find. It seems to live with me and for me. It is my earliest recollection; I know it will be my last, for I shall die in its embrace. Do you think, Nellie," he continued, stopping short and gazing earnestly in her face, "do you think that the chiefs knew this when they called me 'Sleeping Water'?"

To Miss Nellie's several gifts I fear the gods had not added poetry. A slight knowledge of English verse of a select character, unfortunately, did not assist her in the interpretation of the young man's speech, nor relieve her from the momentary feeling that he was at times deficient in intellect. She preferred, however, to take a personal view of the question, and expressed her sarcastic regret that she had not known before that she had been indebted to the great flume and ditch at Excelsior for the pleasure of his acquaintance. This pert remark occasioned some explanation, which ended in the girl's accepting a kiss in lieu of more logical argument. Nevertheless, she was still conscious of an inward irritation, always distinct from her singular and perfectly material passion, which found vent as the difficulties of their undeviating progress through the underbrush increased. At last she lost her shoe again, and stopped short. "It's a pity your Indian friends did not christen you 'Wild Mustard' or 'Clover,'" she said satirically, "that you might have had some sympathies and longings for the open fields instead of these horrid jungles! I know we will not get back in time."

Unfortunately, Low accepted this speech literally and with his remorseless gravity. "If my name annoys you, I can get it changed by the legislature, you know, and I can find out what my father's name was, and take that. My mother, who died in giving me birth, was the daughter of a chief."

"Then your mother was really an Indian?" said Nellie, "and you are" - She stopped short.

"But I told you all this the day we first met," said Low with grave astonishment. "Don't you remember our long talk coming from church?"

"No," said Nellie, coldly, "you didn't tell me." But she was obliged to drop her eyes before the unwavering, undeniable truthfulness of his.

"You have forgotten," he said calmly; "but it is only right you should have your own way in disposing of a name that I have cared little for; and as you're to have a share of it" -

"Yes, but it's getting late, and if we are not going forward", interrupted the girl impatiently.

"We are going forward," said Low imperturbably; "but I wanted to tell you, as we were speaking on that subject" (Nellie looked at her watch), "I've been offered the place of botanist and naturalist in Professor Grant's survey of Mount Shasta, and if I take it, why when I come back, darling, well" -

"But you're not going just yet," broke in Nellie, with a new expression in her face.

"No."

"Then we need not talk of it now," she said with animation.

Her sudden vivacity relieved him. "I see what's the matter," he said gently, looking down at her feet, "these little shoes were not made to keep step with a moccasin. We must try another way." He stooped as if to secure the erring buskin, but suddenly lifted her like a child to his shoulder. "There," he continued, placing her arm around his neck, "you are clear of the ferns and brambles now, and we can go on. Are you comfortable?" He looked up, read her answer in her burning eyes and the warm lips pressed to his forehead at the roots of his straight dark hair, and again moved onward as in a mesmeric dream. But he did not swerve from his direct course, and with a final dash through the undergrowth parted the leafy curtain before the spring.

At first the young girl was dazzled by the strong light that came from a rent in the interwoven arches of the wood. The breach had been caused by the huge bulk of one of the great giants that had half fallen, and was lying at a steep angle against one of its mightiest brethren, having borne down a lesser tree in the arc of its downward path. Two of the roots, as large as younger trees, tossed their blackened and bare limbs high in the air. The spring, the insignificant cause of this vast disruption, gurgled, flashed, and sparkled at the base; the limpid baby fingers that had laid bare the foundations of that fallen column played with the still clinging rootlets, laved the fractured and twisted limbs, and, widening, filled with sleeping water the graves from which they had been torn.

"It had been going on for years, down there," said Low, pointing to a cavity from which the fresh water now slowly welled, "but it had been quickened by the rising of the subterranean springs and rivers which always occurs at a certain stage of the dry season. I remember that on that very night, for it happened a little after midnight, when all sounds are more audible, I was troubled and oppressed in my sleep by what you would call a nightmare; a feeling as if I was kept down by bonds and pinions that I longed to break. And then I heard a crash in this direction, and the first streak of morning brought me the sound and scent of water. Six months afterwards I chanced to find my way here, as I told you, and gave it your name. I did not dream that I should ever stand beside it with you, and have you christen it yourself."

He unloosed the cup from his flask, and filling it at the spring handed it to her. But the young girl leant over the pool, and pouring the water idly back said, "I'd rather put my feet in it. Mayn't I?"

"I don't understand you," he said wonderingly.

"My feet are so hot and dusty. The water looks deliciously cool. May I?"

"Certainly."

He turned away as Nellie, with apparent unconsciousness, seated herself on the bank, and removed her shoes and stockings. When she had dabbled her feet a few moments in the pool, she said over her shoulder -

"We can talk just as well, can't we?"

"Certainly."

"Well, then, why didn't you come to church more often, and why didn't you think of telling father that you were convicted of sin and wanted to be baptized?"

"I don't know," hesitated the young man.

"Well, you lost the chance of having father convert you, baptize you, and take you into full church fellowship."

"I never thought," he began.

"You never thought. Aren't you a Christian?"

"I suppose so."

"He supposes so! Have you no convictions, no professions?"

"But, Nellie, I never thought that you" - "Never thought that I, what? Do you think that I could ever be anything to a man who did not believe in justification by faith, or in the covenant of church fellowship? Do you think father would let me?"

In his eagerness to defend himself he stepped to her side. But seeing her little feet shining through the dark water, like outcroppings of delicately veined quartz, he stopped embarrassed. Miss Nellie, however, leaped to one foot, and, shaking the other over the pool, put her hand on his shoulder to steady herself. "You haven't got a towel, or," she said dubiously, looking at her small handkerchief, "anything to dry them on?"

But Low did not, as she perhaps expected, offer his own handkerchief.

"If you take a bath after our fashion," he said gravely, "you must learn to dry yourself after our fashion."

Lifting her again lightly in his arms, he carried her a few steps to the sunny opening, and bade her bury her feet in the dried mosses and baked withered grasses that were bleaching in a hollow. The young girl uttered a cry of childish delight, as the soft ciliated fibres touched her sensitive skin.

"It is healing, too," continued Low; "a moccasin filled with it after a day on the trail makes you all right again."

But Miss Nellie seemed to be thinking of something else.

"Is that the way the squaws bathe and dry themselves?"

"I don't know; you forget I was a boy when I left them."

"And you're sure you never knew any?"

"None."

The young girl seemed to derive some satisfaction in moving her feet up and down for several minutes among the grasses in the hollow; then, after a pause, said, "You are quite certain I am the first woman that ever touched this spring?"

"Not only the first woman, but the first human being, except myself."

"How nice!"

They had taken each other's hands; seated side by side, they leaned against a curving elastic root that half supported, half encompassed them. The girl's capricious, fitful manner succumbed as before to the near contact of her companion. Looking into her eyes, Low fell into a sweet, selfish lover's monologue, descriptive of his past and present feelings towards her, which she accepted with a heightened color, a slight exchange of sentiment, and a strange curiosity. The sun had painted their half-embraced silhouettes against the slanting tree-trunk, and began to decline unnoticed; the ripple of the water mingling with their whispers came as one sound to the listening ear; even their eloquent silences were as deep, and, I wot, perhaps as dangerous, as the darkened pool that filled so noiselessly a dozen yards away. So quiet were they that the tremor of invading wings once or twice shook the silence, or the quick scamper of frightened feet rustled the dead grass. But in the midst of a prolonged stillness the young man sprang up so suddenly that Nellie was still half clinging to his neck as he stood erect. "Hush!" he whispered; "someone is near!"

He disengaged her anxious hands gently, leaped upon the slanting tree-trunk, and running half-way up its incline with the agility of a squirrel, stretched himself at full length upon it and listened.

To the impatient, inexplicably startled girl, it seemed an age before he rejoined her.

"You are safe," he said; "he's going by the western trail toward Indian Spring."

"Who is he?" she asked, biting her lips with a poorly restrained gesture of mortification and disappointment.

"Some stranger," replied Low.

"As long as he wasn't coming here, why did you give me such a fright?" she said pettishly. "Are you nervous because a single wayfarer happens to stray here?"

"It was no wayfarer, for he tried to keep near the trail," said Low. "He was a stranger to the wood, for he lost his way every now and then. He was seeking or expecting some one, for he stopped frequently and waited or listened. He had not walked far, for he wore spurs that tinkled and caught in the brush; and yet he had not ridden here, for no horse's hoofs passed the road since we have been here. He must have come from Indian Spring."

"And you heard all that when you listened just now?" asked Nellie half disdainfully.

Impervious to her incredulity, Low turned his calm eyes on her face. "Certainly, I'll bet my life on what I say. Tell me: do you know anybody in Indian Spring who would likely spy upon you?"

The young girl was conscious of a certain ill-defined uneasiness, but answered, "No."

"Then it was not you he was seeking," said Low thoughtfully. Miss Nellie had not time to notice the emphasis, for he added, "You must go at once, and lest you have been followed I will show you another way back to Indian Spring. It is longer, and you must hasten. Take your shoes and stockings with you until we are out of the bush."

He raised her again in his arms and strode once more out through the covert into the dim aisles of the wood. They spoke but little; she could not help feeling that some other discordant element, affecting him more strongly than it did her, had come between them, and was half perplexed and half frightened. At the end of ten minutes he seated her upon a fallen branch, and telling her he would return by the time she had resumed her shoes and stockings glided from her like a shadow. She would have uttered an indignant protest at being left alone, but he was gone ere she could detain him. For a moment she thought she hated him. But when she had mechanically shod herself once more, not without nervous shivers at every falling needle, he was at her side.

"Do you know anyone who wears a frieze coat like that?" he asked, handing her a few torn shreds of wool affixed to a splinter of bark.

Miss Nellie instantly recognized the material of a certain sporting-coat worn by Mr. Jack Brace on festive occasions, but a strange yet infallible instinct that was part of her nature made her instantly disclaim all knowledge of it.

"No," she said.

"Not anyone who scents himself with some doctor's stuff like cologne?" continued Low, with the disgust of keen olfactory sensibilities.

Again Miss Nellie recognized the perfume with which the gallant expressman was wont to make redolent her little parlor, but again she avowed no knowledge of its possessor. "Well," returned Low, with some disappointment, "such a man has been here. Be on your guard. Let us go at once."

She required no urging to hasten her steps, but hurried breathlessly at his side. He had taken a new trail by which they left the wood at right angles with the highway, two miles away. Following an almost effaced mule track along a slight depression of the plain, deep enough, however, to hide them from view, he accompanied her, until, rising to the level again, she saw they were beginning to approach the highway and the distant roofs of Indian Spring. "Nobody meeting you now," he whispered, "would suspect where you had been. Good night! until next week, remember."

They pressed each other's hands, and standing on the slight ridge outlined against the paling sky, in full view of the highway, parting carelessly, as if they had been chance met travellers. But Nellie could not restrain a parting backward glance as she left the ridge. Low had descended to the deserted trail, and was running swiftly in the direction of the Carquinez Woods.

CHAPTER IV.

Teresa awoke with a start. It was day already, but how far advanced the even, unchanging, soft twilight of the woods gave no indication. Her companion had vanished, and to her bewildered senses so had the camp-fire, even to its embers and ashes. Was she awake, or had she wandered away unconsciously in the night? One glance at the tree above her dissipated the fancy. There was the opening of her quaint retreat and the hanging strips of bark, and at the foot of the opposite tree lay the carcass of the bear. It had been skinned, and, as Teresa thought with an inward shiver, already looked half its former size.

Not yet accustomed to the fact that a few steps in either direction around the circumference of those great trunks produced the sudden appearance or disappearance of any figure, Teresa uttered a slight scream as her young companion unexpectedly stepped to her side. "You see a change here," he said; "the stamped-out ashes of the camp-fire lie under the brush," and he pointed to some cleverly scattered boughs and strips of bark which completely effaced the traces of last night's bivouac. "We can't afford to call the attention of any packer or hunter who might straggle this way to this particular spot and this particular tree; the more naturally," he added, "as they always prefer to camp over an old fire." Accepting this explanation meekly, as partly a reproach for her caprice of the previous night, Teresa hung her head.

"I'm very sorry," she said, "but wouldn't that," pointing to the carcass of the bear, "have made them curious?"

But Low's logic was relentless.

"By this time there would have been little left to excite curiosity if you had been willing to leave those beasts to their work."

"I'm very sorry," repeated the woman, her lips quivering.

"They are the scavengers of the wood," he continued in a lighter tone; "if you stay here you must try to use them to keep your house clean."

Teresa smiled nervously.

"I mean that they shall finish their work to-night," he added, "and I shall build another camp-fire for us a mile from here until they do."

But Teresa caught his sleeve.

"No," she said hurriedly, "don't, please, for me. You must not take the trouble, nor the risk. Hear me; do, please. I can bear it, I will bear it to-night. I would have borne it last night, but it was so strange - and" she passed her hands over her forehead - "I think I must have been half mad. But I am not so foolish now."

She seemed so broken and despondent that he replied reassuringly: "Perhaps it would be better that I should find another hiding-place for you, until I can dispose of that carcass, so that it will not draw dogs after the wolves, and men after them. Besides, your friend the sheriff will probably remember the bear when he remembers anything, and try to get on its track again."

"He's a conceited fool," broke in Teresa in a high voice, with a slight return of her old fury, "or he'd have guessed where that shot came from; and," she added in a lower tone, looking down at her limp and nerveless fingers, "he wouldn't have let a poor, weak, nervous wretch like me get away."

"But his deputy may put two and two together, and connect your escape with it."

Teresa's eyes flashed. "It would be like the dog, just to save his pride, to swear it was an ambush of my friends, and that he was overpowered by numbers. Oh yes! I see it all!" she almost screamed, lashing herself into a rage at the bare contemplation of this diminution of her glory. "That's the dirty lie he tells everywhere, and is telling now."

She stamped her feet and glanced savagely around, as if at any risk to proclaim the falsehood. Low turned his impassive, truthful face towards her.

"Sheriff Dunn," he began gravely, "is a politician, and a fool when he takes to the trail as a hunter of man or beast. But he is not a coward nor a liar. Your chances would be better if he were, if he laid your escape to an ambush of your friends, than if his pride held you alone responsible."

"If he's such a good man, why do you hesitate?" she replied bitterly. "Why don't you give me up at once, and do a service to one of your friends?"

"I do not even know him," returned Low, opening his clear eyes upon her. "I've promised to hide you here, and I shall hide you as well from him as from anybody."

Teresa did not reply, but suddenly dropping down upon the ground buried her face in her hands and began to sob convulsively. Low turned impassively away, and putting aside the bark curtain climbed into the hollow tree. In a few moments he reappeared, laden with provisions and a few simple cooking utensils, and touched her lightly on the shoulder. She looked up timidly; the paroxysm had passed, but her lashes yet glittered.

"Come," he said, "come and get some breakfast. I find you have eaten nothing since you have been here, twenty-four hours."

"I didn't know it," she said, with a faint smile. Then seeing his burden, and possessed by a new and strange desire for some menial employment, she said hurriedly, "Let me carry something, do, please," and even tried to disencumber him.

Half annoyed, Low at last yielded, and handing his rifle said, "There, then, take that; but be careful, it's loaded!"

A cruel blush burnt the woman's face to the roots of her hair as she took the weapon hesitatingly in her hand.

"No!" she stammered, hurriedly lifting her shame-suffused eyes to his; "no! no!"

He turned away with an impatience which showed her how completely gratuitous had been her agitation and its significance, and said, "Well, then give it back if you are afraid of it." But she as suddenly declined to return it; and shouldering it deftly, took her place by his side. Silently they moved from the hollow tree together.

During their walk she did not attempt to invade his taciturnity. Nevertheless she was as keenly alive and watchful of his every movement and gesture as if she had hung enchanted on his lips. The unerring way with which he pursued a viewless, undeviating path through those trackless woods, his quick reconnaissance of certain trees or openings, his mute inspection of some almost imperceptible footprint of bird or beast, his critical examination of certain plants which he plucked and deposited in his deerskin haversack, were not lost on the quick-witted woman. As they gradually changed the clear, unencumbered aisles of the central woods for a more tangled undergrowth, Teresa felt that subtle admiration which culminates in imitation, and simulating perfectly the step, tread, and easy swing of her companion, followed so accurately his lead that she won a gratified exclamation from him when their goal was reached, a broken, blackened shaft, splintered by long-forgotten lightning, in the centre of a tangled carpet of wood-clover.

"I don't wonder you distanced the deputy," he said cheerfully, throwing down his burden, "if you can take the hunting-path like that. In a few days, if you stay here, I can venture to trust you alone for a little pasear when you are tired of the tree."

Teresa looked pleased, but busied herself with arrangements for the breakfast, while he gathered the fuel for the roaring fire which soon blazed beside the shattered tree.

Teresa's breakfast was a success. It was a revelation to the young nomad, whose ascetic habits and simple tastes were usually content with the most primitive forms of frontier cookery. It was at least a surprise to him to know that without extra trouble kneaded flour, water, and saleratus need not be essentially heavy; that coffee need not be boiled with sugar to the consistency of syrup; that even that rarest delicacy, small shreds of venison covered with ashes and broiled upon the end of a ramrod boldly thrust into the flames, would be better and even more expeditiously cooked upon burning coals. Moved in his practical nature, he was surprised to find this curious creature of disorganized nerves and useless impulses informed with an intelligence that did not preclude the welfare of humanity or the existence of a soul. He respected her for some minutes, until in the midst of a culinary triumph a big tear dropped and spluttered in the saucepan. But he forgave the irrelevancy by taking no notice of it, and by doing full justice to that particular dish.

Nevertheless, he asked several questions based upon these recently discovered qualities. It appeared that in the old days of her wanderings with the circus troupe she had often been forced to undertake this nomadic housekeeping. But she "despised it," had never done it since, and always had refused to do it for "him", the personal pronoun referring, as Low understood, to her lover Curson. Not caring to revive these memories further, Low briefly concluded:

"I don't know what you were, or what you may be, but from what I see of you you've got all the sabe of a frontierman's wife."

She stopped and looked at him, and then, with an impulse of impudence that only half concealed a more serious vanity, asked, "Do you think I might have made a good squaw?"

"I don't know," he replied quietly. "I never saw enough of them to know."

Teresa, confident from his clear eyes that he spoke the truth, but having nothing ready to follow this calm disposal of her curiosity, relapsed into silence.

The meal finished, Teresa washed their scant table equipage in a little spring near the camp-fire; where, catching sight of her disordered dress and collar, she rapidly threw her shawl, after the national fashion, over her shoulder and pinned it quickly. Low cached the remaining provisions and the few cooking-utensils under the dead embers and ashes, obliterating all superficial indication of their camp-fire as deftly and artistically as he had before.

"There isn't the ghost of a chance," he said in explanation, "that anybody but you or I will set foot here before we come back to supper, but it's well to be on guard. I'll take you back to the cabin now, though I bet you could find your way there as well as I can."

On their way back Teresa ran ahead of her companion, and plucking a few tiny leaves from a hidden oasis in the bark-strewn trail brought them to him.

"That's the kind you're looking for, isn't it?" she said, half timidly.

"It is," responded Low, in gratified surprise; "but how did you know it? You're not a botanist, are you?"

"I reckon not," said Teresa; "but you picked some when we came, and I noticed what they were."

Here was indeed another revelation. Low stopped and gazed at her with such frank, open, utterly unabashed curiosity that her black eyes fell before him.

"And do you think," he asked with logical deliberation, "that you could find any plant from another I should give you?"

"Yes."

"Or from a drawing of it?"

"Yes; perhaps even if you described it to me."

A half-confidential, half fraternal silence followed.

"I tell you what. I've got a book" -

"I know it," interrupted Teresa; "full of these things."

"Yes. Do you think you could" -

"Of course I could," broke in Teresa, again.

"But you don't know what I mean," said the imperturbable Low.

"Certainly I do. Why, find 'em, and preserve all the different ones for you to write under, that's it, isn't it?"

Low nodded his head, gratified but not entirely convinced that she had fully estimated the magnitude of the endeavor.

"I suppose," said Teresa, in the feminine postscriptum voice which it would seem entered even the philosophical calm of the aisles they were treading, "I suppose that she places great value on them?"

Low had indeed heard Science personified before, nor was it at all impossible that the singular woman walking by his side had also. He said "Yes;" but added, in mental reference to the Linnean Society of San Francisco, that "they were rather particular about the rarer kinds."

Content as Teresa had been to believe in Low's tender relations with some favored one of her sex, this frank confession of a plural devotion staggered her.

"They?" she repeated.

"Yes," he continued calmly. "The Botanical Society I correspond with are more particular than the Government Survey."

"Then you are doing this for a society?" demanded Teresa, with a stare.

"Certainly. I'm making a collection and classification of specimens. I intend, but what are you looking at?"

Teresa had suddenly turned away. Putting his hand lightly on her shoulder, the young man brought her face to face with him again. She was laughing.

"I thought all the while it was for a girl," she said; "and" - But here the mere effort of speech sent her off into an audible and genuine outburst of laughter. It was the first time he had seen her even smile other than bitterly. Characteristically unconscious of any humor in her error, he remained unembarrassed. But he could not help noticing a change in the expression of her face, her voice, and even her intonation. It seemed as if that fit of laughter had loosed the last ties that bound her to a self-imposed character, had swept away the last barrier between her and her healthier nature, had dispossessed a painful unreality, and relieved the morbid tension of a purely nervous attitude. The change in her utterance and the resumption of her softer Spanish accent seemed to have come with her confidences, and Low took leave of her before their sylvan cabin with a comrade's heartiness, and a complete forgetfulness that her voice had ever irritated him.

When he returned that afternoon he was startled to find the cabin empty. But instead of bearing any appearance of disturbance or hurried flight, the rude interior seemed to have magically assumed a decorous order and cleanliness unknown before. Fresh bark hid the inequalities of the floor. The skins and blankets were folded in the corners, the rude shelves were carefully arranged, even a few tall ferns and bright but quickly fading flowers were disposed around the blackened chimney. She had evidently availed herself of the change of clothing he had brought her, for her late garments were hanging from the hastily-devised wooden pegs driven in the wall. The young man gazed around him with mixed feelings of gratification and uneasiness. His presence had been dispossessed in a single hour; his ten years of lonely habitation had left no trace that this woman had not effaced with a deft move of her hand. More than that, it looked as if she had always occupied it; and it was with a singular conviction that even when she should occupy it no longer it would only revert to him as her dwelling that he dropped the bark shutters athwart the opening, and left it to follow her.

To his quick ear, fine eye, and abnormal senses, this was easy enough. She had gone in the direction of this morning's camp. Once or twice he paused with a half-gesture of recognition and a characteristic "Good!" at the place where she had stopped, but was surprised to find that her main course had been as direct as his own. Deviating from this direct line with Indian precaution he first made a circuit of the camp, and approached the shattered trunk from the opposite direction. He consequently came upon Teresa unawares. But the momentary astonishment and embarrassment were his alone.

He scarcely recognized her. She was wearing the garments he had brought her the day before, a certain discarded gown of Miss Nellie Wynn, which he had hurriedly begged from her under the pretext of clothing the wife of a distressed over-land emigrant then on the way to the mines. Although he had satisfied his conscience with the intention of confessing the pious fraud to her when Teresa was gone and safe from pursuit, it was not without a sense of remorse that he witnessed the sacrilegious transformation. The two women were nearly the same height and size; and although Teresa's maturer figure accented the outlines more strongly, it was still becoming enough to increase his irritation.

Of this becomingness she was doubtless unaware at the moment that he surprised her. She was conscious of having "a change," and this had emboldened her to "do her hair" and otherwise compose herself. After their greeting she was the first to allude to the dress, regretting that it was not more of a rough disguise, and that, as she must now discard the national habit of wearing her shawl "manta" fashion over her head, she wanted a hat. "But you must not," she said, "borrow any more dresses for me from your young woman. Buy them for me at some shop. They left me enough money for that." Low gently put aside the few pieces of gold she had drawn from her pocket, and briefly reminded her of the suspicion such a purchase by him would produce. "That's so," she said, with a laugh. "Caramba! what a mule I'm becoming! Ah! wait a moment. I have it! Buy me a common felt hat, a man's hat, as if for yourself, as a change to that animal," pointing to the fox-tailed cap he wore summer and winter, "and I'll show you a trick. I haven't run a theatrical wardrobe for nothing." Nor had she, for the hat thus procured, a few days later, became, by the aid of a silk handkerchief and a bluejay's feather, a fascinating "pork pie."

Whatever cause of annoyance to Low still lingered in Teresa's dress, it was soon forgotten in a palpable evidence of Teresa's value as botanical assistant. It appeared that during the afternoon she had not only duplicated his specimens, but had discovered one or two rare plants as yet unclassified in the flora of the Carquinez Woods. He was delighted, and in turn, over the camp-fire, yielded up some details of his present life and some of his earlier recollections.

"You don't remember anything of your father?" she asked. "Did he ever try to seek you out?"

"No! Why should he?" replied the imperturbable Low; "he was not a Cherokee."

"No, he was a beast," responded Teresa promptly. "And your mother, do you remember her?"

"No, I think she died."

"You think she died? Don't you know?"

"No!"

"Then you're another!" said Teresa. Notwithstanding this frankness, they shook hands for the night; Teresa nestling like a rabbit in a hollow by the side of the camp-fire; Low with his feet towards it, Indian-wise, and his head and shoulders pillowed on his haversack, only half distinguishable in the darkness beyond.

With such trivial details three uneventful days slipped by. Their retreat was undisturbed, nor could Low detect, by the least evidence to his acute perceptive faculties, that any intruding feet had since crossed the belt of shade. The echoes of passing events at Indian Spring had recorded the escape of Teresa as occurring at a remote and purely imaginative distance, and her probable direction the county of Yolo.

"Can you remember," he one day asked her, "what time it was when you cut the riata and got away?"

Teresa pressed her hands upon her eyes and temples.

"About three, I reckon."

"And you were here at seven; you could have covered some ground in four hours?"

"Perhaps, I don't know," she said, her voice taking up its old quality again. "Don't ask me, I ran all the way."

Her face was quite pale as she removed her hands from her eyes, and her breath came as quickly as if she had just finished that race for life.

"Then you think I am safe here?" she added, after a pause.

"Perfectly, until they find you are not in Yolo. Then they'll look here. And that's the time for you to go there." Teresa smiled timidly.

"It will take them some time to search Yolo, unless," she added, "you're tired of me here." The charming non sequitur did not, however, seem to strike the young man. "I've got time yet to find a few more plants for you," she suggested.

"Oh, certainly!"

"And give you a few more lessons in cooking."

"Perhaps."

The conscientious and literal Low was beginning to doubt if she were really practical. How otherwise could she trifle with such a situation?

It must be confessed that that day and the next she did trifle with it. She gave herself up to a grave and delicious languor that seemed to flow from shadow and silence and permeate her entire being. She passed hours in a thoughtful repose of mind and spirit that seemed to fall like balm from those steadfast guardians, and distill their gentle ether in her soul; or breathed into her listening ear immunity from the forgotten past, and security for the present. If there was no dream of the future in this calm, even recurrence of placid existence, so much the better. The simple details of each succeeding day, the quaint housekeeping, the brief companionship and coming and going of her young host, himself at best a crystallized personification of the sedate and hospitable woods, satisfied her feeble cravings. She no longer regretted the inferior passion that her fears had obliged her to take the first night she came; she began to look up to this young man, so much younger than herself, without knowing what it meant; it was not until she found that this attitude did not detract from his picturesqueness that she discovered herself seeking for reasons to degrade him from this seductive eminence.

A week had elapsed with little change. On two days he had been absent all day, returning only in time to sup in the hollow tree, which, thanks to the final removal of the dead bear from its vicinity, was now considered a safer retreat than the exposed camp-fire. On the first of these occasions she received him with some preoccupation, paying but little heed to the scant gossip he brought from Indian Spring, and retiring early under the plea of fatigue, that he might seek his own distant camp-fire, which, thanks to her stronger nerves and regained courage, she no longer required so near. On the second occasion, he found her writing a letter more or less blotted with her tears. When it was finished, she begged him to post it at Indian Spring, where in two days an answer would be returned, under cover, to him.

"I hope you will be satisfied then," she added.

"Satisfied with what?" queried the young man.

"You'll see," she replied, giving him her cold hand. "Good-night."

"But can't you tell me now?" he remonstrated, retaining her hand.

"Wait two days longer, it isn't much," was all she vouchsafed to answer.

The two days passed. Their former confidence and good fellowship were fully restored when the morning came on which he was to bring the answer from the post-office at Indian Spring. He had talked again of his future, and had recorded his ambition to procure the appointment of naturalist to a Government Surveying Expedition. She had even jocularly proposed to dress herself in man's attire and "enlist" as his assistant.

"But you will be safe with your friends, I hope, by that time," responded Low.

"Safe with my friends," she repeated in a lower voice. "Safe with my friends, yes!" An awkward silence followed; Teresa broke it gayly: "But your girl, your sweetheart, my benefactor, will she let you go?"

"I haven't told her yet," said Low, gravely, "but I don't see why she should object."

"Object, indeed!" interrupted Teresa in a high voice and a sudden and utterly gratuitous indignation; "how should she? I'd like to see her do it!"

She accompanied him some distance to the intersection of the trail, where they parted in good spirits. On the dusty plain without a gale was blowing that rocked the high tree-tops above her, but, tempered and subdued, entered the low aisles with a fluttering breath of morning and a sound like the cooing of doves. Never had the wood before shown so sweet a sense of security from the turmoil and tempest of the world beyond; never before had an intrusion from the outer life, even in the shape of a letter, seemed so wicked a desecration. Tempted by the solicitation of air and shade, she lingered, with Low's herbarium slung on her shoulder.

A strange sensation, like a shiver, suddenly passed across her nerves, and left them in a state of rigid tension. With every sense morbidly acute, with every faculty strained to its utmost, the subtle instincts of Low's woodcraft transformed and possessed her. She knew it now! A new element was in the wood, a strange being, another life, another man approaching! She did not even raise her head to look about her, but darted with the precision and fleetness of an arrow in the direction of her tree. But her feet were arrested, her limbs paralyzed, her very existence suspended, by the sound of a voice:

"Teresa!"

It was a voice that had rung in her ears for the last two years in all phases of intensity, passion, tenderness, and anger; a voice upon whose modulations, rude and unmusical though they were, her heart and soul had hung in transport or anguish. But it was a chime that had rung its last peal to her senses as she entered the Carquinez Woods, and for the last week had been as dead to her as a voice from the grave. It was the voice of her lover - Dick Curson!

CHAPTER V.

The wind was blowing towards the stranger, so that he was nearly upon her when Teresa first took the alarm. He was a man over six feet in height, strongly built, with a slight tendency to a roundness of bulk which suggested reserved rather than impeded energy. His thick beard and moustache were closely cropped around a small and handsome mouth that lisped except when he was excited, but always kept fellowship with his blue eyes in a perpetual smile of half-cynical good-humor. His dress was superior to that of the locality; his general expression that of a man of the world, albeit a world of San Francisco, Sacramento, and Murderer's Bar. He advanced towards her with a laugh and an outstretched hand.

"You here!" she gasped, drawing back.

Apparently neither surprised nor mortified at this reception, he answered frankly, "Yeth. You didn't expect me, I know. But Doloreth showed me the letter you wrote her, and, well, here I am, ready to help you, with two men and a thpare horthe waiting outside the woodth on the blind trail."

"You, you, here?" she only repeated.

Curson shrugged his shoulders. "Yeth. Of courth you never expected to thee me again, and leatht of all here. I'll admit that; I'll thay I wouldn't if I'd been in your plathe. I'll go further, and thay you didn't want to thee me again, anywhere. But it all cometh to the thame thing; here I am; I read the letter you wrote Doloreth. I read how you were hiding here, under Dunn'th very nothe, with his whole pothe out, cavorting round and barkin' up the wrong tree. I made up my mind to come down here with a few nathty friends of mine and cut you out under Dunn'th nothe, and run you over into Yuba, that 'th all."

"How dared she show you my letter, you of all men? How dared she ask your help?" continued Teresa, fiercely.

"But she didn't athk my help," he responded coolly. "Damned if I don't think she jutht calculated I'd be glad to know you were being hunted down and thtarving, that I might put Dunn on your track."

"You lie!" said Teresa, furiously; "she was my friend. A better friend than those who professed more, she added, with a contemptuous drawing away of her skirt as if she feared Curson's contamination.

"All right. Thettle that with her when you go back," continued Curson philosophically. "We can talk of that on the way. The thing now ith to get up and get out of thethe woods. Come!"

Teresa's only reply was a gesture of scorn.

"I know all that," continued Curson half soothingly, "but they're waiting."

"Let them wait. I shall not go."

"What will you do?"

"Stay here, till the wolves eat me."

"Teresa, listen. Damn it all, Teresa! Tita! see here," he said with sudden energy. "I swear to God it's all right. I'm willing to let by-gones be by-gones and take a new deal. You shall come back as if nothing had happened, and take your old place as before. I don't mind doing the square thing, all round. If that's what you mean, if that's all that stands in the way, why, look upon the thing as settled. There, Tita, old girl, come."

Careless or oblivious of her stony silence and starting eyes, he attempted to take her hand. But she disengaged herself with a quick movement, drew back, and suddenly crouched like a wild animal about to spring. Curson folded his arms as she leaped to her feet; the little dagger she had drawn from her garter flashed menacingly in the air, but she stopped.

The man before her remained erect, impassive, and silent; the great trees around and beyond her remained erect, impassive, and silent; there was no sound in the dim aisles but the quick panting of her mad passion, no movement in the calm, motionless shadow but the trembling of her uplifted steel. Her arm bent and slowly sank, her fingers relaxed, the knife fell from her hand.

"That'th quite enough for a thow," he said, with a return to his former cynical ease and a perceptible tone of relief in his voice. "It'th the thame old Teretha. Well, then, if you won't go with me, go without me; take the led horthe and cut away. Dick Athley and Petereth will follow you over the county line. If you want thome money, there it ith." He took a buckskin purse from his pocket. "If you won't take it from me", he hesitated as she made no reply, "Athley'th flush and ready to lend you thome."

She had not seemed to hear him, but had stooped in some embarrassment, picked up the knife and hastily hid it, then with averted face and nervous fingers was beginning to tear strips of loose bark from the nearest trunk.

"Well, what do you thay?"

"I don't want any money, and I shall stay here." She hesitated, looked around her, and then added, with an effort, "I suppose you meant well. Be it so! Let bygones be by-gones. You said just now, 'It's the same old Teresa.' So she is, and seeing she's the same she's better here than anywhere else."

There was enough bitterness in her tone to call for Curson's half-perfunctory sympathy.

"That be damned," he responded quickly. "Jutht thay you'll come, Tita, and" -

She stopped his half-spoken sentence with a negative gesture. "You don't understand. I shall stay here."

"But even if they don't theek you here, you can't live here forever. The friend that you wrote about who wath tho good to you, you know, can't keep you here alwayth; and are you thure you can alwayth trutht her?"

"It isn't a woman; it's a man." She stopped short, and colored to the line of her forehead. "Who said it was a woman?" she continued fiercely, as if to cover her confusion with a burst of gratuitous anger. "Is that another of your lies?"

Curson's lips, which for a moment had completely lost their smile, were now drawn together in a prolonged whistle. He gazed curiously at her gown, at her hat, at the bow of bright ribbon that tied her black hair, and said, "Ah!"

"A poor man who has kept my secret," she went on hurriedly, "a man as friendless and lonely as myself. Yes," disregarding Curson's cynical smile, "a man who has shared everything" -

"Naturally," suggested Curson.

"And turned himself out of his only shelter to give me a roof and covering," she continued mechanically, struggling with the new and horrible fancy that his words awakened.

"And thlept every night at Indian Thpring to save your reputation," said Curson. "Of courthe."

Teresa turned very white. Curson was prepared for an outburst of fury, perhaps even another attack. But the crushed and beaten woman only gazed at him with frightened and imploring eyes. "For God's sake, Dick, don't say that!"

The amiable cynic was staggered. His good-humor and a certain chivalrous instinct he could not repress got the better of him. He shrugged his shoulders. "What I thay, and what you do, Teretha, needn't make us quarrel. I've no claim on you, I know it. Only", a vivid sense of the ridiculous, powerful in men of his stamp, completed her victory, "only don't thay anything about my coming down here to cut you out from the, the, the sheriff." He gave utterance to a short but unaffected laugh, made a slight grimace, and turned to go.

Teresa did not join in his mirth. Awkward as it would have been if he had taken a severer view of the subject, she was mortified even amidst her fears and embarrassment at his levity. Just as she had become convinced that his jealousy had made her over-conscious, his apparent good-humored indifference gave that over-consciousness a guilty significance. Yet this was lost in her sudden alarm as her companion, looking up, uttered an exclamation, and placed his hand upon his revolver. With a sinking conviction that the climax had come, Teresa turned her eyes. From the dim aisles beyond, Low was approaching. The catastrophe seemed complete.

She had barely time to utter an imploring whisper: "In the name of God, not a word to him." But a change had already come over her companion. It was no longer a parley with a foolish woman; he had to deal with a man like himself. As Low's dark face and picturesque figure came nearer, Mr. Curson's proposed method of dealing with him was made audible.

"Ith it a mulatto or a Thircuth, or both?" he asked, with affected anxiety.

Low's Indian phlegm was impervious to such assault. He turned to Teresa, without apparently noticing her companion. "I turned back," he said quietly, "as soon as I knew there were strangers here; I thought you might need me." She noticed for the first time that, in addition to his rifle, he carried a revolver and hunting-knife in his belt.

"Yeth," returned Curson, with an ineffectual attempt to imitate Low's phlegm; "but ath I did n't happen to be a sthranger to thith lady, perhaps it wathn't nethethary, particularly ath I had two friends" -

"Waiting at the edge of the wood with a led horse," interrupted Low, without addressing him, but apparently continuing his explanation to Teresa. But she turned to Low with feverish anxiety.

"That's so, he is an old friend", she gave a quick, imploring glance at Curson, "an old friend who came to help me away, he is very kind," she stammered, turning alternately from the one to the other; "but I told him there was no hurry, at least to-day, that you-were-very good-too, and would hide me a little longer until your plan, you know your plan," she added, with a look of beseeching significance to Low, "could be tried." And then, with a helpless conviction that her excuses, motives, and emotions were equally and perfectly transparent to both men, she stopped in a tremble.

"Perhapth it'th jutht ath well, then, that the gentleman came thraight here, and didn't tackle my two friendth when he pathed them," observed Curson, half sarcastically.

"I have not passed your friends, nor have I been near them," said Low, looking at him for the first time, with the same exasperating calm, "or perhaps I should not be here or they there. I knew that one man entered the wood a few moments ago, and that two men and four horses remained outside."

"That's true," said Teresa to Curson excitedly, "that's true. He knows all. He can see without looking, hear without listening. He, he" - she stammered, colored, and stopped.

The two men had faced each other. Curson, after his first good-natured impulse, had retained no wish to regain Teresa, whom he felt he no longer loved, and yet who, for that very reason perhaps, had awakened his chivalrous instincts. Low, equally on his side, was altogether unconscious of any feeling which might grow into a passion, and prevent him from letting her go with another if for her own safety. They were both men of a certain taste and refinement. Yet, in spite of all this, some vague instinct of the baser male animal remained with them, and they were moved to a mutually aggressive attitude in the presence of the female.

One word more, and the opening chapter of a sylvan Iliad might have begun. But this modern Helen saw it coming, and arrested it with an inspiration of feminine genius. Without being observed, she disengaged her knife from her bosom and let it fall as if by accident. It struck the ground with the point of its keen blade, bounded and rolled between them. The two men started and looked at each other with a foolish air. Curson laughed.

"I reckon she can take care of herthelf," he said, extending his hand to Low. "I'm off. But if I'm wanted she'll know where to find me." Low took the proffered hand, but neither of the two men looked at Teresa. The reserve of antagonism once broken, a few words of caution, advice, and encouragement passed between them, in apparent obliviousness of her presence or her personal responsibility. As Curson at last nodded a farewell to her, Low insisted upon accompanying him as far as the horses, and in another moment she was again alone.

She had saved a quarrel between them at the sacrifice of herself, for her vanity was still keen enough to feel that this exhibition of her old weakness had degraded her in their eyes, and, worse, had lost the respect her late restraint had won from Low. They had treated her like a child or a crazy woman, perhaps even now were exchanging criticisms upon her, perhaps pitying her! Yet she had prevented a quarrel, a fight, possibly the death of either one or the other of these men who despised her, for none better knew than she the trivial beginning and desperate end of these encounters. Would they, would Low ever realize it, and forgive her? Her small, dark hands went up to her eyes and she sank upon the ground. She looked through tear-veiled lashes upon the mute and giant witnesses of her deceit and passion, and tried to draw, from their immovable calm, strength and consolation as before. But even they seemed to stand apart, reserved and forbidding.

When Low returned she hoped to gather from his eyes and manner what had passed between him and her former lover. But beyond a mere gentle abstraction at times he retained his usual calm. She was at last forced to allude to it herself with simulated recklessness.

"I suppose I didn't get a very good character from my last place?" she said, with a laugh.

"I don't understand you," he replied, in evident sincerity.

She bit her lip and was silent. But as they were returning home, she said gently, "I hope you were not angry with me for the lie I told when I spoke of 'your plan.' I could not give the real reason for not returning with, with that man. But it's not all a lie. I have a plan if you haven't. When you are ready to go to Sacramento to take your place, dress me as an Indian boy, paint my face, and let me go with you. You can leave me there, you know."

"It's not a bad idea," he responded gravely. "We will see."

On the next day, and the next, the rencontre seemed to be forgotten. The herbarium was already filled with rare specimens. Teresa had even overcome her feminine repugnance to "bugs" and creeping things so far as to assist in his entomological collection. He had drawn from a sacred cache in the hollow of a tree the few worn textbooks from which he had studied.

"They seem very precious," she said, with a smile.

"Very," he replied gravely. "There was one with plates that the ants ate up, and it will be six months before I can afford to buy another."

Teresa glanced hurriedly over his well-worn buckskin suit, at his calico shirt with its pattern almost obliterated by countless washings, and became thoughtful.

"I suppose you couldn't buy one at Indian Spring?" she said innocently.

For once Low was startled out of his phlegm. "Indian Spring!" he ejaculated; "perhaps not even in San Francisco. These came from the States."

"How did you get them?" persisted Teresa.

"I bought them for skins I got over the ridge."

"I didn't mean that, but no matter. Then you mean to sell that bearskin, don't you?" she added.

Low had, in fact, already sold it, the proceeds having been invested in a gold ring for Miss Nellie, which she scrupulously did not wear except in his presence. In his singular truthfulness he would have frankly confessed it to Teresa, but the secret was not his own. He contented himself with saying that he had disposed of it at Indian Spring. Teresa started, and communicated unconsciously some of her nervousness to her companion. They gazed in each other's eyes with a troubled expression.

"Do you think it was wise to sell that particular skin, which might be identified?" she asked timidly.

Low knitted his arched brows, but felt a strange sense of relief. "Perhaps not," he said carelessly; "but it's too late now to mend matters."

That afternoon she wrote several letters, and tore them up. One, however, she retained, and handed it to Low to post at Indian Spring, whither he was going. She called his attention to the superscription being the same as the previous letter, and added, with affected gayety, "But if the answer isn't as prompt, perhaps it will be pleasanter than the last." Her quick feminine eye noticed a little excitement in his manner and a more studious attention to his dress. Only a few days before she would not have allowed this to pass without some mischievous allusion to his mysterious sweetheart; it troubled her greatly now to find that she could not bring herself to this household pleasantry, and that her lip trembled and her eye grew moist as he parted from her.

The afternoon passed slowly; he had said he might not return to supper until late, nevertheless a strange restlessness took possession of her as the day wore on. She put aside her work, the darning of his stockings, and rambled aimlessly through the woods. She had wandered she knew not how far, when she was suddenly seized with the same vague sense of a foreign presence which she had felt before. Could it be Curson again, with a word of warning? No! she knew it was not he; so subtle had her sense become that she even fancied that she detected in the invisible aura projected by the unknown no significance or relation to herself or Low, and felt no fear. Nevertheless she deemed it wisest to seek the protection of her sylvan bower, and hurried swiftly thither.

But not so quickly nor directly that she did not once or twice pause in her flight to examine the newcomer from behind a friendly trunk. He was a stranger, a young fellow with a brown mustache, wearing heavy Mexican spurs in his riding-boots, whose tinkling he apparently did not care to conceal. He had perceived her, and was evidently pursuing her, but so awkwardly and timidly that she eluded him with ease. When she had reached the security of the hollow tree and had pulled the curtain of bark before the narrow opening, with her eye to the interstices, she waited his coming. He arrived breathlessly in the open space before the tree where the bear once lay; the dazed, bewildered, and half awed expression of his face, as he glanced around him and through the openings of the forest aisles, brought a faint smile to her saddened face. At last he called in a half embarrassed voice:

"Miss Nellie!"

The smile faded from Teresa's cheek. Who was "Miss Nellie"? She pressed her ear to the opening. "Miss Wynn!" the voice again called, but was lost in the echoless woods. Devoured with a new and gratuitous curiosity, in another moment Teresa felt she would have disclosed herself at any risk, but the stranger rose and began to retrace his steps. Long after his tinkling spurs were lost in the distance, Teresa remained like a statue, staring at the place where he had stood. Then she suddenly turned like a mad woman, glanced down at the gown she was wearing, tore it from her back as if it had been a polluted garment, and stamped upon it in a convulsion of rage. And then, with her beautiful bare arms clasped together over her head, she threw herself upon her couch in a tempest of tears.

CHAPTER VI.

When Miss Nellie reached the first mining extension of Indian Spring, which surrounded it like a fosse, she descended for one instant into one of its trenches, opened her parasol, removed her duster, hid it under a bowlder, and with a few shivers and cat-like strokes of her soft hands not only obliterated all material traces of the stolen cream of Carquinez Woods, but assumed a feline demureness quite inconsistent with any moral dereliction. Unfortunately, she forgot to remove at the same time a certain ring from her third finger, which she had put on with her duster and had worn at no other time. With this slight exception, the benignant fate which always protected that young person brought her in contact with the Burnham girls at one end of the main street as the returning coach to Excelsior entered the other, and enabled her to take leave of them before the coach office with a certain ostentation of parting which struck Mr. Jack Brace, who was lingering at the doorway, into a state of utter bewilderment.

Here was Miss Nellie Wynn, the belle of Excelsior, calm, quiet, self-possessed, her chaste cambric skirts and dainty shoes as fresh as when she had left her father's house; but where was the woman of the brown duster, and where the yellow-dressed apparition of the woods? He was feebly repeating to himself his mental adjuration of a few hours before when he caught her eye, and was taken with a blush and a fit of coughing. Could he have been such an egregious fool, and was it not plainly written on his embarrassed face for her to read?

"Are we going down together?" asked Miss Nellie, with an exceptionally gracious smile.

There was neither affectation nor coquetry in this advance. The girl had no idea of Brace's suspicion of her, nor did any uneasy desire to placate or deceive a possible rival of Low's prompt her graciousness. She simply wished to shake off in this encounter the already stale excitement of the past two hours, as she had shaken the dust of the woods from her clothes. It was characteristic of her irresponsible nature and transient susceptibilities that she actually enjoyed the relief of change; more than that, I fear, she looked upon this infidelity to a past dubious pleasure as a moral principle. A mild, open flirtation with a recognized man like Brace, after her secret passionate tryst with a nameless nomad like Low, was an ethical equipoise that seemed proper to one of her religious education.

Brace was only too happy to profit by Miss Nellie's condescension; he at once secured the seat by her side, and spent the four hours and a half of their return journey to Excelsior in blissful but timid communion with her. If he did not dare to confess his past suspicions, he was equally afraid to venture upon the boldness he had premeditated a few hours before. He was therefore obliged to take a middle course of slightly egotistical narration of his own personal adventures, with which he beguiled the young girl's ear. This he only departed from once, to describe to her a valuable grizzly bearskin which he had seen that day for sale at Indian Spring, with a view to divining her possible acceptance of it for a "buggy robe;" and once to comment upon a ring which she had inadvertently disclosed in pulling off her glove.

"It's only an old family keepsake," she added, with easy mendacity; and affecting to recognize in Mr. Brace's curiosity a not unnatural excuse for toying with her charming fingers, she hid them in chaste and virginal seclusion in her lap, until she could recover the ring and resume her glove.

A week passed, a week of peculiar and desiccating heat for even those dry Sierra table-lands. The long days were filled with impalpable dust and acrid haze suspended in the motionless air; the nights were breathless and dewless; the cold wind which usually swept down from the snow line was laid to sleep over a dark monotonous level, whose horizon was pricked with the eating fires of burning forest crests. The lagging coach of Indian Spring drove up at Excelsior, and precipitated its passengers with an accompanying cloud of dust before the Excelsior Hotel. As they emerged from the coach, Mr. Brace, standing in the doorway, closely scanned their begrimed and almost unrecognizable faces. They were the usual type of travelers: a single professional man in dusty black, a few traders in tweeds and flannels, a sprinkling of miners in red and gray shirts, a Chinaman, a negro, and a Mexican packer or muleteer. This latter for a moment mingled with the crowd in the bar-room, and even penetrated the corridor and dining-room of the hotel, as if impelled by a certain semi-civilized curiosity, and then strolled with a lazy, dragging step, half impeded by the enormous leather leggings, chains, and spurs, peculiar to his class, down the main street. The darkness was gathering, but the muleteer indulged in the same childish scrutiny of the dimly lighted shops, magazines, and saloons, and even of the occasional groups of citizens at the street corners. Apparently young, as far as the outlines of his figure could be seen, he seemed to show even more than the usual concern of masculine Excelsior in the charms of womankind. The few female figures about at that hour, or visible at window or veranda, received his marked attention; he respectfully followed the two auburn-haired daughters of Deacon Johnson on their way to choir meeting to the door of the church. Not content with that act of discreet gallantry, after they had entered he managed to slip in unperceived behind them.

The memorial of the Excelsior gamblers' generosity was a modern building, large and pretentious for even Mr. Wynn's popularity, and had been good-humoredly known, in the characteristic language of the generous donors, as one of the "biggest religious bluffs" on record. Its groined rafters, which were so new and spicy that they still suggested their native forest aisles, seldom covered more than a hundred devotees, and in the rambling choir, with its bare space for the future organ, the few choristers, gathered round a small harmonium, were lost in the deepening shadow of that summer evening. The muleteer remained hidden in the obscurity of the vestibule. After a few moments' desultory conversation, in which it appeared that the unexpected absence of Miss Nellie Wynn, their leader, would prevent their practicing, the choristers withdrew. The stranger, who had listened eagerly, drew back in the darkness as they passed out, and remained for a few moments a vague and motionless figure in the silent church. Then coming cautiously to the window, the flapping broad-brimmed hat was put aside, and the faint light of the dying day shone in the black eyes of Teresa! Despite her face, darkened with dye and disfigured with dust, the matted hair piled and twisted around her head, the strange dress and boyish figure, one swift glance from under her raised lashes betrayed her identity.

She turned aside mechanically into the first pew, picked up and opened a hymn-book. Her eyes became riveted on a name written on the title-page, "Nellie Wynn." Her name, and her book. The instinct that had guided her here was right; the slight gossip of her fellow-passengers was right; this was the clergyman's daughter, whose praise filled all mouths. This was the unknown girl the stranger was seeking, but who in her turn perhaps had been seeking Low, the girl who absorbed his fancy, the secret of his absences, his preoccupation, his coldness! This was the girl whom to see, perhaps in his arms, she was now periling her liberty and her life unknown to him! A slight odor, some faint perfume of its owner, came from the book; it was the same she had noticed in the dress Low had given her. She flung the volume to the ground, and, throwing her arms over the back of the pew before her, buried her face in her hands.

In that light and attitude she might have seemed some rapt acolyte abandoned to self-communion. But whatever yearning her soul might have had for higher sympathy or deeper consolation, I fear that the spiritual Tabernacle of Excelsior and the Reverend Mr. Wynn did not meet that requirement. She only felt the dry, oven-like heat of that vast shell, empty of sentiment and beauty, hollow in its pretense and dreary in its desolation. She only saw in it a chief altar for the glorification of this girl who had absorbed even the pure worship of her companion, and converted and degraded his sublime paganism to her petty creed. With a woman's withering contempt for her own art displayed in another woman, she thought how she herself could have touched him with the peace that the majesty of their woodland aisles, so unlike this pillared sham, had taught her own passionate heart, had she but dared. Mingling with this imperfect theology, she felt she could have proved to him also that a brunette and a woman of her experience was better than an immature blonde. She began to loathe herself for coming hither, and dreaded to meet his face. Here a sudden thought struck her. What if he had not come here? What if she had been mistaken? What if her rash interpretation of his absence from the wood that night was simple madness? What if he should return, if he had already returned? She rose to her feet, whitening yet joyful with the thought. She would return at once; what was the girl to her now? Yet there was time to satisfy herself if he were at her house. She had been told where it was; she could find it in the dark; an open door or window would betray some sign or sound of the occupants. She rose, replaced her hat over her eyes, knotted her flaunting scarf around her throat, groped her way to the door, and glided into the outer darkness.

CHAPTER VII.

It was quite dark when Mr. Jack Brace stopped before Father Wynn's open door. The windows were also invitingly open to the wayfarer, as were the pastoral counsels of Father Wynn, delivered to some favored guest within, in a tone of voice loud enough for a pulpit. Jack Brace paused. The visitor was the convalescent sheriff, Jim Dunn, who had publicly commemorated his recovery by making his first call upon the father of his inamorata. The Reverend Mr. Wynn had been expatiating upon the unremitting heat as a possible precursor of forest fires, and exhibiting some catholic knowledge of the designs of a Deity in that regard, and what should be the policy of the Legislature, when Mr. Brace concluded to enter. Mr. Wynn and the wounded man, who occupied an arm-chair by the window, were the only occupants of the room. But in spite of the former's ostentatious greeting, Brace could see that his visit was inopportune and unwelcome. The sheriff nodded a quick, impatient recognition, which, had it not been accompanied by an anathema on the heat, might have been taken as a personal insult. Neither spoke of Miss Nellie, although it was patent to Brace that they were momentarily expecting her. All of which went far to strengthen a certain wavering purpose in his mind.

"Ah, ha! strong language, Mr. Dunn," said Father Wynn, referring to the sheriff's adjuration, "but 'out of the fullness of the heart the mouth speaketh.' Job, sir, cursed, we are told, and even expressed himself in vigorous Hebrew regarding his birthday. Ha, ha! I'm not opposed to that. When I have often wrestled with the spirit I confess I have sometimes said, 'Damn you.' Yes, sir, 'Damn you.'"

There was something so unutterably vile in the reverend gentleman's utterance and emphasis of this oath that the two men, albeit both easy and facile blasphemers, felt shocked; as the purest of actresses is apt to overdo the rakishness of a gay Lothario, Father Wynn's immaculate conception of an imprecation was something terrible. But he added, "The law ought to interfere with the reckless use of camp-fires in the woods in such weather by packers and prospecters."

"It isn't so much the work of white men," broke in Brace, "as it is of Greasers, Chinamen, and Diggers, especially Diggers. There's that blasted Low, ranges the whole Carquinez Woods as if they were his. I reckon he ain't particular just where he throws his matches.'"

"But he's not a Digger; he's a Cherokee, and only a half-breed at that," interpolated Wynn. "Unless," he added, with the artful suggestion of the betrayed trust of a too credulous Christian, "he deceived me in this as in other things."

In what other things Low had deceived him he did not say; but, to the astonishment of both men, Dunn growled a dissent to Brace's proposition. Either from some secret irritation with that possible rival, or impatience at the prolonged absence of Nellie, he had "had enough of that sort of hog-wash ladled out to him for genuine liquor." As to the Carquinez Woods, he [Dunn] "didn't know why Low hadn't as much right there as if he'd grabbed it under a preemption law and didn't live there." With this hint at certain speculations of Father Wynn in public lands for a homestead, he added that "If they [Brace and Wynn] could bring him along any older American settler than an Indian, they might rake down his [Dunn's] pile." Unprepared for this turn in the conversation, Wynn hastened to explain that he did not refer to the pure aborigine, whose gradual extinction no one regretted more than himself, but to the mongrel, who inherited only the vices of civilization. "There should be a law, sir, against the mingling of races. There are men, sir, who violate the laws of the Most High by living with Indian women, squaw men, sir, as they are called."

Dunn rose with a face livid with weakness and passion. "Who dares say that? They are a damned sight better than sneaking Northern Abolitionists, who married their daughters to buck niggers like" - But a spasm of pain withheld this Parthian shot at the politics of his two companions, and he sank back helplessly in his chair.

An awkward silence ensued. The three men looked at each other in embarrassment and confusion. Dunn felt that he had given way to a gratuitous passion; Wynn had a vague presentiment that he had said something that imperiled his daughter's prospects; and Brace was divided between an angry retort and the secret purpose already alluded to.

"It's all the blasted heat," said Dunn, with a forced smile, pushing away the whiskey which Wynn had ostentatiously placed before him.

"Of course," said Wynn hastily; "only it's a pity Nellie ain't here to give you her smelling-salts. She ought to be back now," he added, no longer mindful of Brace's presence; "the coach is over-due now, though I reckon the heat made Yuba Bill take it easy at the up grade."

"If you mean the coach from Indian Spring," said Brace quietly, "it's in already; but Miss Nellie didn't come on it."

"Maybe she got out at the Crossing," said Wynn cheerfully; "she sometimes does."

"She didn't take the coach at Indian Spring," returned Brace, "because I saw it leave, and passed it on Buckskin ten minutes ago, coming up the hills."

"She's stopped over at Burnham's," said Wynn reflectively. Then, in response to the significant silence of his guests, he added, in a tone of chagrin which his forced heartiness could not disguise, "Well, boys, it's a disappointment all round; but we must take the lesson as it comes. I'll go over to the coach office and see if she's sent any word. Make yourselves at home until I return."

When the door had closed behind him, Brace arose and took his hat as if to go. With his hand on the lock, he turned to his rival, who, half-hidden in the gathering darkness, still seemed unable to comprehend his ill-luck.

"If you're waiting for that bald-headed fraud to come back with the truth about his daughter," said Brace coolly, "you'd better send for your things and take up your lodgings here."

"What do you mean?" said Dunn sternly.

"I mean that she's not at the Burnhams'; I mean that he does or does not know where she is, and that in either case he is not likely to give you information. But I can."

"You can?"

"Yes."

"Then, where is she?"

"In the Carquinez Woods, in the arms of the man you were just defending, Low, the half-breed."

The room had become so dark that from the road nothing could be distinguished. Only the momentary sound of struggling feet was heard.

"Sit down," said Brace's voice, "and don't be a fool. You're too weak, and it ain't a fair fight. Let go your hold. I'm not lying, I wish to God I was!"

There was a silence, and Brace resumed, "We've been rivals, I know. Maybe I thought my chance as good as yours. If what I say ain't truth, we'll stand as we stood before; and if you're on the shoot, I'm your man when you like, where you like, or on sight if you choose. But I can't see another man played upon as I've been played upon, given dead away as I have been. It ain't on the square.

"There," he continued, after a pause, "that's right; now steady. Listen. A week ago that girl went down just like this to Indian Spring. It was given out, like this, that she went to the Burnhams'. I don't mind saying, Dunn, that I went down myself, all on the square, thinking I might get a show to talk to her, just as you might have done, you know, if you had my chance. I didn't come across her anywhere. But two men that I met thought they recognized her in a disguise going into the woods. Not suspecting anything, I went after her; saw her at a distance in the middle of the woods in another dress that I can swear to, and was just coming up to her when she vanished, went like a squirrel up a tree, or down like a gopher in the ground, but vanished."

"Is that all?" said Dunn's voice. "And just because you were a damned fool, or had taken a little too much whiskey, you thought" -

"Steady! That's just what I said to myself," interrupted Brace coolly, "particularly when I saw her that same afternoon in another dress, saying good-by to the Burnhams, as fresh as a rose and as cold as those snow-peaks. Only one thing, she had a ring on her finger she never wore before, and didn't expect me to see."

"What if she did? She might have bought it. I reckon she hasn't to consult you," broke in Dunn's voice sternly.

"She didn't buy it," continued Brace quietly. "Low gave that Jew trader a bearskin in exchange for it, and presented it to her. I found that out two days afterwards. I found out that out of the whole afternoon she spent less than an hour with the Burnhams. I found out that she bought a duster like the disguise the two men saw her in. I found the yellow dress she wore that day hanging up in Low's cabin, the place where I saw her go, the rendezvous where she meets him. Oh, you're listenin', are you? Stop! SIT DOWN!

"I discovered it by accident," continued the voice of Brace when all was again quiet; "it was hidden as only a squirrel or an Injin can hide when they improve upon nature. When I was satisfied that the girl had been in the woods, I was determined to find out where she vanished, and went there again. Prospecting around, I picked up at the foot of one of the biggest trees this yer old memorandum-book, with grasses and herbs stuck in it. I remembered that I'd heard old Wynn say that Low, like the damned Digger that he was, collected these herbs; only he pretended it was for science. I reckoned the book was his and that he mightn't be far away. I lay low and waited. Bimeby I saw a lizard running down the root. When he got sight of me he stopped."

"Damn the lizard! What's that got to do with where she is now?"

"Everything. That lizard had a piece of sugar in his mouth. Where did it come from? I made him drop it, and calculated he'd go back for more. He did. He scooted up that tree and slipped in under some hanging strips of bark. I shoved 'em aside, and found an opening to the hollow where they do their housekeeping."

"But you didn't see her there, and how do you know she is there now?"

"I determined to make it sure. When she left to-day, I started an hour ahead of her, and hid myself at the edge of the woods. An hour after the coach arrived at Indian Spring, she came there in a brown duster and was joined by him. I'd have followed them, but the damned hound has the ears of a squirrel, and though I was five hundred yards from him he was on his guard."

"Guard be blessed! Wasn't you armed? Why didn't you go for him?" said Dunn, furiously.

"I reckoned I'd leave that for you," said Brace coolly. "If he'd killed me, and if he'd even covered me with his rifle, he'd be sure to let daylight through me at double the distance. I shouldn't have been any better off, nor you either. If I'd killed him, it would have been your duty as sheriff to put me in jail; and I reckon it wouldn't have broken your heart, Jim Dunn, to have got rid of two rivals instead of one. Hullo! Where are you going?"

"Going?" said Dunn hoarsely. "Going to the Carquinez Woods, by God! to kill him before her. I'll risk it, if you daren't. Let me succeed, and you can hang me and take the girl yourself."

"Sit down, sit down. Don't be a fool, Jim Dunn! You wouldn't keep the saddle a hundred yards. Did I say I wouldn't help you? No. If you're willing, we'll run the risk together, but it must be in my way. Hear me. I'll drive you down there in a buggy before daylight, and we'll surprise them in the cabin or as they leave the wood. But you must come as if to arrest him for some offense, say, as an escaped Digger from the Reservation, a dangerous tramp, a destroyer of public property in the forests, a suspected road agent, or anything to give you the right to hunt him. The exposure of him and Nellie, don't you see, must be accidental. If he resists, kill him on the spot, and nobody'll blame you; if he goes peaceably with you, and you once get him in Excelsior jail, when the story gets out that he's taken the belle of Excelsior for his squaw, if you'd the angels for your posse you couldn't keep the boys from hanging him to the first tree. What's that?"

He walked to the window, and looked out cautiously.

"If it was the old man coming back and listening," he said, after a pause, "it can't be helped. He'll hear it soon enough, if he don't suspect something already."

"Look yer, Brace," broke in Dunn hoarsely. "Damned if I understand you or you me. That dog Low has got to answer to me, not to the law! I'll take my risk of killing him, on sight and on the square. I don't reckon to handicap myself with a warrant, and I am not going to draw him out with a lie. You hear me? That's me all the time!"

"Then you calkilate to go down thar," said Brace contemptuously, "yell out for him and Nellie, and let him line you on a rest from the first tree as if you were a grizzly."

There was a pause. "What's that you were saying just now about a bearskin he sold?" asked Dunn slowly, as if reflecting.

"He exchanged a bearskin," replied Brace, "with a single hole right over the heart. He's a dead shot, I tell you."

"Damn his shooting," said Dunn. "I'm not thinking of that. How long ago did he bring in that bearskin?"

"About two weeks, I reckon. Why?"

"Nothing! Look yer, Brace, you mean well, thar's my hand. I'll go down with you there, but not as the sheriff. I'm going there as Jim Dunn, and you can come along as a white man, to see things fixed on the square. Come!"

Brace hesitated. "You'll think better of my plan before you get there; but I've said I'd stand by you, and I will Come, then. There's no time to lose."

They passed out into the darkness together.

"What are you waiting for?" said Dunn impatiently, as Brace, who was supporting him by the arm, suddenly halted at the corner of the house.

"Someone was listening, did you not see him? Was it the old man?" asked Brace hurriedly.

"Blast the old man! It was only one of them Mexican packers chock-full of whiskey, and trying to hold up the house. What are you thinking of? We shall be late."

In spite of his weakness, the wounded man hurriedly urged Brace forward, until they reached the latter's lodgings. To his surprise, the horse and buggy were already before the door.

"Then you reckoned to go, anyway?" said Dunn, with a searching look at his companion.

"I calkilated somebody would go," returned Brace, evasively, patting the impatient Buckskin; "but come in and take a drink before we leave."

Dunn started out of a momentary abstraction, put his hand on his hip, and mechanically entered the house. They had scarcely raised the glasses to their lips when a sudden rattle of wheels was heard in the street. Brace set down his glass and ran to the window.

"It's the mare bolted," he said, with an oath. "We've kept her too long standing. Follow me;" and he dashed down the staircase into the street. Dunn followed with difficulty; when he reached the door he was confronted by his breathless companion. "She's gone off on a run, and I'll swear there was a man in the buggy!" He stopped and examined the halter-strap, still fastened to the fence. "Cut! by God!"

Dunn turned pale with passion. "Who's got another horse and buggy?" he demanded.

"The new blacksmith in Main Street; but we won't get it by borrowing," said Brace.

"How, then?" asked Dunn savagely.

"Seize it, as the sheriff of Yuba and his deputy, pursuing a confederate of the Injin Low, THE HORSE THIEF!"

CHAPTER VIII.

The brief hour of darkness that preceded the dawn was that night intensified by a dense smoke, which, after blotting out horizon and sky, dropped a thick veil on the highroad and the silent streets of Indian Spring. As the buggy containing Sheriff Dunn and Brace dashed through the obscurity, Brace suddenly turned to his companion.

"Someone ahead!"

The two men bent forward over the dashboard. Above the steady plunging of their own horse-hoofs they could hear the quicker irregular beat of other hoofs in the darkness before them.

"It's that horse thief!" said Dunn, in a savage whisper. "Bear to the right, and hand me the whip."

A dozen cuts of the cruel lash, and their maddened horse, bounding at each stroke, broke into a wild canter. The frail vehicle swayed from side to side at each spring of the elastic shafts. Steadying himself by one hand on the low rail, Dunn drew his revolver with the other. "Sing out to him to pull up, or we'll fire. My voice is clean gone," he added, in a husky whisper.

They were so near that they could distinguish the bulk of a vehicle careering from side to side in the blackness ahead. Dunn deliberately raised his weapon. "Sing out!" he repeated impatiently. But Brace, who was still keeping in the shadow, suddenly grasped his companion's arm.

"Hush! It's not Buckskin," he whispered hurriedly.

"Are you sure?"

"Don't you see we're gaining on him?" replied the other contemptuously. Dunn grasped his companion's hand and pressed it silently. Even in that supreme moment this horseman's tribute to the fugitive Buckskin forestalled all baser considerations of pursuit and capture!

In twenty seconds they were abreast of the stranger, crowding his horse and buggy nearly into the ditch; Brace keenly watchful, Dunn suppressed and pale. In half a minute they were leading him a length; and when their horse again settled down to his steady work, the stranger was already lost in the circling dust that followed them. But the victors seemed disappointed. The obscurity had completely hidden all but the vague outlines of the mysterious driver.

"He's not our game, any way," whispered Dunn. "Drive on."

"But if it was some friend of his," suggested Brace uneasily, "what would you do?"

"What I said I'd do," responded Dunn savagely. "I don't want five minutes to do it in, either; we'll be half an hour ahead of that damned fool, whoever he is. Look here; all you've got to do is to put me in the trail to that cabin. Stand back of me, out of gun-shot, alone, if you like, as my deputy, or with any number you can pick up as my posse. If he gets by me as Nellie's lover, you may shoot him or take him as a horse thief, if you like."

"Then you won't shoot him on sight?"

"Not till I've had a word with him."

"But" -

"I've chirped," said the sheriff gravely. "Drive on."

For a few moments only the plunging hoofs and rattling wheels were heard. A dull, lurid glow began to define the horizon. They were silent until an abatement of the smoke, the vanishing of the gloomy horizon line, and a certain impenetrability in the darkness ahead showed them they were nearing the Carquinez Woods. But they were surprised on entering them to find the dim aisles alight with a faint mystic Aurora. The tops of the towering spires above them had caught the gleam of the distant forest fires, and reflected it as from a gilded dome.

"It would be hot work if the Carquinez Woods should conclude to take a hand in this yer little game that's going on over on the Divide yonder," said Brace, securing his horse and glancing at the spires overhead. "I reckon I'd rather take a back seat at Injin Spring when the show commences."

Dunn did not reply, but, buttoning his coat, placed one hand on his companion's shoulder, and sullenly bade him "lead the way." Advancing slowly and with difficulty, the desperate man might have been taken for a peaceful invalid returning from an early morning stroll. His right hand was buried thoughtfully in the side-pocket of his coat. Only Brace knew that it rested on the handle of his pistol.

From time to time the latter stopped and consulted the faint trail with a minuteness that showed recent careful study. Suddenly he paused. "I made a blaze hereabouts to show where to leave the trail. There it is," he added, pointing to a slight notch cut in the trunk of an adjoining tree.

"But we've just passed one," said Dunn, "if that's what you are looking after, a hundred yards back."

Brace uttered an oath, and ran back in the direction signified by his companion. Presently he returned with a smile of triumph.

"They've suspected something. It's a clever trick, but it won't hold water. That blaze which was done to muddle you was cut with an axe; this which I made was done with a bowie-knife. It's the real one. We're not far off now. Come on."

They proceeded cautiously, at right angles with the "blazed" tree, for ten minutes more. The heat was oppressive; drops of perspiration rolled from the forehead of the sheriff, and at times, when he attempted to steady his uncertain limbs, his hands shrank from the heated, blistering bark he touched with ungloved palms.

"Here we are," said Brace, pausing at last. "Do you see that biggest tree, with the root stretching out half-way across to the opposite one?"

"No; it's further to the right and abreast of the dead brush," interrupted Dunn quickly, with a sudden revelation that this was the spot where he had found the dead bear in the night Teresa escaped.

"That's so," responded Brace, in astonishment.

"And the opening is on the other side, opposite the dead brush," said Dunn.

"Then you know it?" said Brace suspiciously.

"I reckon!" responded Dunn, grimly. "That's enough! Fall back!"

To the surprise of his companion, he lifted his head erect, and with a strong, firm step walked directly to the tree. Reaching it, he planted himself squarely before the opening.

"Halloo!" he said.

There was no reply. A squirrel scampered away close to his feet. Brace, far in the distance, after an ineffectual attempt to distinguish his companion through the intervening trunks, took off his coat, leaned against a tree, and lit a cigar.

"Come out of that cabin!" continued Dunn, in a clear, resonant voice. "Come out before I drag you out!"

"All right, 'Captain Scott.' Don't shoot, and I'll come down," said a voice as clear and as high as his own. The hanging strips of bark were dashed aside, and a woman leaped lightly to the ground.

Dunn staggered back. "Teresa! by the Eternal!"

It was Teresa! the old Teresa! Teresa, a hundred times more vicious, reckless, hysterical, extravagant, and outrageous than before, Teresa, staring with tooth and eye, sunburnt and embrowned, her hair hanging down her shoulders, and her shawl drawn tightly around her neck.

"Teresa it is! the same old gal! Here we are again! Return of the favorite in her original character! For two weeks only! Houp là! Tshk!" and, catching her yellow skirt with her fingers, she pirouetted before the astounded man, and ended in a pose. Recovering himself with an effort, Dunn dashed forward and seized her by the wrist.

"Answer me, woman! Is that Low's cabin?"

"It is."

"Who occupies it besides?"

"I do."

"And who else?"

"Well," drawled Teresa slowly, with an extravagant affectation of modesty, "nobody else but us, I reckon. Two's company, you know, and three's none."

"Stop! Will you swear that there isn't a young girl, his, his sweetheart, concealed there with you?"

The fire in Teresa's eye was genuine as she answered steadily, "Well, it ain't my style to put up with that sort of thing; at least, it wasn't over at Yolo, and you know it, Jim Dunn, or I wouldn't be here."

"Yes, yes," said Dunn hurriedly. "But I'm a damned fool, or worse, the fool of a fool. Tell me, Teresa, is this man Low your lover?"

Teresa lowered her eyes as if in maidenly confusion.

"Well, if I'd known that you had any feeling of your own about it, if you'd spoken sooner" -

"Answer me, you devil!"

"He is."

"And he has been with you here, yesterday, tonight?"

"He has."

"Enough." He laughed a weak, foolish laugh, and turning pale, suddenly lapsed against a tree. He would have fallen, but with a quick instinct Teresa sprang to his side, and supported him gently to a root. The action over they both looked astounded.

"I reckon that wasn't much like either you or me," said Dunn slowly, "was it? But if you'd let me drop then you'd have stretched out the biggest fool in the Sierras." He paused, and looked at her curiously. "What's come over you; blessed if I seem to know you now."

She was very pale again, and quiet; that was all.

"Teresa! damn it, look here! When I was laid up yonder in Excelsior I said I wanted to get well for only two things. One was to hunt you down, the other to marry Nellie Wynn. When I came here I thought that last thing could never be. I came here expecting to find her here with Low, and kill him, perhaps kill her too. I never even thought of you; not once. You might have risen up before me, between me and him, and I'd have passed you by. And now that I find it's all a mistake, and it was you, not her, I was looking for, why" -

"Why," she interrupted bitterly, "you'll just take me, of course, to save your time and earn your salary. I'm ready."

"But I'm not, just yet," he said faintly. "Help me up." She mechanically assisted him to his feet.

"Now stand where you are," he added, "and don't move beyond this tree till I return."

He straightened himself with an effort, clenched his fists until the nails were nearly buried in his palms, and strode with a firm, steady step in the direction he had come. In a few moments he returned and stood before her.

"I've sent away my deputy, the man who brought me here, the fool who thought you were Nellie. He knows now he made a mistake. But who it was he mistook for Nellie he does not know, nor shall ever know, nor shall any living being know, other than myself. And when I leave the wood to-day I shall know it no longer. You are safe here as far as I am concerned, but I cannot screen you from others prying. Let Low take you away from here as soon as he can."

"Let him take me away? Ah, yes. For what?"

"To save you," said Dunn. "Look here, Teresa! Without knowing it, you lifted me out of hell just now; and because of the wrong I might have done her, for her sake, I spare you and shirk my duty."

"For her sake!" gasped the woman, "for her sake! Oh, yes! Go on."

"Well," said Dunn gloomily, "I reckon perhaps you'd as lieve left me in hell, for all the love you bear me. And maybe you've grudge enough agin me still to wish I'd found her and him together."

"You think so?" she said, turning her head away.

"There, damn it! I didn't mean to make you cry. Maybe you wouldn't, then. Only tell that fellow to take you out of this, and not run away the next time he sees a man coming."

"He didn't run," said Teresa, with flashing eyes. "I, I, I sent him away," she stammered. Then, suddenly turning with fury upon him, she broke out, "Run! Run from you! Ha, ha! You said just now I'd a grudge against you. Well, listen, Jim Dunn. I'd only to bring you in range of that young man's rifle, and you'd have dropped in your tracks like" -

"Like that bar, the other night," said Dunn, with a short laugh. "So that was your little game?" He checked his laugh suddenly, a cloud passed over his face. "Look here, Teresa," he said, with an assumption of carelessness that was as transparent as it was utterly incompatible with his frank, open selfishness. "What became of that bar? The skin, eh? That was worth something?"

"Yes," said Teresa quietly. "Low exchanged it and got a ring for me from that trader Isaacs. It was worth more, you bet. And the ring didn't fit either" -

"Yes," interrupted Dunn, with an almost childish eagerness.

"And I made him take it back, and get the value in money. I hear that Isaacs sold it again and made another profit; but that's like those traders." The disingenuous candor of Teresa's manner was in exquisite contrast to Dunn. He rose and grasped her hand so heartily she was forced to turn her eyes away.

"Good-by!" he said.

"You look tired," she murmured, with a sudden gentleness that surprised him; "let me go with you a part of the way."

"It isn't safe for you just now," he said, thinking of the possible consequences of the alarm Brace had raised.

"Not the way you came," she replied; "but one known only to myself."

He hesitated only a moment. "All right, then," he said finally; "let us go at once. It's suffocating here, and I seem to feel this dead bark crinkle under my feet."

She cast a rapid glance around her, and then seemed to sound with her eyes the far-off depths of the aisles, beginning to grow pale with the advancing day, but still holding a strange quiver of heat in the air. When she had finished her half abstracted scrutiny of the distance, she cast one backward glance at her own cabin and stopped.

"Will you wait a moment for me?" she asked gently.

"Yes, but no tricks, Teresa! It isn't worth the time."

She looked him squarely in the eyes without a word.

"Enough," he said; "go!"

She was absent for some moments. He was beginning to become uneasy, when she made her appearance again, clad in her old faded black dress. Her face was very pale, and her eyes were swollen, but she placed his hand on her shoulder, and bidding him not to fear to lean upon her, for she was quite strong, led the way.

"You look more like yourself now, and yet, blast it all! you don't either," said Dunn, looking down upon her. "You've changed in some way. What is it? Is it on account of that Injin? Couldn't you have found a white man in his place?"

"I reckon he's neither worse nor better for that," she replied bitterly; "and perhaps he wasn't as particular in his taste as a white man might have been. But," she added, with a sudden spasm of her old rage, "it's a lie; he's not an Indian, no more than I am. Not unless being born of a mother who scarcely knew him, of a father who never even saw him, and being brought up among white men and wild beasts less cruel than they were, could make him one!"

Dunn looked at her in surprise not unmixed with admiration. "If Nellie," he thought, "could but love me like that!" But he only said:

"For all that, he's an Injin. Why, look at his name. It ain't Low. It's L'Eau Dormante, Sleeping Water, an Injin name."

"And what does that prove?" returned Teresa. "Only that Indians clap a nickname on any stranger, white or red, who may camp with them. Why, even his own father, a white man, the wretch who begot him and abandoned him, he had an Indian name, Loup Noir."

"What name did you say?"

"Le Loup Noir, the Black Wolf. I suppose you'd call him an Indian, too? Eh? What's the matter? We're walking too fast. Stop a moment and rest. There, there, lean on me!"

She was none too soon; for, after holding him upright a moment, his limbs failed, and stooping gently she was obliged to support him half reclining against a tree.

"It's the heat!" he said. "Give me some whiskey from my flask. Never mind the water," he added faintly, with a forced laugh, after he had taken a draught at the strong spirit. "Tell me more about the other water, the Sleeping Water, you know. How do you know all this about him and his father?"

"Partly from him and partly from Curson, who wrote to me about him," she answered, with some hesitation.

But Dunn did not seem to notice this incongruity of correspondence with a former lover. "And he told you?"

"Yes; and I saw the name on an old memorandum-book he has, which he says belonged to his father. It's full of old accounts of some trading post on the frontier. It's been missing for a day or two, but it will turn up. But I can swear I saw it."

Dunn attempted to rise to his feet. "Put your hand in my pocket," he said in a hurried whisper. "No, there! bring out a book. There, I haven't looked at it yet. Is that it?" he added, handing her the book Brace had given him a few hours before.

"Yes," said Teresa, in surprise. "Where did you find it?"

"Never mind! Now let me see it, quick. Open it, for my sight is failing. There, thank you, that's all!"

"Take more whiskey," said Teresa, with a strange anxiety creeping over her. "You are faint again."

"Wait! Listen, Teresa, lower, put your ear lower. Listen! I came near killing that chap Low to-day. Wouldn't it have been ridiculous?"

He tried to smile, but his head fell back. He had fainted.

CHAPTER IX.

For the first time in her life Teresa lost her presence of mind in an emergency. She could only sit staring at the helpless man, scarcely conscious of his condition, her mind filled with a sudden prophetic intuition of the significance of his last words. In the light of that new revelation she looked into his pale, haggard face for some resemblance to Low, but in vain. Yet her swift feminine instinct met the objection. "It's the mother's blood that would show," she murmured, "not this man's."

Recovering herself, she began to chafe his hands and temples, and moistened his lips with the spirit. When his respiration returned with a faint color to his cheeks, she pressed his hand eagerly and leaned over him.

"Are you sure?" she asked.

"Of what?" he whispered faintly.

"That Low is really your son?"

"Who said so?" he asked, opening his round eyes upon her.

"You did yourself, a moment ago," she said quickly. "Don't you remember?"

"Did I?"

"You did. Is it so?"

He smiled faintly. "I reckon."

She held her breath in expectation. But only the ludicrousness of the discovery seemed paramount to his weakened faculties. "Isn't it just about the ridiculousest thing all round?" he said, with a feeble chuckle. "First you nearly kill me before you know I am Low's father; then I'm just spoilin' to kill him before I know he's my son; then that god-forsaken fool Jack Brace mistakes you for Nellie, and Nellie for you. Ain't it just the biggest thing for the boys to get hold of? But we must keep it dark until after I marry Nellie, don't you see? Then we'll have a good time all round, and I'll stand the drinks. Think of it, Teresha! You don'no me, I do'no you, nobody knowsh anybody elsh. I try kill Lo'. Lo' wants kill Nellie. No thath no ri'," but the potent liquor, overtaking his exhausted senses, thickened, impeded, and at last stopped his speech. His head slipped to her shoulder, and he became once more unconscious.

Teresa breathed again. In that brief moment she had abandoned herself to a wild inspiration of hope which she could scarcely define. Not that it was entirely a wild inspiration; she tried to reason calmly. What if she revealed the truth to him? What if she told the wretched man before her that she had deceived him; that she had overheard his conversation with Brace; that she had stolen Brace's horse to bring Low warning; that, failing to find Low in his accustomed haunts, or at the camp-fire, she had left a note for him pinned to the herbarium, imploring him to fly with his companion from the danger that was coming; and that, remaining on watch, she had seen them both, Brace and Dunn, approaching, and had prepared to meet them at the cabin? Would this miserable and maddened man understand her self-abnegation? Would he forgive Low and Nellie? she did not ask for herself. Or would the revelation turn his brain, if it did not kill him outright? She looked at the sunken orbits of his eyes and hectic on his cheek, and shuddered.

Why was this added to the agony she already suffered? She had been willing to stand between them with her life, her liberty and even, the hot blood dyed her cheek at the thought, with the added shame of being thought the cast-off mistress of that man's son. Yet all this she had taken upon herself in expiation of something, she knew not clearly what; no, for nothing, only for him. And yet this very situation offered her that gleam of hope which had thrilled her; a hope so wild in its improbability, so degrading in its possibility, that at first she knew not whether despair was not preferable to its shame. And yet was it unreasonable? She was no longer passionate; she would be calm and think it out fairly.

She would go to Low at once. She would find him somewhere, and even if with that girl, what mattered? and she would tell him all. When he knew that the life and death of his father lay in the scale, would he let his brief, foolish passion for Nellie stand in the way? Even if he were not influenced by filial affection or mere compassion, would his pride let him stoop to a rivalry with the man who had deserted his youth? Could he take Dunn's promised bride, who must have coquetted with him to have brought him to this miserable plight? Was this like the calm, proud young god she knew? Yet she had an uneasy instinct that calm, proud young gods and goddesses did things like this, and felt the weakness of her reasoning flush her own conscious cheek.

"Teresa!"

She started. Dunn was awake, and was gazing at her curiously.

"I was reckoning it was the only square thing for Low to stop this promiscuous picnicking here and marry you out and out."

"Marry me!" said Teresa in a voice that, with all her efforts, she could not make cynical.

"Yes," he repeated, "after I've married Nellie; tote you down to San Angeles, and there take my name like a man, and give it to you. Nobody'll ask after Teresa, sure, you bet your life. And if they do, and he can't stop their jaw, just you call on the old man. It's mighty queer, ain't it, Teresa, to think of you being my daughter-in-law?"

It seemed here as if he was about to lapse again into unconsciousness over the purely ludicrous aspect of the subject, but he haply recovered his seriousness. "He'll have as much money from me as he wants to go into business with. What's his line of business, Teresa?" asked this prospective father-in-law, in a large, liberal way.

"He is a botanist!" said Teresa, with a sudden childish animation that seemed to keep up the grim humor of the paternal suggestion; "and oh, he is too poor to buy books! I sent for one or two for him myself, the other day", she hesitated, "it was all the money I had, but it wasn't enough for him to go on with his studies."

Dunn looked at her sparkling eyes and glowing cheeks, and became thoughtful. "Curson must have been a damned fool," he said finally.

Teresa remained silent. She was beginning to be impatient and uneasy, fearing some mischance that might delay her dreaded yet longed-for meeting with Low. Yet she could not leave this sick and exhausted man, his father, now bound to her by more than mere humanity.

"Couldn't you manage," she said gently, "to lean on me a few steps further, until I could bring you to a cooler spot and nearer assistance?"

He nodded. She lifted him almost like a child to his feet. A spasm of pain passed over his face. "How far is it?" he asked.

"Not more than ten minutes," she replied.

"I can make a spurt for that time," he said coolly, and began to walk slowly but steadily on. Only his face, which was white and set, and the convulsive grip of his hand on her arm, betrayed the effort. At the end of ten minutes she stopped. They stood before the splintered, lightning-scarred shaft in the opening of the woods, where Low had built her first camp-fire. She carefully picked up the herbarium, but her quick eye had already detected in the distance, before she had allowed Dunn to enter the opening with her, that her note was gone. Low had been there before them; he had been warned, as his absence from the cabin showed; he would not return there. They were free from interruption, but where had he gone?

The sick man drew a long breath of relief as she seated him in the clover-grown hollow where she had slept the second night of her stay. "It's cooler than those cursed woods," he said. "I suppose it's because it's a little like a grave. What are you going to do now?" he added, as she brought a cup of water and placed it at his side.

"I am going to leave you here for a little while," she said cheerfully, but with a pale face and nervous hands. "I'm going to leave you while I seek Low."

The sick man raised his head. "I'm good for a spurt, Teresa, like that I've just got through, but I don't think I'm up to a family party. Couldn't you issue cards later on?"

"You don't understand," she said. "I'm going to get Low to send some one of your friends to you here. I don't think he'll begrudge leaving her a moment for that," she added to herself bitterly.

"What's that you're saying?" he queried, with the nervous quickness of an invalid.

"Nothing, but that I'm going now." She turned her face aside to hide her moistened eyes. "Wish me good luck, won't you?" she asked, half sadly, half pettishly.

"Come here!"

She came and bent over him. He suddenly raised his hands, and, drawing her face down to his own, kissed her forehead.

"Give that to him," he whispered, "from me."

She turned and fled, happily for her sentiment, not hearing the feeble laugh that followed, as Dunn, in sheer imbecility, again referred to the extravagant ludicrousness of the situation. "It is about the biggest thing in the way of a sell all round," he repeated, lying on his back, confidentially to the speck of smoke-obscured sky above him. He pictured himself repeating it, not to Nellie, her severe propriety might at last overlook the fact, but would not tolerate the joke, but to her father! It would be just one of those characteristic Californian jokes Father Wynn would admire.

To his exhaustion fever presently succeeded, and he began to grow restless. The heat too seemed to invade his retreat, and from time to time the little patch of blue sky was totally obscured by clouds of smoke. He amused himself with watching a lizard who was investigating a folded piece of paper, whose elasticity gave the little creature lively apprehensions of its vitality. At last he could stand the stillness of his retreat and his supine position no longer, and rolled himself out of the bed of leaves that Teresa had so carefully prepared for him. He rose to his feet stiff and sore, and, supporting himself by the nearest tree, moved a few steps from the dead ashes of the camp-fire. The movement frightened the lizard, who abandoned the paper and fled. With a satirical recollection of Brace and his "ridiculous" discovery through the medium of this animal, he stooped and picked up the paper. "Like as not," he said to himself, with grim irony, "these yer lizards are in the discovery business. P'r'aps this may lead to another mystery;" and he began to unfold the paper with a smile. But the smile ceased as his eye suddenly caught his own name.

A dozen lines were written in pencil on what seemed to be a blank leaf originally torn from some book. He trembled so that he was obliged to sit down to read these words: -

"When you get this keep away from the woods. Dunn and another man are in deadly pursuit of you and your companion. I overheard their plan to surprise you in our cabin. Don't go there, and I will delay them and put them off the scent. Don't mind me. God bless you, and if you never see me again think sometimes of

TERESA."

His trembling ceased; he did not start, but rose in an abstracted way, and made a few deliberate steps in the direction Teresa had gone. Even then he was so confused that he was obliged to refer to the paper again, but with so little effect that he could only repeat the last words, "think sometimes of Teresa." He was conscious that this was not all; he had a full conviction of being deceived, and knew that he held the proof in his hand, but he could not formulate it beyond that sentence. "Teresa", yes, he would think of her. She would think of him. She would explain it. And here she was returning.

In that brief interval her face and manner had again changed. She was pale and quite breathless. She cast a swift glance at Dunn and the paper he mechanically held out, walked up to him, and tore it from his hand.

"Well," she said hoarsely, "what are you going to do about it?"

He attempted to speak, but his voice failed him. Even then he was conscious that if he had spoken he would have only repeated, "think sometimes of Teresa." He looked longingly but helplessly at the spot where she had thrown the paper, as if it had contained his unuttered words.

"Yes," she went on to herself, as if he was a mute, indifferent spectator, "yes, they're gone. That ends it all. The game's played out. Well!" suddenly turning upon him, "now you know it all. Your

Nellie was here with him, and is with him now. Do you hear? Make the most of it; you've lost them, but here I am."

"Yes," he said eagerly, "yes, Teresa."

She stopped, stared at him; then taking him by the hand led him like a child back to his couch. "Well," she said, in half-savage explanation, "I told you the truth when I said the girl wasn't at the cabin last night, and that I didn't know her. What are you glowerin' at? No! I haven't lied to you, I swear to God, except in one thing. Do you know what that was? To save him I took upon me a shame I don't deserve. I let you think I was his mistress. You think so now, don't you? Well, before God to-day, and He may take me when He likes, I'm no more to him than a sister! I reckon your Nellie can't say as much."

She turned away, and with the quick, impatient stride of some caged animal made the narrow circuit of the opening, stopping a moment mechanically before the sick man, and again, without looking at him, continuing her monotonous round. The heat had become excessive, but she held her shawl with both hands drawn tightly over her shoulders. Suddenly a wood-duck darted out of the covert blindly into the opening, struck against the blasted trunk, fell half stunned near her feet, and then, recovering, fluttered away. She had scarcely completed another circuit before the irruption was followed by a whirring bevy of quail, a flight of jays, and a sudden tumult of wings swept through the wood like a tornado. She turned inquiringly to Dunn, who had risen to his feet, but the next moment she caught convulsively at his wrist: a wolf had just dashed through the underbrush not a dozen yards away, and on either side of them they could hear the scamper and rustle of hurrying feet like the outburst of a summer shower. A cold wind arose from the opposite direction, as if to contest this wild exodus, but it was followed by a blast of sickening heat. Teresa sank at Dunn's feet in an agony of terror.

"Don't let them touch me!" she gasped; "keep them off! Tell me, for God's sake, what has happened!"

He laid his hand firmly on her arm, and lifted her in his turn to her feet like a child. In that supreme moment of physical danger, his strength, reason, and manhood returned in their plenitude of power. He pointed coolly to the trail she had quitted, and said:

"The Carquinez Woods are on fire!"

CHAPTER X.

The nest of the tuneful Burnhams, although in the suburbs of Indian Spring, was not in ordinary weather and seasons hidden from the longing eyes of the youth of that settlement. That night, however, it was veiled in the smoke that encompassed the great highway leading to Excelsior. It is presumed that the Burnham brood had long since folded their wings, for there was no sign of life nor movement in the house as a rapidly driven horse and buggy pulled up before it. Fortunately, the paternal Burnham was an early bird, in the habit of picking up the first stirring mining worm, and a resounding knock brought him half dressed to the street door. He was startled at seeing Father Wynn before him, a trifle flushed and abstracted.

"Ah ha! up betimes, I see, and ready. No sluggards here, ha, ha!" he said heartily, slamming the door behind him, and by a series of pokes in the ribs genially backing his host into his own sitting-room.

"I'm up, too, and am here to see Nellie. She's here, eh, of course?" he added, darting a quick look at Burnham.

But Mr. Burnham was one of those large, liberal Western husbands who classified his household under the general title of "woman folk," for the integers of which he was not responsible. He hesitated, and then propounded over the balusters to the upper story the direct query, "You don't happen to have Nellie Wynn up there, do ye?"

There was an interval of inquiry proceeding from half a dozen reluctant throats, more or less cottony and muffled, in those various degrees of grievance and mental distress which indicate too early roused young womanhood. The eventual reply seemed to be affirmative, albeit accompanied with a suppressed giggle, as if the young lady had just been discovered as an answer to an amusing conundrum.

"All right," said Wynn, with an apparent accession of boisterous geniality. "Tell her I must see her, and I've only got a few minutes to spare. Tell her to slip on anything and come down; there's no one here but myself, and I've shut the front door on Brother Burnham. Ha, ha!" and suiting the action to the word, he actually bundled the admiring Brother Burnham out on his own doorstep. There was a light pattering on the staircase, and Nellie Wynn, pink with sleep, very tall, very slim, hastily draped in a white counterpane with a blue border and a general classic suggestion, slipped into the parlor. At the same moment the father shut the door behind her, placed one hand on the knob, and with the other seized her wrist.

"Where were you yesterday?" he asked.

Nellie looked at him, shrugged her shoulders, and said, "Here."

"You were in the Carquinez Woods with Low Dorman; you went there in disguise; you've met him there before. He is your clandestine lover; you have taken pledges of affection from him; you have" -

"Stop!" she said.

He stopped.

"Did he tell you this?" she asked, with an expression of disdain.

"No; I overheard it. Dunn and Brace were at the house waiting for you. When the coach did not bring you, I went to the office to inquire. As I left our door I thought I saw somebody listening at the parlor windows. It was only a drunken Mexican muleteer leaning against the house; but if he heard nothing, I did. Nellie, I heard Brace tell Dunn that he had tracked you in your disguise to the woods, do you hear? that when you pretended to be here with the girls you were with Low, alone; that you wear a ring that Low got of a trader here; that there was a cabin in the woods" -

"Stop!" she repeated.

Wynn again paused.

"And what did you do?" she asked.

"I heard they were starting down there to surprise you and him together, and I harnessed up and got ahead of them in my buggy."

"And found me here," she said, looking full into his eyes.

He understood her and returned the look. He recognized the full importance of the culminating fact conveyed in her words, and was obliged to content himself with its logical and worldly significance. It was too late now to take her to task for mere filial disobedience; they must become allies.

"Yes," he said hurriedly; "but if you value your reputation, if you wish to silence both these men, answer me fully."

"Go on," she said.

"Did you go to the cabin in the woods yesterday?"

"No."

"Did you ever go there with Low?"

"No; I do not know even where it is."

Wynn felt that she was telling the truth. Nellie knew it; but as she would have been equally satisfied with an equally efficacious falsehood, her face remained unchanged.

"And when did he leave you?"

"At nine o'clock, here. He went to the hotel."

"He saved his life, then, for Dunn is on his way to the woods to kill him."

The jeopardy of her lover did not seem to affect the young girl with alarm, although her eyes betrayed some interest.

"Then Dunn has gone to the woods?" she said thoughtfully.

"He has," replied Wynn.

"Is that all?" she asked.

"I want to know what you are going to do?"

"I was going back to bed."

"This is no time for trifling, girl."

"I should think not," she said, with a yawn; "it's too early, or too late."

Wynn grasped her wrist more tightly. "Hear me! Put whatever face you like on this affair, you are compromised, and compromised with a man you can't marry."

"I don't know that I ever wanted to marry Low, if you mean him," she said quietly.

"And Dunn wouldn't marry you now."

"I'm not so sure of that either."

"Nellie," said Wynn excitedly, "do you want to drive me mad? Have you nothing to say, nothing to suggest?"

"Oh, you want me to help you, do you? Why didn't you say that first? Well, go and bring Dunn here."

"Are you mad? The man has gone already in pursuit of your lover, believing you with him."

"Then he will the more readily come and talk with me without him. Will you take the invitation, yes or no?"

"Yes, but" -

"Enough. On your way there you will stop at the hotel and give Low a letter from me."

"Nellie!"

"You shall read it, of course," she said scornfully, "for it will be your text for the conversation you will have with him. Will you please take your hand from the lock and open the door?"

Wynn mechanically opened the door. The young girl flew up-stairs. In a very few moments she returned with two notes: one contained a few lines of formal invitation to Dunn; the other read as follows:

"DEAR MR. DORMAN: My father will tell you how deeply I regret that our recent botanical excursions in the Carquinez Woods have been a source of serious misapprehension to those who had a claim to my consideration, and that I shall be obliged to discontinue them for the future. At the same time he wishes me to express my gratitude for your valuable instruction and assistance in that pleasing study, even though approaching events may compel me to relinquish it for other duties. May I beg you to accept the enclosed ring as a slight recognition of my obligations to you?

"Your grateful pupil,

"NELLIE WYNN."

When he had finished reading the letter, she handed him a ring, which he took mechanically. He raised his eyes to hers with perfectly genuine admiration. "You're a good girl, Nellie," he said, and, in a moment of parental forgetfulness, unconsciously advanced his lips towards her cheek. But she drew back in time to recall him to a sense of that human weakness.

"I suppose I'll have time for a nap yet," she said, as a gentle hint to her embarrassed parent. He nodded and turned towards the door.

"If I were you," she continued, repressing a yawn, "I'd manage to be seen on good terms with Low at the hotel; so perhaps you need not give the letter to him until the last thing. Good-by."

The sitting-room door opened and closed behind her as she slipped up-stairs, and her father, without the formality of leave-taking, quietly let *himselt out by the front door.

When he drove into the highroad again, however, an overlooked possibility threatened for a moment to indefinitely postpone his amiable intentions regarding Low. The hotel was at the farther end of the settlement toward the Carquinez Woods, and as Wynn had nearly reached it he was recalled to himself by the sounds of hoofs and wheels rapidly approaching from the direction of the Excelsior turnpike. Wynn made no doubt it was the sheriff and Brace. To avoid recognition at that moment, he whipped up his horse, intending to keep the lead until he could turn into the first cross-road. But the coming travelers had the fleetest horse; and finding it impossible to distance them, he drove close to the ditch, pulling up suddenly as the strange vehicle was abreast of him, and forcing them to pass him at full speed, with the result already chronicled. When they had vanished in the darkness, Mr. Wynn, with a heart overflowing with Christian thankfulness and universal benevolence, wheeled round, and drove back to the hotel he had already passed. To pull up at the veranda with a stentorian shout, to thump loudly at the deserted bar, to hilariously beat the panels of the landlord's door, and commit a jocose assault and battery upon that half-dressed and half-awakened man, was eminently characteristic of Wynn, and part of his amiable plans that morning.

"Something to wash this wood smoke from my throat, Brother Carter, and about as much again to prop open your eyes," he said, dragging Carter before the bar, "and glasses round for as many of the boys as are up and stirring after a hard-working Christian's rest. How goes the honest publican's trade, and who have we here?"

"Thar's Judge Robinson and two lawyers from Sacramento, Dick Curson over from Yolo," said Carter, "and that ar young Injin yarb doctor from the Carquinez Woods. I reckon he's jist up, I noticed a light under his door as I passed."

"He's my man for a friendly chat before breakfast," said Wynn. "You needn't come up. I'll find the way. I don't want a light; I reckon my eyes ain't as bright nor as young as his, but they'll see almost as far in the dark, he-he!" And, nodding to Brother Carter, he strode along the passage, and with no other introduction than a playful and preliminary "Boo!" burst into one of the rooms. Low, who by the light of a single candle was bending over the plates of a large quarto, merely raised his eyes and looked at the intruder. The young man's natural imperturbability, always exasperating to Wynn, seemed accented that morning by contrast with his own over-acted animation.

"Ah ha! wasting the midnight oil instead of imbibing the morning dews," said Father Wynn archly, illustrating his metaphor with a movement of his hand to his lips. "What have we here?"

"An anonymous gift," replied Low simply, recognizing the father of Nellie by rising from his chair. "It's a volume I've longed to possess, but never could afford to buy. I cannot imagine who sent it to me."

Wynn was for a moment startled by the thought that this recipient of valuable gifts might have influential friends. But a glance at the bare room, which looked like a camp, and the strange, unconventional garb of its occupant, restored his former convictions. There might be a promise of intelligence, but scarcely of prosperity, in the figure before him.

"Ah! We must not forget that we are watched over in the night season," he said, laying his hand on Low's shoulder, with an illustration of celestial guardianship that would have been impious but for its palpable grotesqueness. "No, sir, we know not what a day may bring forth."

Unfortunately, Low's practical mind did not go beyond a mere human interpretation. It was enough, however, to put a new light in his eye and a faint color in his cheek.

"Could it have been Miss Nellie?" he asked, with half-boyish hesitation.

Mr. Wynn was too much of a Christian not to bow before what appeared to him the purely providential interposition of this suggestion. Seizing it and Low at the same moment, he playfully forced him down again in his chair.

"Ah, you rascal!" he said, with infinite archness; "that's your game, is it? You want to trap poor Father Wynn. You want to make him say 'No.' You want to tempt him to commit himself. No, sir! never, sir! no, no!"

Firmly convinced that the present was Nellie's and that her father only good-humoredly guessed it, the young man's simple, truthful nature was embarrassed. He longed to express his gratitude, but feared to betray the young girl's trust. The Reverend Mr. Wynn speedily relieved his mind.

"No," he continued, bestriding a chair, and familiarly confronting Low over its back. "No, sir, no! And you want me to say 'No,' don't you, regarding the little walks of Nellie and a certain young man in the Carquinez Woods? ha, ha! You'd like me to say that I knew nothing of the botanizings, and the herb collectings, and the picnickings there, he-he! you sly dog! Perhaps you'd like to tempt Father Wynn further and make him swear he knows nothing of his daughter disguising herself in a duster and meeting another young man, isn't it another young man? all alone, eh? Perhaps you want poor old Father Wynn to say 'No.' No, sir, nothing of the kind ever occurred. Ah, you young rascal!"

Slightly troubled, in spite of Wynn's hearty manner, Low, with his usual directness however, said, "I do not want anyone to deny that I have seen Miss Nellie."

"Certainly, certainly," said Wynn, abandoning his method, considerably disconcerted by Low's simplicity, and a certain natural reserve that shook off his familiarity. "Certainly it's a noble thing to be able to put your hand on your heart and say to the world, 'Come on, all of you! Observe me; I have nothing to conceal. I walk with Miss Wynn in the woods as her instructor, her teacher, in fact. We cull a flower here and there; we pluck an herb fresh from the hand of the Creator. We look, so to speak, from Nature to Nature's God.' Yes, my young friend, we should be the first to repel the foul calumny that could misinterpret our most innocent actions."

"Calumny?" repeated Low, starting to his feet. "What calumny?"

"My friend, my noble young friend, I recognize your indignation. I know your worth. When I said to Nellie, my only child, my perhaps too simple offspring, a mere wildflower like yourself, when I said to her, 'Go, my child, walk in the woods with this young man, hand in hand. Let him instruct you from the humblest roots, for he has trodden in the ways of the Almighty. Gather wisdom from his lips, and knowledge from his simple woodman's craft. Make, in fact, a collection not only of herbs, but of moral axioms and experience,' I knew I could trust you, and, trusting you, my young friend, I felt I could trust the world. Perhaps I was weak, foolish. But I thought only of her welfare. I even recall how that, to preserve the purity of her garments, I bade her don a simple duster; that, to secure her from the trifling companionship of others, I bade her keep her own counsel, and seek you at seasons known but to yourselves."

"But ... did Nellie ... understand you?" interrupted Low hastily.

"I see you read her simple nature. Understand me? No, not at first! Her maidenly instinct, perhaps her duty to another, took the alarm. I remember her words. 'But what will Dunn say?' she asked. 'Will he not be jealous?'"

"Dunn! jealous! I don't understand," said Low, fixing his eyes on Wynn.

"That's just what I said to Nellie. 'Jealous!' I said. 'What, Dunn, your affianced husband, jealous of a mere friend, a teacher, a guide, a philosopher. It is impossible.' Well, sir, she was right. He is jealous. And, more than that, he has imparted his jealousy to others! In other words, he has made a scandal!"

Low's eyes flashed. "Where is your daughter now?" he said sternly.

"At present in bed, suffering from a nervous attack brought on by these unjust suspicions. She appreciates your anxiety, and, knowing that you could not see her, told me to give you this." He handed Low the ring and the letter.

The climax had been forced, and, it must be confessed, was by no means the one Mr. Wynn had fully arranged in his own inner consciousness. He had intended to take an ostentatious leave of Low in the bar-room, deliver the letter with archness, and escape before a possible explosion. He consequently backed towards the door for an emergency. But he was again at fault. That unaffected stoical fortitude in acute suffering, which was the one remaining pride and glory of Low's race, was yet to be revealed to Wynn's civilized eyes.

The young man took the letter, and read it without changing a muscle, folded the ring in it, and dropped it into his haversack. Then he picked up his blanket, threw it over his shoulder, took his trusty rifle in his hand, and turned toward Wynn as if coldly surprised that he was still standing there.

"Are you, are you going?" stammered Wynn.

"Are you not?" replied Low dryly, leaning on his rifle for a moment as if waiting for Wynn to precede him. The preacher looked at him a moment, mumbled something, and then shambled feebly and ineffectively down the staircase before Low, with a painful suggestion to the ordinary observer of being occasionally urged thereto by the moccasin of the young man behind him.

On reaching the lower hall, however, he endeavored to create a diversion in his favor by dashing into the barroom and clapping the occupants on the back with indiscriminate playfulness. But here again he seemed to be disappointed. To his great discomfiture, a large man not only returned his salutation with powerful levity, but with equal playfulness seized him in his arms, and after an ingenious simulation of depositing him in the horse-trough set him down in affected amazement. "Bleth't if I didn't think from the weight of your hand it wath my old friend, Thacramento Bill," said Curson apologetically, with a wink at the bystanders. "That'th the way Bill alwayth uthed to tackle hith friendth, till he wath one day bounthed by a prithe-fighter in Frithco, whom he had mithtaken for a mithionary." As Mr. Curson's reputation was of a quality that made any form of apology from him instantly acceptable, the amused spectators made way for him as, recognizing Low, who was just leaving the hotel, he turned coolly from them and walked towards him.

"Halloo!" he said, extending his hand. "You're the man I'm waiting for. Did you get a book from the exthpreth offithe latht night?"

"I did. Why?"

"It'th all right. Ath I'm rethponthible for it, I only wanted to know."

"Did you send it?" asked Low, quickly fixing his eyes on his face.

"Well, not exactly me. But it'th not worth making a mythtery of it. Teretha gave me a commithion to buy it and thend it to you anonymouthly. That'th a woman'th nonthenth, for how could thee get a retheipt for it?"

"Then it was her present," said Low gloomily.

"Of courthe. It wathn't mine, my boy. I'd have thent you a Tharp'th rifle in plathe of that muthle loader you carry, or thomething thenthible. But, I thay! what'th up? You look ath if you had been running all night."

Low grasped his hand. "Thank you," he said hurriedly; "but it's nothing. Only I must be back to the woods early. Good-by."

But Curson retained Low's hand in his own powerful grip.

"I'll go with you a bit further," he said. "In fact, I've got thomething to thay to you; only don't be in thuch a hurry; the woodth can wait till you get there." Quietly compelling Low to alter his own characteristic Indian stride to keep pace with his, he went on: "I don't mind thaying I rather cottoned to you from the time you acted like a white man, no offenthe, to Teretha. She thayth you were left when a child lying round, jutht ath promithcuouthly ath she wath; and if I can do anything towardth putting you on the trail of your people, I'll do it. I know thome of the voyageurth who traded with the Cherokeeth, and your father wath one, wasn't he?" He glanced at Low's utterly abstracted and immobile face. "I thay, you don't theem to take a hand in thith game, pardner. What 'th the row? Ith anything wrong over there?" and he pointed to the Carquinez Woods, which were just looming out of the morning horizon in the distance.

Low stopped. The last words of his companion seemed to recall him to himself. He raised his eyes automatically to the woods, and started.

"There is something wrong over there," he said breathlessly. "Look!"

"I thee nothing," said Curson, beginning to doubt Low's sanity; "nothing more than I thaw an hour ago."

"Look again. Don't you see that smoke rising straight up? It isn't blown over from the Divide; it's new smoke! The fire is in the woods!"

"I reckon that 'th so," muttered Curson, shading his eyes with his hand. "But, hullo! wait a minute! We'll get hortheth. I say!" he shouted, forgetting his lisp in his excitement, "stop!" But Low had already lowered his head and darted forward like an arrow.

In a few moments he had left not only his companion but the last straggling houses of the outskirts far behind him, and had struck out in a long, swinging trot for the disused "cut-off." Already he fancied he heard the note of clamor in Indian Spring, and thought he distinguished the sound of hurrying hoofs on the great highway. But the sunken trail hid it from his view. From the column of smoke now plainly visible in the growing morning light he tried to locate the scene of the conflagration. It was evidently not a fire advancing regularly from the outer skirt of the wood, communicated to it from the Divide; it was a local outburst near its centre. It was not in the direction of his cabin in the tree. There was no immediate danger to Teresa, unless fear drove her beyond the confines of the wood into the hands of those who might recognize her. The screaming of jays and ravens above his head quickened his speed, as it heralded the rapid advance of the flames; and the unexpected apparition of a bounding body, flattened and flying over the yellow plain, told him that even the secure retreat of the mountain wild-cat had been invaded. A sudden recollection of Teresa's uncontrollable terror that first night smote him with remorse and redoubled his efforts. Alone in the track of these frantic and bewildered beasts, to what madness might she not be driven!

The sharp crack of a rifle from the highroad turned his course momentarily in that direction. The smoke was curling lazily over the heads of a party of men in the road, while the huge bulk of a grizzly was disappearing in the distance. A battue of the escaping animals had commenced! In the bitterness of his heart he caught at the horrible suggestion, and resolved to save her from them or die with her there.

How fast he ran, or the time it took him to reach the woods, has never been known. Their outlines were already hidden when he entered them. To a sense less keen, a courage less desperate, and a purpose less unaltered than Low's, the wood would have been impenetrable. The central fire was still confined to the lofty tree-tops, but the downward rush of wind from time to time drove the smoke into the aisles in blinding and suffocating volumes. To simulate the creeping animals, and fall to the ground on hands and knees, feel his way through the underbrush when the smoke was densest, or take advantage of its momentary lifting, and without uncertainty, mistake, or hesitation glide from tree to tree in one undeviating course, was possible only to an experienced woodsman. To keep his reason and insight so clear as to be able in the midst of this bewildering confusion to shape that course so as to intersect the wild and unknown tract of an inexperienced, frightened wanderer belonged to Low, and to Low alone. He was making his way against the wind towards the fire. He had reasoned that she was either in comparative safety to windward of it, or he should meet her being driven towards him by it, or find her succumbed and fainting at its feet. To do this he must penetrate the burning belt, and then pass under the blazing dome. He was already upon it; he could see the falling fire dropping like rain or blown like gorgeous blossoms of the conflagration across his path. The space was lit up brilliantly. The vast shafts of dull copper cast no shadow below, but there was no sign nor token of any human being. For a moment the young man was at fault. It was true this hidden heart of the forest bore no undergrowth; the cool matted carpet of the aisles seemed to quench the glowing fragments as they fell. Escape might be difficult, but not impossible; yet every moment was precious. He leaned against a tree, and sent his voice like a clarion before him: "Teresa!" There was no reply. He called again. A faint cry at his back from the trail he had just traversed made him turn. Only a few paces behind him, blinded and staggering, but following like a beaten and wounded animal, Teresa halted, knelt, clasped her hands, and dumbly held them out before her. "Teresa!" he cried again, and sprang to her side.

She caught him by the knees, and lifted her face imploringly to his.

"Say that again!" she cried, passionately. "Tell me it was Teresa you called, and no other! You have come back for me! You would not let me die here alone!"

He lifted her tenderly in his arms, and cast a rapid glance around him. It might have been his fancy, but there seemed a dull glow in the direction he had come.

"You do not speak!" she said. "Tell me! You did not come here to seek her?"

"Whom?" he said quickly.

"Nellie!"

With a sharp cry he let her slip to the ground. All the pent-up agony, rage, and mortification of the last hour broke from him in that inarticulate outburst. Then, catching her hands again, he dragged her to his level.

"Hear me!" he cried, disregarding the whirling smoke and the fiery baptism that sprinkled them, "hear me! If you value your life, if you value your soul, and if you do not want me to cast you to the beasts like Jezebel of old, never, never take that accursed name again upon your lips. Seek her, her? Yes! Seek her to tie her like a witch's daughter of hell to that blazing tree!" He stopped. "Forgive me," he said in a changed voice. "I'm mad, and forgetting myself and you. Come."

Without noticing the expression of half savage delight that had passed across her face, he lifted her in his arms.

"Which way are you going?" she asked, passing her hands vaguely across his breast, as if to reassure herself of his identity.

"To our camp by the scarred tree," he replied.

"Not there, not there," she said, hurriedly. "I was driven from there just now. I thought the fire began there until I came here."

Then it was as he feared. Obeying the same mysterious law that had launched this fatal fire like a thunderbolt from the burning mountain crest five miles away into the heart of the Carquinez Woods, it had again leaped a mile beyond, and was hemming them between two narrowing lines of fire. But Low was not daunted. Retracing his steps through the blinding smoke, he strode off at right angles to the trail near the point where he had entered the wood. It was the spot where he had first lifted Nellie in his arms to carry her to the hidden spring. If any recollection of it crossed his mind at that moment, it was only shown in his redoubled energy. He did not glide through the thick underbrush, as on that day, but seemed to take a savage pleasure in breaking through it with sheer brute force. Once Teresa insisted upon relieving him of the burden of her weight, but after a few steps she staggered blindly against him, and would fain have recourse once more to his strong arms. And so, alternately staggering, bending, crouching, or bounding and crashing on, but always in one direction, they burst through the jealous rampart, and came upon the sylvan haunt of the hidden spring. The great angle of the half fallen tree acted as a barrier to the wind and drifting smoke, and the cool spring sparkled and bubbled in the almost translucent air. He laid her down beside the water, and bathed her face and hands. As he did so his quick eye caught sight of a woman's handkerchief lying at the foot of the disrupted root. Dropping Teresa's hand, he walked towards it, and with the toe of his moccasin gave it one vigorous kick into the ooze at the overflow of the spring. He turned to Teresa, but she evidently had not noticed the act.

"Where are you?" she asked, with a smile.

Something in her movement struck him. He came towards her, and bending down looked into her face.

"Teresa! Good God! look at me! What has happened?"

She raised her eyes to his. There was a slight film across them; the lids were blackened; the beautiful lashes gone forever!

"I see you a little now, I think," she said, with a smile, passing her hands vaguely over his face. "It must have happened when he fainted, and I had to drag him through the blazing brush; both my hands were full, and I could not cover my eyes."

"Drag whom?" said Low, quickly.

"Why, Dunn."

"Dunn! He here?" said Low, hoarsely.

"Yes; didn't you read the note I left on the herbarium? Didn't you come to the camp-fire?" she asked hurriedly, clasping his hands. "Tell me quickly!"

"No!"

"Then you were not there, then you didn't leave me to die?"

"No! I swear it, Teresa!" the stoicism that had upheld his own agony breaking down before her strong emotion.

"Thank God!" She threw her arms around him, and hid her aching eyes in his troubled breast.

"Tell me all, Teresa," he whispered in her listening ear. "Don't move; stay there, and tell me all."

With her face buried in his bosom, as if speaking to his heart alone, she told him part, but not all. With her eyes filled with tears, but a smile on her lips, radiant with new-found happiness, she told him how she had overheard the plans of Dunn and Brace, how she had stolen their conveyance to warn him in time. But here she stopped, dreading to say a word that would shatter the hope she was building upon his sudden revulsion of feeling for Nellie. She could not bring herself to repeat their interview, that would come later, when they were safe and out of danger; now not even the secret of his birth must come between them with its distraction, to mar their perfect communion. She faltered that Dunn had fainted from weakness, and that she had dragged him out of danger. "He will never interfere with us, I mean," she said softly, "with me again. I can promise you that as well as if he had sworn it."

"Let him pass now," said Low; "that will come later on," he added, unconsciously repeating her thought in a tone that made her heart sick. "But tell me, Teresa, why did you go to Excelsior?"

She buried her head still deeper, as if to hide it. He felt her broken heart beat against his own; he was conscious of a depth of feeling her rival had never awakened in him. The possibility of Teresa loving him had never occurred to his simple nature. He bent his head and kissed her. She was frightened, and unloosed her clinging arms; but he retained her hand, and said, "We will leave this accursed place, and you shall go with me as you said you would; nor need you ever leave me, unless you wish it."

She could hear the beating of her own heart through his words; she longed to look at the eyes and lips that told her this, and read the meaning his voice alone could not entirely convey. For the first time she felt the loss of her sight. She did not know that it was, in this moment of happiness, the last blessing vouchsafed to her miserable life.

A few moments of silence followed, broken only by the distant rumor of the conflagration and the crash of falling boughs. "It may be an hour yet," he whispered, "before the fire has swept a path for us to the road below. We are safe here, unless some sudden current should draw the fire down upon us. You are not frightened?" She pressed his hand; she was thinking of the pale face of Dunn, lying in the secure retreat she had purchased for him at such a sacrifice. Yet the possibility of danger to him now for a moment marred her present happiness and security. "You think the fire will not go north of where you found me?" she asked softly.

"I think not," he said; "but I will reconnoitre. Stay where you are."

They pressed hands and parted. He leaped upon the slanting trunk and ascended it rapidly. She waited in mute expectation.

There was a sudden movement of the root on which she sat, a deafening crash, and she was thrown forward on her face.

The vast bulk of the leaning tree, dislodged from its aerial support by the gradual sapping of the spring at its roots, or by the crumbling of the bark from the heat, had slipped, made a half revolution, and, falling, overbore the lesser trees in its path, and tore, in its resistless momentum, a broad opening to the underbrush.

With a cry to Low, Teresa staggered to her feet. There was an interval of hideous silence, but no reply. She called again. There was a sudden deepening roar, the blast of a fiery furnace swept through the opening, a thousand luminous points around her burst into fire, and in an instant she was lost in a whirlwind of smoke and flame! From the onset of its fury to its culmination twenty minutes did not elapse; but in that interval a radius of two hundred yards around the hidden spring was swept of life and light and motion.

For the rest of that day and part of the night a pall of smoke hung above the scene of desolation. It lifted only towards the morning, when the moon, riding high, picked out in black and silver the shrunken and silent columns of those roofless vaults, shorn of base and capital. It flickered on the still, overflowing pool of the hidden spring, and shone upon the white face of Low, who, with a rootlet of the fallen tree holding him down like an arm across his breast, seemed to be sleeping peacefully in the sleeping water.

Contemporaneous history touched him as briefly, but not as gently. "It is now definitely ascertained," said "The Slumgullion Mirror," "that Sheriff Dunn met his fate in the Carquinez Woods in the performance of his duty; that fearless man having received information of the concealment of a band of horse thieves in their recesses. The desperadoes are presumed to have escaped, as the only remains found are those of two wretched tramps, one of whom is said to have been a digger, who supported himself upon roots and herbs, and the other a degraded half-white woman. It is not unreasonable to suppose that the fire originated through their carelessness, although Father Wynn of the First Baptist Church, in his powerful discourse of last Sunday, pointed at the warning and lesson of such catastrophes. It may not be out of place here to say that the rumors regarding an engagement between the pastor's accomplished daughter and the late lamented sheriff are utterly without foundation, as it has been an on dit for some time in all well-informed circles that the indefatigable Mr. Brace, of Wells, Fargo & Co.'s Express, will shortly lead the lady to the hymeneal altar."

AT THE MISSION OF SAN CARMEL.

PROLOGUE.

It was noon of the 10th of August, 1838. The monotonous coast line between Monterey and San Diego had set its hard outlines against the steady glare of the Californian sky and the metallic glitter of the Pacific Ocean. The weary succession of rounded, dome-like hills obliterated all sense of distance; the rare whaling vessel or still rarer trader, drifting past, saw no change in these rusty undulations, barren of distinguishing peak or headland, and bald of wooded crest or timbered ravine. The withered ranks of wild oats gave a dull procession of uniform color to the hills, unbroken by any relief of shadow in their smooth, round curves. As far as the eye could reach, sea and shore met in one bleak monotony, flecked by no passing cloud, stirred by no sign of life or motion. Even sound was absent; the Angelus, rung from the invisible Mission tower far inland, was driven back again by the steady northwest trades, that for half the year had swept the coast line and left it abraded of all umbrage and color.

But even this monotony soon gave way to a change and another monotony as uniform and depressed. The western horizon, slowly contracting before a wall of vapor, by four o'clock had become a mere cold, steely strip of sea, into which gradually the northern trend of the coast faded and was lost. As the fog stole with soft step southward, all distance, space, character, and locality again vanished; the hills upon which the sun still shone bore the same monotonous outlines as those just wiped into space. Last of all, before the red sun sank like the descending Host, it gleamed upon the sails of a trading vessel close in shore. It was the last object visible. A damp breath breathed upon it, a soft hand passed over the slate, the sharp pencilling of the picture faded and became a confused gray cloud.

The wind and waves, too, went down in the fog; the now invisible and hushed breakers occasionally sent the surf over the sand in a quick whisper, with grave intervals of silence, but with no continuous murmur as before. In a curving bight of the shore the creaking of oars in their rowlocks began to be distinctly heard, but the boat itself, although apparently only its length from the sands, was invisible.

"Steady now; way enough!" The voice came from the sea, and was low, as if unconsciously affected by the fog. "Silence!"

The sound of a keel grating the sand was followed by the order, "Stern all!" from the invisible speaker.

"Shall we beach her?" asked another vague voice.

"Not yet. Hail again, and all together."

"Ah hoy, oi, oi, oy!"

There were four voices, but the hail appeared weak and ineffectual, like a cry in a dream, and seemed hardly to reach beyond the surf before it was suffocated in the creeping cloud. A silence followed, but no response.

"It's no use to beach her and go ashore until we find the boat," said the first voice, gravely; "and we'll do that if the current has brought her here. Are you sure you've got the right bearings?"

"As near as a man could off a shore with not a blasted pint to take his bearings by."

There was a long silence again, broken only by the occasional dip of oars, keeping the invisible boat-head to the sea.

"Take my word for it, lads, it's the last we'll see of that boat again, or of Jack Cranch, or the captain's baby."

"It does look mighty queer that the painter should slip. Jack Cranch ain't the man to tie a granny knot."

"Silence!" said the invisible leader. "Listen."

A hail, so faint and uncertain that it might have been the long-deferred, far-off echo of their own, came from the sea, abreast of them.

"It's the captain. He hasn't found anything, or he couldn't be so far north. Hark!"

The hail was repeated again faintly, dreamily. To the seamen's trained ears it seemed to have an intelligent significance, for the first voice gravely responded, "Aye, aye?" and then said softly, "Oars."

The word was followed by a splash. The oars clicked sharply and simultaneously in the rowlocks, then more faintly, then still fainter, and then passed out into the darkness.

The silence and shadow both fell together; for hours sea and shore were impenetrable. Yet at times the air was softly moved and troubled, the surrounding gloom faintly lightened as with a misty dawn, and then was dark again; or drowsy, far-off cries and confused noises seemed to grow out of the silence, and, when they had attracted the weary ear, sank away as in a mocking dream, and showed themselves unreal. Nebulous gatherings in the fog seemed to indicate stationary objects that, even as one gazed, moved away; the recurring lap and ripple on the shingle sometimes took upon itself the semblance of faint articulate laughter or spoken words. But towards morning a certain monotonous grating on the sand, that had for many minutes alternately cheated and piqued the ear, asserted itself more strongly, and a moving, vacillating shadow in the gloom became an opaque object on the shore.

With the first rays of the morning light the fog lifted. As the undraped hills one by one bared their cold bosoms to the sun, the long line of coast struggled back to life again. Everything was unchanged, except that a stranded boat lay upon the sands, and in its stern sheets a sleeping child.

I.

The 10th of August, 1852, brought little change to the dull monotony of wind, fog, and treeless coast line. Only the sea was occasionally flecked with racing sails that outstripped the old, slow-creeping trader, or was at times streaked and blurred with the trailing smoke of a steamer. There were a few strange footprints on those virgin sands, and a fresh track, that led from the beach over the rounded hills, dropped into the bosky recesses of a hidden valley beyond the coast range.

It was here that the refectory windows of the Mission of San Carmel had for years looked upon the reverse of that monotonous picture presented to the sea. It was here that the trade winds, shorn of their fury and strength in the heated, oven-like air that rose from the valley, lost their weary way in the tangled recesses of the wooded slopes, and breathed their last at the foot of the stone cross before the Mission. It was on the crest of those slopes that the fog halted and walled in the sun-illumined plain below; it was in this plain that limitless fields of grain clothed the flat adobe soil; here the Mission garden smiled over its hedges of fruitful vines, and through the leaves of fig and gnarled pear trees; and it was here that Father Pedro had lived for fifty years, found the prospect good, and had smiled also.

Father Pedro's smile was rare. He was not a Las Casas, nor a Junipero Serra, but he had the deep seriousness of all disciples laden with the responsible wording of a gospel not their own. And his smile had an ecclesiastical as well as a human significance, the pleasantest object in his prospect being the fair and curly head of his boy acolyte and chorister, Francisco, which appeared among the vines, and his sweetest pastoral music, the high soprano humming of a chant with which the boy accompanied his gardening.

Suddenly the acolyte's chant changed to a cry of terror. Running rapidly to Father Pedro's side, he grasped his sotana, and even tried to hide his curls among its folds.

"'St! 'st!" said the Padre, disengaging himself with some impatience. "What new alarm is this? Is it Luzbel hiding among our Catalan vines, or one of those heathen Americanos from Monterey? Speak!"

"Neither, holy father," said the boy, the color struggling back into his pale cheeks, and an apologetic, bashful smile lighting his clear eyes. "Neither; but oh! such a gross, lethargic toad! And it almost leaped upon me."

"A toad leaped upon thee!" repeated the good father with evident vexation. "What next? I tell thee, child, those foolish fears are most unmeet for thee, and must be overcome, if necessary, with prayer and penance. Frightened by a toad! Blood of the Martyrs! 'T is like any foolish girl!"

Father Pedro stopped and coughed.

"I am saying that no Christian child should shrink from any of God's harmless creatures. And only last week thou wast disdainful of poor Murieta's pig, forgetting that San Antonio himself did elect one his faithful companion, even in glory."

"Yes, but it was so fat, and so uncleanly, holy father," replied the young acolyte, "and it smelt so."

"Smelt so?" echoed the father doubtfully. "Have a care, child, that this is not luxuriousness of the senses. I have noticed of late you gather over-much of roses and syringa, excellent in their way and in moderation, but still not to be compared with the flower of Holy Church, the lily."

"But lilies don't look well on the refectory table, and against the adobe wall," returned the acolyte, with a pout of a spoilt child; "and surely the flowers cannot help being sweet, any more than myrrh or incense. And I am not frightened of the heathen Americanos either, now. There was a small one in the garden yesterday, a boy like me, and he spoke kindly and with a pleasant face."

"What said he to thee, child?" asked Father Pedro, anxiously.

"Nay, the matter of his speech I could not understand," laughed the boy, "but the manner was as gentle as thine, holy father."

"'St, child," said the Padre, impatiently. "Thy likings are as unreasonable as thy fears. Besides, have I not told thee it ill becomes a child of Christ to chatter with those sons of Belial? But canst thou not repeat the words, the words he said?" he continued suspiciously.

"'T is a harsh tongue the Americanos speak in their throat," replied the boy. "But he said 'Devilishnisse' and 'pretty-as-a-girl,' and looked at me."

The good father made the boy repeat the words gravely, and as gravely repeated them after him with infinite simplicity. "They are but heretical words," he replied, in answer to the boy's inquiring look; "it is well you understand not English. Enough. Run away, child, and be ready for the Angelus. I will commune with myself awhile under the pear trees."

Glad to escape so easily, the young acolyte disappeared down the alley of fig trees, not without a furtive look at the patches of chickweed around their roots, the possible ambuscade of creeping or saltant vermin. The good priest heaved a sigh and glanced round the darkening prospect. The sun had already disappeared over the mountain wall that lay between him and the sea, rimmed with a faint white line of outlying fog. A cool zephyr fanned his cheek; it was the dying breath of the vientos generales beyond the wall. As Father Pedro's eyes were raised to this barrier, which seemed to shut out the boisterous world beyond, he fancied he noticed for the first time a slight breach in the parapet, over which an advanced banner of the fog was fluttering. Was it an omen? His speculations were cut short by a voice at his very side.

He turned quickly and beheld one of those "heathens" against whom he had just warned his young acolyte; one of that straggling band of adventurers whom the recent gold discoveries had scattered along the coast. Luckily the fertile alluvium of these valleys, lying parallel with the sea, offered no "indications" to attract the gold-seekers. Nevertheless, to Father Pedro even the infrequent contact with the Americanos was objectionable: they were at once inquisitive and careless; they asked questions with the sharp perspicacity of controversy; they received his grave replies with the frank indifference of utter worldliness. Powerful enough to have been tyrannical oppressors, they were singularly tolerant and gentle, contenting themselves with a playful, good-natured irreverence, which tormented the good father more than opposition. They were felt to be dangerous and subversive.

The Americano, however, who stood before him did not offensively suggest these national qualities. A man of middle height, strongly built, bronzed and slightly gray from the vicissitudes of years and exposure, he had an air of practical seriousness that commended itself to Father Pedro. To his religious mind it suggested self-consciousness; expressed in the dialect of the stranger, it only meant "business."

"I'm rather glad I found you out here alone," began the latter; "it saves time. I haven't got to take my turn with the rest, in there," he indicated the church with his thumb, "and you haven't got to make an appointment. You have got a clear forty minutes before the Angelus rings," he added, consulting a large silver chronometer, "and I reckon I kin git through my part of the job inside of twenty, leaving you ten minutes for remarks. I want to confess."

Father Pedro drew back with a gesture of dignity. The stranger, however, laid his hand upon the Padre's sleeve with the air of a man anticipating objection, but never refusal, and went on.

"Of course, I know. You want me to come at some other time, and in there. You want it in the reg'lar style. That's your way and your time. My answer is: it ain't my way and my time. The main idea of confession, I take it, is gettin' at the facts. I'm ready to give 'em if you'll take 'em out here, now. If you're willing to drop the Church and confessional, and all that sort o' thing, I, on my side, am willing to give up the absolution, and all that sort o' thing. You might," he added, with an unconscious touch of pathos in the suggestion, "heave in a word or two of advice after I get through; for instance, what you'd do in the circumstances, you see! That's all. But that's as you please. It ain't part of the business."

Irreverent as this speech appeared, there was really no trace of such intention in his manner, and his evident profound conviction that his suggestion was practical, and not at all inconsistent with ecclesiastical dignity, would alone have been enough to touch the Padre, had not the stranger's dominant personality already overridden him. He hesitated. The stranger seized the opportunity to take his arm, and lead him with the half familiarity of powerful protection to a bench beneath the refectory window. Taking out his watch again, he put it in the passive hands of the astonished priest, saying, "Time me," cleared his throat, and began:

"Fourteen years ago there was a ship cruisin' in the Pacific, jest off this range, that was ez nigh on to a Hell afloat as anything rigged kin be. If a chap managed to dodge the cap'en's belaying-pin for a time he was bound to be fetched up in the ribs at last by the mate's boots. There was a chap knocked down the fore hatch with a broken leg in the Gulf, and another jumped overboard off Cape Corrientes, crazy as a loon, along a clip of the head from the cap'en's trumpet. Them's facts. The ship was a brigantine, trading along the Mexican coast. The cap'en had his wife aboard, a little timid Mexican woman he'd picked up at Mazatlan. I reckon she didn't get on with him any better than the men, for she ups and dies one day, leavin' her baby, a year-old gal. One o' the crew was fond o' that baby. He used to get the black nurse to put it in the dingy, and he'd tow it astern, rocking it with the painter like a cradle. He did it, hatin' the cap'en all the same. One day the black nurse got out of the dingy for a moment, when the baby was asleep, leavin' him alone with it. An idea took hold on him, jest from cussedness, you'd say, but it was partly from revenge on the cap'en and partly to get away from the ship. The ship was well in shore, and the current settin' towards it. He slipped the painter, that man, and set himself adrift with the baby. It was a crazy act, you'd reckon, for there was n't any oars in the boat; but he had a crazy man's luck, and he contrived, by sculling the boat with one of the seats he tore out, to keep her out of the breakers, till he could find a bight in the shore to run her in. The alarm was given from the ship, but the fog shut down upon him; he could hear the other boats in pursuit. They seemed to close in on him, and by the sound he judged the cap'en was just abreast of him in the gig, bearing down upon him in the fog. He slipped out of the dingy into the water without a splash, and struck out for the breakers. He got ashore after havin' been knocked down and dragged in four times by the undertow. He had only one idea then, thankfulness that he had not taken the baby with him in the surf. You kin put that down for him; it's a fact. He got off into the hills, and made his way up to Monterey."

"And the child?" asked the Padre, with a sudden and strange asperity that boded no good to the penitent; "the child thus ruthlessly abandoned, what became of it?"

"That's just it, the child," said the stranger, gravely. "Well, if that man was on his death-bed instead of being here talking to you, he'd swear that he thought the cap'en was sure to come up to it the next minit. That's a fact. But it wasn't until one day that he, that's me, ran across one of that crew in Frisco. 'Hallo, Cranch,' sez he to me, 'so you got away, didn't you? And how's the cap'en's baby? Grown a young gal by this time, ain't she?' 'What are you talking about,' sez I; 'how should I know?' He draws away from me, and sez,'Damnit,' sez he, 'you don't mean that you' ... I grabs him by the throat and makes him tell me all. And then it appears that the boat and the baby were never found again, and every man of that crew, cap'en and all, believed I had stolen it."

He paused. Father Pedro was staring at the prospect with an uncompromising rigidity of head and shoulder.

"It's a bad lookout for me, ain't it?" the stranger continued, in serious reflection.

"How do I know," said the priest harshly, without turning his head, "that you did not make away with this child?"

"Beg pardon."

"That you did not complete your revenge by, by killing it, as your comrade suspected you? Ah! Holy Trinity," continued Father Pedro, throwing out his hands with an impatient gesture, as if to take the place of unutterable thought.

"How do you know?" echoed the stranger coldly.

"Yes."

The stranger linked his fingers together and threw them over his knee, drew it up to his chest caressingly, and said quietly, "Because you do know."

The Padre rose to his feet.

"What mean you?" he said, sternly fixing his eyes upon the speaker. Their eyes met. The stranger's were gray and persistent, with hanging corner lids that might have concealed even more purpose than they showed. The Padre's were hollow, open, and the whites slightly brown, as if with tobacco stains. Yet they were the first to turn away.

"I mean," returned the stranger, with the same practical gravity, "that you know it wouldn't pay me to come here, if I'd killed the baby, unless I wanted you to fix things right with me up there," pointing skyward, "and get absolution; and I've told you that wasn't in my line."

"Why do you seek me, then?" demanded the Padre, suspiciously.

"Because I reckon I thought a man might be allowed to confess something short of a murder. If you're going to draw the line below that" -

"This is but sacrilegious levity," interrupted Father Pedro, turning as if to go. But the stranger did not make any movement to detain him.

"Have you implored forgiveness of the father, the man you wronged, before you came here?" asked the priest, lingering.

"Not much. It wouldn't pay if he was living, and he died four years ago."

"You are sure of that?"

"I am."

"There are other relations, perhaps?"

"None."

Father Pedro was silent. When he spoke again, it was with a changed voice. "What is your purpose, then?" he asked, with the first indication of priestly sympathy in his manner. "You cannot ask forgiveness of the earthly father you have injured, you refuse the intercession of Holy Church with the Heavenly Father you have disobeyed. Speak, wretched man! What is it you want?"

"I want to find the child."

"But if it were possible, if she were still living, are you fit to seek her, to even make yourself known to her, to appear before her?"

"Well, if I made it profitable to her, perhaps."

"Perhaps," echoed the priest, scornfully. "So be it. But why come here?"

"To ask your advice. To know how to begin my search. You know this country. You were here when that boat drifted ashore beyond that mountain."

"Ah, indeed. I have much to do with it. It is an affair of the alcalde, the authorities, of your, your police."

"Is it?"

The Padre again met the stranger's eyes. He stopped, with the snuffbox he had somewhat ostentatiously drawn from his pocket still open in his hand.

"Why is it not, Señor?" he demanded.

"If she lives, she is a young lady by this time, and might not want the details of her life known to anyone."

"And how will you recognize your baby in this young lady?" asked Father Pedro, with a rapid gesture, indicating the comparative heights of a baby and an adult.

"I reckon I'll know her, and her clothes too; and whoever found her wouldn't be fool enough to destroy them."

"After fourteen years! Good! You have faith, Señor" -

"Cranch," supplied the stranger, consulting his watch. "But time's up. Business is business. Good-by; don't let me keep you."

He extended his hand.

The Padre met it with a dry, unsympathetic palm, as sere and yellow as the hills. When their hands separated, the father still hesitated, looking at Cranch. If he expected further speech or entreaty from him he was mistaken, for the American, without turning his head, walked in the same serious, practical fashion down the avenue of fig trees, and disappeared beyond the hedge of vines. The outlines of the mountain beyond were already lost in the fog. Father Pedro turned into the refectory.

"Antonio."

A strong flavor of leather, onions, and stable preceded the entrance of a short, stout vaquero from the little patio.

"Saddle Pinto and thine own mule to accompany Francisco, who will take letters from me to the Father Superior at San José to-morrow at daybreak."

"At daybreak, reverend father?"

"At daybreak. Hark ye, go by the mountain trails and avoid the highway. Stop at no posada nor fonda, but if the child is weary, rest then awhile at Don Juan Briones' or at the rancho of the Blessed Fisherman. Have no converse with stragglers, least of all those gentile Americanos. So" ...

The first strokes of the Angelus came from the nearer tower. With a gesture Father Pedro waved Antonio aside, and opened the door of the sacristy.

"Ad Majorem Dei Gloria."

II.

The hacienda of Don Juan Briones, nestling in a wooded cleft of the foot-hills, was hidden, as Father Pedro had wisely reflected, from the straying feet of travelers along the dusty highway to San José. As Francisco, emerging from the cañada, put spurs to his mule at the sight of the whitewashed walls, Antonio grunted:

"Oh aye, little priest! thou wast tired enough a moment ago, and though we are not three leagues from the Blessed Fisherman, thou couldst scarce sit thy saddle longer. Mother of God! and all to see that little mongrel, Juanita."

"But, good Antonio, Juanita was my playfellow, and I may not soon again chance this way. And Juanita is not a mongrel, no more than I am."

"She is a mestiza, and thou art a child of the Church, though this following of gypsy wenches does not show it."

"But Father Pedro does not object," urged the boy.

"The reverend father has forgotten he was ever young," replied Antonio, sententiously, "or he wouldn't set fire and tow together."

"What sayest thou, good Antonio?" asked Francisco quickly, opening his blue eyes in frank curiosity; "who is fire, and who is tow?"

The worthy muleteer, utterly abashed and confounded by this display of the acolyte's direct simplicity, contented himself by shrugging his shoulders, and a vague "Quien sabe?"

"Come," said the boy, gayly, "confess it is only the aguardiente of the Blessed Fisherman thou missest. Never fear, Juanita will find thee some. And see! here she comes."

There was a flash of white flounces along the dark brown corridor, the twinkle of satin slippers, the flying out of long black braids, and with a cry of joy a young girl threw herself upon Francisco as he entered the patio, and nearly dragged him from his mule.

"Have a care, little sister," laughed the acolyte, looking at Antonio, "or there will be a conflagration. Am I the fire?" he continued, submitting to the two sounding kisses the young girl placed upon either cheek, but still keeping his mischievous glance upon the muleteer.

"Quien sabe?" repeated Antonio, gruffly, as the young girl blushed under his significant eyes. "It is no affair of mine," he added to himself, as he led Pinto away. "Perhaps Father Pedro is right, and this young twig of the Church is as dry and sapless as himself. Let the mestiza burn if she likes."

"Quick, Pancho," said the young girl, eagerly leading him along the corridor. "This way. I must talk with thee before thou seest Don Juan; that is why I ran to intercept thee, and not as that fool Antonio would signify, to shame thee. Wast thou ashamed, my Pancho?"

The boy threw his arm familiarly round the supple, stayless little waist, accented only by the belt of the light flounced saya, and said, "But why this haste and feverishness, 'Nita? And now I look at thee, thou hast been crying."

They had emerged from a door in the corridor into the bright sunlight of a walled garden. The girl dropped her eyes, cast a quick glance around her, and said:

"Not here; to the arroyo;" and half leading, half dragging him, made her way through a copse of manzanita and alder until they heard the faint tinkling of water. "Dost thou remember," said the girl, "it was here," pointing to an embayed pool in the dark current, "that I baptized thee, when Father Pedro first brought thee here, when we both played at being monks? They were dear old days, for Father Pedro would trust no one with thee but me, and always kept us near him."

"Aye, and he said I would be profaned by the touch of any other, and so himself always washed and dressed me, and made my bed near his."

"And took thee away again, and I saw thee not till thou camest with Antonio, over a year ago, to the cattle branding. And now, my Pancho, I may never see thee again." She buried her face in her hands and sobbed aloud.

The little acolyte tried to comfort her, but with such abstraction of manner and inadequacy of warmth that she hastily removed his caressing hand.

"But why? What has happened?" he asked eagerly.

The girl's manner had changed. Her eyes flashed, and she put her brown fist on her waist and began to rock from side to side.

"But I'll not go," she said, viciously.

"Go where?" asked the boy.

"Oh, where?" she echoed, impatiently. "Hear me, Francisco. Thou knowest I am, like thee, an orphan; but I have not, like thee, a parent in the Holy Church. For, alas," she added, bitterly, "I am not a boy, and have not a lovely voice borrowed from the angels. I was, like thee, a foundling, kept, by the charity of the reverend fathers, until Don Juan, a childless widower, adopted me. I was happy, not knowing and caring who were the parents who had abandoned me, happy only in the love of him who became my adopted father. And now" - She paused.

"And now?" echoed Francisco, eagerly.

"And now they say it is discovered who are my parents."

"And they live?"

"Mother of God! no," said the girl, with scarcely filial piety. "There is someone, a thing, a mere Don Fulano, who knows it all, it seems, who is to be my guardian."

"But how? Tell me all, dear Juanita," said the boy with a feverish interest, that contrasted so strongly with his previous abstraction that Juanita bit her lips with vexation.

"Ah! How? Santa Barbara! An extravaganza for children. A necklace of lies. I am lost from a ship of which my father, Heaven rest him! is General, and I am picked up among the weeds on the sea-shore, like Moses in the bulrushes. A pretty story, indeed."

"O how beautiful!" exclaimed Francisco enthusiastically. "Ah, Juanita, would it had been me!"

"Thee!" said the girl bitterly, "thee! No! it was a girl wanted. Enough, it was me."

"And when does the guardian come?" persisted the boy, with sparkling eyes.

"He is here even now, with that pompous fool the American alcalde from Monterey, a wretch who knows nothing of the country or the people, but who helped the other American to claim me. I tell thee, Francisco, like as not it is all a folly, some senseless blunder of those Americanos that imposes upon Don Juan's simplicity and love for them."

"How looks he, this Americano who seeks thee?" asked Francisco.

"What care I how he looks," said Juanita, "or what he is? He may have the four S's, for all I care. Yet," she added with a slight touch of coquetry, "he is not bad to look upon, now I recall him."

"Had he a long mustache and a sad, sweet smile, and a voice so gentle and yet so strong that you felt he ordered you to do things without saying it? And did his eye read your thoughts? that very thought that you must obey him?"

"Saints preserve thee, Pancho! Of whom dost thou speak?"

"Listen, Juanita. It was a year ago, the eve of Natividad; he was in the church when I sang. Look where I would, I always met his eye. When the canticle was sung and I was slipping into the sacristy, he was beside me. He spoke kindly, but I understood him not. He put into my hand gold for an aguinaldo. I pretended I understood not that also, and put it into the box for the poor. He smiled and went away. Often have I seen him since; and last night, when I left the Mission, he was there again with Father Pedro."

"And Father Pedro, what said he of him?" asked Juanita.

"Nothing." The boy hesitated. "Perhaps, because I said nothing of the stranger."

Juanita laughed. "So thou canst keep a secret from the good father when thou carest. But why dost thou think this stranger is my new guardian?"

"Dost thou not see, little sister? He was even then seeking thee," said the boy with joyous excitement. "Doubtless he knew we were friends and playmates, maybe the good father has told him thy secret. For it is no idle tale of the alcalde, believe me. I see it all! It is true!"

"Then thou wilt let him take me away," exclaimed the girl bitterly, withdrawing the little hand he had clasped in his excitement.

"Alas, Juanita, what avails it now? I am sent to San José, charged with a letter to the Father Superior, who will give me further orders. What they are, or how long I must stay, I know not. But I know this: the good Father Pedro's eyes were troubled when he gave me his blessing, and he held me long in his embrace. Pray Heaven I have committed no fault. Still it may be that the reputation of my gift hath reached the Father Superior, and he would advance me;" and Francisco's eyes lit up with youthful pride at the thought.

Not so Juanita. Her black eyes snapped suddenly with suspicion, she drew in her breath, and closed her little mouth firmly. Then she began a crescendo.

Mother of God! was that all? Was he a child, to be sent away for such time or for such purpose as best pleased the fathers? Was he to know no more than that? With such gifts as God had given him, was he not at least to have some word in disposing of them? Ah! she would not stand it.

The boy gazed admiringly at the piquant energy of the little figure before him, and envied her courage. "It is the mestizo blood," he murmured to himself. Then aloud, "Thou shouldst have been a man, 'Nita."

"And thou a woman."

"Or a priest. Eh, what is that?"

They had both risen, Juanita defiantly, her black braids flying as she wheeled and suddenly faced the thicket, Francisco clinging to her with trembling hands and whitened lips. A stone, loosened from the hillside, had rolled to their feet; there was a crackling in the alders on the slope above them.

"Is it a bear, or a brigand?" whispered Francisco, hurriedly, sounding the uttermost depths of his terror in the two words.

"It is an eavesdropper," said Juanita, impetuously; "and who and why, I intend to know," and she started towards the thicket.

"Do not leave me, good Juanita;" said the young acolyte, grasping the girl's skirt.

"Nay; run to the hacienda quickly, and leave me to search the thicket. Run!"

The boy did not wait for a second injunction, but scuttled away, his long coat catching in the brambles, while Juanita darted like a kitten into the bushes. Her search was fruitless, however, and she was returning impatiently, when her quick eye fell upon a letter lying amid the dried grass where she and Francisco had been seated the moment before. It had evidently fallen from his breast when he had risen suddenly, and been overlooked in his alarm. It was Father Pedro's letter to the Father Superior of San José.

In an instant she had pounced upon it as viciously as if it had been the interloper she was seeking. She knew that she held in her fingers the secret of Francisco's sudden banishment. She felt instinctively that this yellowish envelope, with its red string and its blotch of red seal, was his sentence and her own. The little mestizo, had not been brought up to respect the integrity of either locks or seals, both being unknown in the patriarchal life of the hacienda. Yet with a certain feminine instinct she looked furtively around her, and even managed to dislodge the clumsy wax without marring the pretty effigy of the crossed keys impressed upon it. Then she opened the letter and read.

Suddenly she stopped and put back her hair from her brown temples. Then a succession of burning blushes followed each other in waves from her neck up, and died in drops of moisture in her eyes. This continued until she was fairly crying, dropping the letter from her hands and rocking to and fro. In the midst of this she quickly stopped again; the clouds broke, a sunshine of laughter started from her eyes, she laughed shyly, she laughed loudly, she laughed hysterically. Then she stopped again as suddenly, knitted her brows, swooped down once more upon the letter, and turned to fly. But at the same moment the letter was quietly but firmly taken from her hand, and Mr. Jack Cranch stood beside her.

Juanita was crimson, but unconquered. She mechanically held out her hand for the letter; the American took her little fingers, kissed them, and said:

"How are you again?"

"The letter," replied Juanita, with a strong disposition to stamp her foot.

"But," said Cranch, with business directness, "you've read enough to know it isn't for you."

"Nor for you either," responded Juanita.

"True. It is for the Reverend Father Superior of San José Mission. I'll give it to him."

Juanita was becoming alarmed, first at this prospect, second at the power the stranger seemed to be gaining over her. She recalled Francisco's description of him with something like superstitious awe.

"But it concerns Francisco. It contains a secret he should know."

"Then you can tell him it. Perhaps it would come easier from you."

Juanita blushed again. "Why?" she asked, half dreading his reply.

"Because," said the American, quietly, "you are old playmates; you are attached to each other."

Juanita bit her lips. "Why don't you read it yourself?" she asked bluntly.

"Because I don't read other people's letters, and if it concerns me you'll tell me."

"What if I don't?"

"Then the Father Superior will."

"I believe you know Francisco's secret already," said the girl, boldly.

"Perhaps."

"Then, Mother of God! Señor Crancho, what do you want?"

"I do not want to separate two such good friends as you and Francisco."

"Perhaps you'd like to claim us both," said the girl, with a sneer that was not devoid of coquetry.

"I should be delighted."

"Then here is your occasion, Senor, for here comes my adopted father, Don Juan, and your friend, Senor Br-r-own, the American alcalde."

Two men appeared in the garden path below them. The stiff, glazed, broad-brimmed black hat, surmounting a dark face of Quixotic gravity and romantic rectitude, indicated Don Juan Briones. His companion, lazy, specious, and red-faced, was Señor Brown, the American alcalde.

"Well, I reckon we kin about call the thing fixed," said Señor Brown, with a large wave of the hand, suggesting a sweeping away of all trivial details. "Ez I was saying to the Don yer, when two high-toned gents like you and him come together in a delicate matter of this kind, it ain't no hoss trade nor sharp practice. The Don is that lofty in principle that he's willin' to sacrifice his affections for the good of the gal; and you, on your hand, kalkilate to see all he's done for her, and go your whole pile better. You'll make the legal formalities good. I reckon that old Injin woman who can swear to the finding of the baby on the shore will set things all right yet. For the matter o' that, if you want anything in the way of a certificate, I'm on hand always."

"Juanita and myself are at your disposition, caballeros," said Don Juan, with a grave exaltation. "Never let it be said that the Mexican nation was outdone by the great Americanos in deeds of courtesy and affection. Let it rather stand that Juanita was a sacred trust put into my hands years ago by the goddess of American liberty, and nurtured in the Mexican eagle's nest. Is it not so, my soul?" he added, more humanly, to the girl, when he had quite recovered from the intoxication of his own speech. "We love thee, little one, but we keep our honor."

"There's nothing mean about the old man," said Brown, admiringly, with a slight dropping of his left eyelid; "his head is level, and he goes with his party."

"Thou takest my daughter, Señor Cranch," continued the old man, carried away by his emotion; "but the American nation gives me a son."

"You know not what you say, father," said the young girl, angrily, exasperated by a slight twinkle in the American's eye.

"Not so," said Cranch. "Perhaps one of the American nation may take him at his word."

"Then, caballeros, you will, for the moment at least, possess yourselves of the house and its poor hospitality," said Don Juan, with time-honored courtesy, producing the rustic key of the gate of the patio. "It is at your disposition, caballeros," he repeated, leading the way as his guests passed into the corridor.

Two hours passed. The hills were darkening on their eastern slopes; the shadows of the few poplars that sparsedly dotted the dusty highway were falling in long black lines that looked like ditches on the dead level of the tawny fields; the shadows of slowly moving cattle were mingling with their own silhouettes, and becoming more and more grotesque. A keen wind rising in the hills was already creeping from the cañada as from the mouth of a funnel, and sweeping the plains. Antonio had forgathered with the servants, had pinched the ears of the maids, had partaken of aguardiente, had saddled the mules, Antonio was becoming impatient.

And then a singular commotion disturbed the peaceful monotony of the patriarchal household of Don Juan Briones. The stagnant courtyard was suddenly alive with peons and servants, running hither and thither. The alleys and gardens were filled with retainers. A confusion of questions, orders, and outcrys rent the air, the plains shook with the galloping of a dozen horsemen. For the acolyte Francisco, of the Mission San Carmel, had disappeared and vanished, and from that day the hacienda of Don Juan Briones knew him no more.

III.

When Father Pedro saw the yellow mules vanish under the low branches of the oaks beside the little graveyard, caught the last glitter of the morning sun on Pinto's shining headstall, and heard the last tinkle of Antonio's spurs, something very like a mundane sigh escaped him. To the simple wonder of the majority of early worshipers, the half-breed converts who rigorously attended the spiritual ministrations of the Mission, and ate the temporal provisions of the reverend fathers, he deputed the functions of the first mass to a coadjutor, and, breviary in hand, sought the orchard of venerable pear trees. Whether there was any occult sympathy in his reflections with the contemplation of their gnarled, twisted, gouty, and knotty limbs, still bearing gracious and goodly fruit, I know not, but it was his private retreat, and under one of the most rheumatic and misshapen trunks there was a rude seat. Here Father Pedro sank, his face toward the mountain wall between him and the invisible sea. The relentless, dry, practical Californian sunlight falling on his face grimly pointed out a night of vigil and suffering. The snuffy yellow of his eyes was injected yet burning, his temples were ridged and veined like a tobacco leaf; the odor of desiccation which his garments always exhaled was hot and feverish, as if the fire had suddenly awakened among the ashes.

Of what was Father Pedro thinking?

He was thinking of his youth, a youth spent under the shade of those pear trees, even then venerable as now. He was thinking of his youthful dreams of heathen conquest, emulating the sacrifices and labors of Junipero Serra; a dream cut short by the orders of the archbishop, that sent his companion, Brother Diego, north on a mission to strange lands, and condemned him to the isolation of San Carmel. He was thinking of that fierce struggle with envy of a fellow-creature's better fortune, that, conquered by prayer and penance, left him patient, submissive, and devoted to his humble work; how he raised up converts to the faith, even taking them from the breast of heretic mothers.

He recalled how once, with the zeal of propagandism quickening in the instincts of a childless man, he had dreamed of perpetuating his work through some sinless creation of his own; of dedicating some virgin soul, one over whom he could have complete control, restricted by no human paternal weakness, to the task he had begun. But how? Of all the boys eagerly offered to the Church by their parents there seemed none sufficiently pure and free from parental taint. He remembered how one night, through the intercession of the Blessed Virgin herself, as he firmly then believed, this dream was fulfilled. An Indian woman brought him a Waugee child, a baby-girl that she had picked up on the sea-shore. There were no parents to divide the responsibility, the child had no past to confront, except the memory of the ignorant Indian woman, who deemed her duty done, and whose interest ceased in giving it to the Padre. The austere conditions of his monkish life compelled him to the first step in his adoption of it, the concealment of its sex. This was easy enough, as he constituted himself from that moment its sole nurse and attendant, and boldly baptized it among the other children by the name of Francisco. No others knew its origin, nor cared to know. Father Pedro had taken a muchacho foundling for adoption; his jealous seclusion of it and his personal care was doubtless some sacerdotal formula at once high and necessary.

He remembered with darkening eyes and impeded breath how his close companionship and daily care of this helpless child had revealed to him the fascinations of that paternity denied to him; how he had deemed it his duty to struggle against the thrill of baby fingers laid upon his yellow cheeks, the pleading of inarticulate words, the eloquence of wonder-seeing and mutely questioning eyes; how he had succumbed again and again, and then struggled no more, seeing only in them the suggestion of childhood made incarnate in the Holy Babe. And yet, even as he thought, he drew from his gown a little shoe, and laid it beside his breviary. It was Francisco's baby slipper, a duplicate to those worn by the miniature waxen figure of the Holy Virgin herself in her niche in the transept.

Had he felt during these years any qualms of conscience at this concealment of the child's sex? None. For to him the babe was sexless, as most befitted one who was to live and die at the foot of the altar. There was no attempt to deceive God; what mattered else? Nor was he withholding the child from the ministrations of the sacred sisters. There was no convent near the Mission, and as each year passed, the difficulty of restoring her to the position and duties of her sex became greater and more dangerous. And then the acolyte's destiny was sealed by what again appeared to Father Pedro as a direct interposition of Providence. The child developed a voice of such exquisite sweetness and purity that an angel seemed to have strayed into the little choir, and kneeling worshipers below, transported, gazed upwards, half expectant of a heavenly light breaking through the gloom of the raftered ceiling. The fame of the little singer filled the valley of San Carmel; it was a miracle vouchsafed the Mission; Don José Peralta remembered, ah yes, to have heard in old Spain of boy choristers with such voices!

And was this sacred trust to be withdrawn from him? Was this life, which he had brought out of an unknown world of sin, unstained and pure, consecrated and dedicated to God, just in the dawn of power and promise for the glory of the Mother Church, to be taken from his side? And at the word of a self-convicted man of sin, a man whose tardy repentance was not yet absolved by the Holy Church? Never! never! Father Pedro dwelt upon the stranger's rejections of the ministrations of the Church with a pitiable satisfaction; had he accepted it, he would have had a sacred claim upon Father Pedro's sympathy and confidence. Yet he rose again, uneasily and with irregular steps returned to the corridor, passing the door of the familiar little cell beside his own. The window, the table, and even the scant toilette utensils were filled with the flowers of yesterday, some of them withered and dry; the white gown of the little chorister was hanging emptily against the wall. Father Pedro started and trembled; it seemed as if the spiritual life of the child had slipped away with its garments.

In that slight chill, which even in the hottest days in California always invests any shadow cast in that white sunlight, Father Pedro shivered in the corridor. Passing again into the garden, he followed in fancy the wayfaring figure of Francisco, saw the child arrive at the rancho of Don Juan, and with the fateful blindness of all dreamers projected a picture most unlike the reality. He followed the pilgrims even to San José, and saw the child deliver the missive which gave the secret of her sex and condition to the Father Superior. That the authority at San José might dissent with the Padre of San Carmel, or decline to carry out his designs, did not occur to the one-idea'd priest. Like all solitary people, isolated from passing events, he made no allowance for occurrences outside of his routine. Yet at this moment a sudden thought whitened his yellow cheek. What if the Father Superior deemed it necessary to impart the secret to Francisco? Would the child recoil at the deception, and, perhaps, cease to love him? It was the first time, in his supreme selfishness, he had taken the acolyte's feelings into account. He had thought of him only as one owing implicit obedience to him as a temporal and spiritual guide.

"Reverend Father!"

He turned impatiently. It was his muleteer, José. Father Pedro's sunken eye brightened.

"Ah, José! Quickly, then; hast thou found Sanchicha?"

"Truly, your reverence! And I have brought her with me, just as she is; though if your reverence make more of her than to fill the six-foot hole and say a prayer over her, I'll give the mule that brought her here for food for the bull's horns. She neither hears nor speaks, but whether from weakness or sheer wantonness, I know not."

"Peace, then! and let thy tongue take example from hers. Bring her with thee into the sacristy and attend without. Go!"

Father Pedro watched the disappearing figure of the muleteer and hurriedly swept his thin, dry hand, veined and ribbed like a brown November leaf, over his stony forehead, with a sound that seemed almost a rustle. Then he suddenly stiffened his fingers over his breviary, dropped his arms perpendicularly before him, and with a rigid step returned to the corridor and passed into the sacristy.

For a moment in the half-darkness the room seemed to be empty. Tossed carelessly in the corner appeared some blankets topped by a few straggling black horsetails, like an unstranded riata. A trembling agitated the mass as Father Pedro approached. He bent over the heap and distinguished in its midst the glowing black eyes of Sanchicha, the Indian centenarian of the Mission San Carmel. Only her eyes lived. Helpless, boneless, and jelly-like, old age had overtaken her with a mild form of deliquescence.

"Listen, Sanchicha," said the father, gravely. "It is important that thou shouldst refresh thy memory for a moment. Look back fourteen years, mother; it is but yesterday to thee. Thou dost remember the baby, a little muchacha thou broughtest me then, fourteen years ago?"

The old woman's eyes became intelligent, and turned with a quick look towards the open door of the church, and thence towards the choir.

The Padre made a motion of irritation. "No, no! Thou dost not understand; thou dost not attend me. Knowest thou of any mark of clothing, trinket, or amulet found upon the babe?"

The light of the old woman's eyes went out. She might have been dead. Father Pedro waited a moment, and then laid his hand impatiently on her shoulder.

"Dost thou mean there are none?"

A ray of light struggled back into her eyes.

"None."

"And thou hast kept back or put away no sign nor mark of her parentage? Tell me, on this crucifix."

The eyes caught the crucifix, and became as empty as the orbits of the carven Christ upon it.

Father Pedro waited patiently. A moment passed; only the sound of the muleteer's spurs was heard in the courtyard.

"It is well," he said at last, with a sigh of relief. "Pepita shall give thee some refreshment, and José will bring thee back again. I will summon him."

He passed out of the sacristy door, leaving it open. A ray of sunlight darted eagerly in, and fell upon the grotesque heap in the corner. Sanchicha's eyes lived again; more than that, a singular movement came over her face. The hideous caverns of her toothless mouth opened, she laughed. The step of José was heard in the corridor, and she became again inert.

The third day, which should have brought the return of Antonio, was nearly spent. Father Pedro was impatient but not alarmed. The good fathers at San José might naturally detain Antonio for the answer, which might require deliberation. If any mischance had occurred to Francisco, Antonio would have returned or sent a special messenger. At sunset he was in his accustomed seat in the orchard, his hands clasped over the breviary in his listless lap, his eyes fixed upon the mountain between him and that mysterious sea that had brought so much into his life. He was filled with a strange desire to see it, a vague curiosity hitherto unknown to his preoccupied life; he wished to gaze upon that strand, perhaps the very spot where she had been found; he doubted not his questioning eyes would discover some forgotten trace of her; under his persistent will and aided by the Holy Virgin, the sea would give up its secret. He looked at the fog creeping along the summit, and recalled the latest gossip of San Carmel; how that since the advent of the Americanos it was gradually encroaching on the Mission. The hated name vividly recalled to him the features of the stranger as he had stood before him three nights ago, in this very garden; so vividly that he sprang to his feet with an exclamation. It was no fancy, but Señor Cranch himself advancing from under the shadow of a pear tree.

"I reckoned I'd catch you here," said Mr. Cranch, with the same dry, practical business fashion, as if he were only resuming an interrupted conversation, "and I reckon I ain't going to keep you a minit longer than I did t'other day." He mutely referred to his watch, which he already held in his hand, and then put it back in his pocket. "Well! we found her!"

"Francisco," interrupted the priest with a single stride, laying his hand upon Cranch's arm, and staring into his eyes.

Mr. Cranch quietly removed Father Pedro's hand. "I reckon that wasn't the name as I caught it," he returned dryly. "Hadn't you better sit down?"

"Pardon me, pardon me, Señor," said the priest, hastily sinking back upon his bench, "I was thinking of other things. You, you came upon me suddenly. I thought it was the acolyte. Go on, Señor! I am interested."

"I thought you'd be," said Cranch, quietly. "That's why I came. And then you might be of service too."

"True, true," said the priest, with rapid accents; "and this girl, Señor, this girl is" -

"Juanita, the mestiza, adopted daughter of Don Juan Briones, over on the Santa Clare Valley," replied Cranch, jerking his thumb over his shoulder, and then sitting down upon the bench beside Father Pedro.

The priest turned his feverish eyes piercingly upon his companion for a few seconds, and then doggedly fixed them upon the ground. Cranch drew a plug of tobacco from his pocket, cut off a portion, placed it in his cheek, and then quietly began to strap the blade of his jack-knife upon his boot. Father Pedro saw it from under his eyelids, and even in his preoccupation despised him.

"Then you are certain she is the babe you seek?" said the father, without looking up.

"I reckon as near as you can be certain of anything. Her age tallies; she was the only foundling girl baby baptized by you, you know," he partly turned round appealingly to the Padre, "that year. Injin woman says she picked up a baby. Looks like a pretty clear case, don't it?"

"And the clothes, friend Cranch?" said the priest, with his eyes still on the ground, and a slight assumption of easy indifference.

"They will be forthcoming, like enough, when the time comes," said Cranch. "The main thing at first was to find the girl; that was my job; the lawyers, I reckon, can fit the proofs and say what's wanted, later on."

"But why lawyers," continued Padre Pedro, with a slight sneer he could not repress, "if the child is found and Señor Cranch is satisfied?"

"On account of the property. Business is business!"

"The property?"

Mr. Cranch pressed the back of his knife-blade on his boot, shut it up with a click, and putting it in his pocket said calmly:

"Well, I reckon the million of dollars that her father left when he died, which naturally belongs to her, will require some proof that she is his daughter."

He had placed both his hands in his pockets, and turned his eyes full upon Father Pedro. The priest arose hurriedly.

"But you said nothing of this before, Señor Cranch," said he, with a gesture of indignation, turning his back quite upon Cranch, and taking a step towards the refectory.

"Why should I? I was looking after the girl, not the property," returned Cranch, following the Padre with watchful eyes, but still keeping his careless, easy attitude.

"Ah, well! Will it be said so, think you? Eh! Bueno. What will the world think of your sacred quest, eh?" continued the Padre Pedro, forgetting himself in his excitement, but still averting his face from his companion.

"The world will look after the proofs, and I reckon not bother if the proofs are all right," replied Cranch, carelessly; "and the girl won't think the worse for me for helping her to a fortune. Hallo! you've dropped something." He leaped to his feet, picked up the breviary which had fallen from the Padre's fingers, and returned it to him with a slight touch of gentleness that was unsuspected in the man.

The priest's dry, tremulous hand grasped the volume without acknowledgment.

"But these proofs?" he said hastily; "these proofs, Señor?"

"Oh, well, you'll testify to the baptism, you know."

"But if I refuse; if I will have nothing to do with this thing! If I will not give my word that there is not some mistake," said the priest, working himself into a feverish indignation. "That there are not slips of memory, eh? Of so many children baptized, is it possible for me to know which, eh? And if this Juanita is not your girl, eh?"

"Then you'll help me to find who is," said Cranch, coolly.

Father Pedro turned furiously on his tormentor. Overcome by his vigil and anxiety, he was oblivious of everything but the presence of the man who seemed to usurp the functions of his own conscience. "Who are you, who speak thus?" he said hoarsely, advancing upon Cranch with outstretched and anathematizing fingers. "Who are you, Señor Heathen, who dare to dictate to me, a Father of Holy Church? I tell you, I will have none of this. Never! I will not! From this moment, you understand--nothing. I will never..."

He stopped. The first stroke of the Angelus rang from the little tower. The first stroke of that bell before whose magic exorcism all human passions fled, the peaceful bell that had for fifty years lulled the little fold of San Carmel to prayer and rest, came to his throbbing ear. His trembling hands groped for the crucifix, carried it to his left breast; his lips moved in prayer. His eyes were turned to the cold, passionless sky, where a few faint, far-spaced stars had silently stolen to their places. The Angelus still rang, his trembling ceased, he remained motionless and rigid.

The American, who had uncovered in deference to the worshiper rather than the rite, waited patiently. The eyes of Father Pedro returned to the earth, moist as if with dew caught from above. He looked half absently at Cranch.

"Forgive me, my son," he said, in a changed voice. "I am only a worn old man. I must talk with thee more of this, but not to-night, not to-night; to-morrow, to-morrow, to-morrow."

He turned slowly and appeared to glide rather than move under the trees, until the dark shadow of the Mission tower met and encompassed him. Cranch followed him with anxious eyes. Then he removed the quid of tobacco from his cheek.

"Just as I reckoned," remarked he, quite audibly. "He's clean gold on the bed rock after all!"

IV.

That night Father Pedro dreamed a strange dream. How much of it was reality, how long it lasted, or when he awoke from it, he could not tell. The morbid excitement of the previous day culminated in a febrile exaltation in which he lived and moved as in a separate existence.

This is what he remembered. He thought he had risen at night in a sudden horror of remorse, and making his way to the darkened church had fallen upon his knees before the high altar, when all at once the acolyte's voice broke from the choir, but in accents so dissonant and unnatural that it seemed a sacrilege, and he trembled. He thought he had confessed the secret of the child's sex to Cranch, but whether the next morning or a week later he did not know. He fancied, too, that Cranch had also confessed some trifling deception to him, but what, or why, he could not remember; so much greater seemed the enormity of his own transgression. He thought Cranch had put in his hands the letter he had written to the Father Superior, saying that his secret was still safe, and that he had been spared the avowal and the scandal that might have ensued. But through all, and above all, he was conscious of one fixed idea: to seek the sea-shore with Sanchicha, and upon the spot where she had found Francisco, meet the young girl who had taken his place, and so part from her forever. He had a dim recollection that this was necessary to some legal identification of her, as arranged by Cranch, but how or why he did not understand; enough that it was a part of his penance.

It was early morning when the faithful Antonio, accompanied by Sanchicha and José, rode forth with him from the Mission of San Carmel. Except on the expressionless features of the old woman, there was anxiety and gloom upon the faces of the little cavalcade. He did not know how heavily his strange abstraction and hallucinations weighed upon their honest hearts. As they wound up the ascent of the mountain he noticed that Antonio and José conversed with bated breath and many pious crossings of themselves, but with eyes always wistfully fixed upon him. He wondered if, as part of his penance, he ought not to proclaim his sin and abase himself before them; but he knew that his devoted followers would insist upon sharing his punishment; and he remembered his promise to Cranch, that for her sake he would say nothing. Before they reached the summit he turned once or twice to look back upon the Mission. How small it looked, lying there in the peaceful valley, contrasted with the broad sweep of the landscape beyond, stopped at the farther east only by the dim, ghost-like outlines of the Sierras. But the strong breath of the sea was beginning to be felt; in a few moments more they were facing it with lowered sombreros and flying serapes, and the vast, glittering, illimitable Pacific opened out beneath them.

Dazed and blinded, as it seemed to him, by the shining, restless expanse, Father Pedro rode forward as if still in a dream. Suddenly he halted, and called Antonio to his side.

"Tell me, child, didst thou say that this coast was wild and desolate of man, beast, and habitation?"

"Truly I did, reverend father."

"Then what is that?" pointing to the shore.

Almost at their feet nestled a cluster of houses, at the head of an arroyo reaching up from the beach. They looked down upon the smoke of a manufactory chimney, upon strange heaps of material and curious engines scattered along the sands, with here and there moving specks of human figures. In a little bay a schooner swung at her cables.

The vaquero crossed himself in stupefied alarm. "I know not, your reverence; it is only two years ago, before the rodeo, that I was here for strayed colts, and I swear by the blessed bones of San Antonio that it was as I said."

"Ah! it is like these Americanos," responded the muleteer. "I have it from my brother Diego that he went from San José to Pescadero two months ago across the plains, with never a hut nor fonda to halt at all the way. He returned in seven days, and in the midst of the plain there were three houses and a mill and many people. And why was it? Ah! Mother of God! one had picked up in the creek where he drank that much of gold;" and the muleteer tapped one of the silver coins that fringed his jacket sleeves in place of buttons.

"And they are washing the sands for gold there now," said Antonio, eagerly pointing to some men gathered round a machine like an enormous cradle. "Let us hasten on."

Father Pedro's momentary interest had passed. The words of his companions fell dull and meaningless upon his dreaming ears. He was conscious only that the child was more a stranger to him as an outcome of this hard, bustling life, than when he believed her borne to him over the mysterious sea. It perplexed his dazed, disturbed mind to think that if such an antagonistic element could exist within a dozen miles of the Mission, and he not know it, could not such an atmosphere have been around him, even in his monastic isolation, and he remain blind to it? Had he really lived in the world without knowing it? Had it been in his blood? Had it impelled him to - He shuddered and rode on.

They were at the last slope of the zigzag descent to the shore, when he saw the figures of a man and woman moving slowly through a field of wild oats, not far from the trail. It seemed to his distorted fancy that the man was Cranch. The woman! His heart stopped beating. Ah! could it be? He had never seen her in her proper garb: would she look like that? Would she be as tall? He thought he bade José and Antonio go on slowly before with Sanchicha, and dismounted, walking slowly between the high stalks of grain lest he should disturb them. They evidently did not hear his approach, but were talking earnestly. It seemed to Father Pedro that they had taken each other's hands, and as he looked Cranch slipped his arm round her waist. With only a blind instinct of some dreadful sacrilege in this act, Father Pedro would have rushed forward, when the girl's voice struck his ear. He stopped, breathless. It was not Francisco, but Juanita, the little mestiza.

"But are you sure you are not pretending to love me now, as you pretended to think I was the muchacha you had run away with and lost? Are you sure it is not pity for the deceit you practiced upon me, upon Don Juan, upon poor Father Pedro?"

It seemed as if Cranch had tried to answer with a kiss, for the girl drew suddenly away from him with a coquettish fling of the black braids, and whipped her little brown hands behind her.

"Well, look here," said Cranch, with the same easy, good-natured, practical directness which the priest remembered, and which would have passed for philosophy in a more thoughtful man, "put it squarely, then. In the first place, it was Don Juan and the alcalde who first suggested you might be the child."

"But you have said you knew it was Francisco all the time," interrupted Juanita.

"I did; but when I found the priest would not assist me at first, and admit that the acolyte was a girl, I preferred to let him think I was deceived in giving a fortune to another, and leave it to his own conscience to permit it or frustrate it. I was right. I reckon it was pretty hard on the old man, at his time of life, and wrapped up as he was in the girl; but at the moment he came up to the scratch like a man."

"And to save him you have deceived me? Thank you, Señor," said the girl with a mock curtsey.

"I reckon I preferred to have you for a wife than a daughter," said Cranch, "if that's what you mean. When you know me better, Juanita," he continued, gravely, "you'll know that I would never have let you believe I sought in you the one if I had not hoped to find in you the other."

"Bueno! And when did you have that pretty hope?"

"When I first saw you."

"And that was two weeks ago."

"A year ago, Juanita. When Francisco visited you at the rancho. I followed and saw you."

Juanita looked at him a moment, and then suddenly darted at him, caught him by the lapels of his coat and shook him like a terrier.

"Are you sure that you did not love that Francisco? Speak!" (She shook him again.) "Swear that you did not follow her!"

"But I did," said Cranch, laughing and shaking between the clenching of the little hands.

"Judas Iscariot! Swear you do not love her all this while."

"But, Juanita!"

"Swear!"

Cranch swore. Then to Father Pedro's intense astonishment she drew the American's face towards her own by the ears and kissed him.

"But you might have loved her, and married a fortune," said Juanita, after a pause.

"Where would have been my reparation, my duty?" returned Cranch, with a laugh.

"Reparation enough for her to have had you," said Juanita, with that rapid disloyalty of one loving woman to another in an emergency. This provoked another kiss from Cranch, and then Juanita said demurely:

"But we are far from the trail. Let us return, or we shall miss Father Pedro. Are you sure he will come?"

"A week ago he promised to be here to see the proofs to-day."

The voices were growing fainter and fainter; they were returning to the trail.

Father Pedro remained motionless. A week ago! Was it a week ago since, since what? And what had he been doing here? Listening! He! Father Pedro, listening like an idle peon to the confidences of two lovers. But they had talked of him, of his crime, and the man had pitied him. Why did he not speak? Why did he not call after them? He tried to raise his voice. It sank in his throat with a horrible choking sensation. The nearest heads of oats began to nod to him, he felt himself swaying backward and forward. He fell heavily, down, down, down, from the summit of the mountain to the floor of the Mission chapel, and there he lay in the dark.

"He moves."

"Blessed Saint Anthony preserve him!"

It was Antonio's voice, it was José's arm, it was the field of wild oats, the sky above his head, all unchanged.

"What has happened?" said the priest feebly.

"A giddiness seized your reverence just now, as we were coming to seek you."

"And you met no one?"

"No one, your reverence."

Father Pedro passed his hand across his forehead.

"But who are these?" he said, pointing to two figures who now appeared upon the trail.

Antonio turned.

"It is the Americano, Señor Cranch, and his adopted daughter, the mestiza Juanita, seeking your reverence, methinks."

"Ah!" said Father Pedro.

Cranch came forward and greeted the priest cordially.

"It was kind of you, Father Pedro," he said, meaningly, with a significant glance at José and Antonio, "to come so far to bid me and my adopted daughter farewell. We depart when the tide serves, but not before you partake of our hospitality in yonder cottage."

Father Pedro gazed at Cranch and then at Juanita.

"I see," he stammered. "But she goes not alone. She will be strange at first. She takes some friend, perhaps some companion?" he continued, tremulously.

"A very old and dear one, Father Pedro, who is waiting for us now."

He led the way to a little white cottage, so little and white and recent, that it seemed a mere fleck of sea-foam cast on the sands. Disposing of José and Antonio in the neighboring workshop and outbuildings, he assisted the venerable Sanchicha to dismount, and, together with Father Pedro and Juanita, entered a white palisaded enclosure beside the cottage, and halted before what appeared to be a large folding trap-door, covering a slight sandy mound. It was locked with a padlock; beside it stood the American alcalde and Don Juan Briones. Father Pedro looked hastily around for another figure, but it was not there.

"Gentlemen," began Cranch, in his practical business way, "I reckon you all know we've come here to identify a young lady, who", he hesitated, "was lately under the care of Father Pedro, with a foundling picked up on this shore fifteen years ago by an Indian woman. How this foundling came here, and how I was concerned in it, you all know. I've told everybody here how I scrambled ashore, leaving the baby in the dingy, supposing it would be picked up by the boat pursuing me. I've told some of you," he looked at Father Pedro, "how I first discovered, from one of the men, three years ago, that the child was not found by its father. But I have never told anyone, before now, I knew it was picked up here.

"I never could tell the exact locality where I came ashore, for the fog was coming on as it is now. But two years ago I came up with a party of gold hunters to work these sands. One day, digging near this creek, I struck something embedded deep below the surface. Well, gentlemen, it wasn't gold, but something worth more to me than gold or silver. Here it is."

At a sign the alcalde unlocked the doors and threw them open. They disclosed an irregular trench, in which, filled with sand, lay the half-excavated stern of a boat.

"It was the dingy of the Trinidad, gentlemen; you can still read her name. I found hidden away, tucked under the stern sheets, moldy and water-worn, some clothes that I recognized to be the baby's. I knew then that the child had been taken away alive for some purpose, and the clothes were left so that she should carry no trace with her. I recognized the hand of an Indian. I set to work quietly. I found Sanchicha here, she confessed to finding a baby, but what she had done with it she would not at first say. But since then she has declared before the alcalde that she gave it to Father Pedro of San Carmel, and that here it stands, Francisco that was! Francisca that it is!"

He stepped aside to make way for a tall girl, who had approached from the cottage.

Father Pedro had neither noticed the concluding words nor the movement of Cranch. His eyes were fixed upon the imbecile Sanchicha, Sanchicha, of whom, to render his rebuke more complete, the Deity seemed to have worked a miracle, and restored intelligence to eye and lip. He passed his hand tremblingly across his forehead, and turned away, when his eye fell upon the last comer.

It was she. The moment he had longed for and dreaded had come. She stood there, animated, handsome, filled with a hurtful consciousness in her new charms, her fresh finery, and the pitiable trinkets that had supplanted her scapulary, and which played under her foolish fingers. The past had no place in her preoccupied mind; her bright eyes were full of eager anticipation of a substantial future. The incarnation of a frivolous world, even as she extended one hand to him in half-coquettish embarrassment she arranged the folds of her dress with the other. At the touch of her fingers he felt himself growing old and cold. Even the penance of parting, which he had looked forward to, was denied him; there was no longer sympathy enough for sorrow. He thought of the empty chorister's robe in the little cell, but not now with regret. He only trembled to think of the flesh that he had once caused to inhabit it.

"That's all, gentlemen," broke in the practical voice of Cranch. "Whether there are proofs enough to make Francisca the heiress of her father's wealth, the lawyers must say. I reckon it's enough for me that they give me the chance of repairing a wrong by taking her father's place. After all, it was a mere chance."

"It was the will of God," said Father Pedro, solemnly.

They were the last words he addressed them. For when the fog had begun to creep in-shore, hastening their departure, he only answered their farewells by a silent pressure of the hand, mute lips, and far-off eyes.

When the sound of their laboring oars grew fainter, he told Antonio to lead him and Sanchicha again to the buried boat. There he bade her kneel beside him. "We will do penance here, thou and I, daughter," he said, gravely. When the fog had drawn its curtain gently around the strange pair, and sea and shore were blotted out, he whispered, "Tell me, it was even so, was it not, daughter, on the night she came?" When the distant clatter of blocks and rattle of cordage came from the unseen vessel, now standing out to sea, he whispered again, "So, this is what thou didst hear, even then." And so during the night he marked, more or less audibly to the half-conscious woman at his side, the low whisper of the waves, the murmur of the far-off breakers, the lightening and thickening of the fog, the phantoms of moving shapes, and the slow coming of the dawn. And when the morning sun had rent the veil over land and sea, Antonio and José found him, haggard but erect, beside the trembling old woman, with a blessing on his lips, pointing to the horizon where a single sail still glimmered:

"Va Usted con Dios."

A BLUE-GRASS PENELOPE

I.

She was barely twenty-three years old. It is probable that up to that age, and the beginning of this episode, her life had been uneventful. Born to the easy mediocrity of such compensating extremes as a small farmhouse and large lands, a good position and no society, in that vast grazing district of Kentucky known as the "Blue Grass" region, all the possibilities of a Western American girl's existence lay before her. A piano in the bare-walled house, the latest patented mower in the limitless meadows, and a silk dress sweeping the rough floor of the unpainted "meeting-house," were already the promise of those possibilities. Beautiful she was, but the power of that beauty was limited by being equally shared with her few neighbors. There were small, narrow, arched feet besides her own that trod the uncarpeted floors of outlying log cabins with equal grace and dignity; bright, clearly opened eyes that were equally capable of looking unabashed upon princes and potentates, as a few later did, and the heiress of the county judge read her own beauty without envy in the frank glances and unlowered crest of the blacksmith's daughter. Eventually she had married the male of her species, a young stranger, who, as schoolmaster in the nearest town, had utilized to some local extent a scant capital of education. In obedience to the unwritten law of the West, after the marriage was celebrated the doors of the ancestral home cheerfully opened, and bride and bridegroom issued forth, without regret and without sentiment, to seek the further possibilities of a life beyond these already too familiar voices. With their departure for California as Mr. and Mrs. Spencer Tucker, the parental nest in the Blue Grass meadows knew them no more.

They submitted with equal cheerfulness to the privations and excesses of their new conditions. Within three years the schoolmaster developed into a lawyer and capitalist, the Blue Grass bride supplying a grace and ease to these transitions that were all her own. She softened the abruptness of sudden wealth, mitigated the austerities of newly acquired power, and made the most glaring incongruity picturesque. Only one thing seemed to limit their progress in the region of these possibilities. They were childless. It was as if they had exhausted the future in their own youth, leaving little or nothing for another generation to do.

A southwesterly storm was beating against the dressing-room windows of their new house in one of the hilly suburbs of San Francisco, and threatening the unseasonable frivolity of the stucco ornamentation of cornice and balcony. Mrs. Tucker had been called from the contemplation of the dreary prospect without by the arrival of a visitor. On entering the drawing-room she found him engaged in a half admiring, half resentful examination of its new furniture and hangings. Mrs. Tucker at once recognized Mr. Calhoun Weaver, a former Blue Grass neighbor; with swift feminine intuition she also felt that his slight antagonism was likely to be transferred from her furniture to herself. Waiving it with the lazy amiability of Southern indifference, she welcomed him by the familiarity of a Christian name.

"I reckoned that mebbee you opined old Blue Grass friends wouldn't naturally hitch on to them fancy doins," he said, glancing around the apartment to avoid her clear eyes, as if resolutely setting himself against the old charm of her manner as he had against the more recent glory of her surroundings, "but I thought I'd just drop in for the sake of old times."

"Why shouldn't you, Cal?" said Mrs. Tucker with a frank smile.

"Especially as I'm going up to Sacramento to-night with some influential friends," he continued, with an ostentation calculated to resist the assumption of her charms and her furniture. "Senator Dyce of Kentucky, and his cousin Judge Briggs; perhaps you know 'em, or maybe Spencer, I mean Mr. Tucker does."

"I reckon," said Mrs. Tucker smiling; "but tell me something about the boys and girls at Vineville, and about yourself. You're looking well, and right smart too." She paused to give due emphasis to this latter recognition of a huge gold chain with which her visitor was somewhat ostentatiously trifling.

"I didn't know as you cared to hear anything about Blue Grass," he returned, a little abashed. "I've been away from there some time myself," he added, his uneasy vanity taking fresh alarm at the faint suspicion of patronage on the part of his hostess. "They're doin' well though; perhaps as well as some others."

"And you're not married yet," continued Mrs. Tucker, oblivious of the innuendo. "Ah Cal," she added archly, "I am afraid you are as fickle as ever. What poor girl in Vineville have you left pining?"

The simple face of the man before her flushed with foolish gratification at this old-fashioned, ambiguous flattery. "Now look yer, Belle," he said, chuckling, "if you're talking of old times and you think I bear malice agin Spencer, why" -

But Mrs. Tucker interrupted what might have been an inopportune sentimental retrospect with a finger of arch but languid warning. "That will do! I'm dying to know all about it, and you must stay to dinner and tell me. It's right mean you can't see Spencer too; but he isn't back from Sacramento yet."

Grateful as a tête-à-tête with his old neighbor in her more prosperous surroundings would have been, if only for the sake of later gossiping about it, he felt it would be inconsistent with his pride and his assumption of present business. More than that, he was uneasily conscious that in Mrs. Tucker's simple and unaffected manner there was a greater superiority than he had ever noticed during their previous acquaintance. He would have felt kinder to her had she shown any "airs and graces," which he could have commented upon and forgiven. He stammered some vague excuse of preoccupation, yet lingered in the hope of saying something which, if not aggressively unpleasant, might at least transfer to her indolent serenity some of his own irritation. "I reckon," he said, as he moved hesitatingly toward the door, "that Spencer has made himself easy and secure in them business risks he's taking. That 'ere Alameda ditch affair they're talking so much about is a mighty big thing, rather too big if it ever got to falling back on him. But I suppose he's accustomed to take risks?"

"Of course he is," said Mrs. Tucker gayly. "He married me."

The visitor smiled feebly, but was not equal to the opportunity offered for gallant repudiation. "But suppose you ain't accustomed to risks?"

"Why not? I married him," said Mrs. Tucker.

Mr. Calhoun Weaver was human, and succumbed to this last charming audacity. He broke into a noisy but genuine laugh, shook Mrs. Tucker's hand with effusion, said, "Now that's regular Blue Grass and no mistake!" and retreated under cover of his hilarity. In the hall he made a rallying stand to repeat confidentially to the servant who had overheard them, "Blue Grass all over, you bet your life," and, opening the door, was apparently swallowed up in the tempest.

Mrs. Tucker's smile kept her lips until she had returned to her room, and even then languidly shone in her eyes for some minutes after, as she gazed abstractedly from her window on the storm-tossed bay in the distance. Perhaps some girlish vision of the peaceful Blue Grass plain momentarily usurped the prospect; but it is to be doubted if there was much romance in that retrospect, or that it was more interesting to her than the positive and sharply cut outlines of the practical life she now led. Howbeit she soon forgot this fancy in lazily watching a boat that, in the teeth of the gale, was beating round Alcatraz Island. Although at times a mere blank speck on the gray waste of foam, a closer scrutiny showed it to be one of those lateen-rigged Italian fishing-boats that so often flecked the distant bay. Lost in the sudden darkening of rain, or reappearing beneath the lifted curtain of the squall, she watched it weather the island, and then turn its laboring but persistent course toward the open channel. A rent in the Indian-inky sky, that showed the narrowing portals of the Golden Gate beyond, revealed, as unexpectedly, the destination of the little craft, a tall ship that hitherto lay hidden in the mist of the Saucelito shore. As the distance lessened between boat and ship, they were again lost in the downward swoop of another squall. When it lifted, the ship was creeping under the headland towards the open sea, but the boat was gone. Mrs. Tucker in vain rubbed the pane with her handkerchief, it had vanished. Meanwhile the ship, as she neared the Gate, drew out from the protecting headland, stood outlined for a moment with spars and canvas hearsed in black against the lurid rent in the horizon, and then seemed to sink slowly into the heaving obscurity beyond. A sudden onset of rain against the windows obliterated the remaining prospect; the entrance of a servant completed the diversion.

"Captain Poindexter, ma'am!"

Mrs. Tucker lifted her pretty eyebrows interrogatively. Captain Poindexter was a legal friend of her husband, and had dined there frequently; nevertheless she asked, "Did you tell him Mr. Tucker was not at home?"

"Yes, 'm."

"Did he ask for me?"

"Yes, 'm."

"Tell him I'll be down directly."

Mrs. Tucker's quiet face did not betray the fact that this second visitor was even less interesting than the first. In her heart she did not like Captain Poindexter. With a clever woman's instinct, she had early detected the fact that he had a superior, stronger nature than her husband; as a loyal wife, she secretly resented the occasional unconscious exhibition of this fact on the part of his intimate friend in their familiar intercourse. Added to this slight jealousy there was a certain moral antagonism between herself and the captain which none but themselves knew. They were both philosophers, but Mrs. Tucker's serene and languid optimism would not tolerate the compassionate and kind-hearted pessimisms of the lawyer. "Knowing what Jack Poindexter does of human nature," her husband had once said, "it's mighty fine in him to be so kind and forgiving. You ought to like him better, Belle." "And qualify myself to be forgiven," said the lady pertly. "I don't see what you're driving at, Belle; I give it up," had responded the puzzled husband. Mrs. Tucker kissed his high but foolish forehead tenderly, and said, "I'm glad you don't, dear."

Meanwhile her second visitor had, like the first, employed the interval in a critical survey of the glories of the new furniture, but with apparently more compassion than resentment in his manner. Once only had his expression changed. Over the fireplace hung a large photograph of Mr. Spencer Tucker. It was retouched, refined, and idealized in the highest style of that polite and diplomatic art. As Captain Poindexter looked upon the fringed hazel eyes, the drooping raven mustache, the clustering ringlets, and the Byronic full throat and turned-down collar of his friend, a smile of exhausted humorous tolerance and affectionate impatience curved his lips. "Well, you are a fool, aren't you?" he apostrophized it half audibly.

He was standing before the picture as she entered. Even in the trying contiguity of that peerless work he would have been called a fine-looking man. As he advanced to greet her, it was evident that his military title was not one of the mere fanciful sobriquets of the locality. In his erect figure and the disciplined composure of limb and attitude there were still traces of the refined academic rigors of West Point. The pliant adaptability of Western civilization, which enabled him, three years before, to leave the army and transfer his executive ability to the more profitable profession of the law, had loosed sash and shoulder-strap, but had not entirely removed the restraint of the one, nor the bearing of the other.

"Spencer is in Sacramento," began Mrs. Tucker in languid explanation, after the first greetings were over.

"I knew he was not here," replied Captain Poindexter gently, as he drew the proffered chair towards her, "but this is business that concerns you both." He stopped and glanced upwards at the picture. "I suppose you know nothing of his business? Of course not," he added reassuringly, "nothing, absolutely nothing, certainly." He said this so kindly, and yet so positively, as if to promptly dispose of that question before going further, that she assented mechanically. "Well, then, he's taken some big risks in the way of business, and, well, things have gone bad with him, you know. Very bad! Really, they couldn't be worse! Of course it was dreadfully rash and all that," he went on, as if commenting upon the amusing waywardness of a child; "but the result is the usual smash-up of everything, money, credit, and all!" He laughed and added, "Yes, he's got cut off, mules and baggage regularly routed and dispersed! I'm in earnest." He raised his eyebrows and frowned slightly, as if to deprecate any corresponding hilarity on the part of Mrs. Tucker, or any attempt to make too light of the subject, and then rising, placed his hands behind his back, beamed half-humorously upon her from beneath her husband's picture, and repeated, "That's so."

Mrs. Tucker instinctively knew that he spoke the truth, and that it was impossible for him to convey it in any other than his natural manner; but between the shock and the singular influence of that manner she could at first only say, "You don't mean it!" fully conscious of the utter inanity of the remark, and that it seemed scarcely less cold-blooded than his own.

Poindexter, still smiling, nodded.

She arose with an effort. She had recovered from the first shock, and pride lent her a determined calmness that more than equaled Poindexter's easy philosophy.

"Where is he?" she asked.

"At sea, and I hope by this time where he cannot be found or followed."

Was her momentary glimpse of the outgoing ship a coincidence or only a vision? She was confused and giddy, but, mastering her weakness, she managed to continue in a lower voice:

"You have no message for me from him? He told you nothing to tell me?"

"Nothing, absolutely nothing," replied Poindexter. "It was as much as he could do, I reckon, to get fairly away before the crash came."

"Then you did not see him go?"

"Well, no," said Poindexter. "I'd hardly have managed things in this way." He checked himself and added, with a forgiving smile, "but he was the best judge of what he needed, of course."

"I suppose I will hear from him," she said quietly, "as soon as he is safe. He must have had enough else to think about, poor fellow."

She said this so naturally and quietly that Poindexter was deceived. He had no idea that the collected woman before him was thinking only of solitude and darkness, of her own room, and madly longing to be there. He said, "Yes, I dare say," in quite another voice, and glanced at the picture. But as she remained standing, he continued more earnestly, "I didn't come here to tell you what you might read in the newspapers to-morrow morning, and what everybody might tell you. Before that time I want you to do something to save a fragment of your property from the ruin; do you understand? I want you to make a rally, and bring off something in good order."

"For him?" said Mrs. Tucker, with brightening eyes.

"Well, yes, of course, if you like, but as if for yourself. Do you know the Rancho de los Cuervos?"

"I do."

"It's almost the only bit of real property your husband hasn't sold, mortgaged, or pledged. Why it was exempt, or whether only forgotten, I can't say."

"I'll tell you why," said Mrs. Tucker, with a slight return of color. "It was the first land we ever bought, and Spencer always said it should be mine and he would build a new house on it."

Captain Poindexter smiled and nodded at the picture. "Oh, he did say that, did he? Well, that's evidence. But you see he never gave you the deed, and by sunrise tomorrow his creditors will attach it, unless -

"Unless" - repeated Mrs. Tucker, with kindling eyes.

"Unless," continued Captain Poindexter, "they happen to find you in possession."

"I'll go," said Mrs. Tucker.

"Of course you will," returned Poindexter, pleasantly. "Only, as it's a big contract to take, suppose we see how you can fill it. It's forty miles to Los Cuervos, and you can't trust yourself to steamboat or stage-coach. The steamboat left an hour ago."

"If I had only known this then!" ejaculated Mrs. Tucker.

"I knew it, but you had company then," said Poindexter, with ironical gallantry, "and I wouldn't disturb you." Without saying how he knew it, he continued, "In the stage-coach you might be recognized. You must go in a private conveyance and alone; even I cannot go with you, for I must go on before and meet you there. Can you drive forty miles?"

Mrs. Tucker lifted up her abstracted pretty lids. "I once drove fifty at home," she returned simply.

"Good! And I dare say you did it then for fun. Do it now for something real and personal, as we lawyers say. You will have relays and a plan of the road. It's rough weather for a pasear, but all the better for that. You'll have less company on the road."

"How soon can I go?" she asked.

"The sooner the better. I've arranged everything for you already," he continued with a laugh. "Come now, that's a compliment to you, isn't it?" He smiled a moment in her steadfast, earnest face, and then said, more gravely, "You'll do. Now listen."

He then carefully detailed his plan. There was so little of excitement or mystery in their manner that the servant, who returned to light the gas, never knew that the ruin and bankruptcy of the house was being told before her, or that its mistress was planning her secret flight.

"Good afternoon. I will see you to-morrow then," said Poindexter, raising his eyes to hers as the servant opened the door for him.

"Good afternoon," repeated Mrs. Tucker, quietly answering his look. "You need not light the gas in my room, Mary," she continued in the same tone of voice as the door closed upon him; "I shall lie down for a few moments, and then I may run over to the Robinsons for the evening."

She regained her room composedly. The longing desire to bury her head in her pillow and "think out" her position had gone. She did not apostrophize her fate, she did not weep; few real women do in the access of calamity, or when there is anything else to be done. She felt that she knew it all; she believed she had sounded the profoundest depths of the disaster, and seemed already so old in her experience that she almost fancied she had been prepared for it. Perhaps she did not fully appreciate it. To a life like hers it was only an incident, the mere turning of a page of the illimitable book of youth; the breaking up of what she now felt had become a monotony. In fact, she was not quite sure she had ever been satisfied with their present success. Had it brought her all she expected? She wanted to say this to her husband, not only to comfort him, poor fellow, but that they might come to a better understanding of life in the future. She was not perhaps different from other loving women, who, believing in this unattainable goal of matrimony, have sought it in the various episodes of fortune or reverses, in the bearing of children, or the loss of friends. In her childless experience there was no other life that had taken root in her circumstances and might suffer transplantation; only she and her husband could lose or profit by the change. The "perfect" understanding would come under other conditions than these.

She would have gone superstitiously to the window to gaze in the direction of the vanished ship, but another instinct restrained her. She would put aside all yearning for him until she had done something to help him, and earned the confidence he seemed to have withheld. Perhaps it was pride, perhaps she never really believed his exodus was distant or complete.

With a full knowledge that to-morrow the various ornaments and pretty trifles around her would be in the hands of the law, she gathered only a few necessaries for her flight and some familiar personal trinkets. I am constrained to say that this self-abnegation was more fastidious than moral. She had no more idea of the ethics of bankruptcy than any other charming woman; she simply did not like to take with her any contagious memory of the chapter of the life just closing. She glanced around the home she was leaving without a lingering regret; there was no sentiment of tradition or custom that might be destroyed; her roots lay too near the surface to suffer dislocation; the happiness of her childless union had depended upon no domestic center, nor was its flame sacred to any local hearthstone. It was without a sigh that, when night had fully fallen, she slipped unnoticed down the staircase. At the door of the drawing-room she paused, and then entered with the first guilty feeling of shame she had known that evening. Looking stealthily around, she mounted a chair before her husband's picture, kissed the irreproachable mustache hurriedly, said, "You foolish darling, you!" and slipped out again. With this touching indorsement of the views of a rival philosopher, she closed the door softly and left her home forever.

II.

The wind and rain had cleared the unfrequented suburb of any observant lounger, and the darkness, lit only by far-spaced, gusty lamps, hid her hastening figure. She had barely crossed the second street when she heard the quick clatter of hoofs behind her; a buggy drove up to the curbstone, and Poindexter leaped out. She entered quickly, but for a moment he still held the reins of the impatient horse. "He's rather fresh," he said, eying her keenly: "are you sure you can manage him?"

"Give me the reins," she said simply.

He placed them in the two firm, well-shaped hands that reached from the depths of the vehicle, and was satisfied. Yet he lingered.

"It's rough work for a lone woman," he said, almost curtly, "I can't go with you, but, speak frankly, is there any man you know whom you can trust well enough to take? It's not too late yet; think a moment!"

He paused over the buttoning of the leather apron of the vehicle.

"No, there is none," answered the voice from the interior; "and it's better so. Is all ready?"

"One moment more." He had recovered his half bantering manner. "You have a friend and countryman already with you, do you know? Your horse is Blue Grass. Good-night."

With these words ringing in her ears she began her journey. The horse, as if eager to maintain the reputation which his native district had given his race, as well as the race of the pretty woman behind him, leaped impatiently forward. But pulled together by the fine and firm fingers that seemed to guide rather than check his exuberance, he presently struck into the long, swinging pace of his kind, and kept it throughout without "break" or acceleration. Over the paved streets the light buggy rattled, and the slender shafts danced around his smooth barrel, but when they touched the level high road, horse and vehicle slipped forward through the night, a swift and noiseless phantom. Mrs. Tucker could see his graceful back dimly rising and falling before her with tireless rhythm, and could feel the intelligent pressure of his mouth until it seemed the responsive grasp of a powerful but kindly hand. The faint glow of conquest came to her cold cheek; the slight stirrings of pride moved her preoccupied heart. A soft light filled her hazel eyes. A desolate woman, bereft of husband and home, and flying through storm and night, she knew not where, she still leaned forward towards her horse. "Was he Blue Grass, then, dear old boy?" she gently cooed at him in the darkness. He evidently was, and responded by blowing her an ostentatious equine kiss. "And he would be good to his own forsaken Belle," she murmured caressingly, "and wouldn't let any one harm her?" But here, overcome by the lazy witchery of her voice, he shook his head so violently that Mrs. Tucker, after the fashion of her sex, had the double satisfaction of demurely restraining the passion she had evoked.

To avoid the more traveled thoroughfare, while the evening was still early, it had been arranged that she should at first take a less direct but less frequented road. This was a famous pleasure-drive from San Francisco, a graveled and sanded stretch of eight miles to the sea, and an ultimate "cocktail," in a "stately pleasure-dome decreed" among the surf and rocks of the Pacific shore. It was deserted now, and left to the unobstructed sweep of the wind and rain. Mrs. Tucker would not have chosen this road. With the instinctive jealousy of a bucolic inland race born by great rivers, she did not like the sea; and again, the dim and dreary waste tended to recall the vision connected with her husband's flight, upon which she had resolutely shut her eyes. But when she had reached it the road suddenly turned, following the trend of the beach, and she was exposed to the full power of its dread fascinations. The combined roar of sea and shore was in her ears. As the direct force of the gale had compelled her to furl the protecting hood of the buggy to keep the light vehicle from oversetting or drifting to leeward, she could no longer shut out the heaving chaos on the right, from which the pallid ghosts of dead and dying breakers dimly rose and sank as if in awful salutation. At times through the darkness a white sheet appeared spread before the path and beneath the wheels of the buggy, which, when withdrawn with a reluctant hiss, seemed striving to drag the exhausted beach seaward with it. But the blind terror of her horse, who swerved at every sweep of the surge, shamed her own half superstitious fears, and with the effort to control his alarm she regained her own self-possession, albeit with eyelashes wet not altogether with the salt spray from the sea. This was followed by a reaction, perhaps stimulated by her victory over the beaten animal, when for a time, she knew not how long, she felt only a mad sense of freedom and power, oblivious of even her sorrows, her lost home and husband, and with intense feminine consciousness she longed to be a man. She was scarcely aware that the track turned again inland until the beat of the horse's hoofs on the firm ground and an acceleration of speed showed her she had left the beach and the mysterious sea behind her, and she remembered that she was near the end of the first stage of her journey. Half an hour later the twinkling lights of the roadside inn where she was to change horses rose out of the darkness.

Happily for her, the hostler considered the horse, who had a local reputation, of more importance than the unknown muffled figure in the shadow of the unfurled hood, and confined his attention to the animal. After a careful examination of his feet and a few comments addressed solely to the superior creation, he led him away. Mrs. Tucker would have liked to part more affectionately from her four-footed compatriot, and felt a sudden sense of loneliness at the loss of her new friend, but a recollection of certain cautions of Captain Poindexter's kept her mute. Nevertheless, the hostler's ostentatious adjuration of "Now then, aren't you going to bring out that mustang for the Señora?" puzzled her. It was not until the fresh horse was put to, and she had flung a piece of gold into the attendant's hand, that the "Gracias" of his unmistakable Saxon speech revealed to her the reason of the lawyer's caution. Poindexter had evidently represented her to these people as a native Californian who did not speak English. In her inconsistency her blood took fire at this first suggestion of deceit, and burned in her face. Why should he try to pass her off as anybody else? Why should she not use her own, her husband's name? She stopped and bit her lip.

It was but the beginning of an uneasy train of thought. She suddenly found herself thinking of her visitor, Calhoun Weaver, and not pleasantly. He would hear of their ruin to-morrow, perhaps of her own flight. He would remember his visit, and what would he think of her deceitful frivolity? Would he believe that she was then ignorant of the failure? It was her first sense of any accountability to others than herself, but even then it was rather owing to an uneasy consciousness of what her husband must feel if he were subjected to the criticisms of men like Calhoun. She wondered if others knew that he had kept her in ignorance of his flight. Did Poindexter know it, or had he only entrapped her into the admission? Why had she not been clever enough to make him think that she knew it already? For the moment she hated Poindexter for sharing that secret. Yet this was again followed by a new impatience of her husband's want of insight into her ability to help him. Of course the poor fellow could not bear to worry her, could not bear to face such men as Calhoun, or even Poindexter (she added exultingly to herself), but he might have sent her a line as he fled, only to prepare her to meet and combat the shame alone. It did not occur to her unsophisticated singleness of nature that she was accepting as an error of feeling what the world would call cowardly selfishness.

At midnight the storm lulled and a few stars trembled through the rent clouds. Her eyes had become accustomed to the darkness, and her country instincts, a little overlaid by the urban experiences of the last few years, came again to the surface. She felt the fresh, cool radiation from outlying, upturned fields, the faint, sad odors from dim stretches of pricking grain and quickening leaf, and wondered if at Los Cuervos it might be possible to reproduce the peculiar verdure of her native district. She beguiled her fancy by an ambitious plan of retrieving their fortunes by farming; her comfortable tastes had lately rebelled against the homeless mechanical cultivation of these desolate but teeming Californian acres, and for a moment indulged in a vision of a vine-clad cottage home that in any other woman would have been sentimental. Her cramped limbs aching, she took advantage of the security of the darkness and the familiar contiguity of the fields to get down from the vehicle, gather her skirts together, and run at the head of the mustang, until her chill blood was thawed, night drawing a modest veil over this charming revelation of the nymph and woman. But the sudden shadow of a coyote checked the scouring feet of this swift Camilla, and sent her back precipitately to the buggy. Nevertheless, she was refreshed and able to pursue her journey, until the cold gray of early morning found her at the end of her second stage.

Her route was changed again from the main highway, rendered dangerous by the approach of day and the contiguity of the neighboring rancheros. The road was rough and hilly, her new horse and vehicle in keeping with the rudeness of the route, by far the most difficult of her whole journey. The rare wagon tracks that indicated her road were often scarcely discernible; at times they led her through openings in the half-cleared woods, skirted suspicious morasses, painfully climbed the smooth, domelike hills, or wound along perilous slopes at a dangerous angle. Twice she had to alight and cling to the sliding wheels on one of those treacherous inclines, or drag them from impending ruts or immovable mire. In the growing light she could distinguish the distant, low-lying marshes eaten by encroaching sloughs and insidious channels, and beyond them the faint gray waste of the Lower Bay. A darker peninsula in the marsh she knew to be the extreme boundary of her future home: the Rancho de los Cuervos. In another hour she began to descend to the plain, and once more to approach the main road, which now ran nearly parallel with her track. She scanned it cautiously for any early traveler; it stretched north and south in apparent unending solitude. She struck into it boldly, and urged her horse to the top of his speed, until she reached the cross-road that led to the rancho. But here she paused and allowed the reins to drop idly on the mustang's back. A singular and unaccountable irresolution seized her. The difficulties of her journey were over; the rancho lay scarcely two miles away; she had achieved the most important part of her task in the appointed time; but she hesitated. What had she come for? She tried to recall Poindexter's words, even her own enthusiasm, but in vain. She was going to take possession of her husband's property, she knew, that was all. But the means she had taken seemed now so exaggerated and mysterious for that simple end, that she began to dread an impending something, or some vague danger she had not considered, that she was rushing blindly to meet. Full of this strange feeling, she almost mechanically stopped her horse as she entered the cross-road.

From this momentary hesitation a singular sound aroused her. It seemed at first like the swift hurrying by of some viewless courier of the air, the vague alarm of some invisible flying herald, or like the inarticulate cry that precedes a storm. It seemed to rise and fall around her as if with some changing urgency of purpose. Raising her eyes she suddenly recognized the two far-stretching lines of telegraph wire above her head, and knew the aeolian cry of the morning wind along its vibrating chords. But it brought another and more practical fear to her active brain. Perhaps even now the telegraph might be anticipating her! Had Poindexter thought of that? She hesitated no longer, but laying the whip on the back of her jaded mustang, again hurried forward.

As the level horizon grew more distinct, her attention was attracted by the white sail of a small boat lazily threading the sinuous channel of the slough. It might be Poindexter arriving by the more direct route from the steamboat that occasionally laid off the ancient embarcadero of the Los Cuervos Rancho. But even while watching it her quick ear caught the sound of galloping hoofs behind her. She turned quickly and saw she was followed by a horseman. But her momentary alarm was succeeded by a feeling of relief as she recognized the erect figure and square shoulders of Poindexter. Yet she could not help thinking that he looked more like a militant scout, and less like a cautious legal adviser, than ever.

With unaffected womanliness she rearranged her slightly disordered hair as he drew up beside her. "I thought you were in yonder boat," she said.

"Not I," he laughed; "I distanced you by the highroad two hours, and have been reconnoitering, until I saw you hesitate at the cross-roads."

"But who is in the boat?" asked Mrs. Tucker, partly to hide her embarrassment.

"Only some early Chinese market gardener, I dare say. But you are safe now. You are on your own land. You passed the boundary monument of the rancho five minutes ago. Look! All you see before you is yours from the embarcadero to yonder Coast Range."

The tone of half raillery did not, however, cheer Mrs. Tucker. She shuddered slightly and cast her eyes over the monotonous sea of tule and meadow.

"It doesn't look pretty, perhaps," continued Poindexter, "but it's the richest land in the State, and the embarcadero will someday be a town. I suppose you'll call it Blue Grassville. But you seem tired!" he said, suddenly dropping his voice to a tone of half humorous sympathy.

Mrs. Tucker managed to get rid of an impending tear under the pretense of clearing her eyes. "Are we nearly there?" she asked.

"Nearly. You know," he added, with the same half mischievous, half sympathizing gayety, "it's not exactly a palace you're coming to, hardly. It's the old casa that has been deserted for years, but I thought it better you should go into possession there than take up your abode at the shanty where your husband's farm-hands are. No one will know when you take possession of the casa, while the very hour of your arrival at the shanty would be known; and if they should make any trouble" -

"If they should make any trouble?" repeated Mrs. Tucker, lifting her frank, inquiring eyes to Poindexter.

His horse suddenly rearing from an apparently accidental prick of the spur, it was a minute or two before he was able to explain. "I mean if this ever comes up as a matter of evidence, you know. But here we are!"

What had seemed to be an overgrown mound rising like an island out of the dead level of the grassy sea now resolved itself into a collection of adobe walls, eaten and incrusted with shrubs and vines, that bore some resemblance to the usual uninhabited-looking exterior of a Spanish-American dwelling. Apertures that might have been lance-shaped windows or only cracks and fissures in the walls were choked up with weeds and grass, and gave no passing glimpse of the interior. Entering a ruinous corral they came to a second entrance, which proved to be the patio or courtyard. The deserted wooden corridor, with beams, rafters, and floors whitened by the sun and wind, contained a few withered leaves, dryly rotting skins, and thongs of leather, as if undisturbed by human care. But among these scattered débris of former life and habitation there was no noisome or unclean suggestion of decay. A faint spiced odor of desiccation filled the bare walls. There was no slime on stone or sun-dried brick. In place of fungus or discolored moisture the dust of efflorescence whitened in the obscured corners. The elements had picked clean the bones of the old and crumbling tenement ere they should finally absorb it.

A withered old peon woman, who in dress, complexion, and fibrous hair might have been an animated fragment of the débris, rustled out of a low vaulted passage and welcomed them with a feeble crepitation. Following her into the dim interior, Mrs. Tucker was surprised to find some slight attempt at comfort and even adornment in the two or three habitable apartments. They were scrupulously clean and dry, two qualities which in her feminine eyes atoned for poverty of material.

"I could not send anything from San Bruno, the nearest village, without attracting attention," explained Poindexter; "but if you can manage to picnic here for a day longer, I'll get one of our Chinese friends here," he pointed to the slough, "to bring over, for his return cargo from across the bay, any necessaries you may want. There is no danger of his betraying you," he added, with an ironical smile; "Chinamen and Indians are, by an ingenious provision of the statute of California, incapable of giving evidence against a white person. You can trust your handmaiden perfectly, even if she can't trust you. That is your sacred privilege under the constitution. And now, as I expect to catch the up boat ten miles from hence. I must say 'good-by' until to-morrow night. I hope to bring you then some more definite plans for the future. The worst is over." He held her hand for a moment, and with a graver voice continued, "You have done it very well, do you know, very well!"

In the slight embarrassment produced by his sudden change of manner she felt that her thanks seemed awkward and restrained. "Don't thank me," he laughed, with a prompt return of his former levity; "that's my trade. I only advised. You have saved yourself like a plucky woman, shall I say like Blue Grass? Good-by!" He mounted his horse, but, as if struck by an after-thought, wheeled and drew up by her side again. "If I were you I wouldn't see many strangers for a day or two, and listen to as little news as a woman possibly can." He laughed again, waved her a half gallant, half military salute, and was gone. The question she had been trying to frame, regarding the probability of communication with her husband, remained unasked. At least she had saved her pride before him.

Addressing herself to the care of her narrow household, she mechanically put away the few things she had brought with her, and began to read just the scant furniture. She was a little discomposed at first at the absence of bolts, locks, and even window-fastenings until assured, by Concha's evident inability to comprehend her concern, that they were quite unknown at Los Cuervos. Her slight knowledge of Spanish was barely sufficient to make her wants known, so that the relief of conversation with her only companion was debarred her, and she was obliged to content herself with the sapless, crackling smiles and withered genuflexions that the old woman dropped like dead leaves in her path. It was staring noon when, the house singing like an empty shell in the monotonous wind, she felt she could stand the solitude no longer, and, crossing the glaring patio and whistling corridor, made her way to the open gateway.

But the view without seemed to intensify her desolation. The broad expanse of the shadowless plain reached apparently to the Coast Range, trackless and unbroken save by one or two clusters of dwarfed oaks, which at that distance were but mossy excrescences on the surface, barely raised above the dead level. On the other side the marsh took up the monotony and carried it, scarcely interrupted by undefined water-courses, to the faintly marked-out horizon line of the remote bay. Scattered and apparently motionless black spots on the meadows that gave a dreary significance to the title of "the Crows" which the rancho bore, and sudden gray clouds of sandpipers on the marshes, that rose and vanished down the wind, were the only signs of life. Even the white sail of the early morning was gone.

She stood there until the aching of her straining eyes and the stiffening of her limbs in the cold wind compelled her to seek the sheltered warmth of the courtyard. Here she endeavored to make friends with a bright-eyed lizard, who was sunning himself in the corridor; a graceful little creature in blue and gold, from whom she felt at other times she might have fled, but whose beauty and harmlessness solitude had made known to her. With misplaced kindness she tempted it with bread-crumbs, with no other effect than to stiffen it into stony astonishment. She wondered if she should become like the prisoners she had read of in books, who poured out their solitary affections on noisome creatures, and she regretted even the mustang, which with the buggy had disappeared under the charge of some unknown retainer on her arrival. Was she not a prisoner? The shutterless windows, yawning doors, and open gate refuted the suggestion, but the encompassing solitude and trackless waste still held her captive. Poindexter had told her it was four miles to the shanty; she might walk there. Why had she given her word that she would remain at the rancho until he returned?

The long day crept monotonously away, and she welcomed the night which shut out the dreary prospect. But it brought no cessation of the harassing wind without, nor surcease of the nervous irritation its perpetual and even activity wrought upon her. It haunted her pillow even in her exhausted sleep, and seemed to impatiently beckon her to rise and follow it. It brought her feverish dreams of her husband, footsore and weary, staggering forward under its pitiless lash and clamorous outcry; she would have gone to his assistance, but when she reached his side and held out her arms to him it hurried her past with merciless power, and, bearing her away, left him hopelessly behind. It was broad day when she awoke. The usual night showers of the waning rainy season had left no trace in sky or meadow; the fervid morning sun had already dried the patio; only the restless, harrying wind remained.

Mrs. Tucker arose with a resolve. She had learned from Concha on the previous evening that a part of the shanty was used as a tienda or shop for the laborers and rancheros. Under the necessity of purchasing some articles, she would go there and for a moment mingle with those people, who would not recognize her. Even if they did, her instinct told her it would be less to be feared than the hopeless uncertainty of another day. As she left the house the wind seemed to seize her as in her dream, and hurry her along with it, until in a few moments the walls of the low casa sank into the earth again and she was alone, but for the breeze on the solitary plain. The level distance glittered in the sharp light, a few crows with slant wings dipped and ran down the wind before her, and a passing gleam on the marsh was explained by the far-off cry of a curlew.

She had walked for an hour, upheld by the stimulus of light and morning air, when the cluster of scrub oaks, which was her destination, opened enough to show two rambling sheds, before one of which was a wooden platform containing a few barrels and bones. As she approached nearer, she could see that one or two horses were tethered under the trees, that their riders were lounging by a horse-trough, and that over an open door the word Tienda was rudely painted on a board, and as rudely illustrated by the wares displayed at door and window. Accustomed as she was to the poverty of frontier architecture, even the crumbling walls of the old hacienda she had just left seemed picturesque to the rigid angles of the thin, blank, unpainted shell before her. One of the loungers, who was reading a newspaper aloud as she advanced, put it aside and stared at her; there was an evident commotion in the shop as she stepped upon the platform, and when she entered, with breathless lips and beating heart, she found herself the object of a dozen curious eyes. Her quick pride resented the scrutiny and recalled her courage, and it was with a slight coldness in her usual lazy indifference that she leaned over the counter and asked for the articles she wanted.

The request was followed by a dead silence. Mrs. Tucker repeated it with some hauteur.

"I reckon you don't seem to know this store is in the hands of the sheriff," said one of the loungers.

Mrs. Tucker was not aware of it.

"Well, I don't know anyone who's a better right to know than Spence Tucker's wife," said another with a coarse laugh. The laugh was echoed by the others. Mrs. Tucker saw the pit into which she had deliberately walked, but did not flinch.

"Is there any one to serve here?" she asked, turning her clear eyes full upon the bystanders.

"You'd better ask the sheriff. He was the last one to sarve here. He sarved an attachment," replied the inevitable humorist of all Californian assemblages.

"Is he here?" asked Mrs. Tucker, disregarding the renewed laughter which followed this subtle witticism.

The loungers at the door made way for one of their party, who was half dragged, half pushed into the shop. "Here he is," said half a dozen eager voices, in the fond belief that his presence might impart additional humor to the situation. He cast a deprecating glance at Mrs. Tucker and said, "It's so, madam! This yer place is attached; but if there's anything you're wanting, why I reckon, boys," he turned half appealingly to the crowd, "we could oblige a lady." There was a vague sound of angry opposition and remonstrance from the back door of the shop, but the majority, partly overcome by Mrs. Tucker's beauty, assented. "Only," continued the officer explanatorily, "ez these yer goods are in the hands of the creditors, they ought to be represented by an equivalent in money. If you're expecting they should be charged" -

"But I wish to, pay for them," interrupted Mrs. Tucker, with a slight flush of indignation; "I have the money."

"Oh, I bet you have!" screamed a voice, as, overturning all opposition, the malcontent at the back door, in the shape of an infuriated woman, forced her way into the shop. "I'll bet you have the money! Look at her, boys! Look at the wife of the thief, with the stolen money in diamonds in her ears and rings on her fingers. She's got money if we've none. She can pay for what she fancies, if we haven't a cent to redeem the bed that's stolen from under us. Oh yes, buy it all, Mrs. Spencer Tucker! buy the whole shop, Mrs. Spencer Tucker, do you hear? And if you ain't satisfied then, buy my clothes, my wedding ring, the only things your husband hasn't stolen."

"I don't understand you," said Mrs. Tucker coldly, turning towards the door. But with a flying leap across the counter her relentless adversary stood between her and retreat.

"You don't understand! Perhaps you don't understand that your husband not only stole the hard labor of these men, but even the little money they brought here and trusted to his thieving hands. Perhaps you don't know that he stole my husband's hard earnings, mortgaged these very goods you want to buy, and that he is to-day a convicted thief, a forger, and a runaway coward. Perhaps, if you can't understand me, you can read the newspaper. Look!" She exultingly opened the paper the sheriff had been reading aloud, and pointed to the displayed headlines. "Look! there are the very words, 'Forgery, Swindling, Embezzlement!' Do you see? And perhaps you can't understand this. Look! 'Shameful Flight. Abandons his Wife. Runs off with a Notorious'" -

"Easy, old gal, easy now. Dann it! Will you dry up? I say. Stop!"

It was too late! The sheriff had dashed the paper from the woman's hand, but not until Mrs. Tucker had read a single line, a line such as she had sometimes turned from with weary scorn in her careless perusal of the daily shameful chronicle of domestic infelicity. Then she had coldly wondered if there could be any such men and women. And now! The crowd fell back before her; even the virago was silenced as she looked at her face. The humorist's face was as white, but not as immobile, as he gasped, "Christ! if I don't believe she knew nothin' of it!"

For a moment the full force of such a supposition, with all its poignancy, its dramatic intensity, and its pathos, possessed the crowd. In the momentary clairvoyance of enthusiasm they caught a glimpse of the truth, and by one of the strange reactions of human passion they only waited for a word of appeal or explanation from her lips to throw themselves at her feet. Had she simply told her story they would have believed her; had she cried, fainted, or gone into hysterics, they would have pitied her. She did neither. Perhaps she thought of neither, or indeed of anything that was then before her eyes. She walked erect to the door and turned upon the threshold. "I mean what I say," she said calmly. "I don't understand you. But whatever just claims you have upon my husband will be paid by me, or by his lawyer, Captain Poindexter."

She had lost the sympathy but not the respect of her hearers. They made way for her with sullen deference as she passed out on the platform. But her adversary, profiting by the last opportunity, burst into an ironical laugh.

"Captain Poindexter, is it? Well, perhaps he's safe to pay your bill; but as for your husband's" -

"That's another matter," interrupted a familiar voice with the greatest cheerfulness; "that's what you were going to say, wasn't it? Ha! ha! Well, Mrs. Patterson," continued Poindexter, stepping from his buggy, "you never spoke a truer word in your life. One moment, Mrs. Tucker. Let me send you back in the buggy. Don't mind me. I can get a fresh horse of the sheriff. I'm quite at home here." Then, turning to one of the bystanders, "I say, Patterson, step a few paces this way, will you? A little further from your wife, please. That will do. You've got a claim of five thousand dollars against the property, haven't you?"

"Yes."

"Well, that woman just driving away is your one solitary chance of getting a cent of it. If your wife insults her again, that chance is gone. And if you do" -

"Well?"

"As sure as there is a God in Israel and a Supreme Court of the State of California, I'll kill you in your tracks!.... Stay!"

Patterson turned. The irrepressible look of humorous tolerance of all human frailty had suffused Poindexter's black eyes with mischievous moisture. "If you think it quite safe to confide to your wife this prospect of her improvement by widowhood, you may!"

III.

Mr. Patterson did not inform his wife of the lawyer's personal threat to himself. But he managed, after Poindexter had left, to make her conscious that Mrs. Tucker might be a power to be placated and feared. "You've shot off your mouth at her," he said argumentatively, "and whether you've hit the mark or not you've had your say. Ef you think it's worth a possible five thousand dollars and interest to keep on, heave ahead. Ef you rather have the chance of getting the rest in cash, you'll let up on her." "You don't suppose," returned Mrs. Patterson contemptuously, "that she's got anything but what that man of hers, Poindexter, lets her have?" "The sheriff says," retorted Patterson surlily, "that she's notified him that she claims the rancho as a gift from her husband three years ago, and she's in possession now, and was so when the execution was out. It don't make no matter," he added, with gloomy philosophy, "who's got a full hand as long as we ain't got the cards to chip in. I wouldn't 'a' minded it," he continued meditatively, "ef Spence Tucker had dropped a hint to me afore he put out." "And I suppose," said Mrs. Patterson angrily, "you'd have put out too?" "I reckon," said Patterson simply.

Twice or thrice during the evening he referred, more or less directly, to this lack of confidence shown by his late debtor and employer, and seemed to feel it more keenly than the loss of property. He confided his sentiments quite openly to the sheriff in possession, over the whiskey and euchre with which these gentlemen avoided the difficulties of their delicate relations. He brooded over it as he handed the keys of the shop to the sheriff when they parted for the night, and was still thinking of it when the house was closed, everybody gone to bed, and he was fetching a fresh jug of water from the well. The moon was at times obscured by flying clouds, the avant-couriers of the regular evening shower. He was stooping over the well, when he sprang suddenly to his feet again. "Who's there?" he demanded sharply.

"Hush!" said a voice so low and faint it might have been a whisper of the wind in the palisades of the corral. But, indistinct as it was, it was the voice of a man he was thinking of as far away, and it sent a thrill of alternate awe and pleasure through his pulses.

He glanced quickly round. The moon was hidden by a passing cloud, and only the faint outlines of the house he had just quitted were visible. "Is that you, Spence?" he said tremulously.

"Yes," replied the voice, and a figure dimly emerged from the corner of the corral.

"Lay low, lay low, for God's sake," said Patterson, hurriedly throwing himself upon the apparition. "The sheriff and his posse are in there."

"But I must speak to you a moment," said the figure.

"Wait," said Patterson, glancing toward the building. Its blank, shutterless windows revealed no inner light; a profound silence encompassed it. "Come quick," he whispered. Letting his grasp slip down to the unresisting hand of the stranger, he half dragged, half led him, brushing against the wall, into the open door of the deserted bar-room he had just quitted, locked the inner door, poured a glass of whiskey from a decanter, gave it to him, and then watched him drain it at a single draught.

The moon came out, and falling through the bare windows full upon the stranger's face, revealed the artistic but slightly disheveled curls and mustache of the fugitive, Spencer Tucker.

Whatever may have been the real influence of this unfortunate man upon his fellows, it seemed to find expression in a singular unanimity of criticism. Patterson looked at him with a half dismal, half welcoming smile. "Well, you are a hell of a fellow, ain't you?"

Spencer Tucker passed his hand through his hair and lifted it from his forehead, with a gesture at once emotional and theatrical. "I am a man with a price on me!" he said bitterly. "Give me up to the sheriff, and you'll get five thousand dollars. Help me, and you'll get nothing. That's my damned luck, and yours too, I suppose."

"I reckon you're right there," said Patterson gloomily. "But I thought you got clean away, went off in a ship" -

"Went off in a boat to a ship," interrupted Tucker savagely; "went off to a ship that had all my things on board, everything. The cursed boat capsized in a squall just off the Heads. The ship, damn her, sailed away, the men thinking I was drowned, likely, and that they'd make a good thing off my goods, I reckon."

"But the girl, Inez, who was with you, didn't she make a row?"

"Quien sabe?" returned Tucker, with a reckless laugh. "Well, I hung on like grim death to that boat's keel until one of those Chinese fishermen, in a 'dug-out,' hauled me in opposite Saucelito. I chartered him and his dug-out to bring me down here."

"Why here?" asked Patterson, with a certain ostentatious caution that ill concealed his pensive satisfaction.

"You may well ask," returned Tucker, with an equal ostentation of bitterness, as he slightly waved his companion away. "But I reckoned I could trust a white man that I'd been kind to, and who wouldn't go back on me. No, no, let me go! Hand me over to the sheriff!"

Patterson had suddenly grasped both the hands of the picturesque scamp before him, with an affection that for an instant almost shamed the man who had ruined him. But Tucker's egotism whispered that this affection was only a recognition of his own superiority, and felt flattered. He was beginning to believe that he was really the injured party.

"What I have and what I have had is yours, Spence," returned Patterson, with a sad and simple directness that made any further discussion a gratuitous insult. "I only wanted to know what you reckoned to do here."

"I want to get over across the Coast Range to Monterey," said Tucker. "Once there, one of those coasting schooners will bring me down to Acapulco, where the ship will put in."

Patterson remained silent for a moment. "There's a mustang in the corral you can take, leastways, I shan't know that it's gone, until to-morrow afternoon. In an hour from now," he added, looking from the window, "these clouds will settle down to business. It will rain; there will be light enough for you to find your way by the regular trail over the mountain, but not enough for any one to know you. If you can't push through to-night, you can lie over at the posada on the summit. Them greasers that keep it won't know you, And if they did they won't go back on you. And if they did go back on you, nobody would believe them. It's mighty curious," he added, with gloomy philosophy, "but I reckon it's the reason why Providence allows this kind of cattle to live among white men and others made in his image. Take a piece of pie, won't you?" he continued, abandoning this abstract reflection and producing half a flat pumpkin pie from the bar. Spencer Tucker grasped the pie with one hand and his friend's fingers with the other, and for a few moments was silent from the hurried deglutition of viand and sentiment. "You're a white man, Patterson, any way," he resumed. "I'll take your horse, and put it down in our account at your own figure. As soon as this cursed thing is blown over, I'll be back here and see you through, you bet! I don't desert my friends, however rough things go with me."

"I see you don't," returned Patterson, with an unconscious and serious simplicity that had the effect of the most exquisite irony. "I was only just saying to the sheriff that if there was anything I could have done for you, you wouldn't have cut away without letting me know." Tucker glanced uneasily at Patterson, who continued, "Ye ain't wanting anything else?" Then observing that his former friend and patron was roughly but newly clothed, and betrayed no trace of his last escapade, he added, "I see you've got a fresh harness."

"That damned Chinaman bought me these at the landing. They're not much in style or fit," he continued, trying to get a moonlight view of himself in the mirror behind the bar, "but that don't matter here." He filled another glass of spirits, jauntily settled himself back in his chair, and added, "I don't suppose there are any girls around, anyway."

"'Cept your wife; she was down here this afternoon," said Patterson meditatively.

Mr. Tucker paused with the pie in his hand. "Ah, yes!" He essayed a reckless laugh, but that evident simulation failed before Patterson's melancholy. With an assumption of falling in with his friend's manner, rather than from any personal anxiety, he continued, "Well?"

"That man Poindexter was down here with her. Put her in the hacienda to hold possession afore the news came out."

"Impossible!" said Tucker, rising hastily. "It don't belong, that is" - he hesitated.

"Yer thinking the creditors'll get it, mebbe," returned Patterson, gazing at the floor. "Not as long as she's in it; no sir! Whether it's really hers, or she's only keeping house for Poindexter, she's a fixture, you bet. They are a team when they pull together, they are!"

The smile slowly faded from Tucker's face, that now looked quite rigid in the moonlight. He put down his glass and walked to the window as Patterson gloomily continued: "But that's nothing to you. You've got ahead of 'em both, and had your revenge by going off with the gal. That's what I said all along. When folks, specially women folks, wondered how you could leave a woman like your wife, and go off with a scallawag like that gal, I allers said they'd find out there was a reason. And when your wife came flaunting down here with Poindexter before she'd quite got quit of you, I reckon they began to see the whole little game. No, sir! I knew it wasn't on account of the gal! Why, when you came here to-night and told me quite nat'ral-like and easy how she went off in the ship, and then calmly ate your pie and drank your whiskey after it, I knew you didn't care for her. There's my hand, Spence; you're a trump, even if you are a little looney, eh? Why, what's up?"

Shallow and selfish as Tucker was, Patterson's words seemed like a revelation that shocked him as profoundly as it might have shocked a nobler nature. The simple vanity and selfishness that made him unable to conceive any higher reason for his wife's loyalty than his own personal popularity and success, now that he no longer possessed that éclat, made him equally capable of the lowest suspicions. He was a dishonored fugitive, broken in fortune and reputation, why should she not desert him? He had been unfaithful to her from wildness, from caprice, from the effect of those fascinating qualities; it seemed to him natural that she should be disloyal from more deliberate motives, and he hugged himself with that belief. Yet there was enough doubt, enough of haunting suspicion, that he had lost or alienated a powerful affection, to make him thoroughly miserable. He returned his friend's grasp convulsively and buried his face upon his shoulder. But he was above feeling a certain exultation in the effect of his misery upon the dog-like, unreasoning affection of Patterson, nor could he entirely refrain from slightly posing his affliction before that sympathetic but melancholy man. Suddenly he raised his head, drew back, and thrust his hand into his bosom with a theatrical gesture.

"What's to keep me from killing Poindexter in his tracks?" he said wildly.

"Nothin' but his shooting first," returned Patterson, with dismal practicality. "He's mighty quick, like all them army men. It's about even, I reckon, that he don't get me first," he added in an ominous voice.

"No!" returned Tucker, grasping his hand again. "This is not your affair, Patterson; leave him to me when I come back."

"If he ever gets the drop on me, I reckon he won't wait," continued Patterson lugubriously. "He seems to object to my passin' criticism on your wife, as if she was a queen or an angel."

The blood came to Spencer's cheek, and he turned uneasily to the window. "It's dark enough now for a start," he said hurriedly, "and if I could get across the mountain without lying over at the summit, it would be a day gained."

Patterson arose without a word, filled a flask of spirit, handed it to his friend, and silently led the way through the slowly falling rain and the now settled darkness. The mustang was quickly secured and saddled; a heavy poncho afforded Tucker a disguise as well as a protection from the rain. With a few hurried, disconnected words, and an abstracted air, he once more shook his friend's hand and issued cautiously from the corral. When out of earshot from the house he put spurs to the mustang, and dashed into a gallop.

To intersect the mountain road he was obliged to traverse part of the highway his wife had walked that afternoon, and to pass within a mile of the casa where she was. Long before he reached that point his eyes were straining the darkness in that direction for some indication of the house which was to him familiar. Becoming now accustomed to the even obscurity, less trying to the vision than the alternate light and shadow of cloud or the full glare of the moonlight, he fancied he could distinguish its low walls over the monotonous level. One of those impulses which had so often taken the place of resolution in his character suddenly possessed him to diverge from his course and approach the house. Why, he could not have explained. It was not from any feeling of jealous suspicion or contemplated revenge, that had passed with the presence of Patterson; it was not from any vague lingering sentiment for the woman he had wronged, he would have shrunk from meeting her at that moment. But it was full of these and more possibilities by which he might or might not be guided, and was at least a movement towards some vague end, and a distraction from certain thoughts he dared not entertain and could not entirely dismiss. Inconceivable and inexplicable to human reason, it might have been acceptable to the Divine omniscience for its predestined result.

He left the road at a point where the marsh encroached upon the meadow, familiar to him already as near the spot where he had debarked from the Chinaman's boat the day before. He remembered that the walls of the hacienda were distinctly visible from the tules where he had hidden all day, and he now knew that the figures he had observed near the building, which had deterred his first attempts at landing, must have been his wife and his friend. He knew that a long tongue of the slough filled by the rising tide followed the marsh, and lay between him and the hacienda. The sinking of his horse's hoofs in the spongy soil determined its proximity, and he made a detour to the right to avoid it. In doing so, a light suddenly rose above the distant horizon ahead of him, trembled faintly, and then burned with a steady lustre. It was a light at the hacienda. Guiding his horse half abstractedly in this direction, his progress was presently checked by the splashing of the animal's hoofs in the water. But the turf below was firm, and a salt drop that had spattered to his lips told him that it was only the encroaching of the tide in the meadow. With his eyes on the light, he again urged his horse forward. The rain lulled, the clouds began to break, the landscape alternately lightened and grew dark; the outlines of the crumbling hacienda walls that enshrined the light grew more visible. A strange and dreamy resemblance to the long blue-grass plain before his wife's paternal house, as seen by him during his evening rides to courtship, pressed itself upon him. He remembered, too, that she used to put a light in the window to indicate her presence. Following this retrospect, the moon came boldly out, sparkled upon the overflow of silver at his feet, seemed to show the dark, opaque meadow beyond for a moment, and then disappeared. It was dark now, but the lesser earthly star still shone before him as a guide, and pushing towards it, he passed in the all-embracing shadow.

IV.

As Mrs. Tucker, erect, white, and rigid, drove away from the tienda, it seemed to her to sink again into the monotonous plain, with all its horrible realities. Except that there was now a new and heart-breaking significance to the solitude and loneliness of the landscape, all that had passed might have been a dream. But as the blood came back to her cheek, and little by little her tingling consciousness returned, it seemed as if her life had been the dream, and this last scene the awakening reality. With eyes smarting with the moisture of shame, the scarlet blood at times dyeing her very neck and temples, she muffled her lowered crest in her shawl and bent over the reins. Bit by bit she recalled, in Poindexter's mysterious caution and strange allusions, the corroboration of her husband's shame and her own disgrace. This was why she was brought hither, the deserted wife, the abandoned confederate! The mocking glitter of the concave vault above her, scoured by the incessant wind, the cold stare of the shining pools beyond, the hard outlines of the Coast Range, and the jarring accompaniment of her horse's hoofs and rattling buggy-wheels, alternately goaded and distracted her. She found herself repeating "No! no! no!" with the dogged reiteration of fever. She scarcely knew when or how she reached the hacienda. She was only conscious that as she entered the patio the dusky solitude that had before filled her with unrest now came to her like balm. A benumbing peace seemed to fall from the crumbling walls; the peace of utter seclusion, isolation, oblivion, death! Nevertheless, an hour later, when the jingle of spurs and bridle were again heard in the road, she started to her feet with bent brows and a kindling eye, and confronted Captain Poindexter in the corridor.

"I would not have intruded upon you so soon again," he said gravely, "but I thought I might perhaps spare you a repetition of the scene of this morning. Hear me out, please," he added, with a gentle, half deprecating gesture, as she lifted the beautiful scorn of her eyes to his. "I have just heard that your neighbor, Don José Santierra, of Los Gatos, is on his way to this house. He once claimed this land, and hated your husband, who bought of the rival claimant, whose grant was confirmed. I tell you this," he added, slightly flushing as Mrs. Tucker turned impatiently away, "only to show you that legally he has no rights, and you need not see him unless you choose. I could not stop his coming without perhaps doing you more harm than good; but when he does come, my presence under this roof as your legal counsel will enable you to refer him to me." He stopped. She was pacing the corridor with short, impatient steps, her arms dropped, and her hands clasped rigidly before her. "Have I your permission to stay?"

She suddenly stopped in her walk, approached him rapidly, and fixing her eyes on his, said:

"Do I know all, now, everything?"

He could only reply that she had not yet told him what she had heard.

"Well," she said scornfully, "that my husband has been cruelly imposed upon, imposed upon by some wretched woman, who has made him sacrifice his property, his friends, his honor, everything but me!"

"Everything but whom?" gasped Poindexter.

"But ME!"

Poindexter gazed at the sky, the air, the deserted corridor, the stones of the patio itself, and then at the inexplicable woman before him. Then he said gravely, "I think you know everything."

"Then if my husband has left me all he could, this property," she went on rapidly, twisting her handkerchief between her fingers, "I can do with it what I like, can't I?"

"You certainly can."

"Then sell it," she said, with passionate vehemence. "Sell it all! everything! And sell these." She darted into her bedroom, and returned with the diamond rings she had torn from her fingers and ears when she entered the house. "Sell them for anything they'll bring, only sell them at once."

"But for what?" asked Poindexter, with demure lips but twinkling eyes.

"To pay the debts that this, this woman has led him into; to return the money she has stolen!" she went on rapidly; "to keep him from sharing infamy! Can't you understand?"

"But, my dear madam," began Poindexter, "even if this could be done" -

"Don't tell me 'if it could', it must be done. Do you think I could sleep under this roof, propped up by the timbers of that ruined tienda? Do you think I could wear those diamonds again, while that termagant shop-woman can say that her money bought them? No! If you are my husband's friend you will do this for, for his sake." She stopped, locked and interlocked her cold fingers before her, and said, hesitating and mechanically, "You meant well, Captain Poindexter, in bringing me here, I know! You must not think that I blame you for it, or for the miserable result of it that you have just witnessed. But if I have gained anything by it, for God's sake let me reap it quickly, that I may give it to these people and go! I have a friend who can aid me to get to my husband or to my home in Kentucky, where Spencer will yet find me, I know. I want nothing more." She stopped again. With another woman the pause would have been one of tears. But she kept her head above the flood that filled her heart, and the clear eyes fixed upon Poindexter, albeit pained, were undimmed.

"But this would require time," said Poindexter, with a smile of compassionate explanation; "you could not sell now, nobody would buy. You are safe to hold this property while you are in actual possession, but you are not strong enough to guarantee it to another. There may still be litigation; your husband has other creditors than these people you have talked with. But while nobody could oust you, the wife who would have the sympathies of judge and jury, it might be a different case with anyone who derived title from you. Any purchaser would know that you could not sell, or if you did, it would be at a ridiculous sacrifice."

She listened to him abstractedly, walked to the end of the corridor, returned, and without looking up, said:

"I suppose you know her?"

"I beg your pardon?"

"This woman. You have seen her?"

"Never, to my knowledge."

"And you are his friend! That's strange." She raised her eyes to his. "Well," she continued impatiently, "who is she? and what is she? You know that surely."

"I know no more of her than what I have said." said Poindexter. "She is a notorious woman."

The swift color came to Mrs. Tucker's face as if the epithet had been applied to herself. "I suppose," she said in a dry voice, as if she were asking a business question, but with an eye that showed her rising anger, "I suppose there is some law by which creatures of this kind can be followed and brought to justice, some law that would keep innocent people from suffering for their crimes?"

"I am afraid," said Poindexter, "that arresting her would hardly help these people over in the tienda."

"I am not speaking of them," responded Mrs. Tucker, with a sudden sublime contempt for the people whose cause she had espoused; "I am talking of my husband."

Poindexter bit his lip. "You'd hardly think of bringing back the strongest witness against him," he said bluntly.

Mrs. Tucker dropped her eyes and was silent. A sudden shame suffused Poindexter's cheek; he felt as if he had struck that woman a blow. "I beg your pardon," he said hastily; "I am talking like a lawyer to a lawyer." He would have taken any other woman by the hand in the honest fullness of his apology, but something restrained him here. He only looked down gently on her lowered lashes, and repeated his question if he should remain during the coming interview with Don José. "I must beg you to determine quickly," he added, "for I already hear him entering the gate."

"Stay," said Mrs. Tucker, as the ringing of spurs and clatter of hoofs came from the corral. "One moment." She looked up suddenly, and said, "How long had he known her?" But before he could reply there was a step in the doorway, and the figure of Don José Santierra emerged from the archway.

He was a man slightly past middle age, fair, and well shaven, wearing a black broadcloth serape, the deeply embroidered opening of which formed a collar of silver rays around his neck, while a row of silver buttons down the side seams of his riding-trousers, and silver spurs completed his singular equipment. Mrs. Tucker's swift feminine glance took in these details, as well as the deep salutation, more formal than the exuberant frontier politeness she was accustomed to, with which he greeted her. It was enough to arrest her first impulse to retreat. She hesitated and stopped as Poindexter stepped forward, partly interposing between them, acknowledging Don José's distant recognition of himself with an ironical accession of his usual humorous tolerance. The Spaniard did not seem to notice it, but remained gravely silent before Mrs. Tucker, gazing at her with an expression of intent and unconscious absorption.

"You are quite right, Don José," said Poindexter, with ironical concern, "it is Mrs. Tucker. Your eyes do not deceive you. She will be glad to do the honors of her house," he continued, with a simulation of appealing to her, "unless you visit her on business, when I need not say I shall be only too happy to attend you, as before."

Don José, with a slight lifting of the eyebrows, allowed himself to become conscious of the lawyer's meaning. "It is not of business that I come to kiss the Señora's hand to-day," he replied, with a melancholy softness; "it is as her neighbor, to put myself at her disposition. Ah! what have we here fit for a lady?" he continued, raising his eyes in deprecation of the surroundings; "a house of nothing, a place of winds and dry bones, without refreshments, or satisfaction, or delicacy. The Señora will not refuse to make us proud this day to send her of that which we have in our poor home at Los Gatos, to make her more complete. Of what shall it be? Let her make choice. Or if she would commemorate this day by accepting of our hospitality at Los Gatos, until she shall arrange herself the more to receive us here, we shall have too much honor."

"The Señora would only find it the more difficult to return to this humble roof again, after once leaving it for Don José's hospitality," said Poindexter, with a demure glance at Mrs. Tucker. But the innuendo seemed to lapse equally unheeded by his fair client and the stranger. Raising her eyes with a certain timid dignity which Don José's presence seemed to have called out, she addressed herself to him.

"You are very kind and considerate, Mister Santierra, and I thank you. I know that my husband", she let the clear beauty of her translucent eyes rest full on both men, "would thank you too. But I shall not be here long enough to accept your kindness in this house nor in your own. I have but one desire and object now. It is to dispose of this property, and indeed all I possess, to pay the debt of my husband. It is in your power, perhaps, to help me. I am told that you wish to possess Los Cuervos," she went on, equally oblivious of the consciousness that appeared in Don José's face, and a humorous perplexity on the brow of Poindexter. "If you can arrange it with Mr. Poindexter, you will find me a liberal vendor. That much you can do, and I know you will believe I shall be grateful. You can do no more, unless it be to say to your friends that Mrs. Belle Tucker remains here only for that purpose, and to carry out what she knows to be the wishes of her husband." She paused, bent her pretty crest, dropped a quaint curtsey to the superior age, the silver braid, and the gentlemanly bearing of Don José, and with the passing sunshine of a smile disappeared from the corridor.

The two men remained silent for a moment, Don José gazing abstractedly on the door through which she had vanished, until Poindexter, with a return of his tolerant smile, said, "You have heard the views of Mrs. Tucker. You know the situation as well as she does."

"Ah, yes; possibly better."

Poindexter darted a quick glance at the grave, sallow face of Don José, but detecting no unusual significance in his manner, continued, "As you see, she leaves this matter in my hands. Let us talk like business men. Have you any idea of purchasing this property?"

"Of purchasing? ah, no."

Poindexter bent his brows, but quickly relaxed them with a smile of humorous forgiveness. "If you have any other idea, Don José, I ought to warn you, as Mrs. Tucker's lawyer, that she is in legal possession here, and that nothing but her own act can change that position."

"Ah, so."

Irritated at the shrug which accompanied this, Poindexter continued haughtily, "If I am to understand, you have nothing to say" -

"To say, ah, yes, possibly. But" - he glanced toward the door of Mrs. Tucker's room, "not here." He stopped, appeared to recall himself, and with an apologetic smile and a studied but graceful gesture of invitation, he motioned to the gateway, and said, "Will you ride?"

"What can the fellow be up to?" muttered Poindexter, as with an assenting nod he proceeded to remount his horse. "If he wasn't an old hidalgo, I'd mistrust him. No matter! here goes!"

The Don also remounted his half-broken mustang; they proceeded in solemn silence through the corral, and side by side emerged on the open plain. Poindexter glanced round; no other being was in sight. It was not until the lonely hacienda had also sunk behind them that Don José broke the silence.

"You say just now we shall speak as business men. I say no, Don Marco; I will not. I shall speak, we shall speak, as gentlemen."

"Go on," said Poindexter, who was beginning to be amused.

"I say just now I will not purchase the rancho from the Señora. And why? Look you, Don Marco;" he reined in his horse, thrust his hand under his serape, and drew out a folded document: "this is why."

With a smile, Poindexter took the paper from his hand and opened it. But the smile faded from his lips as he read. With blazing eyes he spurred his horse beside the Spaniard, almost unseating him, and said sternly, "What does this mean?"

"What does it mean?" repeated Don José, with equally flashing eyes; "I'll tell you. It means that your client, this man Spencer Tucker, is a Judas, a traitor! It means that he gave Los Cuervos to his mistress a year ago, and that she sold it to me, to me, you hear! me, José Santierra, the day before she left! It means that the coyote of a Spencer, the thief, who bought these lands of a thief and gave them to a thief, has tricked you all. Look," he said, rising in his saddle, holding the paper like a bâton, and defining with a sweep of his arm the whole level plain, "all these lands were once mine, they are mine again to-day. Do I want to purchase Los Cuervos? you ask, for you will speak of the business. Well, listen. I have purchased Los Cuervos, and here is the deed."

"But it has never been recorded," said Poindexter, with a carelessness he was far from feeling.

"Of a verity, no. Do you wish that I should record it?" asked Don José, with a return of his simple gravity.

Poindexter bit his lip. "You said we were to talk like gentlemen," he returned. "Do you think you have come into possession of this alleged deed like a gentleman?"

Don José shrugged his shoulders, "I found it tossed in the lap of a harlot. I bought it for a song. Eh, what would you?"

"Would you sell it again for a song?" asked Poindexter.

"Ah! what is this?" said Don José, lifting his iron-gray brows; "but a moment ago we would sell everything, for any money. Now we would buy. Is it so?"

"One moment, Don José," said Poindexter, with a baleful light in his dark eyes. "Do I understand that you are the ally of Spencer Tucker and his mistress, that you intend to turn this doubly betrayed wife from the only roof she has to cover her?"

"Ah, I comprehend not. You heard her say she wished to go. Perhaps it may please me to distribute largess to these cattle yonder, I do not say no. More she does not ask. But you, Don Marco, of whom are you advocate? You abandon your client's mistress for the wife, is it so?"

"What I may do you will learn hereafter," said Poindexter, who had regained his composure, suddenly reining up his horse. "As our paths seem likely to diverge, they had better begin now. Good morning."

"Patience, my friend, patience! Ah, blessed St. Anthony, what these Americans are! Listen. For what you shall do, I do not inquire. The question is to me what I" - he emphasized the pronoun by tapping himself on the breast - "I, José Santierra, will do. Well, I shall tell you. To-day, nothing. To-morrow, nothing. For a week, for a month, nothing! After, we shall see."

Poindexter paused thoughtfully. "Will you give your word, Don José, that you will not press the claim for a month?"

"Truly, on one condition. Observe! I do not ask you for an equal promise, that you will not take this time to defend yourself." He shrugged his shoulder. "No! It is only this. You shall promise that during that time the Señora Tucker shall remain ignorant of this document."

Poindexter hesitated a moment. "I promise," he said at last.

"Good. Adios, Don Marco."

"Adios, Don José"

The Spaniard put spurs to his mustang and galloped off in the direction of Los Gatos. The lawyer remained for a moment gazing on his retreating but victorious figure. For the first time the old look of humorous toleration with which Mr. Poindexter was in the habit of regarding all human infirmity gave way to something like bitterness. "I might have guessed it," he said, with a slight rise of color. "He's an old fool; and she, well, perhaps it's all the better for her!" He glanced backwards almost tenderly in the direction of Los Cuervos, and then turned his head towards the embarcadero.

As the afternoon wore on, a creaking, antiquated oxcart arrived at Los Cuervos, bearing several articles of furniture, and some tasteful ornaments from Los Gatos, at the same time that a young Mexican girl mysteriously appeared in the kitchen, as a temporary assistant to the decrepit Concha. These were both clearly attributable to Don José, whose visit was not so remote but that these delicate attentions might have been already projected before Mrs. Tucker had declined them, and she could not, without marked discourtesy, return them now. She did not wish to seem discourteous; she would like to have been more civil to this old gentleman, who still retained the evidences of a picturesque and decorous past, and a repose so different from the life that was perplexing her. Reflecting that if he bought the estate these things would be ready to his hand, and with a woman's instinct recognizing their value in setting off the house to other purchasers' eyes, she took a pleasure in tastefully arranging them, and even found herself speculating how she might have enjoyed them herself had she been able to keep possession of the property. After all, it would not have been so lonely if refined and gentle neighbors, like this old man, would have sympathized with her; she had an instinctive feeling that, in their own hopeless decay and hereditary unfitness for this new civilization, they would have been more tolerant of her husband's failure than his own kind. She could not believe that Don José really hated her husband for buying of the successful claimant, as there was no other legal title. Allowing herself to become interested in the guileless gossip of the new handmaiden, proud of her broken English, she was drawn into a sympathy with the grave simplicity of Don José's character, a relic of that true nobility which placed this descendant of the Castilians and the daughter of a free people on the same level.

In this way the second day of her occupancy of Los Cuervos closed, with dumb clouds along the gray horizon, and the paroxysms of hysterical wind growing fainter and fainter outside the walls; with the moon rising after nightfall, and losing itself in silent and mysterious confidences with drifting scud. She went to bed early, but woke past midnight, hearing, as she thought, her own name called. The impression was so strong upon her that she rose, and, hastily enwrapping herself, went to the dark embrasures of the oven-shaped windows, and looked out. The dwarfed oak beside the window was still dropping from a past shower, but the level waste of marsh and meadow beyond seemed to advance and recede with the coming and going of the moon. Again she heard her name called, and this time in accents so strangely familiar that with a slight cry she ran into the corridor, crossed the patio, and reached the open gate. The darkness that had, even in this brief interval, again fallen upon the prospect she tried in vain to pierce with eye and voice. A blank silence followed. Then the veil was suddenly withdrawn; the vast plain, stretching from the mountain to the sea, shone as clearly as in the light of day; the moving current of the channel glittered like black pearls, the stagnant pools like molten lead; but not a sign of life nor motion broke the monotony of the broad expanse. She must have surely dreamed it. A chill wind drove her back to the house again; she entered her bedroom, and in half an hour she was in a peaceful sleep.

V.

The two men kept their secret. Mr. Poindexter convinced Mrs. Tucker that the sale of Los Cuervos could not be effected until the notoriety of her husband's flight had been fairly forgotten, and she was forced to accept her fate. The sale of her diamonds, which seemed to her to have realized a singularly extravagant sum, enabled her to quietly reinstate the Pattersons in the tienda and to discharge in full her husband's liabilities to the rancheros and his humbler retainers.

Meanwhile the winter rains had ceased. It seemed to her as if the clouds had suddenly one night struck their white tents and stolen away, leaving the unvanquished sun to mount the vacant sky the next morning alone, and possess it thenceforward unchallenged. One afternoon she thought the long sad waste before her window had caught some tint of grayer color from the sunset; a week later she found it a blazing landscape of poppies, broken here and there by blue lagoons of lupine, by pools of daisies, by banks of dog-roses, by broad outlying shores of dandelions that scattered their lavish gold to the foot of the hills, where the green billows of wild oats carried it on and upwards to the darker crests of pines. For two months she was dazzled and bewildered with color. She had never before been face to face with this spendthrift Californian Flora, in her virgin wastefulness, her more than goddess-like prodigality. The teeming earth seemed to quicken and throb beneath her feet; the few circuits of a plow around the outlying corral was enough to call out a jungle growth of giant grain that almost hid the low walls of the hacienda. In this glorious fecundity of the earth, in this joyous renewal of life and color, in this opulent youth and freshness of soil and sky, it alone remained, the dead and sterile Past, left in the midst of buoyant rejuvenescence and resurrection, like an empty churchyard skull upturned on the springing turf. Its bronzed adobe walls mocked the green vine that embraced them, the crumbling dust of its courtyard remained ungerminating and unfruitful; to the thousand; stirring voices without, its dry lips alone remained mute, unresponsive, and unchanged.

During this time Don José had become a frequent visitor at Los Cuervos, bringing with him at first his niece and sister in a stately precision of politeness that was not lost on the proud Blue Grass stranger. She returned their visit at Los Gatos, and there made the formal acquaintance of Don José's grandmother, a lady who still regarded the decrepit Concha as a giddy muchacha, and who herself glittered as with the phosphorescence of refined decay. Through this circumstance she learned that Don José was not yet fifty, and that his gravity of manner and sedateness was more the result of fastidious isolation and temperament than years. She could not tell why the information gave her a feeling of annoyance, but it caused her to regret the absence of Poindexter, and to wonder, also somewhat nervously, why he had lately avoided her presence. The thought that he might be doing so from a recollection of the innuendoes of Mrs. Patterson caused a little tremor of indignation in her pulses. "As if", but she did not finish the sentence even to herself, and her eyes filled with bitter tears.

Yet she had thought of the husband who had so cruelly wronged her less feverishly, less impatiently than before. For she thought she loved him now the more deeply, because, although she was not reconciled to his absence, it seemed to keep alive the memory of what he had been before his one wild act separated them. She had never seen the reflection of another woman's eyes in his; the past contained no haunting recollection of waning or alienated affection; she could meet him again, and, clasping her arms around him, awaken as if from a troubled dream without reproach or explanation. Her strong belief in this made her patient; she no longer sought to know the particulars of his flight, and never dreamed that her passive submission to his absence was partly due to a fear that something in his actual presence at that moment would have destroyed that belief forever.

For this reason the delicate reticence of the people at Los Gatos, and their seclusion from the world which knew of her husband's fault, had made her encourage the visits of Don José, until from the instinct already alluded to she one day summoned Poindexter to Los Cuervos, on the day that Don José usually called. But to her surprise the two men met more or less awkwardly and coldly, and her tact as hostess was tried to the utmost to keep their evident antagonism from being too apparent. The effort to reconcile their mutual discontent, and some other feeling she did not quite understand, produced a nervous excitement which called the blood to her cheek and gave a dangerous brilliancy to her eyes, two circumstances not unnoticed nor unappreciated by her two guests. But instead of reuniting them, the prettier Mrs. Tucker became, the more distant and reserved grew the men, until Don José rose before his usual hour, and with more than usual ceremoniousness departed.

"Then my business does not seem to be with him!" said Poindexter, with quiet coolness, as Mrs. Tucker turned her somewhat mystified face towards him. "Or have you anything to say to me about him in private?"

"I am sure I don't know what you both mean," she returned with a slight tremor of voice. "I had no idea you were not on good terms. I thought you were! It's very awkward." Without coquetry and unconsciously she raised her blue eyes under her lids until the clear pupils coyly and softly hid themselves in the corners of the brown lashes, and added, "You have both been so kind to me."

"Perhaps that is the reason," said Poindexter, gravely. But Mrs. Tucker refused to accept the suggestion with equal gravity, and began to laugh. The laugh, which was at first frank, spontaneous, and almost child-like, was becoming hysterical and nervous as she went on, until it was suddenly checked by Poindexter.

"I have had no difficulties with Don José Santierra," he said, somewhat coldly ignoring her hilarity, "but perhaps he is not inclined to be as polite to the friend of the husband as he is to the wife."

"Mr. Poindexter!" said Mrs. Tucker quickly, her face becoming pale again.

"I beg your pardon!" said Poindexter, flushing; "but" -

"You want to say," she interrupted coolly, "that you are not friends, I see. Is that the reason why you have avoided this house?" she continued gently.

"I thought I could be of more service to you elsewhere," he replied evasively. "I have been lately following up a certain clue rather closely. I think I am on the track of a confidante of, of that woman."

A quick shadow passed over Mrs. Tucker's face. "Indeed!" she said coldly. "Then I am to believe that you prefer to spend your leisure moments in looking after that creature to calling here?"

Poindexter was stupefied. Was this the woman who only four months ago was almost vindictively eager to pursue her husband's paramour! There could be but one answer to it, Don José! Four months ago he would have smiled compassionately at it from his cynical preeminence. Now he managed with difficulty to stifle the bitterness of his reply.

"If you do not wish the inquiry carried on," he began, "of course" -

"I? What does it matter to me?" she said coolly. "Do as you please."

Nevertheless, half an hour later, as he was leaving, she said, with a certain hesitating timidity, "Do not leave me so much alone here, and let that woman go."

This was not the only unlooked-for sequel to her innocent desire to propitiate her best friends. Don José did not call again upon his usual day, but in his place came Doña Clara, his younger sister. When Mrs. Tucker had politely asked after the absent Don José, Doña Clara wound her swarthy arms around the fair American's waist and replied, "But why did you send for the abogado Poindexter when my brother called?"

"But Captain Poindexter calls as one of my friends," said the amazed Mrs. Tucker. "He is a gentleman, and has been a soldier and an officer," she added with some warmth.

"Ah, yes, a soldier of the law, what you call an oficial de policia, a chief of gendarmes, my sister, but not a gentleman, a camarero to protect a lady."

Mrs. Tucker would have uttered a hasty reply, but the perfect and good-natured simplicity of Doña Clara withheld her. Nevertheless, she treated Don José with a certain reserve at their next meeting, until it brought the simple-minded Castilian so dangerously near the point of demanding an explanation which implied too much that she was obliged to restore him temporarily to his old footing. Meantime she had a brilliant idea. She would write to Calhoun Weaver, whom she had avoided since that memorable day. She would say she wished to consult him. He would come to Los Cuervos; he might suggest something to lighten this weary waiting; at least she would show them all that she had still old friends. Yet she did not dream of returning to her Blue Grass home; her parents had died since she left; she shrank from the thought of dragging her ruined life before the hopeful youth of her girlhood's companions.

Mr. Calhoun Weaver arrived promptly, ostentatiously, oracularly, and cordially, but a little coarsely. He had, did she remember? expected this from the first. Spercer had lost his head through vanity, and had attempted too much. It required foresight and firmness, as he himself, who had lately made successful "combinations" which she might perhaps have heard of, well knew. But Spencer had got the "big head." "As to that woman, a devilish handsome woman too! well, everybody knew that Spencer always had a weakness that way, and he would say, but if she didn't care to hear any more about her, well, perhaps she was right. That was the best way to take it." Sitting before her, prosperous, weak, egotistical, incompetent, unavailable, and yet filled with a vague kindliness of intent, Mrs. Tucker loathed him. A sickening perception of her own weakness in sending for him, a new and aching sense of her utter isolation and helplessness, seemed to paralyze her.

"Nat'rally you feel bad," he continued, with the large air of a profound student of human nature. "Nat'rally, nat'rally you're kept in an uncomfortable state, not knowing jist how you stand. There ain't but one thing to do. Jist rise up, quiet like, and get a divorce agin Spencer. Hold on! There ain't a judge or jury in California that wouldn't give it to you right off the nail, without asking questions. Why, you'd get it by default if you wanted to; you'd just have to walk over the course! And then, Belle," he drew his chair still nearer her, "when you've settled down again, well! I don't mind renewing that offer I once made ye, before Spencer ever came round ye, I don't mind, Belle, I swear I don't! Honest Injin! I'm in earnest, there's my hand."

Mrs. Tucker's reply has not been recorded. Enough that half an hour later Mr. Weaver appeared in the courtyard with traces of tears on his foolish face, a broken falsetto voice, and other evidence of mental and moral disturbance. His cordiality and oracular predisposition remained sufficiently to enable him to suggest the magical words "Blue Grass" mysteriously to Concha, with an indication of his hand to the erect figure of her pale mistress in the doorway, who waved to him a silent but half compassionate farewell.

At about this time a slight change in her manner was noticed by the few who saw her more frequently. Her apparently invincible girlishness of spirit had given way to a certain matronly seriousness. She applied herself to her household cares and the improvement of the hacienda with a new sense of duty and a settled earnestness, until by degrees she wrought into it not only her instinctive delicacy and taste, but part of her own individuality. Even the rude rancheros and tradesmen who were permitted to enter the walls in the exercise of their calling began to speak mysteriously of the beauty of this garden of the almarjal. She went out but seldom, and then accompanied by one or the other of her female servants, in long drives on unfrequented roads. On Sundays she sometimes drove to the half ruined mission church of Santa Inez, and hid herself, during mass, in the dim monastic shadows of the choir. Gradually the poorer people whom she met in these journeys began to show an almost devotional reverence for her, stopping in the roads with uncovered heads for her to pass, or making way for her in the tienda or plaza of the wretched town with dumb courtesy. She began to feel a strange sense of widowhood, that, while it at times brought tears to her eyes, was not without a certain tender solace. In the sympathy and simpleness of this impulse she went as far as to revive the mourning she had worn for her parents, but with such a fatal accenting of her beauty, and dangerous misinterpreting of her condition to eligible bachelors strange to the country, that she was obliged to put it off again. Her reserved and dignified manner caused others to mistake her nationality for that of the Santierras, and in "Doña Bella" the simple Mrs. Tucker was for a while forgotten. At times she even forgot it herself. Accustomed now almost entirely to the accents of another language and the features of another race, she would sit for hours in the corridor, whose massive bronzed enclosure even her tasteful care could only make an embowered mausoleum of the Past, or gaze abstractedly from the dark embrasures of her windows across the stretching almarjal to the shining lagoon beyond that terminated the estuary. She had a strange fondness for this tranquil mirror, which under sun or stars always retained the passive reflex of the sky above, and seemed to rest her weary eyes. She had objected to one of the plans projected by Poindexter to redeem the land and deepen the water at the embarcadero, as it would have drained the lagoon, and the lawyer had postponed the improvement to gratify her fancy. So she kept it through the long summer unchanged save by the shadows of passing wings or the lazy files of sleeping sea-fowl.

On one of these afternoons she noticed a slowly moving carriage leave the highroad and cross the almarjal skirting the edge of the lagoon. If it contained visitors for Los Cuervos they had evidently taken a shorter cut without waiting to go on to the regular road which intersected the highway at right angles a mile farther on. It was with some sense of annoyance and irritation that she watched the trespass, and finally saw the vehicle approach the house. A few moments later the servant informed her that Mr. Patterson would like to see her alone. When she entered the corridor, which in the dry season served as a reception hall, she was surprised to see that Patterson was not alone. Near him stood a well-dressed handsome woman, gazing about her with good-humored admiration of Mrs. Tucker's taste and ingenuity.

"It don't look much like it did two years ago," said the stranger cheerfully. "You've improved it wonderfully."

Stiffening slightly, Mrs. Tucker turned inquiringly to Mr. Patterson. But that gentleman's usual profound melancholy appeared to be intensified by the hilarity of his companion. He only sighed deeply and rubbed his leg with the brim of his hat in gloomy abstraction.

"Well! go on, then," said the woman, laughing and nudging him. "Go on, introduce me, can't you? Don't stand there like a tombstone. You won't? Well, I'll introduce myself." She laughed again, and then, with an excellent imitation of Patterson's lugubrious accents, said, "Mr. Spencer Tucker's wife that is, allow me to introduce you to Mr. Spencer Tucker's sweetheart that was! Hold on! I said that was. For true as I stand here, ma'am, and I reckon I wouldn't stand here if it wasn't true, I haven't set eyes on him since the day he left you."

"It's the gospel truth, every word," said Patterson, stirred into a sudden activity by Mrs. Tucker's white and rigid face. "It's the frozen truth, and I kin prove it. For I kin swear that when that there young woman was sailin' outer the Golden Gate, Spencer Tucker was in my bar-room; I kin swear that I fed him, lickered him, give him a hoss and set him in his road to Monterey that very night."

"Then, where is he now?" said Mrs. Tucker, suddenly facing them.

They looked at each other, and then looked at Mrs. Tucker. Then both together replied slowly and in perfect unison, "That's-what-we-want-to-know." They seemed so satisfied with this effect that they as deliberately repeated, "Yes-that's-what-we-want-to-know."

Between the shock of meeting the partner of her husband's guilt and the unexpected revelation to her inexperience, that in suggestion and appearance there was nothing beyond the recollection of that guilt that was really shocking in the woman, between the extravagant extremes of hope and fear suggested by their words, there was something so grotesquely absurd in the melodramatic chorus that she with difficulty suppressed an hysterical laugh.

"That's the way to take it," said the woman, putting her own good-humored interpretation upon Mrs. Tucker's expression. "Now, look here! I'll tell you all about it," She carefully selected the most comfortable chair, and sitting down, lightly crossed her hands in her lap. "Well, I left here on the 13th of last January on the ship Argo, calculating that your husband would join the ship just inside the Heads. That was our arrangement, but if anything happened to prevent him, he was to join me at Acapulco. Well! he didn't come aboard, and we sailed without him. But it appears now he did attempt to join the ship, but his boat was capsized. There now, don't be alarmed! he wasn't drowned, as Patterson can swear to, no, catch him! not a hair of him was hurt. But I, I was bundled off to the end of the earth in Mexico alone, without a cent to bless me. For true as you live, that hound of a captain, when he found, as he thought, that Spencer was nabbed, he just confiscated all his trunks and valuables and left me in the lurch. If I had not met a man down there that offered to marry me and brought me here, I might have died there, I reckon. But I did, and here I am. I went down there as your husband's sweetheart, I've come back as the wife of an honest man, and I reckon it's about square!"

There was something so startlingly frank, so hopelessly self-satisfied, so contagiously good-humored in the woman's perfect moral unconsciousness, that even if Mrs. Tucker had been less preoccupied her resentment would have abated. But her eyes were fixed on the gloomy face of Patterson, who was beginning to unlock the sepulchers of his memory and disinter his deeply buried thoughts.

"You kin bet your whole pile on what this Mrs. Capting Baxter, ez used to be French Inez of New Orleans, hez told ye. Ye kin take everything she's onloaded. And it's only doin' the square thing to her to say, she hain't done it out o' no cussedness, but just to satisfy herself, now she's a married woman and past such foolishness. But that ain't neither here nor there. The gist of the whole matter is that Spencer Tucker was at the tienda the day after she sailed and after his boat capsized." He then gave a detailed account of the interview, with the unnecessary but truthful minutiae of his class, adding to the particulars already known that the following week he visited the Summit House and was surprised to find that Spencer had never been there, nor had he ever sailed from Monterey.

"But why was this not told to me before?" said Mrs. Tucker, suddenly. "Why not at the time? Why," she demanded almost fiercely, turning from the one to the other, "has this been kept from me?"

"I'll tell ye why," said Patterson, sinking with crashed submission into a chair. "When I found he wasn't where he ought to be, I got to lookin' elsewhere. I knew the track of the hoss I lent him by a loose shoe. I examined, and found he had turned off the highroad somewhere beyond the lagoon, jist as if he was makin' a bee line here."

"Well," said Mrs. Tucker breathlessly.

"Well," said Patterson, with the resigned tone of an accustomed martyr, "mebbe I'm a God-forsaken idiot, but I reckon he did come yer. And mebbe I'm that much of a habitooal lunatic, but thinking so, I calkilated you'd know it without tellin'."

With their eyes fixed upon her, Mrs. Tucker felt the quick blood rush to her cheeks, although she knew not why. But they were apparently satisfied with her ignorance, for Patterson resumed, yet more gloomily:

"Then if he wasn't hidin' here beknownst to you, he must have changed his mind agin and got away by the embarcadero. The only thing wantin' to prove that idea is to know how he got a boat, and what he did with the hoss. And thar's one more idea, and ez that can't be proved," continued Patterson, sinking his voice still lower, "mebbe it's accordin' to God's laws."

Unsympathetic to her as the speaker had always been and still was, Mrs. Tucker felt a vague chill creep over her that seemed to be the result of his manner more than his words. "And that idea is -?" she suggested with pale lips.

"It's this! Fust, I don't say it means much to anybody but me. I've heard of these warnings afore now, ez comin' only to folks ez hear them for themselves alone, and I reckon I kin stand it, if it's the will o' God. The idea is then, that, Spencer Tucker, was drownded in that boat; the idea is", his voice was almost lost in a hoarse whisper, "that it was no living man that kem to me that night, but a spirit that kem out of the darkness and went back into it! No eye saw him but mine, no ears heard him but mine. I reckon it weren't intended it should." He paused, and passed the flap of his hat across his eyes. "The pie, you'll say, is agin it," he continued in the same tone of voice, "the whiskey is agin it, a few cuss words that dropped from him, accidental like, may have been agin it. All the same they mout have been only the little signs and tokens that it was him."

But Mrs. Baxter's ready laugh somewhat rudely dispelled the infection of Patterson's gloom. "I reckon the only spirit was that which you and Spencer consumed," she said, cheerfully. "I don't wonder you're a little mixed. Like as not you've misunderstood his plans."

Patterson shook his head. "He'll turn up yet, alive and kicking! Like as not, then, Poindexter knows where he is all the time."

"Impossible! He would have told me," said Mrs. Tucker, quickly.

Mrs. Baxter looked at Patterson without speaking. Patterson replied by a long lugubrious whistle.

"I don't understand you," said Mrs. Tucker, drawing back with cold dignity.

"You don't?" returned Mrs. Baxter. "Bless your innocent heart! Why was he so keen to hunt me up at first, shadowing my friends and all that, and why has he dropped it now he knows I'm here, if he didn't know where Spencer was?"

"I can explain that," interrupted Mrs. Tucker, hastily, with a blush of confusion. "That is, I" -

"Then mebbe you kin explain too," broke in Patterson with gloomy significance, "why he has bought up most of Spencer's debts himself, and perhaps you're satisfied it is n't to hold the whip hand of him and keep him from coming back openly. Pr'aps you know why he's movin' heaven and earth to make Don José Santierra sell the ranch, and why the Don don't see it all."

"Don José sell Los Cuervos! Buy it, you mean?" said Mrs. Tucker. "I offered to sell it to him."

Patterson arose from the chair, looked despairingly around him, passed his hand sadly across his forehead, and said: "It's come! I knew it would. It's the warning! It's suthing betwixt jim-jams and doddering idjiocy. Here I'd hev been willin' to swear that Mrs. Baxter here told me she had sold this yer ranch nearly two years ago to Don José, and now you" -

"Stop!" said Mrs. Tucker, in a voice that chilled them.

She was standing upright and rigid, as if stricken to stone. "I command you to tell me what this means!" she said, turning only her blazing eyes upon the woman.

Even the ready smile faded from Mrs. Baxter's lips as she replied hesitatingly and submissively: "I thought you knew already that Spencer had given this ranch to me. I sold it to Don José to get the money for us to go away with. It was Spencer's idea" -

"You lie!" said Mrs. Tucker.

There was a dead silence. The wrathful blood that had quickly mounted to Mrs. Baxter's cheek, to Patterson's additional bewilderment, faded as quickly. She did not lift her eyes again to Mrs. Tucker's, but, slowly raising herself from her seat, said, "I wish to God I did lie; but it's true. And it's true that I never touched a cent of the money, but gave it all to him!" She laid her hand on

Patterson's arm, and said, "Come! let us go," and led him a few steps toward the gateway. But here Patterson paused, and again passed his hand over his melancholy brow. The necessity of coherently and logically closing the conversation impressed itself upon his darkening mind. "Then you don't happen to have heard anything of Spencer?" he said sadly, and vanished with Mrs. Baxter through the gate.

Left alone to herself, Mrs. Tucker raised her hands above her head with a little cry, interlocked her rigid fingers, and slowly brought her palms down upon her upturned face and eyes, pressing hard as if to crush out all light and sense of life before her. She stood thus for a moment motionless and silent, with the rising wind whispering without and flecking her white morning dress with gusty shadows from the arbor. Then, with closed eyes, dropping her hands to her breast, still pressing hard, she slowly passed them down the shapely contours of her figure to the waist, and with another cry cast them off as if she were stripping herself of some loathsome garment. Then she walked quickly to the gateway, looked out, returned to the corridor, unloosening and taking off her wedding-ring from her finger as she walked. Here she paused, then slowly and deliberately rearranged the chairs and adjusted the gay-colored rugs that draped them, and quietly reëntered her chamber.

Two days afterwards the sweating steed of Captain Poindexter was turned loose in the corral, and a moment later the captain entered the corridor. Handing a letter to the decrepit Concha, who seemed to be utterly disorganized by its contents and the few curt words with which it was delivered, he gazed silently upon the vacant bower, still fresh and redolent with the delicacy and perfume of its graceful occupant, until his dark eyes filled with unaccustomed moisture. But his reverie was interrupted by the sound of jingling spurs without, and the old humor struggled back into his eyes as Don José impetuously entered. The Spaniard started back, but instantly recovered himself.

"So, I find you here. Ah! it is well!" he said passionately, producing a letter from his bosom. "Look! Do you call this honor? Look how you keep your compact!"

Poindexter coolly took the letter. It contained a few words of gentle dignity from Mrs. Tucker, informing Don José that she had only that instant learned of his just claims upon Los Cuervos, tendering him her gratitude for his delicate intentions, but pointing out with respectful firmness that he must know that a moment's further acceptance of his courtesy was impossible.

"She has gained this knowledge from no word of mine," said Poindexter, calmly. "Right or wrong, I have kept my promise to you. I have as much reason to accuse you of betraying my secret in this," he added coldly, as he took another letter from his pocket and handed it to Don José.

It seemed briefer and colder, but was neither. It reminded Poindexter that as he had again deceived her she must take the government of her affairs in her own hands henceforth. She abandoned all the furniture and improvements she had put in Los Cuervos to him, to whom she now knew she was indebted for them. She could not thank him for what his habitual generosity impelled him to do for any woman, but she could forgive him for misunderstanding her like any other woman, perhaps she should say, like a child. When he received this she would be already on her way to her old home in Kentucky, where she still hoped to be able by her own efforts to amass enough to discharge her obligations to him.

"She does not speak of her husband, this woman," said Don José, scanning Poindexter's face. "It is possible she rejoins him, eh?"

"Perhaps in one way she has never left him, Don José," said Poindexter, with grave significance.

Don José's face flushed, but he returned carelessly, "And the rancho, naturally you will not buy it now?"

"On the contrary, I shall abide by my offer," said Poindexter, quietly.

Don José eyed him narrowly, and then said, "Ah, we shall consider of it."

He did consider it, and accepted the offer. With the full control of the land, Captain Poindexter's improvements, so indefinitely postponed, were actively pushed forward. The thick walls of the hacienda were the first to melt away before them; the low lines of corral were effaced, and the early breath of the summer trade winds swept uninterruptedly across the now leveled plain to the embarcadero, where a newer structure arose. A more vivid green alone marked the spot where the crumbling adobe walls of the casa had returned to the parent soil that gave it. The channel was deepened, the lagoon was drained, until one evening the magic mirror that had so long reflected the weary waiting of the Blue Grass Penelope lay dull, dead, lusterless, an opaque quagmire of noisome corruption and decay to be put away from the sight of man forever. On this spot the crows, the titular tenants of Los Cuervos, assembled in tumultuous congress, coming and going in mysterious clouds, or laboring in thick and writhing masses, as if they were continuing the work of improvement begun by human agency. So well had they done the work that by the end of a week only a few scattered white objects remained glittering on the surface of the quickly drying soil. But they were the bones of the missing outcast, Spencer Tucker!

The same spring a breath of war swept over a foul, decaying quagmire of the whole land, before which such passing deeds as these were blown as vapor. It called men of all rank and condition to battle for a nation's life, and among the first to respond were those into whose boyish hands had been placed the nation's honor. It returned the epaulets to Poindexter's shoulder with the addition of a double star, carried him triumphantly to the front, and left him, at the end of a summer's day and a hard-won fight, sorely wounded, at the door of a Blue Grass farmhouse. And the woman who sought him out and ministered to his wants said timidly, as she left her hand in his, "I told you I should live to repay you."

LEFT OUT ON LONE STAR MOUNTAIN.

I.

There was little doubt that the Lone Star claim was "played out." Not dug out, worked out, washed out, but played out. For two years its five sanguine proprietors had gone through the various stages of mining enthusiasm; had prospected and planned, dug and doubted. They had borrowed money with hearty but unredeeming frankness, established a credit with unselfish abnegation of all responsibility, and had borne the disappointment of their creditors with a cheerful resignation which only the consciousness of some deep Compensating Future could give. Giving little else, however, a singular dissatisfaction obtained with the traders, and, being accompanied with a reluctance to make further advances, at last touched the gentle stoicism of the proprietors themselves. The youthful enthusiasm which had at first lifted the most ineffectual trial, the most useless essay, to the plane of actual achievement, died out, leaving them only the dull, prosaic record of half-finished ditches, purposeless shafts, untenable pits, abandoned engines, and meaningless disruptions of the soil upon the Lone Star claim, and empty flour sacks and pork barrels in the Lone Star cabin.

They had borne their poverty, if that term could be applied to a light renunciation of all superfluities in food, dress, or ornament, ameliorated by the gentle depredations already alluded to, with unassuming levity. More than that: having segregated themselves from their fellow-miners of Red Gulch, and entered upon the possession of the little manzanita-thicketed valley five miles away, the failure of their enterprise had assumed in their eyes only the vague significance of the decline and fall of a general community, and to that extent relieved them of individual responsibility. It was easier for them to admit that the Lone Star claim was "played out" than confess to a personal bankruptcy. Moreover, they still retained the sacred right of criticism of government, and rose superior in their private opinions to their own collective wisdom. Each one experienced a grateful sense of the entire responsibility of the other four in the fate of their enterprise.

On December 24, 1863, a gentle rain was still falling over the length and breadth of the Lone Star claim. It had been falling for several days, had already called a faint spring color to the wan landscape, repairing with tender touches the ravages wrought by the proprietors, or charitably covering their faults. The ragged seams in gulch and cañon lost their harsh outlines, a thin green mantle faintly clothed the torn and abraded hillside. A few weeks more, and a veil of forgetfulness would be drawn over the feeble failures of the Lone Star claim. The charming derelicts themselves, listening to the raindrops on the roof of their little cabin, gazed philosophically from the open door, and accepted the prospect as a moral discharge from their obligations. Four of the five partners were present. The Right and Left Bowers, Union Mills, and the Judge.

It is scarcely necessary to say that not one of these titles was the genuine name of its possessor. The Right and Left Bowers were two brothers; their sobriquets, a cheerful adaptation from the favorite game of euchre, expressing their relative value in the camp. The mere fact that Union Mills had at one time patched his trousers with an old flour-sack legibly bearing that brand of its fabrication, was a tempting baptismal suggestion that the other partners could not forego. The Judge, a singularly inequitable Missourian, with no knowledge whatever of the law, was an inspiration of gratuitous irony.

Union Mills, who had been for some time sitting placidly on the threshold with one leg exposed to the rain, from a sheer indolent inability to change his position, finally withdrew that weather-beaten member, and stood up. The movement more or less deranged the attitudes of the other partners, and was received with cynical disfavor. It was somewhat remarkable that, although generally giving the appearance of healthy youth and perfect physical condition, they one and all simulated the decrepitude of age and invalidism, and after limping about for a few moments, settled back again upon their bunks and stools in their former positions. The Left Bower lazily replaced a bandage that he had worn around his ankle for weeks without any apparent necessity, and the Judge scrutinized with tender solicitude the faded cicatrix of a scratch upon his arm. A passive hypochondria, born of their isolation, was the last ludicrously pathetic touch of their situation.

The immediate cause of this commotion felt the necessity of an explanation.

"It would have been just as easy for you to have stayed outside with your business leg, instead of dragging it into private life in that obtrusive way," retorted the Right Bower; "but that exhaustive effort is n't going to fill the pork barrel. The grocery man at Dalton says, what's that he said?" he appealed lazily to the Judge.

"Said he reckoned the Lone Star was about played out, and he didn't want any more in his, thank you!" repeated the Judge with a mechanical effort of memory utterly devoid of personal or present interest.

"I always suspected that man, after Grimshaw begun to deal with him," said the Left Bower. "They're just mean enough to join hands against us." It was a fixed belief of the Lone Star partners that they were pursued by personal enmities.

"More than likely those new strangers over in the Fork have been paying cash and filled him up with conceit," said Union Mills, trying to dry his leg by alternately beating it or rubbing it against the cabin wall. "Once begin wrong with that kind of snipe and you drag everybody down with you."

This vague conclusion was received with dead silence. Everybody had become interested in the speaker's peculiar method of drying his leg, to the exclusion of the previous topic. A few offered criticism, no one assistance.

"Who did the grocery man say that to?" asked the Right Bower, finally returning to the question.

"The Old Man," answered the Judge.

"Of course," ejaculated the Right Bower sarcastically.

"Of course," echoed the other partners together. "That's like him. The Old Man all over!"

It did not appear exactly what was like the Old Man, or why it was like him, but generally that he alone was responsible for the grocery man's defection. It was put more concisely by Union Mills.

"That comes of letting him go there! It's just a fair provocation to any man to have the Old Man sent to him. They can't, sorter, restrain themselves at him. He's enough to spoil the credit of the Rothschilds."

"That's so," chimed in the Judge. "And look at his prospecting. Why, he was out two nights last week, all night, prospecting in the moonlight for blind leads, just out of sheer foolishness."

"It was quite enough for me," broke in the Left Bower, "when the other day, you remember when, he proposed to us white men to settle down to plain ground sluicing, making 'grub' wages just like any Chinaman. It just showed his idea of the Lone Star claim."

"Well, I never said it afore," added Union Mills, "but when that one of the Mattison boys came over here to examine the claim with an eye to purchasin', it was the Old Man that took the conceit out of him. He just as good as admitted that a lot of work had got to be done afore any pay ore could be realized. Never even asked him over to the shanty here to jine us in a friendly game; just kept him, so to speak, to himself. And naturally the Mattisons didn't see it."

A silence followed, broken only by the rain monotonously falling on the roof, and occasionally through the broad adobe chimney, where it provoked a retaliating hiss and splutter from the dying embers of the hearth. The Right Bower, with a sudden access of energy, drew the empty barrel before him, and taking a pack of well-worn cards from his pocket, began to make a "solitaire" upon the lid. The others gazed at him with languid interest.

"Makin' it for anythin'?" asked Mills.

The Right Bower nodded.

The Judge and Left Bower, who were partly lying in their respective bunks, sat up to get a better view of the game. Union Mills slowly disengaged himself from the wall and leaned over the "solitaire" player. The Right Bower turned the last card in a pause of almost thrilling suspense, and clapped it down on the lid with fateful emphasis.

"It went!" said the Judge in a voice of hushed respect. "What did you make it for?" he almost whispered.

"To know if we'd make the break we talked about and vamose the ranch. It's the fifth time to-day," continued the Right Bower in a voice of gloomy significance. "And it went agin bad cards too."

"I ain't superstitious," said the Judge, with awe and fatuity beaming from every line of his credulous face, "but it's flyin' in the face of Providence to go agin such signs as that."

"Make it again, to see if the Old Man must go," suggested the Left Bower.

The suggestion was received with favor, the three men gathering breathlessly around the player. Again the fateful cards were shuffled deliberately, placed in their mysterious combination, with the same ominous result. Yet everybody seemed to breathe more freely, as if relieved from some responsibility, the Judge accepting this manifest expression of Providence with resigned self-righteousness.

"Yes, gentlemen," resumed the Left Bower, serenely, as if a calm legal decision had just been recorded, "we must not let any foolishness or sentiment get mixed up with this thing, but look at it like business men. The only sensible move is to get up and get out of the camp."

"And the Old Man?" queried the Judge.

"The Old Man, hush! he's coming."

The doorway was darkened by a slight lissome shadow. It was the absent partner, otherwise known as "the Old Man." Need it be added that he was a boy of nineteen, with a slight down just clothing his upper lip!

"The creek is up over the ford, and I had to 'shin' up a willow on the bank and swing myself across," he said, with a quick, frank laugh; "but all the same, boys, it's going to clear up in about an hour, you bet. It's breaking away over Bald Mountain, and there's a sun flash on a bit of snow on Lone Peak. Look! you can see it from here. It's for all the world like Noah's dove just landed on Mount Ararat. It's a good omen."

From sheer force of habit the men had momentarily brightened up at the Old Man's entrance. But the unblushing exhibition of degrading superstition shown in the last sentence recalled their just severity. They exchanged meaning glances. Union Mills uttered hopelessly to himself: "Hell's full of such omens."

Too occupied with his subject to notice this ominous reception, the Old Man continued: "I reckon I struck a fresh lead in the new grocery man at the Crossing. He says he'll let the Judge have a pair of boots on credit, but he can't send them over here; and considering that the Judge has got to try them anyway, it don't seem to be asking too much for the Judge to go over there. He says he'll give us a barrel of pork and a bag of flour if we'll give him the right of using our tail-race and clean out the lower end of it."

"It's the work of a Chinaman, and a four days' job," broke in the Left Bower.

"It took one white man only two hours to clean out a third of it," retorted the Old Man triumphantly, "for I pitched in at once with a pick he let me have on credit, and did that amount of work this morning, and told him the rest of you boys would finish it this afternoon."

A slight gesture from the Right Bower checked an angry exclamation from the Left. The Old Man did not notice either, but, knitting his smooth young brow in a paternally reflective fashion, went on: "You'll have to get a new pair of trousers, Mills, but as he doesn't keep clothing, we'll have to get some canvas and cut you out a pair. I traded off the beans he let me have for some tobacco for the Right Bower at the other shop, and got them to throw in a new pack of cards. These are about played out. We'll be wanting some brushwood for the fire; there's a heap in the hollow. Who's going to bring it in? It's the Judge's turn, isn't it? Why, what's the matter with you all?"

The restraint and evident uneasiness of his companions had at last touched him. He turned his frank young eyes upon them; they glanced helplessly at each other. Yet his first concern was for them, his first instinct paternal and protecting. He ran his eyes quickly over them; they were all there and apparently in their usual condition. "Anything wrong with the claim?" he suggested.

Without looking at him the Right Bower rose, leaned against the open door with his hands behind him and his face towards the landscape, and said, apparently to the distant prospect: "The claim's played out, the partnership's played out, and the sooner we skedaddle out of this the better. If," he added, turning to the Old Man, "if you want to stay, if you want to do Chinaman's work at Chinaman's wages, if you want to hang on to the charity of the traders at the Crossing, you can do it, and enjoy the prospects and the Noah's doves alone. But we're calculatin' to step out of it."

"But I haven't said I wanted to do it alone" protested the Old Man with a gesture of bewilderment.

"If these are your general ideas of the partnership," continued the Right Bower, clinging to the established hypothesis of the other partners for support, "it ain't ours, and the only way we can prove it is to stop the foolishness right here. We calculated to dissolve the partnership and strike out for ourselves elsewhere. You're no longer responsible for us, nor we for you. And we reckon it's the square thing to leave you the claim and the cabin and all it contains. To prevent any trouble with the traders, we've drawn up a paper here" -

"With a bonus of fifty thousand dollars each down, and the rest to be settled on my children," interrupted the Old Man, with a half uneasy laugh. "Of course. But", he stopped suddenly, the blood dropped from his fresh cheek, and he again glanced quickly round the group. "I don't think, I, I quite sabe, boys," he added, with a slight tremor of voice and lip. "If it's a conundrum, ask me an easier one."

Any lingering doubt he might have had of their meaning was dispelled by the Judge. "It's about the softest thing you kin drop into, Old Man," he said confidentially; "if I had n't promised the other boys to go with them, and if I did n't need the best medical advice in Sacramento for my lungs, I'd just enjoy staying with you."

"It gives a sorter freedom to a young fellow like you, Old Man, like goin' into the world on your own capital, that every Californian boy has n't got," said Union Mills, patronizingly.

"Of course it's rather hard papers on us, you know, givin' up everything, so to speak; but it's for your good, and we ain't goin' back on you," said the Left Bower, "are we, boys?"

The color had returned to the Old Man's face a little more quickly and freely than usual. He picked up the hat he had cast down, put it on carefully over his brown curls, drew the flap down on the side towards his companions, and put his hands in his pockets. "All right," he said, in a slightly altered voice. "When do you go?"

"To-day," answered the Left Bower. "We calculate to take a moonlight pasear over to the Cross Roads and meet the down stage at about twelve to-night. There's plenty of time yet," he added, with a slight laugh; "it's only three o'clock now."

There was a dead silence. Even the rain withheld its continuous patter, a dumb, gray film covered the ashes of the hushed hearth. For the first time the Right Bower exhibited some slight embarrassment.

"I reckon it's held up for a spell," he said, ostentatiously examining the weather, "and we might as well take a run round the claim to see if we've forgotten nothing. Of course, we'll be back again," he added hastily, without looking at the Old Man, "before we go, you know."

The others began to look for their hats, but so awkwardly and with such evident preoccupation of mind that it was not at first discovered that the Judge had his already on. This raised a laugh, as did also a clumsy stumble of Union Mills against the pork barrel, although that gentleman took refuge from his confusion and secured a decent retreat by a gross exaggeration of his lameness, as he limped after the Right Bower. The Judge whistled feebly. The Left Bower, in a more ambitious effort to impart a certain gayety to his exit, stopped on the threshold and said, as if in arch confidence to his companions, "Darned if the Old Man don't look two inches higher since he became a proprietor," laughed patronizingly, and vanished.

If the newly-made proprietor had increased in stature, he had not otherwise changed his demeanor. He remained in the same attitude until the last figure disappeared behind the fringe of buckeye that hid the distant highway. Then he walked slowly to the fireplace, and, leaning against the chimney, kicked the dying embers together with his foot. Something dropped and spattered in the film of hot ashes. Surely the rain had not yet ceased!

His high color had already fled except for a spot on either cheekbone that lent a brightness to his eyes. He glanced around the cabin. It looked familiar and yet strange. Rather, it looked strange because still familiar, and therefore incongruous with the new atmosphere that surrounded it, discordant with the echo of their last meeting, and painfully accenting the change. There were the four "bunks," or sleeping berths, of his companions, each still bearing some traces of the individuality of its late occupant with a dumb loyalty that seemed to make their light-hearted defection monstrous. In the dead ashes of the Judge's pipe, scattered on his shelf, still lived his old fire; in the whittled and carved edges of the Left Bower's bunk still were the memories of bygone days of delicious indolence; in the bullet-holes clustered round a knot of one of the beams there was still the record of the Right Bower's old-time skill and practice; in the few engravings of female loveliness stuck upon each headboard there were the proofs of their old extravagant devotion, all a mute protest to the change.

He remembered how, a fatherless, truant schoolboy, he had drifted into their adventurous, nomadic life, itself a life of grown-up truancy like his own, and became one of that gypsy family. How they had taken the place of relations and household in his boyish fancy, filling it with the unsubstantial pageantry of a child's play at grown-up existence, he knew only too well. But how, from being a pet and protégé, he had gradually and unconsciously asserted his own individuality and taken upon his younger shoulders not only a poet's keen appreciation of that life, but its actual responsibilities and half-childish burdens, he never suspected. He had fondly believed that he was a neophyte in their ways, a novice in their charming faith and indolent creed, and they had encouraged it; now their renunciation of that faith could only be an excuse for a renunciation of him. The poetry that had for two years invested the material and sometimes even mean details of their existence was too much a part of himself to be lightly dispelled. The lesson of those ingenuous moralists failed, as such lessons are apt to fail; their discipline provoked but did not subdue; a rising indignation, stirred by a sense of injury, mounted to his cheek and eyes. It was slow to come, but was none the less violent that it had been preceded by the benumbing shock of shame and pride.

I hope I shall not prejudice the reader's sympathies if my duty as a simple chronicler compels me to state, therefore, that the sober second thought of this gentle poet was to burn down the cabin on the spot with all its contents. This yielded to a milder counsel, waiting for the return of the party, challenging the Right Bower, a duel to the death, perhaps himself the victim, with the crushing explanation in extremis, "It seems we are one too many. No matter; it is settled now. Farewell!" Dimly remembering, however, that there was something of this in the last well-worn novel they had read together, and that his antagonist might recognize it, or even worse, anticipate it himself, the idea was quickly rejected. Besides, the opportunity for an apotheosis of self-sacrifice was past. Nothing remained now but to refuse the proffered bribe of claim and cabin by letter, for he must not wait their return. He tore a leaf from a blotted diary, begun and abandoned long since, and essayed to write. Scrawl after scrawl was torn up, until his fury had cooled down to a frigid third personality. "Mr. John Ford regrets to inform his late partners that their tender of house, of furniture," however, seemed too inconsistent with the pork-barrel table he was writing on; a more eloquent renunciation of their offer became frivolous and idiotic from a caricature of Union Mills, label and all, that appeared suddenly on the other side of the leaf; and when he at last indited a satisfactory and impassioned exposition of his feelings, the legible addendum of "Oh, ain't you glad you're out of the wilderness!" the forgotten first line of a popular song, which no scratching would erase, seemed too like an ironical postscript to be thought of for a moment. He threw aside his pen and cast the discordant record of past foolish pastime into the dead ashes of the hearth.

How quiet it was! With the cessation of the rain the wind too had gone down, and scarcely a breath of air came through the open door. He walked to the threshold and gazed on the hushed prospect. In this listless attitude he was faintly conscious of a distant reverberation, a mere phantom of sound, perhaps the explosion of a distant blast in the hills, that left the silence more marked and oppressive. As he turned again into the cabin a change seemed to have come over it. It already looked old and decayed. The loneliness of years of desertion seemed to have taken possession of it; the atmosphere of dry rot was in the beams and rafters. To his excited fancy the few disordered blankets and articles of clothing seemed dropping to pieces; in one of the bunks there was a hideous resemblance in the longitudinal heap of clothing to a withered and mummied corpse. So it might look in after-years when some passing stranger, but he stopped. A dread of the place was beginning to creep over him; a dread of the days to come, when the monotonous sunshine should lay bare the loneliness of these walls; the long, long days of endless blue and cloudless, overhanging solitude; summer days when the wearying, incessant trade winds should sing around that empty shell and voice its desolation. He gathered together hastily a few articles that were especially his own, rather that the free communion of the camp, from indifference or accident, had left wholly to him. He hesitated for a moment over his rifle, but, scrupulous in his wounded pride, turned away and left the familiar weapon that in the dark days had so often provided the dinner or breakfast of the little household. Candor compels me to state that his equipment was not large nor eminently practical.

His scant pack was a light weight for even his young shoulders, but I fear he thought more of getting away from the Past than providing for the Future.

With this vague but sole purpose he left the cabin, and almost mechanically turned his steps towards the creek he had crossed that morning. He knew that by this route he would avoid meeting his companions; its difficulties and circuitousness would exercise his feverish limbs and give him time for reflection. He had determined to leave the claim, but whence he had not yet considered. He reached the bank of the creek where he had stood two hours before; it seemed to him two years. He looked curiously at his reflection in one of the broad pools of overflow, and fancied he looked older. He watched the rush and outset of the turbid current hurrying to meet the South Fork, and to eventually lose itself in the yellow Sacramento. Even in his preoccupation he was impressed with a likeness to himself and his companions in this flood that had burst its peaceful boundaries. In the drifting fragments of one of their forgotten flumes washed from the bank, he fancied he saw an omen of the disintegration and decay of the Lone Star claim.

The strange hush in the air that he had noticed before, a calm so inconsistent with that hour and the season as to seem portentous, became more marked in contrast to the feverish rush of the turbulent watercourse. A few clouds lazily huddled in the west apparently had gone to rest with the sun on beds of somnolent poppies. There was a gleam as of golden water everywhere along the horizon, washing out the cold snow-peaks, and drowning even the rising moon. The creek caught it here and there, until, in grim irony, it seemed to bear their broken sluice-boxes and useless engines on the very Pactolian stream they had been hopefully created to direct and carry. But by some peculiar trick of the atmosphere the perfect plenitude of that golden sunset glory was lavished on the rugged sides and tangled crest of the Lone Star Mountain. That isolated peak, the landmark of their claim, the gaunt monument of their folly, transfigured in the evening splendor, kept its radiance unquenched long after the glow had fallen from the encompassing skies, and when at last the rising moon, step by step, put out the fires along the winding valley and plains, and crept up the bosky sides of the cañon, the vanishing sunset was lost only to reappear as a golden crown.

The eyes of the young man were fixed upon it with more than a momentary picturesque interest. It had been the favorite ground of his prospecting exploits, its lowest flank had been scarred in the old enthusiastic days with hydraulic engines, or pierced with shafts, but its central position in the claim and its superior height had always given it a commanding view of the extent of their valley and its approaches, and it was this practical preeminence that alone attracted him at that moment. He knew that from its crest he would be able to distinguish the figures of his companions, as they crossed the valley near the cabin, in the growing moonlight. Thus he could avoid encountering them on his way to the highroad, and yet see them, perhaps, for the last time. Even in his sense of injury there was a strange satisfaction in the thought.

The ascent was toilsome, but familiar. All along the dim trail he was accompanied by gentler memories of the past, that seemed, like the faint odor of spiced leaves and fragrant grasses wet with the rain and crushed beneath his ascending tread, to exhale the sweeter perfume in his effort to subdue or rise above them. There was the thicket of manzanita, where they had broken noonday bread together; here was the rock beside their maiden shafts, where they had poured a wild libation in boyish enthusiasm of success; and here the ledge where their first flag, a red shirt heroically sacrificed, was displayed from a long-handled shovel to the gaze of admirers below. When he at last reached the summit, the mysterious hush was still in the air, as if in breathless sympathy with his expedition. In the west, the plain was faintly illuminated, but disclosed no moving figures. He turned towards the rising moon, and moved slowly to the eastern edge. Suddenly he stopped. Another step would have been his last! He stood upon the crumbling edge of a precipice. A landslip had taken place on the eastern flank, leaving the gaunt ribs and fleshless bones of Lone Star Mountain bare in the moonlight. He understood now the strange rumble and reverberation he had heard; he understood now the strange hush of bird and beast in brake and thicket!

Although a single rapid glance convinced him that the slide had taken place in an unfrequented part of the mountain, above an inaccessible cañon, and reflection assured him his companions could not have reached that distance when it took place, a feverish impulse led him to descend a few rods in the track of the avalanche. The frequent recurrence of outcrop and angle made this comparatively easy. Here he called aloud; the feeble echo of his own voice seemed only a dull impertinence to the significant silence. He turned to reascend; the furrowed flank of the mountain before him lay full in the moonlight. To his excited fancy a dozen luminous star-like points in the rocky crevices started into life as he faced them. Throwing his arm over the ledge above him, he supported himself for a moment by what appeared to be a projection of the solid rock. It trembled slightly. As he raised himself to its level, his heart stopped beating. It was simply a fragment detached from the outcrop, lying loosely on the ledge but upholding him by its own weight only. He examined it with trembling fingers; the encumbering soil fell from its sides and left its smoothed and worn protuberances glistening in the moonlight. It was virgin gold!

Looking back upon that moment afterwards, he remembered that he was not dazed, dazzled, or startled. It did not come to him as a discovery or an accident, a stroke of chance or a caprice of fortune. He saw it all in that supreme moment; Nature had worked out their poor deduction. What their feeble engines had essayed spasmodically and helplessly against the curtain of soil that hid the treasure, the elements had achieved with mightier but more patient forces. The slow sapping of the winter rains had loosened the soil from the auriferous rock, even while the swollen stream was carrying their impotent and shattered engines to the sea. What mattered that his single arm could not lift the treasure he had found; what mattered that to unfix those glittering stars would still tax both skill and patience! The work was done, the goal was reached! even his boyish impatience was content with that. He rose slowly to his feet, unstrapped his long-handled shovel from his back, secured it in the crevice, and quietly regained the summit.

It was all his own! His own by right of discovery under the law of the land, and without accepting a favor from them. He recalled even the fact that it was his prospecting on the mountain that first suggested the existence of gold in the outcrop and the use of the hydraulic. He had never abandoned that belief, whatever the others had done. He dwelt somewhat indignantly to himself on this circumstance, and half unconsciously faced defiantly towards the plain below. But it was sleeping peacefully in the full sight of the moon, without life or motion. He looked at the stars, it was still far from midnight. His companions had no doubt long since returned to the cabin to prepare for their midnight journey. They were discussing him, perhaps laughing at him, or worse, pitying him and his bargain. Yet here was his bargain! A slight laugh he gave vent to here startled him a little, it sounded so hard and so unmirthful, and so unlike, as he oddly fancied what he really thought. But what did he think?

Nothing mean or revengeful; no, they never would say that. When he had taken out all the surface gold and put the mine in working order, he would send them each a draft for a thousand dollars. Of course, if they were ever ill or poor he would do more. One of the first, the very first things he should do would be to send them each a handsome gun and tell them that he only asked in return the old-fashioned rifle that once was his. Looking back at the moment in after-years, he wondered that, with this exception, he made no plans for his own future, or the way he should dispose of his newly acquired wealth. This was the more singular as it had been the custom of the five partners to lie awake at night, audibly comparing with each other what they would do in case they made a strike. He remembered how, Alnaschar-like, they nearly separated once over a difference in the disposal of a hundred thousand dollars that they never had, nor expected to have. He remembered how Union Mills always began his career as a millionaire by a "square meal" at Delmonico's; how the Right Bower's initial step was always a trip home "to see his mother;" how the Left Bower would immediately placate the parents of his beloved with priceless gifts (it may be parenthetically remarked that the parents and the beloved one were as hypothetical as the fortune); and how the Judge would make his first start as a capitalist by breaking a certain faro bank in Sacramento. He himself had been equally eloquent in extravagant fancy in those penniless days, he who now was quite cold and impassive beside the more extravagant reality.

How different it might have been! If they had only waited a day longer! if they had only broken their resolves to him kindly and parted in good will! How he would long ere this have rushed to greet them with the joyful news! How they would have danced around it, sung themselves hoarse, laughed down their enemies, and run up the flag triumphantly on the summit of the Lone Star Mountain! How they would have crowned him "the Old Man," "the hero of the camp!" How he would have told them the whole story; how some strange instinct had impelled him to ascend the summit, and how another step on that summit would have precipitated him into the cañon! And how, but what if somebody else, Union Mills or the Judge, had been the first discoverer? Might they not have meanly kept the secret from him; have selfishly helped themselves and done -

"What you are doing now."

The hot blood rushed to his cheek, as if a strange voice were at his ear. For a moment he could not believe that it came from his own pale lips until he found himself speaking. He rose to his feet, tingling with shame, and began hurriedly to descend the mountain.

He would go to them, tell them of his discovery, let them give him his share, and leave them forever. It was the only thing to be done, strange that he had not thought of it at once. Yet it was hard, very hard and cruel, to be forced to meet them again. What had he done to suffer this mortification? For a moment he actually hated this vulgar treasure that had forever buried under its gross ponderability the light and careless past, and utterly crushed out the poetry of their old, indolent, happy existence.

He was sure to find them waiting at the Cross Roads where the coach came past. It was three miles away, yet he could get there in time if he hastened. It was a wise and practical conclusion of his evening's work, a lame and impotent conclusion to his evening's indignation.

No matter. They would perhaps at first think he had come to weakly follow them, perhaps they would at first doubt his story. No matter. He bit his lips to keep down the foolish rising tears, but still went blindly forward.

He saw not the beautiful night, cradled in the dark hills, swathed in luminous mists, and hushed in the awe of its own loveliness! Here and there the moon had laid her calm face on lake and overflow, and gone to sleep embracing them, until the whole plain seemed to be lifted into infinite quiet. Walking on as in a dream, the black, impenetrable barriers of skirting thickets opened and gave way to vague distances that it appeared impossible to reach, dim vistas that seemed unapproachable. Gradually he seemed himself to become a part of the mysterious night. He was becoming as pulseless, as calm, as passionless.

What was that? A shot in the direction of the cabin! yet so faint, so echoless, so ineffective in the vast silence, that he would have thought it his fancy but for the strange instinctive jar upon his sensitive nerves. Was it an accident, or was it an intentional signal to him? He stopped; it was not repeated, the silence reasserted itself, but this time with an ominous deathlike suggestion. A sudden and terrible thought crossed his mind. He cast aside his pack and all encumbering weight, took a deep breath, lowered his head, and darted like a deer in the direction of the challenge.

II.

The exodus of the seceding partners of the Lone Star claim had been scarcely an imposing one. For the first five minutes after quitting the cabin the procession was straggling and vagabond. Unwonted exertion had exaggerated the lameness of some, and feebleness of moral purpose had predisposed the others to obtrusive musical exhibition. Union Mills limped and whistled with affected abstraction; the Judge whistled and limped with affected earnestness. The Right Bower led the way with some show of definite design; the Left Bower followed with his hands in his pockets. The two feebler natures, drawn together in unconscious sympathy, looked vaguely at each other for support.

"You see," said the Judge, suddenly, as if triumphantly concluding an argument, "there ain't anything better for a young fellow than independence. Nature, so to speak, points the way. Look at the animals."

"There's a skunk hereabouts," said Union Mills, who was supposed to be gifted with aristocratically sensitive nostrils, "within ten miles of this place; like as not crossing the Ridge. It's always my luck to happen out just at such times. I don't see the necessity anyhow of trapesing round the claim now, if we calculate to leave it to-night."

Both men waited to observe if the suggestion was taken up by the Right and Left Bower moodily plodding ahead. No response following, the Judge shamelessly abandoned his companion.

"You wouldn't stand snoopin' round instead of lettin' the Old Man get used to the idea alone? No; I could see all along that he was takin' it in, takin' it in kindly but slowly, and I reckoned the best thing for us to do was to git up and git until he'd got round it." The Judge's voice was slightly raised for the benefit of the two before him.

"Didn't he say," remarked the Right Bower, stopping suddenly and facing the others, "didn't he say that that new trader was goin' to let him have some provisions anyway?"

Union Mills turned appealingly to the Judge; that gentleman was forced to reply, "Yes; I remember distinctly he said it. It was one of the things I was particular about on his account," responded the Judge, with the air of having arranged it all himself with the new trader. "I remember I was easier in my mind about it."

"But didn't he say," queried the Left Bower, also stopping short, "suthin' about its being contingent on our doing some work on the race?"

The Judge turned for support to Union Mills, who, however, under the hollow pretense of preparing for a long conference, had luxuriously seated himself on a stump. The Judge sat down also, and replied, hesitatingly, "Well, yes! Us or him."

"Us or him," repeated the Right Bower, with gloomy irony. "And you ain't quite clear in your mind, are you, if you haven't done the work already? You're just killing yourself with this spontaneous, promiscuous, and premature overwork; that's what's the matter with you."

"I reckon I heard somebody say suthin' about its being a Chinaman's three-day job," interpolated the Left Bower, with equal irony, "but I ain't quite clear in my mind about that."

"It'll be a sorter distraction for the Old Man," said Union Mills, feebly, "kinder take his mind off his loneliness."

Nobody taking the least notice of the remark, Union Mills stretched out his legs more comfortably and took out his pipe. He had scarcely done so when the Right Bower, wheeling suddenly, set off in the direction of the creek. The Left Bower, after a slight pause, followed without a word. The Judge, wisely conceiving it better to join the stronger party, ran feebly after him, and left Union Mills to bring up a weak and vacillating rear.

Their course, diverging from Lone Star Mountain, led them now directly to the bend of the creek, the base of their old ineffectual operations. Here was the beginning of the famous tail-race that skirted the new trader's claim, and then lost its way in a swampy hollow. It was choked with debris; a thin, yellow stream that once ran through it seemed to have stopped work when they did, and gone into greenish liquidation.

They had scarcely spoken during this brief journey, and had received no other explanation from the Right Bower, who led them, than that afforded by his mute example when he reached the race. Leaping into it without a word, he at once began to clear away the broken timbers and drift-wood. Fired by the spectacle of what appeared to be a new and utterly frivolous game, the men gayly leaped after him, and were soon engaged in a fascinating struggle with the impeded race. The Judge forgot his lameness in springing over a broken sluice-box; Union Mills forgot his whistle in a happy imitation of a Chinese coolie's song. Nevertheless, after ten minutes of this mild dissipation, the pastime flagged; Union Mills was beginning to rub his leg, when a distant rumble shook the earth. The men looked at each other; the diversion was complete; a languid discussion of the probabilities of its being an earthquake or a blast followed, in the midst of which the Right Bower, who was working a little in advance of the others, uttered a warning cry and leaped from the race. His companions had barely time to follow before a sudden and inexplicable rise in the waters of the creek sent a swift irruption of the flood through the race. In an instant its choked and impeded channel was cleared, the race was free, and the scattered debris of logs and timber floated upon its easy current. Quick to take advantage of this labor-saving phenomenon, the Lone Star partners sprang into the water, and by disentangling and directing the eddying fragments completed their work.

"The Old Man oughter been here to see this," said the Left Bower; "it's just one o' them climaxes of poetic justice he's always huntin' up. It's easy to see what's happened. One o' them high-toned shrimps over in the Excelsior claim has put a blast in too near the creek. He's tumbled the bank into the creek and sent the back water down here just to wash out our race. That's what I call poetical retribution."

"And who was it advised us to dam the creek below the race and make it do the thing?" asked the Right Bower, moodily.

"That was one of the Old Man's ideas, I reckon," said the Left Bower, dubiously.

"And you remember," broke in the Judge with animation, "I allus said, 'Go slow, go slow. You just hold on and suthin' will happen.' And," he added, triumphantly, "you see suthin' has happened. I don't want to take credit to myself, but I reckoned on them Excelsior boys bein' fools, and took the chances."

"And what if I happen to know that the Excelsior boys ain't blastin' to-day?" said the Right Bower, sarcastically.

As the Judge had evidently based his hypothesis on the alleged fact of a blast, he deftly evaded the point. "I ain't sayin' the Old Man's head ain't level on some things; he wants a little more sabe of the world. He's improved a good deal in euchre lately, and in poker, well! he's got that sorter dreamy, listenin'-to-the-angels kind o' way that you can't exactly tell whether he's bluffin' or has got a full hand. Hasn't he?" he asked, appealing to Union Mills.

But that gentleman, who had been watching the dark face of the Right Bower, preferred to take what he believed to be his cue from him. "That ain't the question," he said virtuously; "we ain't takin' this step to make a card sharp out of him. We're not doin' Chinamen's work in this race to-day for that. No, sir! We're teachin' him to paddle his own canoe." Not finding the sympathetic response he looked for in the Right Bower's face, he turned to the Left.

"I reckon we were teachin' him our canoe was too full," was the Left Bower's unexpected reply. "That's about the size of it."

The Right Bower shot a rapid glance under his brows at his brother. The latter, with his hands in his pockets, stared unconsciously at the rushing water, and then quietly turned away. The Right Bower followed him. "Are you goin' back on us?" he asked.

"Are you?" responded the other.

"No!"

"No, then it is," returned the Left Bower quietly. The elder brother hesitated in half-angry embarrassment.

"Then what did you mean by saying we reckoned our canoe was too full?"

"Wasn't that our idea?" returned the Left Bower, indifferently. Confounded by this practical expression of his own unformulated good intentions, the Right Bower was staggered.

"Speakin' of the Old Man," broke in the Judge, with characteristic infelicity, "I reckon he'll sort o' miss us, times like these. We were allers runnin' him and bedevilin' him, after work, just to get him excited and amusin', and he'll kinder miss that sort o' stimulatin'. I reckon we'll miss it too, somewhat. Don't you remember, boys, the night we put up that little sell on him and made him believe we'd struck it rich in the bank of the creek, and got him so conceited, he wanted to go off and settle all our debts at once?"

"And how I came bustin' into the cabin with a pan full of iron pyrites and black sand," chuckled Union Mills, continuing the reminiscences, "and how them big gray eyes of his nearly bulged out of his head. Well, it's some satisfaction to know we did our duty by the young fellow even in those little things." He turned for confirmation of their general disinterestedness to the Right Bower, but he was already striding away, uneasily conscious of the lazy following of the Left Bower, like a laggard conscience at his back. This movement again threw Union Mills and the Judge into feeble complicity in the rear, as the procession slowly straggled homeward from the creek.

Night had fallen. Their way lay through the shadow of Lone Star Mountain, deepened here and there by the slight, bosky ridges that, starting from its base, crept across the plain like vast roots of its swelling trunk. The shadows were growing blacker as the moon began to assert itself over the rest of the valley, when the Right Bower halted suddenly on one of these ridges. The Left Bower lounged up to him and stopped also, while the two others came up and completed the group.

"There's no light in the shanty," said the Right Bower in a low voice, half to himself and half in answer to their inquiring attitude. The men followed the direction of his finger. In the distance the black outline of the Lone Star cabin stood out distinctly in the illumined space. There was the blank, sightless, external glitter of moonlight on its two windows that seemed to reflect its dim vacancy, empty alike of light and warmth and motion.

"That's sing'lar," said the Judge in an awed whisper.

The Left Bower, by simply altering the position of his hands in his trousers' pockets, managed to suggest that he knew perfectly the meaning of it, had always known it; but that being now, so to speak, in the hands of Fate, he was callous to it. This much, at least, the elder brother read in his attitude. But anxiety at that moment was the controlling impulse of the Right Bower, as a certain superstitious remorse was the instinct of the two others, and without heeding the cynic, the three started at a rapid pace for the cabin.

They reached it silently, as the moon, now riding high in the heavens, seemed to touch it with the tender grace and hushed repose of a tomb. It was with something of this feeling that the Right Bower softly pushed open the door; it was with something of this dread that the two others lingered on the threshold, until the Right Bower, after vainly trying to stir the dead embers on the hearth into life with his foot, struck a match and lit their solitary candle. Its flickering light revealed the familiar interior unchanged in aught but one thing. The bunk that the Old Man had occupied was stripped of its blankets; the few cheap ornaments and photographs were gone; the rude poverty of the bare boards and scant pallet looked up at them unrelieved by the bright face and gracious youth that had once made them tolerable. In the grim irony of that exposure, their own penury was doubly conscious. The little knapsack, the tea-cup and coffee-pot that had hung near his bed, were gone also. The most indignant protest, the most pathetic of the letters he had composed and rejected, whose torn fragments still littered the floor, could never have spoken with the eloquence of this empty space! The men exchanged no words; the solitude of the cabin, instead of drawing them together, seemed to isolate each one in selfish distrust of the others. Even the unthinking garrulity of Union Mills and the Judge was checked. A moment later, when the Left Bower entered the cabin, his presence was scarcely noticed.

The silence was broken by a joyous exclamation from the Judge. He had discovered the Old Man's rifle in the corner, where it had been at first overlooked. "He ain't gone yet, gentlemen, for yer's his rifle," he broke in, with a feverish return of volubility, and a high excited falsetto. "He wouldn't have left this behind. No! I knowed it from the first. He's just outside a bit, foraging for wood and water. No, sir! Coming along here I said to Union Mills, didn't I? 'Bet your life the Old Man's not far off, even if he ain't in the cabin.' Why, the moment I stepped foot" -

"And I said coming along," interrupted Union Mills, with equally reviving mendacity, 'Like as not he's hangin' round yer and lyin' low just to give us a surprise.' He! ho!"

"He's gone for good, and he left that rifle here on purpose," said the Left Bower in a low voice, taking the weapon almost tenderly in his hands.

"Drop it, then!" said the Right Bower. The voice was that of his brother, but suddenly changed with passion. The two other partners drew back in alarm.

"I'll not leave it here for the first comer," said the Left Bower, calmly, "because we've been fools and he too. It's too good a weapon for that."

"Drop it, I say!" said the Right Bower, with a savage stride towards him.

The younger brother brought the rifle to a half charge with a white face but a steady eye.

"Stop where you are!" he said collectedly. "Don't row with me, because you haven't either the grit to stick to your ideas or the heart to confess them wrong. We've followed your lead, and here we are! The camp's broken up, the Old Man's gone, and we're going. And as for the damned rifle" -

"Drop it, do you hear!" shouted the Right Bower, clinging to that one idea with the blind pertinacity of rage and a losing cause. "Drop it!"

The Left Bower drew back, but his brother had seized the barrel with both hands. There was a momentary struggle, a flash through the half-lighted cabin, and a shattering report. The two men fell back from each other; the rifle dropped on the floor between them.

The whole thing was over so quickly that the other two partners had not had time to obey their common impulse to separate them, and consequently even now could scarcely understand what had passed. It was over so quickly that the two actors themselves walked back to their places, scarcely realizing their own act.

A dead silence followed. The Judge and Union Mills looked at each other in dazed astonishment, and then nervously set about their former habits, apparently in that fatuous belief common to such natures, that they were ignoring a painful situation. The Judge drew the barrel towards him, picked up the cards, and began mechanically to "make a patience," on which Union Mills gazed with ostentatious interest, but with eyes furtively conscious of the rigid figure of the Right Bower by the chimney and the abstracted face of the Left Bower at the door. Ten minutes had passed in this occupation, the Judge and Union Mills conversing in the furtive whispers of children unavoidably but fascinatedly present at a family quarrel, when a light step was heard upon the crackling brushwood outside, and the bright panting face of the Old Man appeared upon the threshold. There was a shout of joy; in another moment he was half-buried in the bosom of the Right Bower's shirt, half-dragged into the lap of the Judge, upsetting the barrel, and completely encompassed by the Left Bower and Union Mills. With the enthusiastic utterance of his name the spell was broken.

Happily unconscious of the previous excitement that had provoked this spontaneous unanimity of greeting, the Old Man, equally relieved, at once broke into a feverish announcement of his discovery. He painted the details with, I fear, a slight exaggeration of coloring, due partly to his own excitement, and partly to justify their own. But he was strangely conscious that these bankrupt men appeared less elated with their personal interest in their stroke of fortune than with his own success. "I told you he'd do it," said the Judge, with a reckless unscrupulousness of the statement that carried everybody with it; "look at him! the game little pup." "Oh, no! he ain't the right breed, is he?" echoed Union Mills with arch irony, while the Right and Left Bower, grasping either hand, pressed a proud but silent greeting that was half new to him, but wholly delicious. It was not without difficulty that he could at last prevail upon them to return with him to the scene of his discovery, or even then restrain them from attempting to carry him thither on their shoulders on the plea of his previous prolonged exertions. Once only there was a momentary embarrassment. "Then you fired that shot to bring me back?" said the Old Man, gratefully. In the awkward silence that followed, the hands of the two brothers sought and grasped each other, penitently. "Yes," interposed the Judge with delicate tact, "ye see the Right and Left Bower almost quarreled to see which should be the first to fire for ye. I disremember which did" - "I never touched the trigger," said the Left Bower, hastily. With a hurried backward kick, the Judge resumed, "It went off sorter spontaneous."

The difference in the sentiment of the procession that once more issued from the Lone Star cabin did not fail to show itself in each individual partner according to his temperament. The subtle tact of Union Mills, however, in expressing an awakened respect for their fortunate partner by addressing him, as if unconsciously, as "Mr. Ford" was at first discomposing, but even this was forgotten in their breathless excitement as they neared the base of the mountain. When they had crossed the creek the Right Bower stopped reflectively.

"You say you heard the slide come down before you left the cabin?" he said, turning to the Old Man.

"Yes; but I did not know then what it was. It was about an hour and a half after you left," was the reply.

"Then look here, boys," continued the Right Bower with superstitious exultation; "it was the slide that tumbled into the creek, overflowed it, and helped us clear out the race!"

It seemed so clear that Providence had taken the partners of the Lone Star directly in hand that they faced the toilsome ascent of the mountain with the assurance of conquerors. They paused only on the summit to allow the Old Man to lead the way to the slope that held their treasure. He advanced cautiously to the edge of the crumbling cliff, stopped, looked bewildered, advanced again, and then remained white and immovable. In an instant the Right Bower was at his side.

"Is anything the matter? Don't, don't look so, Old Man, for God's sake!"

The Old Man pointed to the dull, smooth, black side of the mountain, without a crag, break, or protuberance, and said with ashen lips:

"It's gone!"

And it was gone! A second slide had taken place, stripping the flank of the mountain, and burying the treasure and the weak implement that had marked its side deep under a chaos of rock and débris at its base.

"Thank God!" The blank faces of his companions turned quickly to the Right Bower. "Thank God!" he repeated, with his arm round the neck of the Old Man.

"Had he stayed behind he would have been buried too." He paused, and, pointing solemnly to the depths below, said, "And thank God for showing us where we may yet labor for it in hope and patience like honest men."

The men silently bowed their heads and slowly descended the mountain. But when they had reached the plain, one of them called out to the others to watch a star that seemed to be rising and moving towards them over the hushed and sleeping valley.

"It's only the stage-coach, boys," said the Left Bower, smiling; "the coach that was to take us away."

In the security of their new-found fraternity they resolved to wait and see it pass. As it swept by with flash of light, beat of hoofs, and jingle of harness, the only real presence in the dreamy landscape, the driver shouted a hoarse greeting to the phantom partners, audible only to the Judge, who was nearest the vehicle.

"Did you hear, did you hear what he said, boys?" he gasped, turning to his companions. "No? Shake hands all round, boys! God bless you all, boys! To think we didn't know it all this while!"

"Know what?"

"Merry Christmas!"

A SHIP OF '49.

It had rained so persistently in San Francisco during the first week of January, 1854, that a certain quagmire in the roadway of Long Wharf had become impassable, and a plank was thrown over its dangerous depth. Indeed, so treacherous was the spot that it was alleged, on good authority, that a hastily embarking traveler had once hopelessly lost his portmanteau, and was fain to dispose of his entire interest in it for the sum of two dollars and fifty cents to a speculative stranger on the wharf. As the stranger's search was rewarded afterwards only by the discovery of the body of a casual Chinaman, who had evidently endeavored wickedly to anticipate him, a feeling of commercial insecurity was added to the other eccentricities of the locality.

The plank led to the door of a building that was a marvel even in the chaotic frontier architecture of the street. The houses on either side, irregular frames of wood or corrugated iron, bore evidence of having been quickly thrown together, to meet the requirements of the goods and passengers who were once disembarked on what was the muddy beach of the infant city. But the building in question exhibited a certain elaboration of form and design utterly inconsistent with this idea. The structure obtruded a bowed front to the street, with a curving line of small windows, surmounted by elaborate carvings and scroll work of vines and leaves, while below, in faded gilt letters, appeared the legend "Pontiac, Marseilles." The effect of this incongruity was startling.

It is related that an inebriated miner, impeded by mud and drink before its door, was found gazing at its remarkable façade with an expression of the deepest despondency. "I hev lived a free life, pardner," he explained thickly to the Samaritan who succored him, "and every time since I've been on this six weeks' jamboree might have kalkilated it would come to this. Snakes I've seen afore now, and rats I'm not unfamiliar with, but when it comes to the starn of a ship risin' up out of the street, I reckon it's time to pass in my checks."

"It is a ship, you blasted old soaker," said the Samaritan curtly.

It was indeed a ship. A ship run ashore and abandoned on the beach years before by her gold-seeking crew, with the débris of her scattered stores and cargo, overtaken by the wild growth of the strange city and the reclamation of the muddy flat, wherein she lay hopelessly imbedded; her retreat cut off by wharves and quays and breakwater, jostled at first by sheds, and then impacted in a block of solid warehouses and dwellings, her rudder, port, and counter boarded in, and now gazing hopelessly through her cabin windows upon the busy street before her. But still a ship despite her transformation. The faintest line of contour yet left visible spoke of the buoyancy of another element; the balustrade of her roof was unmistakably a taffrail. The rain slipped from her swelling sides with a certain lingering touch of the sea; the soil around her was still treacherous with its suggestions, and even the wind whistled nautically over her chimney. If, in the fury of some southwesterly gale, she had one night slipped her strange moorings and left a shining track through the lower town to the distant sea, no one would have been surprised.

Least of all, perhaps, her present owner and possessor, Mr. Abner Nott. For by the irony of circumstances, Mr. Nott was a Far Western farmer who had never seen a ship before, nor a larger stream of water than a tributary of the Missouri River. In a spirit, half of fascination, half of speculation, he had bought her at the time of her abandonment, and had since mortgaged his ranch at Petaluma with his live stock, to defray the expenses of filling in the land where she stood, and the improvements of the vicinity. He had transferred his household goods and his only daughter to her cabin, and had divided the space "between decks" and her hold into lodging-rooms, and lofts for the storage of goods. It could hardly be said that the investment had been profitable. His tenants vaguely recognized that his occupancy was a sentimental rather than a commercial speculation, and often generously lent themselves to the illusion by not paying their rent. Others treated their own tenancy as a joke, a quaint recreation born of the childlike familiarity of frontier intercourse. A few had left; carelessly abandoning their unsalable goods to their landlord, with great cheerfulness and a sense of favor. Occasionally Mr. Abner Nott, in a practical relapse, raged against the derelicts, and talked of dispossessing them, or even dismantling his tenement, but he was easily placated by a compliment to the "dear old ship," or an effort made by some tenant to idealize his apartment. A photographer who had ingeniously utilized the forecastle for a gallery (accessible from the bows in the next street), paid no further tribute than a portrait of the pretty face of Rosey Nott. The superstitious reverence in which Abner Nott held his monstrous fancy was naturally enhanced by his purely bucolic exaggeration of its real functions and its native element. "This yer keel has sailed, and sailed, and sailed," he would explain with some incongruity of illustration, "in a bee line, makin' tracks for days runnin'. I reckon more storms and blizzards hez tackled her than you ken shake a stick at. She's stampeded whales afore now, and sloshed round with pirates and freebooters in and outer the Spanish Main, and across lots from Marcelleys where she was rared. And yer she sits peaceful-like just ez if she'd never been outer a pertater patch, and hadn't ploughed the sea with fo'sails and studdin' sails and them things cavortin' round her masts."

Abner Nott's enthusiasm was shared by his daughter, but with more imagination, and an intelligence stimulated by the scant literature of her father's emigrant wagon and the few books found on the cabin shelves. But to her the strange shell she inhabited suggested more of the great world than the rude, chaotic civilization she saw from the cabin windows or met in the persons of her father's lodgers. Shut up for days in this quaint tenement, she had seen it change from the enchanted playground of her childish fancy to the theater of her active maidenhood, but without losing her ideal romance in it. She had translated its history in her own way, read its quaint nautical hieroglyphics after her own fashion, and possessed herself of its secrets. She had in fancy made voyages in it to foreign lands, had heard the accents of a softer tongue on its decks, and on summer nights, from the roof of the quarter-deck, had seen mellower constellations take the place of the hard metallic glitter of the Californian skies. Sometimes, in her isolation, the long, cylindrical vault she inhabited seemed, like some vast sea-shell, to become musical with the murmurings of the distant sea. So completely had it taken the place of the usual instincts of feminine youth that she had forgotten she was pretty, or that her dresses were old in fashion and scant in quantity. After the first surprise of admiration her father's lodgers ceased to follow the abstracted nymph except with their eyes, partly respecting her spiritual shyness, partly respecting the jealous supervision of the paternal Nott. She seldom penetrated the crowded center of the growing city; her rare excursions were confined to the old ranch at Petaluma, whence she brought flowers and plants, and even extemporized a hanging-garden on the quarter-deck.

It was still raining, and the wind, which had increased to a gale, was dashing the drops against the slanting cabin windows with a sound like spray when Mr. Abner Nott sat before a table seriously engaged with his accounts. For it was "steamer night," as that momentous day of reckoning before the sailing of the regular mail steamer was briefly known to commercial San Francisco, and Mr. Nott was subject at such times to severely practical relapses. A swinging light seemed to bring into greater relief that peculiar encased casket-like security of the low-timbered, tightly-fitting apartment, with its toy-like utilities of space, and made the pretty oval face of Rosey Nott appear a characteristic ornament. The sliding door of the cabin communicated with the main deck, now roofed in and partitioned off so as to form a small passage that led to the open starboard gangway, where a narrow, enclosed staircase built on the ship's side took the place of the ship's ladder under her counter, and opened in the street.

A dash of rain against the window caused Rosey to lift her eyes from her book.

"It's much nicer here than at the ranch, father," she said coaxingly, "even leaving alone its being a beautiful ship instead of a shanty; the wind don't whistle through the cracks and blow out the candle when you're reading, nor the rain spoil your things hung up against the wall. And you look more like a gentleman sitting in his own ship, you know, looking over his bills and getting ready to give his orders."

Vague and general as Miss Rosey's compliment was, it had its full effect upon her father, who was at times dimly conscious of his hopeless rusticity and its incongruity with his surroundings. "Yes," he said awkwardly, with a slight relaxation of his aggressive attitude; "yes, in course it's more bang-up style, but it don't pay, Rosey, it don't pay. Yer's the Pontiac that oughter be bringin' in, ez rents go, at least three hundred a month, don't make her taxes. I bin thinkin' seriously of sellin' her."

As Rosey knew her father had experienced this serious contemplation on the first of every month for the last two years, and cheerfully ignored it the next day, she only said, "I'm sure the vacant rooms and lofts are all rented, father."

"That's it," returned Mr. Nott thoughtfully, plucking at his bushy whiskers with his fingers and thumb as if he were removing dead and sapless incumbrances in their growth, "that's just what it is, them's ez in it themselves don't pay, and them ez haz left their goods, the goods don't pay. The feller ez stored them iron sugar kettles in the forehold, after trying to get me to make another advance on 'em, sez he believes he'll have to sacrifice 'em to me after all, and only begs I'd give him a chance of buying back the half of 'em ten years from now, at double what I advanced him. The chap that left them five hundred cases of hair dye 'tween decks and then skipped out to Sacramento, met me the other day in the street and advised me to use a bottle ez an advertisement, or try it on the starn of the Pontiac for fireproof paint. That foolishness ez all he's good for. And yet thar might be suthin' in the paint, if a feller had nigger luck. Ther's that New York chap ez bought up them damaged boxes of plug terbakker for fifty dollars a thousand, and sold 'em for foundations for that new building in Sansome Street at a thousand clear profit. It's all luck, Rosey."

The girl's eyes had wandered again to the pages of her book. Perhaps she was already familiar with the text of her father's monologue. But recognizing an additional querulousness in his voice, she laid the book aside and patiently folded her hands in her lap.

"That's right, for I've suthin' to tell ye. The fact is Sleight wants to buy the Pontiac out and out just ez she stands with the two fifty vara lots she stands on."

"Sleight wants to buy her? Sleight?" echoed Rosey incredulously.

"You bet! Sleight, the big financier, the smartest man in 'Frisco."

"What does he want to buy her for?" asked Rosey, knitting her pretty brows.

The apparently simple question suddenly puzzled Mr. Nott. He glanced feebly at his daughter's face, and frowned in vacant irritation. "That's so," he said, drawing a long breath; "there's suthin' in that."

"What did he say?" continued the young girl, impatiently.

"Not much. 'You've got the Pontiac, Nott,' sez he. 'You bet!' sez I. 'What'll you take for her and the lot she stands on?' sez he, short and sharp. Some fellers, Rosey," said Nott, with a cunning smile, "would hev blurted out a big figger and been cotched. That ain't my style. I just looked at him. 'I'll wait fur your figgers until next steamer day,' sez he, and off he goes like a shot. He's awfully sharp, Rosey."

"But if he is sharp, father, and he really wants to buy the ship," returned Rosey, thoughtfully, "it's only because he knows it's valuable property, and not because he likes it as we do. He can't take that value away even if we don't sell it to him, and all the while we have the comfort of the dear old Pontiac, don't you see?"

This exhaustive commercial' reasoning was so sympathetic to Mr. Nott's instincts that he accepted it as conclusive. He, however, deemed it wise to still preserve his practical attitude. "But that don't make it pay by the month, Rosey. Suthin' must be done. I'm thinking I'll clean out that photographer."

"Not just after he's taken such a pretty view of the cabin front of the Pontiac from the street, father! No! He's going to give us a copy, and put the other in a shop window in Montgomery Street."

"That's so," said Mr. Nott, musingly; "it's no slouch of an advertisement. 'The Pontiac,' the property of A. Nott, Esq., of St. Jo, Missouri. Send it on to your aunt Phoebe; sorter make the old folks open their eyes, oh? Well, seem' he's been to some expense fittin' up an entrance from the other street, we'll let him slide. But as to that damned old Frenchman Ferrers, in the next loft, with his stuck-up airs and high-falutin style, we must get quit of him; he's regularly gouged me in that ere horsehair spekilation."

"How can you say that, father!" said Rosey, with a slight increase of color. "It was your own offer. You know those bales of curled horsehair were left behind by the late tenant to pay his rent. When Mr. De Ferrières rented the room afterwards, you told him you'd throw them in in the place of repairs and furniture. It was your own offer."

"Yes, but I didn't reckon ther'd ever be a big price per pound paid for the darned stuff for sofys and cushions and sich."

"How do you know he knew it, father?" responded Rosey.

"Then why did he look so silly at first, and then put on airs when I joked him about it, eh?"

"Perhaps he didn't understand your joking, father. He's a foreigner, and shy and proud, and not like the others. I don't think he knew what you meant then, any more than he believed he was making a bargain before. He may be poor, but I think he's been, a, a gentleman."

The young girl's animation penetrated even Mr. Nott's slow comprehension. Her novel opposition, and even the prettiness it enhanced, gave him a dull premonition of pain. His small round eyes became abstracted, his mouth remained partly open, even his fresh color slightly paled.

"You seem to have been takin' stock of this yer man, Rosey," he said, with a faint attempt at archness; "if he warn't ez old ez a crow, for all his young feathers, I'd think he was makin' up to you."

But the passing glow had faded from her young cheeks, and her eyes wandered again to her book. "He pays his rent regularly every steamer night," she said, quietly, as if dismissing an exhausted subject, "and he'll be here in a moment, I dare say." She took up her book, and leaning her head on her hand, once more became absorbed in its pages.

An uneasy silence followed. The rain beat against the windows, the ticking of a clock became audible, but still Mr. Nott sat with vacant eyes fixed on his daughter's face, and the constrained smile on his lips. He was conscious that he had never seen her look so pretty before, yet he could not tell why this was no longer an unalloyed satisfaction. Not but that he had always accepted the admiration of others for her as a matter of course, but for the first time he became conscious that she not only had an interest in others, but apparently a superior knowledge of them. How did she know these things about this man, and why had she only now accidentally spoken of them? He would have done so. All this passed so vaguely through his unreflective mind, that he was unable to retain any decided impression, but the far-reaching one that his lodger had obtained some occult influence over her through the exhibition of his baleful skill in the horsehair speculation. "Them tricks is likely to take a young girl's fancy. I must look arter her," he said to himself softly.

A slow regular step in the gangway interrupted his paternal reflections. Hastily buttoning across his chest the pea-jacket which he usually wore at home as a single concession to his nautical surroundings, he drew himself up with something of the assumption of a shipmaster, despite certain bucolic suggestions of his boots and legs. The footsteps approached nearer, and a tall figure suddenly stood in the doorway.

It was a figure so extraordinary that even in the strange masquerade of that early civilization it was remarkable; a figure with whom father and daughter were already familiar without abatement of wonder, the figure of a rejuvenated old man, padded, powdered, dyed, and painted to the verge of caricature, but without a single suggestion of ludicrousness or humor. A face so artificial that it seemed almost a mask, but, like a mask, more pathetic than amusing. He was dressed in the extreme of fashion of a dozen years before; his pearl-gray trousers strapped tightly over his varnished boots, his voluminous satin cravat and high collar embraced his rouged cheeks and dyed whiskers, his closely-buttoned frock coat clinging to a waist that seemed accented by stays.

He advanced two steps into the cabin with an upright precision of motion that might have hid the infirmities of age, and said deliberately with a foreign accent:

"You-r-r ac-coumpt?"

In the actual presence of the apparition Mr. Nott's dignified resistance wavered. But glancing uneasily at his daughter and seeing her calm eyes fixed on the speaker without embarrassment, he folded his arms stiffly, and with a lofty simulation of examining the ceiling, said:

"Ahem! Rosa! The gentleman's account."

It was an infelicitous action. For the stranger, who evidently had not noticed the presence of the young girl before, started, took a step quickly forward, bent stiffly but profoundly over the little hand that held the account, raised it to his lips, and with "a thousand pardons, mademoiselle," laid a small canvas bag containing the rent before the disorganized Mr. Nott and stiffly vanished.

The night was a troubled one to the simple-minded proprietor of the good ship Pontiac. Unable to voice his uneasiness by further discussion, but feeling that his late discomposing interview with his lodger demanded some marked protest, he absented himself on the plea of business during the rest of the evening, happily to his daughter's utter obliviousness of the reason. Lights were burning brilliantly in counting-rooms and offices, the feverish life of the mercantile city was at its height. With a vague idea of entering into immediate negotiations with Mr. Sleight for the sale of the ship, as a direct way out of his present perplexity, he bent his steps towards the financier's office, but paused and turned back before reaching the door. He made his way to the wharf and gazed abstractedly at the lights reflected in the dark, tremulous, jelly-like water. But wherever he went he was accompanied by the absurd figure of his lodger, a figure he had hitherto laughed at or half pitied, but which now, to his bewildered comprehension, seemed to have a fateful significance. Here a new idea seized him, and he hurried back to the ship, slackening his pace only when he arrived at his own doorway. Here he paused a moment and slowly ascended the staircase. When he reached the passage he coughed slightly and paused again. Then he pushed open the door of the darkened cabin and called softly:

"Rosey!"

"What is it, father?" said Rosey's voice from the little state-room on the right, Rosey's own bower.

"Nothing!" said Mr. Nott, with an affectation of languid calmness; "I only wanted to know if you was comfortable. It's an awful busy night in town."

"Yes, father."

"I reckon thar's tons o' gold goin' to the States tomorrow."

"Yes, father."

"Pretty comfortable, eh?"

"Yes, father."

"Well, I'll browse round a spell, and turn in myself soon."

"Yes, father."

Mr. Nott took down a hanging lantern, lighted it, and passed out into the gangway. Another lamp hung from the companion hatch to light the tenants to the lower deck, whence he descended. This deck was divided fore and aft by a partitioned passage, the lofts or apartments being lighted from the ports, and one or two by a door cut through the ship's side communicating with an alley on either side. This was the case with the loft occupied by Mr. Nott's strange lodger, which, besides a door in the passage, had this independent communication with the alley. Nott had never known him to make use of the latter door; on the contrary, it was his regular habit to issue from his apartment at three o'clock every afternoon, dressed as he has been described, stride deliberately through the passage to the upper deck and thence into the street, where his strange figure was a feature of the principal promenade for two or three hours, returning as regularly at eight o'clock to the ship and the seclusion of his loft. Mr. Nott paused before the door, under the pretense of throwing the light before him into the shadows of the forecastle: all was silent within. He was turning back when he was impressed by the regular recurrence of a peculiar rustling sound which he had at first referred to the rubbing of the wires of the swinging lantern against his clothing. He set down the light and listened; the sound was evidently on the other side of the partition; the sound of some prolonged, rustling, scraping movement, with regular intervals. Was it due to another of Mr. Nott's unprofitable tenants, the rats? No. A bright idea flashed upon Mr. Nott's troubled mind. It was De Ferrières snoring! He smiled grimly. "Wonder if Rosey'd call him a gentleman if she heard that," he chuckled to himself as he slowly made his way back to the cabin and the small state-room opposite to his daughter's. During the rest of the night he dreamed of being compelled to give Rosey in marriage to his lodger, who added insult to the outrage by snoring audibly through the marriage service.

Meantime, in her cradle-like nest in her nautical bower, Miss Rosey slumbered as lightly. Waking from a vivid dream of Venice, a child's Venice, seen from the swelling deck of the proudly-riding Pontiac, she was so impressed as to rise and cross on tiptoe to the little slanting port-hole. Morning was already dawning over the flat, straggling city, but from every counting-house and magazine the votive tapers of the feverish worshipers of trade and mammon were still flaring fiercely.

II.

The day following "steamer night" was usually stale and flat at San Francisco. The reaction from the feverish exaltation of the previous twenty-four hours was seen in the listless faces and lounging feet of promenaders, and was notable in the deserted offices and warehouses still redolent of last night's gas, and strewn with the dead ashes of last night's fires. There was a brief pause before the busy life which ran its course from "steamer day" to steamer day was once more taken up. In that interval a few anxious speculators and investors breathed freely, some critical situation was relieved, or some impending catastrophe momentarily averted. In particular, a singular stroke of good fortune that morning befell Mr. Nott. He not only secured a new tenant, but, as he sagaciously believed, introduced into the Pontiac a counteracting influence to the subtle fascinations of De Ferrières.

The new tenant apparently possessed a combination of business shrewdness and brusque frankness that strongly impressed his landlord. "You see, Rosey," said Nott, complacently describing the interview to his daughter, "when I sorter intimated in a keerless kind o' way that sugar kettles and hair dye was about played out ez securities, he just planked down the money for two months in advance. 'There,' sez he, 'that's your security, now where's mine?' 'I reckon I don't hitch on, pardner,' sez I; 'security what for?' "Spose you sell the ship?' sez he, 'afore the two months is up. I've heard that old Sleight wants to buy her.' 'Then you gets back your money,' sez I. 'And lose my room,' sez he; 'not much, old man. You sign a paper that whoever buys the ship inside o' two months hez to buy me ez a tenant with it; that's on the square.' So I sign the paper. It was mighty cute in the young feller, wasn't it?" he said, scanning his daughter's pretty puzzled face a little anxiously; "and don't you see, ez I ain't goin' to sell the Pontiac, it's just about ez cute in me, eh? He's a contractor somewhere around yer, and wants to be near his work. So he takes the room next to the Frenchman, that that ship-captain quit for the mines, and succeeds naterally to his chest and things. He's mighty peart-looking, that young feller, Rosey, long black mustaches, all his own color, Rosey, and he's a regular high-stepper, you bet. I reckon he's not only been a gentleman, but ez now. Some o' them contractors are very high-toned!"

"I don't think we have any right to give him the captain's chest, father," said Rosey; "there may be some private things in it. There were some letters and photographs in the hair-dye man's trunk that you gave the photographer."

"That's just it, Rosey," returned Abner Nott with sublime unconsciousness, "photographs and love letters you can't sell for cash, and I don't mind givin' 'em away, if they kin make a feller-creature happy."

"But, father, have we the right to give 'em away?"

"They're collateral security, Rosey." said her father grimly. "Co-la-te-ral," he continued, emphasizing each syllable by tapping the fist of one hand in the open palm of the other. "Co-la-te-ral is the word the big business sharps yer about call 'em. You can't get round that." He paused a moment, and then, as a new idea seemed to be painfully borne in his round eyes, continued cautiously: "Was that the reason why you wouldn't touch any of them dresses from the trunks of that opery gal ez skedaddled for Sacramento? And yet them trunks I regularly bought at auction, Rosey, at auction, on spec, and they didn't realize the cost of drayage."

A slight color mounted to Rosey's face. "No," she said, hastily, "not that." Hesitating a moment, she then drew softly to his side, and, placing her arms around his neck, turned his broad, foolish face towards her own. "Father," she began, "when mother died, would you have liked anybody to take her trunks and paw round her things and wear them?"

"When your mother died, just this side o' Sweetwater, Rosey," said Mr. Nott, with beaming unconsciousness, "she had n't any trunks. I reckon she had n't even an extra gown hanging up in the wagin, 'cept the petticoat ez she had wrapped around yer. It was about ez much ez we could do to skirmish round with Injins, alkali, and cold, and we sorter forgot to dress for dinner. She never thought, Rosey, that you and me would live to be inhabitin' a paliss of a real ship. Ef she had she would have died a proud woman."

He turned his small, loving, boar-like eyes upon her as a preternaturally innocent and trusting companion of Ulysses might have regarded the transforming Circe. Rosey turned away with the faintest sigh. The habitual look of abstraction returned to her eyes as if she had once more taken refuge in her own ideal world. Unfortunately the change did not escape either the sensitive observation or the fatuous misconception of the sagacious parent. "Ye'll be mountin' a few furbelows and fixins, Rosey, I reckon, ez only natural. Mebbee ye'll have to prink up a little now that we've got a gentleman contractor in the ship. I'll see what I kin pick up in Montgomery Street." And indeed he succeeded a few hours later in accomplishing with equal infelicity his generous design. When she returned from her household tasks she found on her berth a purple velvet bonnet of extraordinary make, and a pair of white satin slippers. "They'll do for a start-off, Rosey," he explained, "and I got 'em at my figgers."

"But I go out so seldom, father; and a bonnet" -

"That's so," interrupted Mr. Nott, complacently, "it might be jest ez well for a young gal like yer to appear ez if she did go out, or would go out if she wanted to. So you kin be wearin' that ar headstall kinder like this evening when the contractor's here, ez if you'd jest come in from a pasear."

Miss Rosey did not however immediately avail herself of her father's purchase, but contented herself with the usual scarlet ribbon that like a snood confined her brown hair, when she returned to her tasks. The space between the galley and the bulwarks had been her favorite resort in summer when not actually engaged in household work. It was now lightly roofed over with boards and tarpaulin against the winter rain, but still afforded her a veranda-like space before the galley door, where she could read or sew, looking over the bow of the Pontiac to the tossing bay or the farther range of the Contra Costa hills.

Hither Miss Rosey brought the purple prodigy, partly to please her father, partly with a view of subjecting it to violent radical changes. But after trying it on before the tiny mirror in the galley once or twice, her thoughts wandered away, and she fell into one of her habitual reveries seated on a little stool before the galley door.

She was aroused from it by the slight shaking and rattling of the doors of a small hatch on the deck, not a dozen yards from where she sat. It had been evidently fastened from below during the wet weather, but as she gazed, the fastenings were removed, the doors were suddenly lifted, and the head and shoulders of a young man emerged from the deck. Partly from her father's description, and partly from the impossibility of its being anybody else, she at once conceived it to be the new lodger. She had time to note that he was young and good-looking, graver perhaps than became his sudden pantomimic appearance, but before she could observe him closely, he had turned, closed the hatch with a certain familiar dexterity, and walked slowly towards the bows. Even in her slight bewilderment she observed that his step upon the deck seemed different to her father's or the photographer's, and that he laid his hand on various objects with a half-caressing ease and habit. Presently he paused and turned back, and glancing at the galley door for the first time encountered her wondering eyes.

It seemed so evident that she had been a curious spectator of his abrupt entrance on deck that he was at first disconcerted and confused. But after a second glance at her he appeared to resume his composure, and advanced a little defiantly towards the galley.

"I suppose I frightened you, popping up the fore hatch just now?"

"The what?" asked Rosey.

"The fore hatch," he repeated impatiently, indicating it with a gesture.

"And that's the fore hatch?" she said abstractedly. "You seem to know ships."

"Yes, a little," he said quietly. "I was below, and unfastened the hatch to come up the quickest way and take a look round. I've just hired a room here," he added explanatorily.

"I thought so," said Rosey simply; "you're the contractor?"

"The contractor! oh, yes! You seem to know it all."

"Father's told me."

"Oh, he's your father, Nott? Certainly. I see now," he continued, looking at her with a half repressed smile. "Certainly, Miss Nott, good morning," he half added and walked towards the companion-way. Something in the direction of his eyes as he turned away made Rosey lift her hands to her head. She had forgotten to remove her father's baleful gift.

She snatched it off and ran quickly to the companion-way.

"Sir!" she called.

The young man turned half-way down the steps and looked up. There was a faint color in her cheeks, and her pretty brown hair was slightly disheveled from the hasty removal of the bonnet.

"Father's very particular about strangers being on this deck," she said a little sharply.

"Oh, ah, I'm sorry I intruded."

"I, I thought I'd tell you," said Rosey, frightened by her boldness into a feeble anti-climax.

"Thank you."

She came back slowly to the galley and picked up the unfortunate bonnet with a slight sense of remorse. Why should she feel angry with her poor father's unhappy offering? And what business had this strange young man to use the ship so familiarly? Yet she was vaguely conscious that she and her father, with all their love and their domestic experience of it, lacked a certain instinctive ease in its possession that the half indifferent stranger had shown on first treading its deck. She walked to the hatchway and examined it with a new interest. Succeeding in lifting the hatch, she gazed at the lower deck. As she already knew the ladder had long since been removed to make room for one of the partitions, the only way the stranger could have reached it was by leaping to one of the rings. To make sure of this she let herself down holding on to the rings, and dropped a couple of feet to the deck below. She was in the narrow passage her father had penetrated the previous night. Before her was the door leading to De Ferrières' loft, always locked. It was silent within; it was the hour when the old Frenchman made his habitual promenade in the city. But the light from the newly-opened hatch allowed her to see more of the mysterious recesses of the forward bulkhead than she had known before, and she was startled by observing another yawning hatchway at her feet from which the closely-fitting door had been lifted, and which the new lodger had evidently forgotten to close again. The young girl stooped down and peered cautiously into the black abyss. Nothing was to be seen, nothing heard but the distant gurgle and click of water in some remoter depth. She replaced the hatch and returned by way of the passage to the cabin.

When her father came home that night she briefly recounted the interview with the new lodger, and her discovery of his curiosity. She did this with a possible increase of her usual shyness and abstraction, and apparently more as a duty than a colloquial recreation. But it pleased Mr. Nott also to give it more than his usual misconception. "Looking round the ship, was he, eh, Rosey?" he said with infinite archness. "In course, kinder sweepin' round the galley, and offerin' to fetch you wood and water, eh?" Even when the young girl had picked up her book with the usual faint smile of affectionate tolerance, and then drifted away in its pages, Mr. Nott chuckled audibly. "I reckon old Frenchy didn't come by when the young one was bedevlin' you there."

"What, father?" said Rosey, lifting her abstracted eyes to his face.

At the moment it seemed impossible that any human intelligence could have suspected deceit or duplicity in Rosey's clear gaze. But Mr. Nott's intelligence was superhuman. "I was sayin' that Mr. Ferrières didn't happen in while the young feller was there, eh?"

"No, father," answered Rosey, with an effort to follow him out of the pages of her book. "Why?"

But Mr. Nott did not reply. Later in the evening he awkwardly waylaid the new lodger before the cabin-door as that gentleman would have passed on to his room.

"I'm afraid," said the young man, glancing at Rosey, "that I intruded upon your daughter to-day. I was a little curious to see the old ship, and I didn't know what part of it was private."

"There ain't no private part to this yer ship, that ez, 'cepting the rooms and lofts," said Mr. Nott, authoritatively. Then, subjecting the anxious look of his daughter to his usual faculty for misconception, he added, "Thar ain't no place whar you haven't as much right to go ez any other man; thar ain't any man, furriner or Amerykan, young or old, dyed or undyed, ez hev got any better rights. You hear me, young fellow. Mr. Renshaw, my darter. My darter, Mr. Renshaw. Rosey, give the gentleman a chair. She's only jest come in from a promeynade, and hez jest taken off her bonnet," he added, with an arch look at Rosey and a hurried look around the cabin, as if he hoped to see the missing gift visible to the general eye. "So take a seat a minit, won't ye?"

But Mr. Renshaw, after an observant glance at the young girl's abstracted face, brusquely excused himself. "I've got a letter to write," he said, with a half bow to Rosey. "Good night."

He crossed the passage to the room that had been assigned to him, and closing the door gave way to some irritability of temper in his efforts to light the lamp and adjust his writing materials. For his excuse to Mr. Nott was more truthful than most polite pretexts. He had, indeed, a letter to write, and one that, being yet young in duplicity, the near presence of his host rendered difficult. For it ran as follows:

DEAR SLEIGHT: As I found I couldn't get a chance to make any examination of the ship except as occasion offered, I just went in to rent lodgings in her from the God-forsaken old ass who owns her, and here I am a tenant for two months. I contracted for that time in case the old fool should sell out to someone else before. Except that she's cut up a little between decks by the partitions for lofts that that Pike County idiot has put into her, she looks but little changed, and her fore-hold, as far as I can judge, is intact. It seems that Nott bought her just as she stands, with her cargo half out, but he wasn't here when she broke cargo. If anybody else had bought her but this cursed Missourian, who hasn't got the hayseed out of his hair, I might have found out something from him, and saved myself this kind of fooling, which isn't in my line. If I could get possession of a loft on the main deck, well forward, just over the fore-hold, I could satisfy myself in a few hours, but the loft is rented by that crazy Frenchman who parades Montgomery Street every afternoon, and though old Pike County wants to turn him out, I'm afraid I can't get it for a week to come.

If anything should happen to me, just you waltz down here and corral my things at once, for this old frontier pirate has a way of confiscating his lodgers' trunks.

Yours, DICK.

III.

If Mr. Renshaw indulged in any further curiosity regarding the interior of the Pontiac, he did not make his active researches manifest to Rosey. Nor, in spite of her father's invitation, did he again approach the galley, a fact which gave her her first vague impression in his favor. He seemed also to avoid the various advances which Mr. Nott appeared impelled to make, whenever they met in the passage, but did so without seemingly avoiding her, and marked his half contemptuous indifference to the elder Nott by an increase of respect to the young girl. She would have liked to ask him something about ships, and was sure his conversation would have been more interesting than that of old Captain Bower, to whose cabin he had succeeded, who had once told her a ship was the "devil's hencoop." She would have liked also to explain to him that she was not in the habit of wearing a purple bonnet. But her thoughts were presently engrossed by an experience which interrupted the even tenor of her young life.

She had been, as she afterwards remembered, impressed with a nervous restlessness one afternoon, which made it impossible for her to perform her ordinary household duties, or even to indulge her favorite recreation of reading or castle-building. She wandered over the ship, and, impelled by the same vague feeling of unrest, descended to the lower deck and the forward bulkhead where she had discovered the open hatch. It had not been again disturbed, nor was there any trace of further exploration. A little ashamed, she knew not why, of revisiting the scene of Mr. Renshaw's researches, she was turning back when she noticed that the door which communicated with De Ferrières' loft was partly open. The circumstance was so unusual that she stopped before it in surprise. There was no sound from within; it was the hour when its queer occupant was always absent; he must have forgotten to lock the door, or it had been unfastened by other hands. After a moment of hesitation she pushed it further open and stepped into the room.

By the dim light of two port-holes she could see that the floor was strewn and piled with the contents of a broken bale of curled horse-hair, of which a few untouched bales still remained against the wall. A heap of morocco skins, some already cut in the form of chair-cushion covers, and a few cushions unfinished and unstuffed, lay in the light of the ports, and gave the apartment the appearance of a cheap workshop. A rude instrument for combining the horse-hair, awls, buttons, and thread, heaped on a small bench, showed that active work had been but recently interrupted. A cheap earthenware ewer and basin on the floor, and a pallet made of an open bale of horse-hair, on which a ragged quilt and blanket were flung, indicated that the solitary worker dwelt and slept beside his work.

The truth flashed upon the young girl's active brain, quickened by seclusion and fed by solitary books. She read with keen eyes the miserable secret of her father's strange guest in the poverty-stricken walls, in the mute evidences of menial handicraft performed in loneliness and privation, in this piteous adaptation of an accident to save the conscious shame of premeditated toil. She knew now why he had stammeringly refused to receive her father's offer to buy back the goods he had given him; she knew now how hardly gained was the pittance that paid his rent and supported his childish vanity and grotesque pride. From a peg in the corner hung the familiar masquerade that hid his poverty, the pearl-gray trousers, the black frock-coat, the tall shining hat, in hideous contrast to the penury of his surroundings. But if they were here, where was he, and in what new disguise had he escaped from his poverty? A vague uneasiness caused her to hesitate and return to the open door. She had nearly reached it when her eye fell on the pallet which it partly illuminated. A singular resemblance in the ragged heap made her draw closer. The faded quilt was a dressing-gown, and clutching its folds lay a white, wasted hand.

The emigrant childhood of Rose Nott had been more than once shadowed by scalping-knives, and she was acquainted with Death. She went fearlessly to the couch, and found that the dressing-gown was only an enwrapping of the emaciated and lifeless body of De Ferrières. She did not retreat or call for help, but examined him closely. He was unconscious, but not pulseless; he had evidently been strong enough to open the door for air or succor, but had afterwards fallen into a fit on the couch. She flew to her father's locker and the galley fire, returned, and shut the door behind her, and by the skillful use of hot water and whiskey soon had the satisfaction of seeing a faint color take the place of the faded rouge in the ghastly cheeks. She was still chafing his hands when he slowly opened his eyes. With a start, he made a quick attempt to push aside her hand and rise. But she gently restrained him.

"Eh, what!" he stammered, throwing his face back from hers with an effort and trying to turn it to the wall.

"You have been ill," she said quietly. "Drink this."

With his face still turned away he lifted the cup to his chattering teeth. When he had drained it he threw a trembling glance round the room and at the door.

"There's no one been here but myself," she said quickly. "I happened to see the door open as I passed. I didn't think it worthwhile to call any one."

The searching look he gave her turned into an expression of relief, which, to her infinite uneasiness, again feebly lightened into one of antiquated gallantry. He drew the dressing-gown around him with an air.

"Ah! it is a goddess, Mademoiselle, that has deigned to enter the cell where, where I amuse myself. It is droll, is it not? I came here to make, what you call, the experiment of your father's fabric. I make myself, ha! ha! like a workman. Ah, bah! the heat, the darkness, the plebeian motion make my head to go round. I stagger, I faint, I cry out, I fall. But what of that? The great God hears my cry and sends me an angel. Voilà!"

He attempted an easy gesture of gallantry, but overbalanced himself and fell sideways on the pallet with a gasp. Yet there was so much genuine feeling mixed with his grotesque affectation, so much piteous consciousness of the ineffectiveness of his falsehood, that the young girl, who had turned away, came back and laid her hand upon his arm.

"You must lie still and try to sleep," she said gently. "I will return again. Perhaps," she added, "there is someone I can send for?"

He shook his head violently. Then in his old manner added, "After Mademoiselle, no one."

"I mean", she hesitated; "have you no friends?"

"Friends, ah! without doubt." He shrugged his shoulders. "But Mademoiselle will comprehend" -

"You are better now," said Rosey quickly, "and no one need know anything if you don't wish it. Try to sleep. You need not lock the door when I go; I will see that no one comes in."

He flushed faintly and averted his eyes. "It is too droll, Mademoiselle, is it not?"

"Of course it is," said Rosey, glancing round the miserable room.

"And Mademoiselle is an angel."

He carried her hand to his lips humbly, his first purely unaffected action. She slipped through the door, and softly closed it behind her.

Reaching the upper deck she was relieved to find her father had not returned, and her absence had been unnoticed. For she had resolved to keep De Ferrières' secret to herself from the moment that she had unwittingly discovered it, and to do this and still be able to watch over him without her father's knowledge required some caution. She was conscious of his strange aversion to the unfortunate man without understanding the reason, but as she was in the habit of entertaining his caprices more from affectionate tolerance of his weakness than reverence of his judgment, she saw no disloyalty to him in withholding a confidence that might be disloyal to another. "It won't do father any good to know it," she said to herself, "and if it did it oughtn't to," she added with triumphant feminine logic. But the impression made upon her by the spectacle she had just witnessed was stronger than any other consideration. The revelation of De Ferrièfres' secret poverty seemed a chapter from a romance of her own weaving; for a moment it lifted the miserable hero out of the depths of his folly and selfishness. She forgot the weakness of the man in the strength of his dramatic surroundings. It partly satisfied a craving she had felt; it was not exactly the story of the ship, as she had dreamed it, but it was an episode in her experience of it that broke its monotony. That she should soon learn, perhaps from De Ferrières' own lips, the true reason of his strange seclusion, and that it involved more than appeared to her now, she never for a moment doubted.

At the end of an hour she again knocked softly at the door, carrying some light nourishment she had prepared for him. He was asleep, but she was astounded to find that in the interval he had managed to dress himself completely in his antiquated finery. It was a momentary shock to the allusion she had been fostering, but she forgot it in the pitiable contrast between his haggard face and his pomatumed hair and beard, the jauntiness of his attire and the collapse of his invalid figure. When she had satisfied herself that his sleep was natural, she busied herself softly in arranging the miserable apartment. With a few feminine touches she removed the slovenliness of misery, and placed the loose material and ostentatious evidences of his work on one side. Finding that he still slept, and knowing the importance of this natural medication, she placed the refreshment she had brought by his side and noiselessly quitted the apartment. Hurrying through the gathering darkness between decks, she once or twice thought she heard footsteps, and paused, but encountering no one, attributed the impression to her over-consciousness. Yet she thought it prudent to go to the galley first, where she lingered a few moments before returning to the cabin. On entering she was a little startled at observing a figure seated at her father's desk, but was relieved at finding it was Mr. Renshaw.

He rose and put aside the book he had idly picked up. "I am afraid I am an intentional intruder this time, Miss Nott. But I found no one here, and I was tempted to look into this ship-shape little snuggery. You see the temptation got the better of me."

His voice and smile were so frank and pleasant, so free from his previous restraint, yet still respectful, so youthful yet manly, that Rosey was affected by them even in her preoccupation. Her eyes brightened and then dropped before his admiring glance. Had she known that the excitement of the last few hours had brought a wonderful charm into her pretty face, had aroused the slumbering life of her half-wakened beauty, she would have been more confused. As it was, she was only glad that the young man should turn out to be "nice." Perhaps he might tell her something about ships; perhaps if she had only known him longer she might, with De Ferrières' permission, have shared her confidence with him, and enlisted his sympathy and assistance. She contented herself with showing this anticipatory gratitude in her face as she begged him, with the timidity of a maiden hostess, to resume his seat.

But Mr. Renshaw seemed to talk only to make her talk, and I am forced to admit that Rosey found this almost as pleasant. It was not long before he was in possession of her simple history from the day of her baby emigration to California to the transfer of her childish life to the old ship, and even of much of the romantic fancies she had woven into her existence there. Whatever ulterior purpose he had in view, he listened as attentively as if her artless chronicle was filled with practical information. Once, when she had paused for breath, he said gravely, "I must ask you to show me over this wonderful ship some day that I may see it with your eyes."

"But I think you know it already better than I do," said Rosey with a smile.

Mr. Renshaw's brow clouded slightly. "Ah," he said, with a touch of his former restraint; "and why?"

"Well," said Rosey timidly, "I thought you went round and touched things in a familiar way as if you had handled them before."

The young man raised his eyes to Rosey's and kept them there long enough to bring back his gentler expression. "Then, because I found you trying on a very queer bonnet the first day I saw you," he said, mischievously, "I ought to believe you were in the habit of wearing one."

In the first flush of mutual admiration young people are apt to find a laugh quite as significant as a sigh for an expression of sympathetic communion, and this master-stroke of wit convulsed them both. In the midst of it Mr. Nott entered the cabin. But the complacency with which he viewed the evident perfect understanding of the pair was destined to suffer some abatement. Rosey, suddenly conscious that she was in some way participating in the ridicule of her father through his unhappy gift, became embarrassed. Mr. Renshaw's restraint returned with the presence of the old man. In vain, at first, Abner Nott strove with profound levity to indicate his arch comprehension of the situation, and in vain, later, becoming alarmed, he endeavored, with cheerful gravity, to indicate his utter obliviousness of any but a business significance in their tête-à-tête.

"I oughtn't to hev intruded, Rosey," he said, "when you and the gentleman were talkin' of contracts, mebbee; but don't mind me. I'm on the fly, anyhow, Rosey dear, hevin' to see a man round the corner."

But even the attitude of withdrawing did not prevent the exit of Renshaw to his apartment and of Rosey to the galley. Left alone in the cabin, Abner Nott felt in the knots and tangles of his beard for a reason. Glancing down at his prodigious boots, which, covered with mud and gravel, strongly emphasized his agricultural origin, and gave him a general appearance of standing on his own broad acres, he was struck with an idea. "It's them boots," he whispered to himself, softly; "they somehow don't seem 'xactly to trump or follow suit in this yer cabin; they don't hitch into anythin' but jist slosh round loose, and so to speak play it alone. And them young critters nat'rally feels it and gets out o' the way." Acting upon this instinct with his usual precipitate caution, he at once proceeded to the nearest second-hand shop, and, purchasing a pair of enormous carpet slippers, originally the property of a gouty sea-captain, reappeared with a strong suggestion of newly upholstering the cabin. The improvement, however, was fraught with a portentous circumstance. Mr. Nott's footsteps, which usually announced his approach all over the ship, became stealthy and inaudible.

Meantime Miss Rosey had taken advantage of the absence of her father to visit her patient. To avoid attracting attention she did not take a light, but groped her way to the lower deck and rapped softly at the door. It was instantly opened by De Ferrières. He had apparently appreciated the few changes she had already made in the room, and had himself cleared away the pallet from which he had risen to make two low seats against the wall. Two bits of candle placed on the floor illuminated the beams above, the dressing-gown was artistically draped over the solitary chair, and a pile of cushions formed another seat. With elaborate courtesy he handed Miss Rosey to the chair. He looked pale and weak, though the gravity of the attack had evidently passed. Yet he persisted in remaining standing. "If I sit," he explained with a gesture, "I shall again disgrace myself by sleeping in Mademoiselle's presence. Yes! I shall sleep, I shall dream, and wake to find her gone!"

More embarrassed by his recovery than when he was lying helplessly before her, she said hesitatingly that she was glad he was better, and that she hoped he liked the broth.

"It was manna from heaven, Mademoiselle. See, I have taken it all, every precious drop. What else could I have done for Mademoiselle's kindness?"

He showed her the empty bowl. A swift conviction came upon her that the man had been suffering from want of food. The thought restored her self-possession even while it brought the tears to her eyes. "I wish you would let me speak to father, or someone," she said impulsively, and stopped.

A quick and half insane gleam of terror and suspicion lit up his deep eyes. "For what, Mademoiselle! For an accident, that is nothing, absolutely nothing, for I am strong and well now, see!" he said tremblingly. "Or for a whim, for a folly you may say, that they will misunderstand. No, Mademoiselle is good, is wise. She will say to herself, 'I understand, my friend Monsieur de Ferrières for the moment has a secret. He would seem poor, he would take the rôle of artisan, he would shut himself up in these walls, perhaps I may guess why, but it is his secret. I think of it no more.'" He caught her hand in his with a gesture that he would have made one of gallantry, but that in its tremulous intensity became a piteous supplication.

"I have said nothing, and will say nothing, if you wish it," said Rosey hastily; "but others may find out how you live here. This is not fit work for you. You seem to be a, a gentleman. You ought to be a lawyer, or a doctor, or in a bank," she continued timidly, with a vague enumeration of the prevailing degrees of local gentility.

He dropped her hand. "Ah! does not Mademoiselle comprehend that it is because I am a gentleman that there is nothing between it and this? Look!" he continued almost fiercely. "What if I told you it is the lawyer, it is the doctor, it is the banker that brings me, a gentleman, to this, eh? Ah, bah! What do I say? This is honest, what I do! But the lawyer, the banker, the doctor, what are they?" He shrugged his shoulders, and pacing the apartment with a furtive glance at the half anxious, half frightened girl, suddenly stopped, dragged a small portmanteau from behind the heap of bales and opened it. "Look, Mademoiselle," he said, tremulously lifting a handful of worn and soiled letters and papers. "Look, these are the tools of your banker, your lawyer, your doctor. With this the banker will make you poor, the lawyer will prove you a thief, the doctor will swear you are crazy, eh? What shall you call the work of a gentleman, this", he dragged the pile of cushions forward, "or this?"

To the young girl's observant eyes some of the papers appeared to be of a legal or official character, and others like bills of lading, with which she was familiar. Their half theatrical exhibition reminded her of some play she had seen; they might be the clue to some story, or the mere worthless hoardings of some diseased fancy. Whatever they were, De Ferrières did not apparently care to explain further; indeed, the next moment his manner changed to his old absurd extravagance. "But this is stupid for Mademoiselle to hear. What shall we speak of? Ah! what should we speak of in Mademoiselle's presence?"

"But are not these papers valuable?" asked Rosey, partly to draw her host's thoughts back to their former channel.

"Perhaps." He paused and regarded the young girl fixedly. "Does Mademoiselle think so?"

"I don't know," said Rosey. "How should I?"

"Ah! if Mademoiselle thought so, if Mademoiselle would deign", He stopped again and placed his hand upon his forehead. "It might be so!" he muttered.

"I must go now," said Rosey hurriedly, rising with an awkward sense of constraint. "Father will wonder where I am."

"I shall explain. I will accompany you, Mademoiselle."

"No, no," said Rosey, quickly; "he must not know I have been here!" She stopped. The honest blush flew to her cheek, and then returned again, because she had blushed.

De Ferrières gazed at her with an exalted look. Then drawing himself to his full height, he said, with an exaggerated and indescribable gesture, "Go, my child, go. Tell your father that you have been alone and unprotected in the abode of poverty and suffering, but that it was in the presence of Armand de Ferrières."

He threw open the door with a bow that nearly swept the ground, but did not again offer to take her hand. At once impressed and embarrassed at this crowning incongruity, her pretty lips trembled between a smile and a cry as she said, "Good-night," and slipped away into the darkness.

Erect and grotesque De Ferrières retained the same attitude until the sound of her footsteps was lost, when he slowly began to close the door. But a strong arm arrested it from without, and a large carpeted foot appeared at the bottom of the narrowing opening. The door yielded, and Mr. Abner Nott entered the room.

IV.

With an exclamation and a hurried glance around him, De Ferrières threw himself before the intruder. But slowly lifting his large hand, and placing it on his lodger's breast, he quietly overbore the sick man's feeble resistance with an impact of power that seemed almost as moral as it was physical. He did not appear to take any notice of the room or its miserable surroundings; indeed, scarcely of the occupant. Still pushing him, with abstracted eyes and immobile face, to the chair that Rosey had just quitted, he made him sit down, and then took up his own position on the pile of cushions opposite. His usually underdone complexion was of watery blueness; but his dull, abstracted glance appeared to exercise a certain dumb, narcotic fascination on his lodger.

"I mout," said Nott, slowly, "hev laid ye out here on sight, without enny warnin', or dropped ye in yer tracks in Montgomery Street, wherever there was room to work a six-shooter in comf'ably? Johnson, of Petaluny, him, ye know, ez hed a game eye, fetched Flynn comin' outer meetin' one Sunday, and it was only on account of his wife, and she a second-hand one, so to speak. There was Walker, of Contra Costa, plugged that young Sacramento chap, whose name I disremember, full o' holes jest ez he was sayin' 'Good-by' to his darter. I mout hev done all this if it had settled things to please me. For while you and Flynn and that Sacramento chap ez all about the same sort o' men, Rosey's a different kind from their sort o' women."

"Mademoiselle is an angel!" said De Ferrières, suddenly rising, with an excess of extravagance. "A saint! Look! I cram the lie, ha! down his throat who challenges it."

"Ef by mam'selle ye mean my Rosey," said Nott, quietly laying his powerful hands on De Ferrières' shoulders, and slowly pinning him down again upon his chair, "ye're about right, though she ain't mam'selle yet. Ez I was sayin', I might hev killed you off-hand ef I hed thought it would hev been a good thing for Rosey."

"For, her? Ah, well! Look, I am ready," interrupted De Ferrières, again springing to his feet, and throwing open his coat with both hands. "See! here at my heart, fire!"

"Ez I was sayin'," continued Nott, once more pressing the excited man down in his chair, "I might hev wiped ye out, and mebbee ye wouldn't hev keered, or you might hev wiped me out, and I mout hev said. 'Thank'ee,' but I reckon this ain't a case for what's comfable for you and me. It's what's good for Rosey. And the thing to kalkilate is, what's to be done."

His small round eyes for the first time rested on De Ferrières' face, and were quickly withdrawn. It was evident that this abstracted look, which had fascinated his lodger, was merely a resolute avoidance of De Ferrières' glance, and it became apparent later that this avoidance was due to a ludicrous appreciation of De Ferrières' attractions.

"And after we've done that we must kalkilate what Rosey is, and what Rosey wants. P'r'aps, ye allow, you know what Rosey is? P'r'aps you've seen her prance round in velvet bonnets and white satin slippers, and sich. P'r'aps you've seen her readin' tracks and v'yages, without waitin' to spell a word, or catch her breath. But that ain't the Rosey ez I knows. It's a little child ez uster crawl in and out the tail-board of a Mizzouri wagon on the alcali-pizoned plains, where there wasn't another bit of God's mercy on yearth to be seen for miles and miles. It's a little gal as uster hunger and thirst ez quiet and mannerly ez she now eats and drinks in plenty; whose voice was ez steady with Injins yellin' round yer nest in the leaves on Sweetwater ez in her purty cabin up yonder. That's the gal ez I knows! That's the Rosey ez my ole woman puts into my arms one night arter we left Laramie when the fever was high, and sez, 'Abner,' sez she, 'the chariot is swingin' low for me to-night, but thar ain't room in it for her or you to git in or hitch on. Take her and rare her, so we kin all jine on the other shore,' sez she. And I'd knowed the other shore wasn't no Kaliforny. And that night, p'r'aps, the chariot swung lower than ever before, and my ole woman stepped into it, and left me and Rosey to creep on in the old wagon alone. It's them kind o' things," added Mr. Nott thoughtfully, "that seem to pint to my killin' you on sight ez the best thing to be done. And yet Rosey mightn't like it."

He had slipped one of his feet out of his huge carpet slippers, and, as he reached down to put it on again, he added calmly: "And ez to yer marrying her it ain't to be done."

The utterly bewildered expression which transfigured De Ferrières' face at this announcement was unobserved by Nott's averted eyes, nor did he perceive that his listener the next moment straightened his erect figure and adjusted his cravat.

"Ef Rosey," he continued, "hez read in v'yages and tracks in Eyetalian and French countries of such chaps ez you and kalkilates you're the right kind to tie to, mebbee it mout hev done if you'd been livin' over thar in a pallis, but somehow it don't jibe in over here and agree with a ship, and that ship lying comf'able ashore in San Francisco. You don't seem to suit the climate, you see, and your general gait is likely to stampede the other cattle. Agin," said Nott, with an ostentation of looking at his companion but really gazing on vacancy, "this fixed-up, antique style of yours goes better with them ivy-kivered ruins in Rome and Palmyry that Rosey's mixed you up with, than it would yere. I ain't sayin'," he added as De Ferrières was about to speak, "ez that child ain't smitten with ye. It ain't no use to lie and say she don't prefer you to her old father, or young chaps of her own age and kind. I've seed it afor now. I suspicioned it afor I seed her slip out o' this place to-night.

Thar! keep your hair on, such ez it is!" he added, as De Ferrières attempted a quick deprecatory gesture. "I ain't askin' yer how often she comes here, nor what she sez to you nor you to her. I ain't asked her and I don't ask you. I'll allow ez you've settled all the preliminaries and bought her the ring and sich; I'm only askin' you now, kalkilatin' you've got all the keerds in your own hand, what you'll take to step out and leave the board?"

The dazed look of De Ferrières might have forced itself even upon Nott's one-idead fatuity, had it not been a part of that gentleman's system delicately to look another way at that moment so as not to embarrass his adversary's calculation. "Pardon," stammered De Ferrières, "but I do not comprehend!" He raised his hand to his head. "I am not well, I am stupid. Ah, mon Dieu!"

"I ain't sayin'," added Nott more gently, "ez you don't feel bad. It's nat'ral. But it ain't business. I'm asking you," he continued, taking from his breast-pocket a large wallet, "how much you'll take in cash now, and the rest next steamer day, to give up Rosey and leave the ship."

De Ferrières staggered to his feet despite Nott's restraining hand. "To leave Mademoiselle and leave the ship?" he said huskily, "is it not?"

"In course. Yer can leave things yer just ez you found 'em when you came, you know," continued Nott, for the first time looking round the miserable apartment. "It's a business job. I'll take the bales back agin, and you kin reckon up what you're out, countin' Rosey and loss o' time."

"He wishes me to go, he has said," repeated De Ferrières to himself thickly.

"Ef you mean me when you say him, and ez thar ain't any other man around, I reckon you do, 'yes!'"

"And he asks me, he, this man of the feet and the daughter, asks me, De Ferrières, what I will take," continued De Ferrières, buttoning his coat. "No! it is a dream!" He walked stiffly to the corner where his portmanteau lay, lifted it, and going to the outer door, a cut through the ship's side that communicated with the alley, unlocked it and flung it open to the night. A thick mist like the breath of the ocean flowed into the room.

"You ask me what I shall take to go," he said as he stood on the threshold. "I shall take what you cannot give, Monsieur, but what I would not keep if I stood here another moment. I take my Honor, Monsieur, and I take my leave!"

For a moment his grotesque figure was outlined in the opening, and then disappeared as if he had dropped into an invisible ocean below. Stupefied and disconcerted a this complete success of his overtures, Abner Nott remained speechless, gazing at the vacant space until a cold influx of the mist recalled him. Then he rose and shuffled quickly to the door.

"Hi! Ferrers! Look yer - Say! Wot's your hurry, pardner?"

But there was no response. The thick mist, which hid the surrounding objects, seemed to deaden all sound also. After a moment's pause he closed the door, but did not lock it, and retreating to the center of the room remained blinking at the two candles and plucking some perplexing problem from his beard. Suddenly an idea seized him. Rosey! Where was she? Perhaps it had been a preconcerted plan, and she had fled with him. Putting out the lights he stumbled hurriedly through the passage to the gangway above. The cabin door was open; there was the sound of voices, Renshaw's and Rosey's. Mr. Nott felt relieved but not unembarrassed. He would have avoided his daughter's presence that evening. But even while making this resolution with characteristic infelicity he blundered into the room. Rosey looked up with a slight start; Renshaw's animated face was changed to its former expression of inward discontent.

"You came in so like a ghost, father," said Rosey with a slight peevishness that was new to her. "And I thought you were in town. Don't go, Mr. Renshaw."

But Mr. Renshaw intimated that he had already trespassed upon Miss Nott's time, and that no doubt her father wanted to talk with her. To his surprise and annoyance, however, Mr. Nott insisted on accompanying him to his room, and without heeding Renshaw's cold "Goodnight," entered and closed the door behind him.

"P'raps," said Mr. Nott with a troubled air, "you disremember that when you first kem here you asked me if you could hev that 'er loft that the Frenchman had downstairs."

"No, I don't remember it," said Renshaw almost rudely. "But," he added, after a pause, with the air of a man obliged to revive a stale and unpleasant memory, "if I did, what about it?"

"Nuthin', only that you kin hev it to-morrow, ez that 'ere Frenchman is movin' out," responded Nott. "I thought you was sorter keen about it when you first kem."

"Umph! we'll talk about it to-morrow." Something in the look of wearied perplexity with which Mr. Nott was beginning to regard his own mal à propos presence, arrested the young man's attention. "What's the reason you didn't sell this old ship long ago, take a decent house in the town, and bring up your daughter like a lady?" he asked, with a sudden blunt good-humor. But even this implied blasphemy against the habitation he worshiped did not prevent Mr. Nott from his usual misconstruction of the question.

"I reckon, now, Rosey's got high-flown ideas of livin' in a castle with ruins, eh?" he said cunningly.

"Haven't heard her say," returned Renshaw abruptly. "Good-night."

Firmly convinced that Rosey had been unable to conceal from Mr. Renshaw the influence of her dreams of a castellated future with De Ferrières, he regained the cabin. Satisfying himself that his daughter had retired, he sought his own couch. But not to sleep. The figure of De Ferrières, standing in the ship side and melting into the outer darkness, haunted him, and compelled him in dreams to rise and follow him through the alleys and byways of the crowded city. Again, it was a part of his morbid suspicion that he now invested the absent man with a potential significance and an unknown power.

What deep-laid plans might he not form to possess himself of Rosey, of which he, Abner Nott, would be ignorant? Unchecked by the restraint of a father's roof, he would now give full license to his power. "Said he'd take his Honor with him," muttered Abner to himself in the dim watches of the night; "lookin' at that sayin' in its right light, it looks bad."

V.

The elaborately untruthful account which Mr. Nott gave his daughter of De Ferrières' sudden departure was more fortunate than his usual equivocations. While it disappointed and slightly mortified her, it did not seem to her inconsistent with what she already knew of him. "Said his doctor had ordered him to quit town under an hour, owing to a comin' attack of hay fever, and he had a friend from furrin parts waitin' him at the Springs, Rosey," explained Nott, hesitating between his desire to avoid his daughter's eyes and his wish to observe her countenance.

"Was he worse? I mean did he look badly, father?" inquired Rosey, thoughtfully.

"I reckon not exactly bad. Kinder looked as if he mout be worse soon ef he didn't hump hisself."

"Did you see him? in his room?" asked Rosey anxiously. Upon the answer to this simple question depended the future confidential relations of father and daughter. If her father had himself detected the means by which his lodger existed, she felt that her own obligations to secrecy had been removed. But Mr. Nott's answer disposed of this vain hope. It was a response after his usual fashion to the question he imagined she artfully wished to ask, i.e. if he had discovered their rendezvous of the previous night. This it was part of his peculiar delicacy to ignore. Yet his reply showed that he had been unconscious of the one miserable secret that he might have read easily.

"I was there an hour or so, him and me alone, discussin' trade. I reckon he's got a good thing outer that curled horse-hair, for I see he's got in an invoice o' cushions. I've stowed 'em all in the forrard bulkhead until he sends for 'em, ez Mr. Renshaw hez taken the loft."

But although Mr. Renshaw had taken the loft, he did not seem in haste to occupy it. He spent part of the morning in uneasily pacing his room, in occasional sallies into the street from which he purposelessly returned, and once or twice in distant and furtive contemplation of Rosey at work in the galley. This last observation was not unnoticed by the astute Nott, who at once conceiving that he was nourishing a secret and hopeless passion for Rosey, began to consider whether it was not his duty to warn the young man of her preoccupied affections. But Mr. Renshaw's final disappearance obliged him to withhold his confidence till morning.

This time Mr. Renshaw left the ship with the evident determination of some settled purpose. He walked rapidly until he reached the counting-house of Mr. Sleight, when he was at once shown into a private office. In a few moments Mr. Sleight, a brusque but passionless man, joined him.

"Well," said Sleight, closing the door carefully. "What news?"

"None," said Renshaw bluntly. "Look here, Sleight," he added, turning to him suddenly. "Let me out of this game. I don't like it."

"Does that mean you've found nothing?" asked Sleight, sarcastically.

"It means that I haven't looked for anything, and that I don't intend to without the full knowledge of that damned fool who owns the ship."

"You've changed your mind since you wrote that letter," said Sleight coolly, producing from a drawer the note already known to the reader. Renshaw mechanically extended his hand to take it. Mr. Sleight dropped the letter back into the drawer, which he quietly locked. The apparently simple act dyed Mr. Renshaw's cheek with color, but it vanished quickly, and with it any token of his previous embarrassment. He looked at Sleight with the convinced air of a resolute man who had at last taken a disagreeable step but was willing to stand by the consequences.

"I have changed my mind," he said coolly. "I found out that it was one thing to go down there as a skilled prospector might go to examine a mine that was to be valued according to his report of the indications, but that it was entirely another thing to go and play the spy in a poor devil's house in order to buy something he didn't know he was selling and wouldn't sell if he did."

"And something that the man he bought of didn't think of selling; something he himself never paid for, and never expected to buy," sneered Sleight.

"But something that we expect to buy from our knowledge of all this, and it is that which makes all the difference."

"But you knew all this before."

"I never saw it in this light before. I never thought of it until I was living there face to face with the old fool I was intending to overreach. I never was sure of it until this morning, when he actually turned out one of his lodgers that I might have the very room I required to play off our little game in comfortably. When he did that, I made up my mind to drop the whole thing, and I'm here to do it."

"And let somebody else take the responsibility, with the percentage, unless you've also felt it your duty to warn Nott too," said Sleight with a sneer.

"You only dare say that to me, Sleight," said Renshaw quietly, "because you have in that drawer an equal evidence of my folly and my confidence; but if you are wise you will not presume too far on either. Let us see how we stand. Through the yarn of a drunken captain and a mutinous sailor you became aware of an unclaimed shipment of treasure, concealed in an unknown ship that entered this harbor. You are enabled, through me, to corroborate some facts and identify the ship. You proposed to me, as a speculation, to identify the treasure if possible before you purchased the ship. I accepted the offer without consideration; on consideration I now decline it, but without prejudice or loss to any one but myself. As to your insinuation I need not remind you that my presence here to-day refutes it. I would not require your permission to make a much better bargain with a good-natured fool like Nott than I could with you. Or if I did not care for the business I could have warned the girl" -

"The girl, what girl?"

Renshaw bit his lip, but answered boldly: "The old man's daughter, a poor girl, whom this act would rob as well as her father."

Sleight looked at his companion attentively. "You might have said so at first, and let up on this camp-meetin' exhortation. Well then, admitting you've got the old man and the young girl on the same string, and that you've played it pretty low down in the short time you've been there, I suppose, Dick Renshaw, I've got to see your bluff. Well, how much is it? What's the figure you and she have settled on?"

For an instant Mr. Sleight was in physical danger.

But before he had finished speaking Renshaw's quick sense of the ludicrous had so far overcome his first indignation as to enable him even to admire the perfect moral insensibility of his companion. As he rose and walked towards the door, he half wondered that he had ever treated the affair seriously. With a smile he replied:

"Far from bluffing, Sleight, I am throwing my cards on the table. Consider that I've passed out. Let some other man take my hand. Rake down the pot if you like, old man, I leave for Sacramento to-night. Adios."

When the door had closed behind him Mr. Sleight summoned his clerk.

"Is that petition for grading Pontiac Street ready?"

"I've seen the largest property holders, sir; they're only waiting for you to sign first," Mr. Sleight paused and then affixed his signature to the paper his clerk laid before him. "Get the other names and send it up at once."

"If Mr. Nott doesn't sign, sir?"

"No matter. He will be assessed all the same." Mr. Sleight took up his hat.

"The Lascar seaman that was here the other day has been wanting to see you, sir. I said you were busy."

Mr. Sleight put down his hat. "Send him up."

Nevertheless Mr. Sleight sat down and at once abstracted himself so completely as to be apparently in utter oblivion of the man who entered. He was lithe and Indian-looking; bearing in dress and manner the careless slouch without the easy frankness of a sailor.

"Well!" said Sleight without looking up.

"I was only wantin' to know ef you had any news for me, boss?"

"News?" echoed Sleight as if absently; "news of what?"

"That little matter of the Pontiac we talked about, boss," returned the Lascar with an uneasy servility in the whites of his teeth and eyes.

"Oh," said Sleight, "that's played out. It's a regular fraud. It's an old forecastle yarn, my man, that you can't reel off in the cabin."

The sailor's face darkened.

"The man who was looking into it has thrown the whole thing up. I tell you it's played out!" repeated Sleight, without raising his head.

"It's true, boss, every word," said the Lascar, with an appealing insinuation that seemed to struggle hard with savage earnestness. "You can swear me, boss; I wouldn't lie to a gentleman like you. Your man hasn't half looked, or else, it must be there, or" -

"That's just it," said Sleight slowly; "who's to know that your friends haven't been there already, that seems to have been your style."

"But no one knew it but me, until I told you, I swear to God. I ain't lying, boss, and I ain't drunk. Say, don't give it up, boss. That man of yours likely don't believe it, because he don't know anything about it. I do, I could find it."

A silence followed. Mr. Sleight remained completely absorbed in his papers for some moments. Then glancing at the Lascar, he took his pen, wrote a hurried note, folded it, addressed it, and, holding it between his fingers, leaned back in his chair.

"If you choose to take this note to my man, he may give it another show. Mind, I don't say that he will. He's going to Sacramento to-night, but you could go down there and find him before he starts. He's got a room there, I believe. While you're waiting for him you might keep your eyes open to satisfy yourself."

"Ay, ay, sir," said the sailor, eagerly endeavoring to catch the eye of his employer. But Mr. Sleight looked straight before him, and he turned to go.

"The Sacramento boat goes at nine," said Mr. Sleight quietly.

This time their glances met, and the Lascar's eye glistened with subtle intelligence. The next moment he was gone, and Mr. Sleight again became absorbed in his papers.

Meanwhile Renshaw was making his way back to the Pontiac with that light-hearted optimism that had characterized his parting with Sleight. It was this quality of his nature, fostered perhaps by the easy civilization in which he moved, that had originally drawn him into relations with the man he just quitted; a quality that had been troubled and darkened by those relations, yet, when they were broken, at once returned. It consequently did not occur to him that he had only selfishly compromised with the difficulty; it seemed to him enough that he had withdrawn from a compact he thought dishonorable; he was not called upon to betray his partner in that compact merely to benefit others. He had been willing to incur suspicion and loss to reinstate himself in his self-respect, more he could not do without justifying that suspicion. The view taken by Sleight was, after all, that which most business men would take, which even the unbusinesslike Nott would take, which the girl herself might be tempted to listen to. Clearly he could do nothing but abandon the Pontiac and her owner to the fate he could not in honor avert. And even that fate was problematical. It did not follow that the treasure was still concealed in the Pontiac, nor that Nott would be willing to sell her. He would make some excuse to Nott, he smiled to think he would probably be classed in the long line of absconding tenants, he would say good-by to Rosey, and leave for Sacramento that night. He ascended the stairs to the gangway with a freer breast than when he first entered the ship.

Mr. Nott was evidently absent, and after a quick glance at the half-open cabin-door, Renshaw turned towards the galley. But Miss Rosey was not in her accustomed haunt, and with a feeling of disappointment, which seemed inconsistent with so slight a cause, he crossed the deck impatiently and entered his room. He was about to close the door when the prolonged rustle of a trailing skirt in the passage attracted his attention. The sound was so unlike that made by any garment worn by Rosey that he remained motionless, with his hand on the door. The sound approached nearer, and the next moment a white veiled figure with a trailing skirt slowly swept past the room. Renshaw's pulses halted for an instant in half superstitious awe. As the apparition glided on and vanished in the cabin-door he could only see that it was the form of a beautiful and graceful woman, but nothing more. Bewildered and curious, he forgot himself so far as to follow it, and impulsively entered the cabin. The figure turned, uttered a little cry, threw the veil aside, and showed the half troubled, half blushing face of Rosey.

"I-beg-your pardon," stammered Renshaw; "I didn't know it was you."

"I was trying on some things," said Rosey, recovering her composure and pointing to an open trunk that seemed to contain a theatrical wardrobe, "some things father gave me long ago. I wanted to see if there was anything I could use. I thought I was all alone in the ship, but fancying I heard a noise forward I came out to see what it was. I suppose it must have been you."

She raised her clear eyes to his, with a slight touch of womanly reserve that was so incompatible with any vulgar vanity or girlish coquetry that he became the more embarrassed. Her dress, too, of a slightly antique shape, rich but simple, seemed to reveal and accent a certain repose of gentlewomanliness, that he was now wishing to believe he had always noticed. Conscious of a superiority in her that now seemed to change their relations completely, he alone remained silent, awkward, and embarrassed before the girl who had taken care of his room, and who cooked in the galley! What he had thoughtlessly considered a merely vulgar business intrigue against her stupid father, now to his extravagant fancy assumed the proportions of a sacrilege to herself.

"You've had your revenge, Miss Nott, for the fright I once gave you," he said a little uneasily, "for you quite startled me just now as you passed. I began to think the Pontiac was haunted. I thought you were a ghost. I don't know why such a ghost should frighten anybody," he went on with a desperate attempt to recover his position by gallantry. "Let me see, that's Donna Elvira's dress, is it not?"

"I don't think that was the poor woman's name," said Rosey simply; "she died of yellow fever at New Orleans as Signora Somebody."

Her ignorance seemed to Mr. Renshaw so plainly to partake more of the nun than the provincial, that he hesitated to explain to her that he meant the heroine of an opera.

"It seems dreadful to put on the poor thing's clothes, doesn't it?" she added.

Mr. Renshaw's eyes showed so plainly that he thought otherwise, that she drew a little austerely towards the door of her state-room.

"I must change these things before any one comes," she said dryly.

"That means I must go, I suppose. But couldn't you let me wait here or in the gangway until then, Miss Nott? I am going away to-night, and I mayn't see you again." He had not intended to say this, but it slipped from his embarrassed tongue. She stopped with her hand on the door.

"You are going away?"

"I think I must leave to-night. I have some important business in Sacramento."

She raised her frank eyes to his. The unmistakable look of disappointment that he saw in them gave his heart a sudden throb and sent the quick blood to his cheeks.

"It's too bad," she said, abstractedly. "Nobody ever seems to stay here long. Captain Bower promised to tell me all about the ship, and he went away the second week. The photographer left before he finished the picture of the Pontiac; Monsieur de Ferrières has only just gone; and now you are going."

"Perhaps, unlike them, I have finished my season of usefulness here," he replied, with a bitterness he would have recalled the next moment. But Rosey, with a faint sigh, saying, "I won't be long," entered the state-room and closed the door behind her.

Renshaw bit his lip and pulled at the long silken threads of his mustache until they smarted. Why had he not gone at once? Why was it necessary to say he might not see her again, and if he had said it, why should he add anything more? What was he waiting for now? To endeavor to prove to her that he really bore no resemblance to Captain Bower, the photographer, the crazy Frenchman De Ferrières? Or would he be forced to tell her that he was running away from a conspiracy to defraud her father, merely for something to say? Was there ever such folly? Rosey was "not long," as she had said, but he was beginning to pace the narrow cabin impatiently when the door opened and she returned.

She had resumed her ordinary calico gown, but such was the impression left upon Renshaw's fancy that she seemed to wear it with a new grace. At any other time he might have recognized the change as due to a new corset, which strict veracity compels me to record Rosey had adopted for the first time that morning. Howbeit, her slight coquetry seemed to have passed, for she closed the open trunk with a return of her old listless air, and sitting on it rested her elbows on her knees and her oval chin in her hands.

"I wish you would do me a favor," she said after a reflective pause.

"Let me know what it is and it shall be done," replied Renshaw quickly.

"If you should come across Monsieur de Ferrières, or hear of him, I wish you would let me know. He was very poorly when he left here, and I should like to know if he was better. He didn't say where he was going. At least, he didn't tell father; but I fancy he and father don't agree."

"I shall be very glad of having even that opportunity of making you remember me, Miss Nott," returned Renshaw with a faint smile. "I don't suppose either that it would be very difficult to get news of your friend, everybody seems to know him."

"But not as I did," said Rosey, with an abstracted little sigh.

Mr. Renshaw opened his brown eyes upon her. Was he mistaken? Was this romantic girl only a little coquette playing her provincial airs on him? "You say he and your father didn't agree? That means, I suppose, that you and he agreed? and that was the result."

"I don't think father knew anything about it," said Rosey simply.

Mr. Renshaw rose. And this was what he had been waiting to hear! "Perhaps," he said grimly, "you would also like news of the photographer and Captain Bower, or did your father agree with them better?"

"No," said Rosey quietly. She remained silent for a moment, and lifting her lashes said, "Father always seemed to agree with you, and that", she hesitated.

"That's why you don't."

"I didn't say that," said Rosey, with an incongruous increase of coldness and color. "I only meant to say it was that which makes it seem so hard you should go now."

Notwithstanding his previous determination Renshaw found himself sitting down again. Confused and pleased, wishing he had said more, or less, he said nothing, and Rosey was forced to continue.

"It's strange, isn't it, but father was urging me this morning to make a visit to some friends at the old Ranch. I didn't want to go. I like it much better here."

"But you cannot bury yourself here forever, Miss Nott," said Renshaw, with a sudden burst of honest enthusiasm. "Sooner or later you will be forced to go where you will be properly appreciated, where you will be admired and courted, where your slightest wish will be law. Believe me, without flattery, you don't know your own power."

"It doesn't seem strong enough to keep even the little I like here," said Rosey, with a slight glistening of the eyes. "But," she added hastily, "you don't know how much the dear old ship is to me. It's the only home I think I ever had."

"But the Ranch?" said Renshaw.

"The Ranch seemed to be only the old wagon halted in the road. It was a very little improvement on out-doors," said Rosey, with a little shiver. "But this is so cosy and snug, and yet so strange and foreign. Do you know I think I began to understand why I like it so since you taught me so much about ships and voyages. Before that I only learned from books. Books deceive you, I think, more than people do. Don't you think so?"

She evidently did not notice the quick flush that covered his cheeks and apparently dazzled his troubled eyelids, for she went on confidentially:

"I was thinking of you yesterday. I was sitting by the galley door, looking forward. You remember the first day I saw you when you startled me by coming up out of the hatch?"

"I wish you wouldn't think of that," said Renshaw, with more earnestness than he would have made apparent.

"I don't want to, either," said Rosey, gravely, "for I've had a strange fancy about it. I saw once, when I was younger, a picture in a print shop in Montgomery Street that haunted me. I think it was called 'The Pirate.' There were a number of wicked-looking sailors lying around the deck, and coming out of the hatch was one figure, with his hands on the deck and a cutlass in his mouth."

"Thank you," said Renshaw.

"You don't understand. He was horrid-looking, not at all like you. I never thought of him when I first saw you; but the other day I thought how dreadful it would have been if some one like him and not like you had come up then. That made me nervous sometimes of being alone. I think father is too. He often goes about stealthily at night, as if he was watching for something."

Renshaw's face grew suddenly dark. Could it be possible that Sleight had always suspected him, and set spies to watch, or was he guilty of some double intrigue?

"He thinks," continued Rosey, with a faint smile, "that some one is looking round the ship, and talks of setting bear-traps. I hope you're not mad, Mr. Renshaw," she added, suddenly catching sight of his changed expression, "at my foolishness in saying you reminded me of the pirate. I meant nothing."

"I know you're incapable of meaning anything but good to anybody, Miss Nott, perhaps to me more than I deserve," said Renshaw, with a sudden burst of feeling. "I wish, I wish you would do me a favor. You asked me one just now." He had taken her hand. It seemed so like a mere illustration of his earnestness, that she did not withdraw it. "Your father tells you everything. If he has any offer to dispose of the ship, will you write to me at once before anything is concluded?" He winced a little, the sentence of Sleight, "What's the figure you and she have settled upon?" flashed across his mind. He scarcely noticed that Rosey had withdrawn her hand coldly.

"Perhaps you had better speak to father, as it is his business. Besides, I shall not be here. I shall be at the Ranch."

"But you said you didn't want to go?"

"I've changed my mind," said Rosey, listlessly. "I shall go to-night."

She rose as if to indicate that the interview was ended. With an overpowering instinct that his whole future happiness depended upon his next act, he made a step towards her, with eager outstretched hands. But she slightly lifted her own with a warning gesture, "I hear father coming, you will have a chance to talk business with him," she said, and vanished into her state-room.

VI.

The heavy tread of Abner Nott echoed in the passage. Confused and embarrassed, Renshaw remained standing at the door that had closed upon Rosey as her father entered the cabin. Providence, which always fostered Mr. Nott's characteristic misconceptions, left that perspicacious parent but one interpretation of the situation. Rosey had evidently just informed Mr. Renshaw that she loved another!

"I was just saying good-by to Miss Nott," said Renshaw, hastily regaining his composure with an effort. "I am going to Sacramento to-night, and will not return. I" -

"In course, in course," interrupted Nott, soothingly; "that's wot you say now, and that's wot you allow to do. That's wot they allus do."

"I mean," said Renshaw, reddening at what he conceived to be an allusion to the absconding propensities of Nott's previous tenants, "I mean that you shall keep the advance to cover any loss you might suffer through my giving up the rooms."

"Certingly," said Nott, laying his hand with a large sympathy on Renshaw's shoulder; "but we'll drop that just now. We won't swap hosses in the middle of the river. We'll square up accounts in your room," he added, raising his voice that Rosey might overhear him, after a preliminary wink at the young man. "Yes, sir, we'll just square up and settle in there. Come along, Mr. Renshaw." Pushing him with paternal gentleness from the cabin, with his hand still upon his shoulder, he followed him into the passage. Half annoyed at his familiarity, yet not altogether displeased by this illustration of Rosey's belief of his preference, Renshaw wonderingly accompanied him. Nott closed the door, and pushing the young man into a chair, deliberately seated himself at the table opposite. "It's jist as well that Rosey reckons that you and me is settlin' our accounts," he began, cunningly, "and mebbee it's just ez well ez she should reckon you're goin' away."

"But I am going," interrupted Renshaw, impatiently. "I leave to-night."

"Surely, surely," said Nott, gently, "that's wot you kalkilate to do; that's just nat'ral in a young feller. That's about what I reckon I'd hev done to her mother if anythin' like this hed ever cropped up, which it didn't. Not but what Almiry Jane had young fellers enough round her, but, 'cept ole Judge Peter, ez was lamed in the War of 1812, there ain't no similarity ez I kin see," he added, musingly.

"I am afraid I can't see any similarity either, Mr. Nott," said Renshaw, struggling between a dawning sense of some impending absurdity and his growing passion for Rosey. "For Heaven's sake, speak out if you've got anything to say."

Mr. Nott leaned forward and placed his large hand on the young man's shoulder. "That's it. That's what I sed to myself when I seed how things were pintin'. 'Speak out,' sez I, 'Abner! Speak out if you've got anything to say. You kin trust this yer Mr. Renshaw. He ain't the kind of man to creep into the bosom of a man's ship for pupposes of his own. He ain't a man that would hunt round until he discovered a poor man's treasure, and then try to rob'" -

"Stop!" said Renshaw, with a set face and darkening eyes. "What treasure? what man are you speaking of?"

"Why Rosey and Mr. Ferrers," returned Nott, simply.

Renshaw sank into his seat again. But the expression of relief which here passed swiftly over his face gave way to one of uneasy interest as Nott went on.

"P'r'aps it's a little high-falutin' talkin' of Rosey ez a treasure. But, considerin', Mr. Renshaw, ez she's the only prop'ty I've kept by me for seventeen years ez hez paid interest and increased in valoo, it ain't sayin' too much to call her so. And ez Ferrers knows this, he oughter been content with gougin' me in that horse-hair spec, without goin' for Rosey. P'r'aps yer surprised at hearing me speak o' my own flesh and blood ez if I was talkin' hoss-trade, but you and me is bus'ness men, Mr. Renshaw, and we discusses ez such. We ain't goin' to slosh round and slop over in po'try and sentiment," continued Nott, with a tremulous voice, and a hand that slightly shook on Renshaw's shoulder. "We ain't goin' to git up and sing, 'Thou 'st lamed to love another thou 'st broken every vow we've parted from each other and my bozom's lonely now oh is it well to sever such hearts as ourn forever kin I forget thee never farewell farewell farewell.' Ye never happen'd to hear Jim Baker sing that at the moosic hall on Dupont Street, Mr. Renshaw," continued Mr. Nott, enthusiastically, when he had recovered from that complete absence of punctuation which alone suggested verse to his intellect. "He sorter struck water down here," indicating his heart, "every time."

"But what has Miss Nott to do with M. de Ferrières?" asked Renshaw, with a faint smile.

Mr. Nott regarded him with, dumb, round, astonished eyes. "Hezn't she told yer?"

"Certainly not."

"And she didn't let on anythin' about him?" he continued, feebly.

"She said she'd like to know where" - He stopped, with the reflection that he was betraying her confidences.

A dim foreboding of some new form of deceit, to which even the man before him was a consenting party, almost paralyzed Nott's faculties. "Then she didn't tell yer that she and Ferrers was sparkin' and keepin' kimpany together; that she and him was engaged, and was kalkilatin' to run away to furrin parts; that she cottoned to him more than to the ship or her father?"

"She certainly did not, and I shouldn't believe it," said Renshaw, quickly.

Nott smiled. He was amused; he astutely recognized the usual trustfulness of love and youth. There was clearly no deceit here! Renshaw's attentive eyes saw the smile, and his brow darkened.

"I like to hear yer say that, Mr. Renshaw," said Nott, "and it's no more than Rosey deserves, ez it's suthing onnat'ral and spell-like that's come over her through Ferrers. It ain't my Rosey. But it's Gospel truth, whether she's bewitched or not; whether it's them damn fool stories she reads, and it's like ez not he's just the kind o' snipe to write 'em hisself, and sorter advertise hisself, don't yer see, she's allus stuck up for Lim. They've had clandesent interviews, and when I taxed him with it he ez much ez allowed it was so, and reckoned he must leave, so ez he could run her off, you know, kinder stampede her with 'honor.' Them's his very words."

"But that is all past; he is gone, and Miss Nott does not even know where he is!" said Renshaw, with a laugh, which, however, concealed a vague uneasiness.

Mr. Nott rose and opened the door carefully. When he had satisfied himself that no one was listening, he came back and said in a whisper, "That's a lie. Not ez Rosey means to lie, but it's a trick he's put upon that poor child. That man, Mr. Renshaw, hez been hangin' round the Pontiac ever since. I've seed him twice with my own eyes pass the cabin windys. More than that, I've heard strange noises at night, and seen strange faces in the alley over yer. And only jist now ez I kem in I ketched sight of a furrin-lookin' Chinee nigger slinking round the back door of what useter be Ferrers' loft."

"Did he look like a sailor?" asked Renshaw quickly, with a return of his former suspicion.

"Not more than I do," said Nott, glancing complacently at his pea-jacket. "He had rings on his yeers like a wench."

Mr. Renshaw started. But seeing Nott's eyes fixed on him, he said lightly, "But what have these strange faces and this strange man, probably only a Lascar sailor out of a job, to do with Ferrières?"

"Friends o' his, feller furrin citizens, spies on Rosey, don't you see? But they can't play the old man, Mr. Renshaw. I've told Rosey she must make a visit to the old Ranch. Once I've got her thar safe, I reckon I kin manage Mr. Ferrers and any number of Chinee niggers he kin bring along."

Renshaw remained for a few moments lost in thought. Then rising suddenly, he grasped Mr. Nott's hand with a frank smile but determined eyes. "I haven't got the hang of this, Mr. Nott, the whole thing gets me! I only know that I've changed my mind. I'm not going to Sacramento. I shall stay here, old man, until I see you safe through the business, or my name's not Dick Renshaw. There's my hand on it! Don't say a word. Maybe it is no more than I ought to do, perhaps not half enough. Only remember, not a word of this to your daughter. She must believe that I leave to-night. And the sooner you get her out of this cursed ship the better."

"Deacon Flint's girls are goin' up in to-night's boat. I'll send Rosey with them," said Nott, with a cunning twinkle. Renshaw nodded. Nott seized his hand with a wink of unutterable significance.

Left to himself, Renshaw tried to review more calmly the circumstances in these strange revelations that had impelled him to change his resolution so suddenly. That the ship was under the surveillance of unknown parties, and that the description of them tallied with his own knowledge of a certain Lascar sailor, who was one of Sleight's informants, seemed to be more than probable. That this seemed to point to Sleight's disloyalty to himself while he was acting as his agent, or a double treachery on the part of Sleight's informants, was in either case a reason and an excuse for his own interference. But the connection of the absurd Frenchman with the case, which at first seemed a characteristic imbecility of his landlord, bewildered him the more he thought of it. Rejecting any hypothesis of the girl's affection for the antiquated figure whose sanity was a question of public criticism, he was forced to the equally alarming theory that Ferrières was cognizant of the treasure, and that his attentions to Rosey were to gain possession of it by marrying her. Might she not be dazzled by a picture of this wealth? Was it not possible that she was already in part possession of the secret, and her strange attraction to the ship, and what he had deemed her innocent craving for information concerning it, a consequence? Why had he not thought of this before? Perhaps she had detected his purpose from the first, and had deliberately checkmated him. The thought did not increase his complacency as Nott softly returned:

"It's all right," he began with a certain satisfaction in this rare opportunity for Machiavellian diplomacy, "it's all fixed now. Rosey tumbled to it at once, partiklerly when I said you was bound to go. 'But wot makes Mr. Renshaw go, father,' sez she; 'wot makes everybody run away from the ship?' sez she, rather peart-like and sassy for her. 'Mr. Renshaw hez contractin' business,' sez I; 'got a big thing up in Sacramento that'll make his fortun','sez I, for I wasn't goin' to give yer away, don't ye see?' He had some business to talk to you about the ship,' sez she, lookin' at me under the corner of her pocket-handkerchief. 'Lots o' business,' sez I. 'Then I reckon he don't care to hev me write to him,' sez she. 'Not a bit,' sez I; 'he wouldn't answer ye if ye did. Ye'll never hear from that chap agin.'"

"But what the devil", interrupted the young man impetuously.

"Keep yer hair on!" remonstrated the old man with dark intelligence. "Ef you'd seen the way she flounced into her state-room! she, Rosey, ez allus moves ez softly ez a spirit, you'd hev wished I'd hev unloaded a little more. No sir, gals is gals in some things all the time."

Renshaw rose and paced the room rapidly. "Perhaps I'd better speak to her again before she goes," he said, impulsively.

"P'r'aps you'd better not," replied the imperturbable Nott.

Irritated as he was, Renshaw could not avoid the reflection that the old man was right. What, indeed, could he say to her with his present imperfect knowledge? How could she write to him if that knowledge was correct?

"Ef," said Nott, kindly, with a laying on of large benedictory and paternal hands, "ef ye're willin' to see Rosey agin, without speakin' to her, I reckon I ken fix it for yer. I'm goin' to take her down to the boat in half an hour. Ef yer should happen mind, ef yer should happen to be down there, seein' some friends off and sorter promenadin' up and down the wharf like them high-toned chaps on Montgomery Street, ye might ketch her eye unconscious like. Or, ye might do this!" He rose after a moment's cogitation and with a face of profound mystery opened the door and beckoned Renshaw to follow him. Leading the way cautiously, he brought the young man into an open unpartitioned recess beside her state-room. It seemed to be used as a store-room, and Renshaw's eye was caught by a trunk the size and shape of the one that had provided Rosey with the materials of her masquerade. Pointing to it, Mr. Nott said in a grave whisper: "This yer trunk is the companion trunk to Rosey's. She's got the things them opery women wears; this yer contains the he things, the duds and fixins o' the men o' the same stripe." Throwing it open he continued: "Now, Mr, Renshaw, gals is gals; it's nat'ral they should be took by fancy dress and store clothes on young chaps as on theirselves. That man Ferrers hez got the dead wood on all of ye in this sort of thing, and hez been playing, so to speak, a lone hand all along. And ef thar's anythin' in thar," he added, lifting part of a theatrical wardrobe, "that you think you'd fancy, anythin' you'd like to put on when ye promenade the wharf down yonder, it's yours. Don't ye be bashful, but help yourself."

It was fully a minute before Renshaw fairly grasped the old man's meaning. But when he did, when the suggested spectacle of himself arrayed à la Ferrières, gravely promenading the wharf as a last gorgeous appeal to the affections of Rosey, rose before his fancy, he gave way to a fit of genuine laughter. The nervous tension of the past few hours relaxed; he laughed until the tears came into his eyes; he was still laughing when the door of the cabin suddenly opened and Rosey appeared cold and distant on the threshold.

"I-beg your pardon," stammered Renshaw hastily. "I didn't mean to disturb you-I" -

Without looking at him Rosey turned to her father. "I am ready," she said coldly, and closed the door again.

A glance of artful intelligence came into Nott's eyes, which had remained blankly staring at Renshaw's apparently causeless hilarity. Turning to him he winked solemnly. "That keerless kind o' hoss-laff jist fetched her," he whispered, and vanished before his chagrined companion could reply.

When Mr. Nott and his daughter departed, Renshaw was not in the ship, neither did he make a spectacular appearance on the wharf as Mr. Nott had fondly expected, nor did he turn up again until after nine o'clock, when he found the old man in the cabin awaiting his return with some agitation. "A minit ago," he said, mysteriously closing the door behind Renshaw, "I heard a voice in the passage, and goin' out, who should I see agin but that darned furrin nigger ez I told yer 'bout, kinder hidin' in the dark, his eyes shinin' like a catamount. I was jist reachin' for my weppins when he riz up with a grin and handed me this yer letter. I told him I reckoned you'd gone to Sacramento, but he said he wez sure you was in your room, and to prove it I went thar. But when I kem back the damned skunk had vamosed, got frightened I reckon, and wasn't nowhar to be seen."

Renshaw took the letter hastily. It contained only a line in Sleight's hand. "If you change your mind, the bearer may be of service to you."

He turned abruptly to Nott. "You say it was the same Lascar you saw before?"

"It was."

"Then all I can say is, he is no agent of De Ferrières'," said Renshaw, turning away with a disappointed air. Mr. Nott would have asked another question, but with an abrupt "Good-night" the young man entered his room, locked the door, and threw himself on his bed to reflect without interruption.

But if he was in no mood to stand Nott's fatuous conjectures, he was less inclined to be satisfied with his own. Had he been again carried away through his impulses evoked by the caprices of a pretty coquette and the absurd theories of her half imbecile father? Had he broken faith with Sleight and remained in the ship for nothing, and would not his change of resolution appear to be the result of Sleight's note? But why had the Lascar been haunting the ship before? In the midst of these conjectures he fell asleep.

VII.

Between three and four in the morning the clouds broke over the Pontiac, and the moon, riding high, picked out in black and silver the long hulk that lay cradled between the iron shells and warehouses and the wooden frames and tenements on either side. The galley and covered gangway presented a mass of undefined shadow, against which the white deck shone brightly, stretching to the forecastle and bows, where the tiny glass roof of the photographer glistened like a gem in the Pontiac's crest. So peaceful and motionless she lay that she might have been some petrifaction of a past age now first exhumed and laid bare to the cold light of the stars.

Nevertheless, this calm security was presently invaded by a sense of stealthy life and motion. What had seemed a fixed shadow suddenly detached itself from the deck and began to slip stanchion by stanchion along the bulwarks toward the companion-way. At the cabin-door it halted and crouched motionless. Then rising, it glided forward with the same staccato movement until opposite the slight elevation of the forehatch. Suddenly it darted to the hatch, unfastened and lifted it with a swift, familiar dexterity, and disappeared in the opening. But as the moon shone upon its vanishing face, it revealed the whitening eyes and teeth of the Lascar seaman.

Dropping to the lower deck lightly, he felt his way through the dark passage between the partitions, evidently less familiar to him, halting before each door to listen.

Returning forward he reached the second hatchway that had attracted Rosey's attention, and noiselessly unclosed its fastenings. A penetrating smell of bilge arose from the opening. Drawing a small bull's-eye lantern from his breast he lit it, and unhesitatingly let himself down to the further depth. The moving flash of his light revealed the recesses of the upper hold, the abyss of the well amidships, and glanced from the shining backs of moving zigzags of rats that seemed to outline the shadowy beams and transoms. Disregarding those curious spectators of his movements, he turned his attention eagerly to the inner casings of the hold, that seemed in one spot to have been strengthened by fresh timbers. Attacking this stealthily with the aid of some tools hidden in his oil-skin clothing, in the light of the lantern he bore a fanciful resemblance to the predatory animals around him. The low continuous sound of rasping and gnawing of timber which followed heightened the resemblance. At the end of a few minutes he had succeeded in removing enough of the outer planking to show that the entire filling of the casing between the stanchions was composed of small boxes. Dragging out one of them with feverish eagerness to the light, the Lascar forced it open. In the rays of the bull's-eye, a wedged mass of discolored coins showed with a lurid glow. The story of the Pontiac was true, the treasure was there!

But Mr. Sleight had overlooked the logical effect of this discovery on the natural villainy of his tool. In the very moment of his triumphant execution of his patron's suggestions the idea of keeping the treasure to himself flashed upon his mind. He had discovered it, why should he give it up to anybody? He had run all the risks; if he were detected at that moment, who would believe that his purpose there at midnight was only to satisfy some one else that the treasure was still intact? No. The circumstances were propitious; he would get the treasure out of the ship at once, drop it over her side, hastily conceal it in the nearest lot adjacent, and take it away at his convenience. Who would be the wiser for it?

But it was necessary to reconnoiter first. He knew that the loft overhead was empty. He knew that it communicated with the alley, for he had tried the door that morning. He would convey the treasure there and drop it into the alley. The boxes were heavy. Each one would require a separate journey to the ship's side, but he would at least secure something if he were interrupted, He stripped the casing, and gathered the boxes together in a pile.

Ah, yes, it was funny too that he, the Lascar hound, the damned nigger, should get what bigger and bullier men than he had died for! The mate's blood was on those boxes, if the salt water had not washed it out. It was a hell of a fight when they dragged the captain, Oh, what was that? Was it the splash of a rat in the bilge, or what?

A superstitious terror had begun to seize him at the thought of blood. The stifling hold seemed again filled with struggling figures he had known, the air thick with cries and blasphemies that he had forgotten. He rose to his feet, and running quickly to the hatchway, leaped to the deck above. All was quiet. The door leading to the empty loft yielded to his touch. He entered, and, gliding through, unbarred and opened the door that gave upon the alley. The cold air and moonlight flowed in silently; the way of escape was clear. Bah! He would go back for the treasure.

He had reached the passage when the door he had just opened was suddenly darkened. Turning rapidly, he was conscious of a gaunt figure, grotesque, silent, and erect, looming on the threshold between him and the sky. Hidden in the shadow, he made a stealthy step towards it, with an iron wrench in his uplifted hand. But the next moment his eyes dilated with superstitious horror; the iron fell from his hand, and with a scream, like a frightened animal, he turned and fled into the passage. In the first access of his blind terror he tried to reach the deck above through the forehatch, but was stopped by the sound of a heavy tread overhead. The immediate fear of detection now overcame his superstition; he would have even faced the apparition again to escape through the loft; but, before he could return there, other footsteps approached rapidly from the end of the passage he would have to traverse. There was but one chance of escape left now, the forehold he had just quitted. He might hide there until the alarm was over. He glided back to the hatch, lifted it, and closed it softly over his head as the upper hatch was simultaneously raised, and the small round eyes of Abner Nott peered down upon it. The other footsteps proved to be Renshaw's, but, attracted by the open door of the loft, he turned aside and entered. As soon as he disappeared Mr. Nott cautiously dropped through the opening to the deck below, and, going to the other hatch through which the Lascar had vanished, deliberately refastened it. In a few moments Renshaw returned with a light, and found the old man sitting on the hatch.

"The loft-door was open," said Renshaw. "There's little doubt whoever was here escaped that way."

"Surely," said Nott. There was a peculiar look of Machiavellian sagacity in his face which irritated Renshaw.

"Then you're sure it was Ferriferes you saw pass by your window before you called me?" he asked.

Nott nodded his head with an expression of infinite profundity.

"But you say he was going from the ship. Then it could not have been he who made the noise we heard down here."

"Mebbee no, and mebbee yes," returned Nott, cautiously.

"But if he was already concealed inside the ship, as that open door, which you say you barred from the inside, would indicate, what the devil did he want with this?" said Renshaw, producing the monkey wrench he had picked up.

Mr. Nott examined the tool carefully, and shook his head with momentous significance. Nevertheless, his eyes wandered to the hatch on which he was seated.

"Did you find anything disturbed there?" said Renshaw, following the direction of his eye. "Was that hatch fastened as it is now?"

"It was," said Nott, calmly. "But ye wouldn't mind fetchin' me a hammer and some o' them big nails from the locker, would yer, while I hang round here just so ez to make sure against another attack."

Renshaw complied with his request; but as Nott proceeded to gravely nail down the fastenings of the hatch, he turned impatiently away to complete his examination of the ship. The doors of the other lofts and their fastenings appeared secure and undisturbed. Yet it was undeniable that a felonious entrance had been made, but by whom or for what purpose, still remained uncertain. Even now, Renshaw found it difficult to accept Nott's theory that De Ferrières was the aggressor and Rosey the object, nor could he justify his own suspicion that the Lascar had obtained a surreptitious entrance under Sleight's directions. With a feeling that if Rosey had been present he would have confessed all, and demanded from her an equal confidence, he began to hate his feeble, purposeless, and inefficient alliance with her father, who believed but dared not tax his daughter with complicity in this outrage. What could be done with a man whose only idea of action at such a moment was to nail up an undisturbed entrance in his invaded house! He was so preoccupied with these thoughts that when Nott rejoined him in the cabin he scarcely heeded his presence, and was entirely oblivious of the furtive looks which the old man from time to time cast upon his face.

"I reckon ye wouldn't mind," broke in Nott, suddenly, "ef I asked a favor of ye, Mr. Renshaw. Mebbee ye'll allow it's askin' too much in the matter of expense; mebbee ye'll allow it's askin' too much in the matter o' time. But I kalkilate to pay all the expense, and if you'd let me know what yer vally yer time at, I reckon I could stand that. What I'd be askin' is this. Would ye mind takin' a letter from me to Rosey, and bringin' back an answer?"

Renshaw stared speechlessly at this absurd realization of his wish of a moment before. "I don't think I understand you," he stammered.

"P'r'aps not," returned Nott, with great gravity. "But that's not so much matter to you ez your time and expenses."

"I meant I should be glad to go if I can be of any service to you," said Renshaw, hastily.

"You kin ketch the seven-o'clock boat this morning, and you'll reach San Rafael at ten" -

"But I thought Miss Rosey went to Petaluma," interrupted Renshaw quickly.

Nott regarded him with an expression of patronizing superiority. "That's what we ladled out to the public gin'rally, and to Ferrers and his gang in partickler. We said Petalumey, but if you go to Madrono Cottage, San Rafael, you'll find Rosey thar."

If Mr. Renshaw required anything more to convince him of the necessity of coming to some understanding with Rosey at once it would have been this last evidence of her father's utterly dark and supremely inscrutable designs. He assented quickly, and Nott handed him a note.

"Ye'll be partickler to give this inter her own hands, and wait for an answer," said Nott gravely.

Resisting the proposition to enter then and there into an elaborate calculation of the value of his time and the expenses of the trip, Renshaw found himself at seven o'clock on the San Rafael boat. Brief as was the journey it gave him time to reflect upon his coming interview with Rosey. He had resolved to begin by confessing all; the attempt of last night had released him from any sense of duty to Sleight. Besides, he did not doubt that Nott's letter contained some reference to this affair only known to Nott's dark and tortuous intelligence.

VIII.

Madroño Cottage lay at the entrance of a little cañada already green with the early winter rains, and nestled in a thicket of the harlequin painted trees that gave it a name. The young man was a little relieved to find that Rosey had gone to the post-office a mile away, and that he would probably overtake her or meet her returning alone. The road, little more than a trail, wound along the crest of the hill looking across the cañada to the long, dark, heavily-wooded flank of Mount Tamalpais that rose from the valley a dozen miles away. A cessation of the warm rain, a rift in the sky, and the rare spectacle of cloud scenery, combined with a certain sense of freedom, restored that light-hearted gayety that became him most. At a sudden turn of the road he caught sight of Rosey's figure coming towards him, and quickened his step with the impulsiveness of a boy. But she suddenly disappeared, and when he again saw her she was on the other side of the trail apparently picking the leaves of a manzanita. She had already seen him.

Somehow the frankness of his greeting was checked. She looked up at him with cheeks that retained enough of their color to suggest why she had hesitated, and said, "You here, Mr. Renshaw? I thought you were in Sacramento."

"And I thought you were in Petaluma," he retorted gayly. "I have a letter from your father. The fact is, one of those gentlemen who has been haunting the ship actually made an entry last night. Who he was, and what he came for, nobody knows. Perhaps your father gives you his suspicions." He could not help looking at her narrowly as he handed her the note. Except that her pretty eyebrows were slightly raised in curiosity she seemed undisturbed as she opened the letter. Presently she raised her eyes to his.

"Is this all father gave you?"

"All."

"You're sure you haven't dropped anything?"

"Nothing. I have given you all he gave me."

"And that is all it is." She exhibited the missive, a perfectly blank sheet of paper folded like a note!

Renshaw felt the angry blood glow in his cheeks. "This is unpardonable! I assure you, Miss Nott, there must be some mistake. He himself has probably forgotten the inclosure," he continued, yet with an inward conviction that the act was perfectly premeditated on the part of the old man.

The young girl held out her hand frankly. "Don't think any more of it, Mr. Renshaw. Father is forgetful at times. But tell me about last night."

In a few words Mr. Renshaw briefly but plainly related the details of the attempt upon the Pontiac, from the moment that he had been awakened by Nott, to his discovery of the unknown trespasser's flight by the open door to the loft. When he had finished, he hesitated, and then taking Rosey's hand, said impulsively, "You will not be angry with me if I tell you all? Your father firmly believes that the attempt was made by the old Frenchman, De Ferrières, with a view of carrying you off."

A dozen reasons other than the one her father would have attributed it to might have called the blood to her face. But only innocence could have brought the look of astonished indignation to her eyes as she answered quickly:

"So that was what you were laughing at?"

"Not that, Miss Nott," said the young man eagerly; "though I wish to God I could accuse myself of nothing more disloyal. Do not speak, I beg," he added impatiently, as Rosey was about to reply. "I have no right to hear you; I have no right to even stand in your presence until I have confessed everything. I came to the Pontiac; I made your acquaintance, Miss Nott, through a fraud as wicked as anything your father charges to De Ferrières. I am not a contractor. I never was an honest lodger in the Pontiac. I was simply a spy."

"But you didn't mean to be, it was some mistake, wasn't it?" said Rosey, quite white, but more from sympathy with the offender's emotion than horror at the offense.

"I am afraid I did mean it. But bear with me for a few moments longer and you shall know all. It's a long story. Will you walk on, and take my arm? You do not shrink from me, Miss Nott. Thank you. I scarcely deserve the kindness."

Indeed so little did Rosey shrink that he was conscious of a slight reassuring pressure on his arm as they moved forward, and for the moment I fear the young man felt like exaggerating his offense for the sake of proportionate sympathy. "Do you remember," he continued, "one evening when I told you some sea tales, you said you always thought there must be some story about the Pontiac? There was a story of the Pontiac, Miss Nott, a wicked story, a terrible story, which I might have told you, which I ought to have told you, which was the story that brought me there. You were right, too, in saying that you thought I had known the Pontiac before I stepped first on her deck that day. I had."

He laid his disengaged hand across lightly on Rosey's, as if to assure himself that she was listening.

"I was at that time a sailor. I had been fool enough to run away from college, thinking it a fine romantic thing to ship before the mast for a voyage round the world. I was a little disappointed, perhaps, but I made the best of it, and in two years I was the second mate of a whaler lying in a little harbor of one of the uncivilized islands of the Pacific. While we were at anchor there a French trading vessel put in, apparently for water. She had the dregs of a mixed crew of Lascars and Portuguese, who said they had lost the rest of their men by desertion, and that the captain and mate had been carried off by fever. There was something so queer in their story that our skipper took the law in his own hands, and put me on board of her with a salvage crew. But that night the French crew mutinied, cut the cables, and would have got to sea if we had not been armed and prepared, and managed to drive them below. When we had got them under hatches for a few hours they parleyed, and offered to go quietly ashore. As we were short of hands and unable to take them with us, and as we had no evidence against them, we let them go, took the ship to Callao, turned her over to the authorities, lodged a claim for salvage, and continued our voyage. When we returned we found the truth of the story was known. She had been a French trader from Marseilles, owned by her captain; her crew had mutinied in the Pacific, killed their officers and the only passenger, the owner of the cargo. They had made away with the cargo and a treasure of nearly half a million of Spanish gold for trading purposes which belonged to the passenger. In course of time the ship was sold for salvage and put into the South American trade until the breaking out of the Californian gold excitement, when she was sent with a cargo to San Francisco. That ship was the Pontiac which your father bought."

A slight shudder ran through the girl's frame. "I wish, I wish you hadn't told me," she said. I shall never close my eyes again comfortably on board of her, I know."

"I would say that you had purified her of all stains of her past, but there may be one that remains. And that in most people's eyes would be no detraction. You look puzzled, Miss Nott, but I am coming to the explanation and the end of my story. A ship of war was sent to the island to punish the mutineers and pirates, for such they were, but they could not be found. A private expedition was sent to discover the treasure which they were supposed to have buried, but in vain. About two months ago Mr. Sleight told me one of his shipmasters had sent him a Lascar sailor who had to dispose of a valuable secret regarding the Pontiac for a percentage. That secret was that the treasure was never taken by the mutineers out of the Pontiac! They were about to land and bury it when we boarded them. They took advantage of their imprisonment under hatches to bury it in the ship. They hid it in the hold so securely and safely that it was never detected by us or the Callao authorities. I was then asked, as one who knew the vessel, to undertake a private examination of her, with a view of purchasing her from your father without awakening his suspicions. I assented. You have my confession now, Miss Nott. You know my crime. I am at your mercy."

Rosey's arm only tightened around his own. Her eyes sought his. "And you didn't find anything?" she said.

The question sounded so oddly like Sleight's, that Renshaw returned a little stiffly:

"I didn't look."

"Why?" asked Rosey simply.

"Because," stammered Renshaw, with an uneasy consciousness of having exaggerated his sentiment, "it didn't seem honorable; it didn't seem fair to you."

"Oh you silly! you might have looked and told me."

"But," said Renshaw, "do you think that would have been fair to Sleight?"

"As fair to him as to us. For, don't you see, it wouldn't belong to any of us. It would belong to the friends or the family of the man who lost it."

"But there were no heirs," replied Renshaw. "That was proved by some impostor who pretended to be his brother, and libelled the Pontiac at Callao, but the courts decided he was a lunatic."

"Then it belongs to the poor pirates who risked their own lives for it, rather than to Sleight, who did nothing." She was silent for a moment, and then resumed with energy, "I believe he was at the bottom of that attack last night."

"I have thought so too," said Renshaw.

"Then I must go back at once," she continued, impulsively. "Father must not be left alone."

"Nor must you," said Renshaw, quickly. "Do let me return with you, and share with you and your father the trouble I have brought upon you. Do not," he added in a lower tone, "deprive me of the only chance of expiating my offense, of making myself worthy your forgiveness."

"I am sure," said Rosey, lowering her lids and half withdrawing her arm, "I am sure I have nothing to forgive. You did not believe the treasure belonged to us any more than to anybody else, until you knew me" -

"That is true," said the young man, attempting to take her hand.

"I mean," said Rosey, blushing, and showing a distracting row of little teeth in one of her infrequent laughs, "oh, you know what I mean." She withdrew her arm gently, and became interested in the selection of certain wayside bay leaves as they passed along. "All the same, I don't believe in this treasure," she said abruptly, as if to change the subject. "I don't believe it ever was hidden inside the Pontiac."

"That can be easily ascertained now," said Renshaw.

"But it's a pity you didn't find it out while you were about it," said Rosey. "It would have saved so much talk and trouble."

"I have told you why I didn't search the ship," responded Renshaw, with a slight bitterness. "But it seems I could only avoid being a great rascal by becoming a great fool."

"You never intended to be a rascal," said Rosey, earnestly, "and you couldn't be a fool, except in heeding what a silly girl says. I only meant if you had taken me into your confidence it would have been better."

"Might I not say the same to you regarding your friend, the old Frenchman?" returned Renshaw. "What if I were to confess to you that I lately suspected him of knowing the secret, and of trying to gain your assistance?"

Instead of indignantly repudiating the suggestion, to the young man's great discomfiture, Rosey only knit her pretty brows, and remained for some moments silent. Presently she asked timidly:

"Do you think it wrong to tell another person's secret for their own good?"

"No," said Renshaw, promptly.

"Then I'll tell you Monsieur de Ferrières'! But only because I believe from what you have just said that he will turn out to have some right to the treasure."

Then with kindling eyes, and a voice eloquent with sympathy, Rosey told the story of her accidental discovery of De Ferrières' miserable existence in the loft. Clothing it with the unconscious poetry of her fresh, young imagination, she lightly passed over his antique gallantry and grotesque weakness, exalting only his lonely sufferings and mysterious wrongs. Renshaw listened, lost between shame for his late suspicions and admiration for her thoughtful delicacy, until she began to speak of De Ferrières' strange allusions to the foreign papers in his portmanteau. "I think some were law papers, and I am almost certain I saw the word Callao printed on one of them."

"It may be so," said Renshaw, thoughtfully. "The old Frenchman has always passed for a harmless, wandering eccentric. I hardly think public curiosity has ever even sought to know his name, much less his history. But had we not better first try to find if there is any property before we examine his claims to it?"

"As you please," said Rosey, with a slight pout; "but you will find it much easier to discover him than his treasure. It's always easier to find the thing you're not looking for."

"Until you want it," said Renshaw, with sudden gravity.

"How pretty it looks over there," said Rosey, turning her conscious eyes to the opposite mountain.

"Very."

They had reached the top of the hill, and in the near distance the chimney of Madroño Cottage was even now visible. At the expected sight they unconsciously stopped, unconsciously disappointed. Rosey broke the embarrassing silence.

"There's another way home, but it's a roundabout way," she said timidly.

"Let us take it," said Renshaw.

She hesitated. "The boat goes at four, and we must return to-night."

"The more reason why we should make the most of our time now," said Renshaw with a faint smile. "To-morrow all things may be changed; to-morrow you may find yourself an heiress, Miss Nott. To-morrow," he added, with a slight tremor in his voice, "I may have earned your forgiveness, only to say farewell to you forever. Let me keep this sunshine, this picture, this companionship with you long enough to say now what perhaps I must not say to-morrow."

They were silent for a moment, and then by a common instinct turned together into a narrow trail, scarce wide enough for two, that diverged from the straight practical path before them. It was indeed a roundabout way home, so roundabout, in fact, that as they wandered on it seemed even to double on its track, occasionally lingering long and becoming indistinct under the shadow of madroño and willow; at one time stopping blindly before a fallen tree in the hollow, where they had quite lost it, and had to sit down to recall it; a rough way, often requiring the mutual help of each other's hands and eyes to tread together in security; an uncertain way, not to be found Without whispered consultation and concession, and yet a way eventually bringing them hand in hand, happy and hopeful, to the gate of Madroño Cottage. And if there was only just time for Rosey to prepare to take the boat, it was due to the deviousness of the way. If a stray curl was lying loose on Rosey's cheek, and a long hair had caught in Renshaw's button, it was owing to the roughness of the way; and if in the tones of their voices and in the glances of their eyes there was a maturer seriousness, it was due to the dim uncertainty of the path they had traveled, and would hereafter tread together.

When Mr. Nott had satisfied himself of Renshaw's departure, he coolly bolted the door at the head of the companion-way, thus cutting off any communication with the lower deck. Taking a long rifle from the rack above his berth, he carefully examined the hammer and cap, and then cautiously let himself down through the forehatch to the deck below. After a deliberate survey of the still intact fastenings of the hatch over the forehold, he proceeded quietly to unloose them again with the aid of the tools that still lay there. When the hatch was once more free he lifted it, and, withdrawing a few feet from the opening, sat himself down, rifle in hand. A profound silence reigned throughout the lower deck.

"Ye kin rize up out o' that," said Nott gently.

There was a stealthy rustle below that seemed to approach the hatch, and then with a sudden bound the Lascar leaped on the deck. But at the same instant Nott covered him with his rifle. A slight shade of disappointment and surprise had crossed the old man's face, and clouded his small round eyes at the apparition of the Lascar, but his hand was none the less firm upon the trigger as the frightened prisoner sank on his knees, with his hands clasped in the attitude of supplication for mercy.

"Ef you're thinkin' o' skippin' afore I've done with yer," said Nott with labored gentleness, "I oughter warn ye that it's my style to drop Injins at two hundred yards, and this deck ain't anywhere more 'n fifty. It's an uncomfortable style, a nasty style, but it's my style. I thought I'd tell yer, so yer could take it easy where you air. Where's Ferrers?"

Even in the man's insane terror, his utter bewilderment at the question was evident. "Ferrers?" he gasped; "don't know him, I swear to God, boss."

"P'r'aps," said Nott, with infinite cunning, "yer don't know the man ez kem into the loft from the alley last night, p'r'aps yer didn't see an airy Frenchman with a dyed mustache, eh? I thought that would fetch ye!" he continued, as the man started at the evidence that his vision of last night was a living man. "P'r'aps you and him didn't break into this ship last night, jist to run off with my darter Rosey? P'r'aps yer don't know Rosey, eh? P'r'aps yer don't know ez Ferrers wants to marry her, and hez been hangin' round yer ever since he left, eh?"

Scarcely believing the evidence of his senses that the old man whose treasure he had been trying to steal was utterly ignorant of his real offense, and yet uncertain of the penalty of the other crime of which he was accused, the Lascar writhed his body and stammered vaguely, "Mercy! Mercy!"

"Well," said Nott, cautiously, "ez I reckon the hide of a dead Chinee nigger ain't any more vallyble than that of a dead Injin, I don't care ef I let up on yer, seein' the cussedness ain't yours. But ef I let yer off this once, you must take a message to Ferrers from me."

"Let me off this time, boss, and I swear to God I will," said the Lascar eagerly.

"Ye kin say to Ferrers, let me see", deliberated Nott, leaning on his rifle with cautious reflection. "Ye kin say to Ferrers like this, sez you, 'Ferrers,' sez you, 'the old man sez that afore you went away you sez to him, sez you, "I take my honor with me," sez you', have you got that?" interrupted Nott suddenly.

"Yes, boss."

"'I take my honor with me,' sez you," repeated Nott slowly. "'Now,' sez you, 'the old man sez, sez he, tell Ferrers, sez he, that his honor havin' run away agin, he sends it back to him, and ef he ever ketches it around after this, he'll shoot it on sight.' Hev yer got that?"

"Yes," stammered the bewildered captive.

"Then git!"

The Lascar sprang to his feet with the agility of a panther, leaped through the hatch above him, and disappeared over the bow of the ship with an unhesitating directness that showed that every avenue of escape had been already contemplated by him. Slipping lightly from the cutwater to the ground, he continued his flight, only stopping at the private office of Mr. Sleight.

When Mr. Renshaw and Rosey Nott arrived on board the Pontiac that evening, they were astonished to find the passage before the cabin completely occupied with trunks and boxes, and the bulk of their household goods apparently in the process of removal. Mr. Nott, who was superintending the work of two Chinamen, betrayed not only no surprise at the appearance of the young people, but not the remotest recognition of their own bewilderment at his occupation.

"Kalkilatin'," he remarked casually to his daughter, "you'd rather look arter your fixins, Rosey; I've left 'em till the last. P'r'aps yer and Mr. Renshaw wouldn't mind sittin' down on that locker until I've strapped this yer box."

"But what does it all mean, father?" said Rosey, taking the old man by the lappels of his pea-jacket, and slightly emphasizing her question. "What in the name of goodness are you doing?"

"Breakin' camp, Rosey dear, breakin' camp, jist ez we uster," replied Nott with cheerful philosophy. "Kinder like ole times, ain't it? Lord, Rosey," he continued, stopping and following up the reminiscence, with the end of the rope in his hand as if it were a clue, "don't ye mind that day we started outer Livermore Pass, and seed the hull o' the Kaliforny coast stretchin' yonder, eh? But don't ye be skeered, Rosey dear," he added quickly, as if in recognition of the alarm expressed in her face. "I ain't turning ye outer house and home; I've jist hired that 'ere Madroño Cottage from the Peters ontil we kin look round."

"But you're not leaving the ship, father," continued Rosey, impetuously. "You haven't sold it to that man Sleight?"

Mr. Nott rose and carefully closed the cabin-door. Then drawing a large wallet from his pocket, he said, "It's sing'lar ye should hev got the name right the first pop, ain't it, Rosey? but it's Sleight, sure enough, all the time. This yer check," he added, producing a paper from the depths of the wallet, "this yer check for 25,000 dollars is wot he paid for it only two hours ago."

"But," said Renshaw, springing to his feet furiously, "you're duped, swindled, betrayed!"

"Young man," said Nott, throwing a certain dignity into his habitual gesture of placing his hands on Renshaw's shoulders, "I bought this yer ship five years ago jist ez she stood for 8,000 dollars. Kalkilatin' wot she cost me in repairs and taxes, and wot she brought me in since then, accordin' to my figgerin', I don't call a clear profit of 15,000 dollars much of a swindle."

"Tell him all," said Rosey, quickly, more alarmed at Renshaw's despairing face than at the news itself. "Tell him everything, Dick, Mr. Renshaw; it may not be too late."

In a voice half choked with passionate indignation Renshaw hurriedly repeated the story of the hidden treasure, and the plot to rescue it, prompted frequently by Rosey's tenacious memory and assisted by her deft and tactful explanations. But to their surprise the imperturbable countenance of Abner Nott never altered; a slight moisture of kindly paternal tolerance of their extravagance glistened in his little eyes, but nothing more.

"Ef there was a part o' this ship, a plank or a bolt, ez I don't know, ez I hevn't touched with my own hand, and looked into with my own eyes, thar might be suthin' in that story. I don't let on to be a sailor like you, but ez I know the ship ez a boy knows his first boss, as a woman knows her first babby, I reckon thar ain't no treasure yer, unless it was brought into the Pontiac last night by them chaps."

"But are you mad? Sleight would not pay three times the value of the ship to-day if he were not positive! And that positive knowledge was gained last night by the villain who broke into the Pontiac, no doubt the Lascar."

"Surely," said Nott, meditatively. "The Lascar! There's suthin' in that. That Lascar I fastened down in the hold last night unbeknownst to you, Mr. Renshaw, and let him out again this morning ekally unbeknownst."

"And you let him carry his information to Sleight, without a word!" said Renshaw, with a sickening sense of Nott's utter fatuity.

"I sent him back with a message to the man he kem from," said Nott, winking both his eyes at Renshaw significantly, and making signs behind his daughter's back.

Rosey, conscious of her lover's irritation, and more eager to soothe his impatience than from any faith in her suggestion, interfered. "Why not examine the place where he was concealed? he may have left some traces of his search."

The two men looked at each other. "Seein' ez I've turned the Pontiac over to Sleight jist as it stands, I don't know ez it's 'zactly on the square," said Nott doubtfully.

"You've a right to know at least what you deliver to him," interrupted Renshaw, brusquely. "Bring a lantern."

Followed by Rosey, Renshaw and Nott hurriedly sought the lower deck and the open hatch of the forehold. The two men leaped down first with the lantern, and then assisted Rosey to descend. Renshaw took a step forward and uttered a cry.

The rays of the lantern fell on the ship's side. The Lascar had, during his forced seclusion, put back the boxes of treasure and replaced the planking, yet not so carefully but that the quick eye of Renshaw had discovered it. The next moment he had stripped away the planking again, and the hurriedly restored box which the Lascar had found fell to the deck, scattering part of its ringing contents. Rosey turned pale; Renshaw's eyes flashed fire; only Abner Nott remained quiet and impassive.

"Are you satisfied you have been duped?" said Renshaw, passionately.

To their surprise Mr. Nott stooped down, and picking up one of the coins handed it gravely to Renshaw. "Would ye mind heftin' that 'ere coin in your hand, feelin' it, bitin' it, scrapin' it with a knife, and kinder seem' how it compares with other coins?"

"What do you mean?" said Renshaw.

"I mean that that yer coin, that all the coins in this yer box, that all the coins in them other boxes, and thar's forty on 'em, is all and every one of 'em counterfeits!"

The piece dropped unconsciously from Renshaw's hand, and striking another that lay on the deck gave out a dull, suspicious ring.

"They waz counterfeits got up by them Dutch supercargo sharps for dealin' with the Injins and cannibals and South Sea heathens ez bows down to wood and stone. It satisfied them ez well ez them buttons ye puts in missionary boxes, I reckon, and, 'cepting ez freight, don't cost nothin'. I found 'em tucked in the ribs o' the old Pontiac when I bought her, and I nailed 'em up in thar lest they should fall into dishonest hands. It's a lucky thing, Mr. Renshaw, that they comes into the honest fingers of a square man like Sleight, ain't it?"

He turned his small, guileless eyes upon Renshaw with such child-like simplicity that it checked the hysterical laugh that was rising to the young man's lips.

"But did any one know of this but yourself?"

"I reckon not. I once suspicioned that old Cap'en Bowers, who was always foolin' round the hold yer, must hev noticed the bulge in the casin', but when he took to axin' questions I axed others, ye know my style, Rosey? Come."

He led the way grimly back to the cabin, the young people following; but turning suddenly at the companion way he observed Renshaw's arm around the waist of his daughter. He said nothing until they had reached the cabin, when he closed the door softly, and looking at them both gently, said with infinite cunning:

"Ef it is n't too late, Rosey, ye kin tell this young man ez how I forgive him for havin' diskivered THE TREASURE of the Pontiac."

It was nearly eighteen months afterwards that Mr. Nott one morning entered the room of his son-in-law at Mandroño Cottage. Drawing him aside, he said with his old air of mystery, "Now ez Rosey's ailin' and don't seem to be so eager to diskiver what's become of Mr. Ferrers, I don't mind tellin' ye that over a year ago I heard he died suddenly in Sacramento. Thar was suthin' in the paper about his bein' a lunatic and claimin' to be a relation to somebody on the Pontiac; but likes ez not it's only the way those newspaper fellows got hold of the story of his wantin' to marry Rosey."